THE [illegible] ON

DETECTIVE INSPECTOR MARC FAGAN

Jason Chapman

ACKNOWLEDGEMENTS

I would like to thank all my beta readers for helping make this book possible. Thank you for putting in the time and effort to read my work and tell me where I am going wrong.

Many thanks to the guys at the UK Crime book club Facebook group for your support. And also a big thank you to Abergavenny Voice and all the people who have helped me in my research.

Special thanks

I would like to thank all the ex-police officers who have given me advice, so that the story you are about to read has a sense of realism.

Authors notes

This novel is a work of complete fiction. The names, characters and incidents portrayed in it are the work of the author's imagination. Any resemblance to actual persons, living or dead, events or localities is entirely coincidental.

Obscene language and sexual abuse warning

This story contains language that some will find offensive. Also references to sexual abuse some will find upsetting.

For mum

Thank you for the gift of storytelling

CHAPTER 1

DAY 1
Bailey Park – Abergavenny – 6:38am

Even in death, her face was beautiful. Unblemished by the relentless march of time.

Detective Inspector Marc Fagan stared down at the woman's body. Her lifeless eyes seemed to stare through the canvass of the CSI tent and across the landscape. A popular spot early in the morning with joggers and dog walkers, especially in the summer months. The woman was slim build, in her mid-fifties. But it was her face that hit home with Fagan. It seemed like time had stopped. The last time he had seen her was thirty-eight years ago.

Fagan glanced at his watch. He had been at the park for just over half an hour. He had been woken and been informed that he was the leading scene of crimes officer regarding the discovery.

Night Detective Inspector, Nathan Saddler, pulled back the entrance to the tent. 'DI Scouser.' He mocked. Saddler was in his early thirties, athletic and totally in love with himself. Single, with a reputation for eyeing up the young female police constables that came in and out of Newport police HQ. He looked down at the woman's body. 'Smart looking piece, you know, for her age.'

Fagan flashed a look of disapproval, but remained silent.

Saddler held out the paperwork he had collated. 'Looks

like you're going to have a busy day with this.'

Fagan took the file.

Saddler hurried out of the tent, and headed towards the park gates, lighting a rolled cigarette.

'Oi, you dull twat!' Fagan shouted after him.

Saddler turned.

'Just in case you didn't realise, this is a fucking crime scene. I'll kick your bloody arse all the way to the chief super's office for a reprimand. Stub that out. Log your name with one of the uniform. Someone will interview you later.'

Saddler stared back, like a scalded schoolchild. Before stubbing out the cigarette on a stone pillar.

'Prick.' Fagan sighed.

Saddler was typical of the new generation of detectives making their way up through the ranks. Not interested in the job, but the salary that comes with it.

The park had been sealed off on immediate discovery of the body. Crime scene investigators descended on the area. Uniformed officers guarded each entrance, taking names from scene of crimes officers and members of the public who were stupid enough to go near the gates. A number of inner and outer cordons had been put in place. A path had been laid out leading directly to the CSI tent.

Cars driving by the main gates slowed to a crawl. Curious early morning commuters tried to peer through the railings. Trying to catch a glimmer of the CSI tent.

Detective Sergeant Sean Watkins was a few hundred yards away talking to the man who had discovered the body. The man's dog provided a constant irritation. Tugging on its lead, barking, demanding to return to the body it had discovered less than two hours earlier.

Normally witnesses were ushered away. However, this wasn't how Fagan worked a crime scene. Any potential witnesses were detained within close proximity. A routine he had picked up while serving with Merseyside police. Fagan had thirty-five years under his belt as a serving police officer. Thirty years on Liverpool homicide. Never committed to a marriage, but involved with a string of women. The job always came first. Marriage was for people who wanted to throw away their careers. At least, that's what Fagan always believed.

The lengthy hours and multiple homicides had eventually taken their toll. The police force was also damaged during the pandemic. Officers had to work from home, instead of on the streets dealing with serious crime.

Fagan's last murder case generated national headlines. Six-year-old Aron Miller. A child with a troubled family history. Social services had placed Aron on the child at risk register. However, after a meeting with his stepmother and father, he had been downgraded to a child in need. Just over a week following the judgment was passed, Aron's body was discovered on waste ground notorious for fly tipping. Aron's father, stepmother and fifteen-year-old stepsister were charged with his murder.

Aron's body was found under an old mattress by council workers. It was part of an eight day search for the young boy after his father reported him missing. A fund had been set up and Aron's parents had spearheaded the campaign to find their missing son. There media interest was massive as cameras followed the couple around. Following their arrest it didn't take long for all three suspects to turn on each other. Blaming one another for Aron's murder. An analysis of Aron's body had determined he had died of internal injuries after being frequently beaten. Swelling of the brain had also contributed to Aron's death.

The trial dragged on for six harrowing weeks. Witness after witness had been called to give evidence. Aron's father and stepmother were both given a whole life sentence. His stepsister had been given a twenty-five-year custodial sentence. When the trial ended, Fagan gave a brief statement about how social services had worked hard to protect Aron. But this wasn't enough to quash anger from the local community. Merseyside social services head office had been targeted several times by angered residents. Especially when evidence had emerged about a series of failings and cover-ups by social services. One social worker involved with the case had been attacked outside her home.

After the trial, Fagan decided it was time for change. A position had opened for a Detective Inspector with Gwent police. Operating mainly around the Monmouthshire area. After seeing the ad, Fagan found himself longing for the town he had spent the first twenty years of his life, Abergavenny.

A town set amongst majestic mountains. Bordering the Brecon Beacons. With a population of over thirteen thousand, Abergavenny has a history stretching back before the Roman period. A fort once guarded a major Roman road that linked several key military positions in the South Wales region.

The day after he had applied for the new position, Fagan drove down to Abergavenny from his Liverpool home. He circled the main roundabout on the outskirts of town. A dual carriageway had replaced the old heads of the valley road. He exited the roundabout, spotting a sign, Welcome to Abergavenny – Gateway to Wales. A 20 mile per hour speed limit sign stood guard just beyond the welcome sign.

As he dropped money into a parking machine, he was dismayed to see a Morrisons supermarket where the old cattle market once stood. As a young teenager Fagan and his friends would watch the live cattle being herded into the slaughter shed. They would sneak into the shed where the cattle was hung for blood draining after being slaughtered.

Fagan strolled through the town centre taking in the changes that had taken place through the decades. Roads were now pedestrianised and a shopping precinct had replaced old Victorian buildings. Many of the pubs were gone. The Farmers Arms, the Black lion, the Vine Tree and the Guardsman. Now a collection of restaurants, cafes and opticians. Abergavenny was now a café culture town. Reinventing itself over the years, unlike other towns in the South Wales valleys that fell into disrepair.

As he wandered the side streets, Fagan came across a small estate agent. A new build house was available for rent. After an hour meeting and a tour with an agent the property was secured. Six weeks later, Fagan said goodbye to Merseyside police. A wave of relief flooded over him as he settled into his new surroundings. Finally, he was home. He was settled. He was happy, until that fateful morning.

Watkins stepped into the evidence tent. 'The dog owner said his dog clocked the body straight away. He's being taken back to Newport to give a more detailed statement. Looks like we'll have to examine the dog. The owner said it pissed on the body before he could pull it away. Other uniform are going door to door on Park Lane and Park avenue. One of these houses is bound to have a camera.'

'I want door to door on the Hereford Road, right up to the Londis at the top of the hill.' Fagan instructed.

Watkins held up a plastic bag containing a blood-stained driver's licence. 'Her name was Rebecca Jenkins, fifty-four years of age. Home address, a hundred and thirty Llwynu Lane.'

A CSI was examining the body.

'Any ideas how she died?' Fagan asked.

The CSI pointed at her neck. 'At first glance it appears to be strangulation. Looks like our murderer had considerable strength.' He then pointed at her blonde hair, which was tied in a neat ponytail that stretched down her back. 'As you can see, there are traces of blood matted into the victim's hair. Indicating trauma to the back of the head.' He indicated to the shoes on her feet. 'A heel is also missing from one of her shoes. She may have been running from her attacker when her heel broke. It's not anywhere close.'

'How long before you can move the body?'

The CSI puffed out his cheeks looking at the body. 'Within the hour hopefully. It looks like she was dragged to this position before being dumped. There are also fresh tire tracks on the rugby pitch. The murderer drove here, dumped her body then drove back the way they came. I've already contacted the duty pathologist. He said he'll be able to set things up at Nevil Hall.'

'Don't you have to take her to the Heath in Cardiff.'

'Not since covid came along. Due to the pandemic Nevil Hall has been given home office clearance. Because of risk of infection, each county in Wales has their own home office approved pathologist.' He looked down at her body. 'I found one peculiarity. The victim's head has been positioned to face the park.'

Fagan studied her for a few moments before peeling away tent entrance. Her dead eyes stared towards where Bailey Park outdoor swimming pool used to be. Beyond that was Park Avenue, and the house that Fagan spent most of his childhood.

The pathologist held a plastic bag with a phone case with a picture of the band Spandau Ballet. 'Someone removed her phone from its casing, then discarded it near the body. But there is no sign of the phone.' He pointed at the corner of the phone case. 'Looks like it was torn from the phone.' He indicated to the bag Watkins was holding. 'My guess is the driver's licence was slipped between the phone and the cover. My wife is forever doing that with her credit cards. Pisses me off big time.'

Watkins looked at the driver's license. 'I'll run this through the DVLA. Get a confirmation it's her.'

'There's no need.'

Watkins looked at Fagan. 'Boss?'

'I know her, or rather I knew her forty years ago.'

'Is that an official identification, boss?' Watkins asked.

Fagan hesitated. 'No, she has a sister, or used to have a sister who lived locally. Ask around, see if her parents are still alive. They lived on Lansdown Road. I want everything in this area bagged and tagged. I also noticed a CCTV camera bolted to the side of the pub overlooking this area. See if you can get hold of the landlord. Also contact the ESSO garage down the road. See if they have anything on their camera system.'

C H A P T E R 2

Incident room – 7:23am

Fagan felt his heart sink, surveying the tiny office they had been stuffed into. The room was in the fire station, across the road from the murder scene. The bustling offices of Edge Lane police HQ in Liverpool seemed like a pleasant memory.

'It's cramped I know.' Watkins said entering the room.

'What happened to the police station and courthouse in Tudor Street?'

'Knocked down several years back. Gwent police said they had to cut the number of stations. It was all about streamlining and saving money. They have a police surgery office in the town hall. Suspects are detained at Newport central HQ. They're supposed to be building a station by the tip in Llanfoist. But no one knows when that will happen.'

Fagan smiled, recalling a past memory. 'I spent a few nights in the Tudor Street drunk tank back in the day.' He quickly refocussed on the task at hand. 'Why have we been given this broom cupboard instead of an incident room in Cwmbran?'

'They've decommissioned Cwmbran and are building a new station in Llantarnam. We're lucky we've got this. Newport central is overrun and there are quite a few detectives working from home.'

'Jesus.' Fagan cursed. 'It was bad enough during the lockdown. Now after covid working from home is the preferred option. What about extra bodies?'

'Despite the CSIs and the door to door officers there's just us two.'

Fagan sat down in an unstable swivel chair. 'Where are we at with everything?'

'The Landlord is at the pub. He arrived ten minutes after we left.'

'Doesn't he live at the property?'

'No. The upstairs is used for offices and the downstairs is a full bar and restaurant.'

'What about the victim?'

'Looks like It will be a little while more before CSI move her to Nevil Hall.'

'Have you tracked any family?'

'No, but we have gained access to her flat in Llwynu Lane. A neighbour had a spare key.'

'Anything?'

'So far clean as a whistle. The victim has a son called Ricky. He does live with her but he's not in the area.'

Fagan picked up the two plastic bags, examining them. The face of Rebecca stared out from her bloodied driver's licence. A face from the past, long ago past. Memories swirled around Fagan's mind. A time many would class as ancient. He then studied the bag containing the phone case. He spotted the difference right away. 'Look at this.' He held the two bags side by side.

'It's a driver's licence and a phone case.' Watkins observed.

'Exactly, but the license is covered in blood and the phone case is clean.'

'Damn. I never clocked it. What's your thinking boss?'

'I reckon this case wasn't with the phone. Meaning the phone is somewhere else, and this case has been deliberately planted.'

'Bit of a wild guess boss.'

Fagan held out the bag. 'Trust me, something doesn't add up here. I want a full fingerprint analysis of this case, asap.'

Watkins took the phone case. 'I'll give CSIs a bell.'

Fagan grabbed his jacket off the back of the chair. 'I'll have a chat with the landlord at the Bailey.'

CHAPTER 3

7:32am

The police had sealed off the entrance to the park and a police cordon had been imposed around the pub.

'We couldn't close the road. It's too busy at this time of the day. People heading to work or doing the school run.' Watkins explained.

Fagan looked back up the Hereford Road towards the fire station. A long line of vehicles waited patiently at the traffic lights.

'Most people are fucked off with the twenty mile per hour speed limit they have enforced everywhere.'

Fagan looked back down the road towards the petrol station. He smiled briefly, recalling jumping over the wall to steal the pears that grew on a tree in the garden of a bungalow next door.

CSIs were examining the area around the main gates to the park, picking up stray litter. Another group was inside the entrance looking around a long-abandoned toilet building where the body of Rebecca had been found.

'I'll see if CSIs has found anything else belonging to the victim.' Watkins offered.

The entrance to the pub was open.

Fagan strolled through the main door and up to the bar.

'Can't you see we're bloody closed?' A voice called out from a corner of the bar. 'The only reason I left the door open, is because plod has been in and out.'

Fagan looked in the man's direction. He was sitting at a

table reading a newspaper.

The man stared back for several seconds before standing. He broke out into a smile and approached Fagan. 'Jesus bloody Christ, the prodigal son returns.'

Fagan stared back at his old friend, Simon Edwards. 'Simon, my god. You're the last person I expected to find running this place.'

They embraced each other as two old friends would, who hadn't seen each other in a very long time.

'Guess who I saw the other day? Paul Archer.'

Fagan laughed. 'There's a name I never thought I'd hear again. I see he stayed out of prison. He must have broken into every house in Abergavenny.'

'He's the caretaker up at the school now.'

'It's suits him.' Fagan remarked. 'If anyone would know his way around that place better than anyone, it's Archer. He broke in there enough times.'

They burst into laughter.

'It's good to see you Fagan.' Edwards beamed. 'Archer said he saw you several weeks ago in Wetherspoons, but I said he was full of it.'

'It was me.' Fagan confessed. 'I was looking for a place to live. Popped in for a spot of lunch.'

Edwards leant back in his seat. 'You're moving back home? I'll close the pub for the night. We'll have everyone round for a reunion.' Edwards sighed. 'Everyone who's left, that is.'

'Who've we lost?'

'The Smith brothers for a start.'

'Robbie and Sam, how?'

'Suicide.'

'Both of them.' Fagan gasped. 'They were the two best young football players in Abergavenny.'

Edwards nodded. 'Robbie killed himself first and then

Sam a few years later. Tore us all to shreds, especially the King twins, Melissa and Andrea.'

'The four of them were inseparable. We all thought they would get married and live happily ever after.'

'Andrew Dire threw himself off the Llanfoist bridge a couple of decades back. It was during a really bad flood.'

'Why?'

'Apparently he'd fallen head over heels with this girl from university. But she was a total dick to him. You know what Andy was like. He'd fall in love with anything with two legs.'

'I remember him being besotted with Diane Marks, the local bike.'

'She's another one who's gone. Drugs and all that shit.'

Fagan shook his head. 'Jesus, the past really catches up with you.'

'Unfortunately, Benny the pervert Nelson is still around.'

Fagan rolled his eyes. 'I thought he would have been banged up by now. Or six feet under because someone had the good sense to kill him.'

'Afraid not, and the girl he's with can't be much older than twenty-five. He's been with her since she was sixteen.'

'You're joking. How old is Benny?'

'Fast approaching sixty-three. She's one of these, Thai imports.'

Fagan shook his head. 'I can't believe that prick is still walking around.'

'Anyway, that's enough doom and gloom.' Edwards looked over towards the bar. 'Can I get an old friend a drink?'

'It's early, but go on, just a small one.'

Fagan sat at the bar, while Edwards poured a brandy.

'So, why have you returned to your roots? The last time we spoke, you said you were done with this shithole of a town.' Edwards placed the glass down on the bar.

Fagan reached into his pocket, pulling out his ID.

'Wow, a detective inspector. Some of us thought you'd spend most of your time in the clink. You know, after your little stint at Usk prison.'

Fagan sipped from his glass. 'To be honest, I thought the same. I wasn't in a good place after dad died.'

'Is your mam still around?'

'No. She passed just before covid came along. When she died I took a long hard look in the mirror. I considered moving back. Then along came the pandemic, which stranded me. When things got better, I thought about how I was going to spend my remaining years in the force. I saw a position in Monmouthshire so I thought, what the hell.'

'Have you seen anyone from the good old days?'

'I haven't really had time. Have had to sort a lot of things out. My furniture turned up three days ago. I've been sleeping on an airbed. The house in Liverpool is on the market.' Fagan looked around the bar. 'What about you? How come you stayed here? I thought you hated this place.'

Edwards inhaled. 'I did, but after dad drank himself into an early grave, our mam convinced me to take it on. So here I am, over thirty years later. It hasn't been easy over the last few years. I moved out from upstairs and turned it into offices to make extra money. I'm one of only two original families in Abergavenny still running pubs.'

'Who are the others?'

'The Mills still run the Cantreff on the Brecon Road.'

'I drove past there when I came back. It hasn't changed a bit.'

'Jackie Mills runs it now. She promised her nan before

she died she wouldn't change a thing.'

'Do you remember that hammering Tommy Mills gave you that day?'

Edwards rubbed his jaw. 'Had a hell of a left hook.'

'Perhaps you shouldn't have shagged Jackie on the floor of the bar.'

Edwards burst into laughter.

'Is it just you running the pub?'

'My daughter, Cara, will be in shortly. Guess who I ended up with, Samantha Hemming.'

'Wow, how did you hook her? I remember her being up her own arse. None of us boys from town were good enough.'

'We got talking up the Chevron one night and went from there. Unfortunately, it wasn't to be. We divorced about ten years ago.'

'Christ the Chevron.' Fagan remarked. 'What a shit hole that was, sticky carpets. Do you remember the Wetton brothers?'

'I remember them throwing you down the stairs on more than one occasion.'

Fagan gurned, remembering how much it hurt. 'Are they still about?'

'Andrew is running a gym where the chocolate factory used to be. Pete did twenty-five years for the murder of an old man up at Underhill. He was told never to come back to Abergavenny.'

'Underhill, the no-go zone of Abergavenny, along with Rother Avenue, Charles Close and Charles Crescent.'

'Things have changed now Fagan. Most people have bought their house. The no-go zones of yesterday are mostly respectable. There are still a few families left, but no one is kicking up a fuss now. People have moved on and grown up.'

'Or grown old.' Fagan added.

A brief silence followed.

'So, can I ask, is it Rebecca they found in the park earlier?'

Fagan stared back at his old friend. 'You know I can't tell you that.'

Edwards fished his phone out of his pocket. 'It's all over Abergavenny's Facebook page.'

'Give me your phone.'

Edwards handed over his phone.

Fagan scrolled through the newsfeed. 'Who runs this Facebook page?'

'Old man George Walker.'

'Wow, George Walker is still alive?'

'Yeah, I see him most days. He'll be in later this evening for his mid-week pint.'

'My mother told me he'd passed away about ten years after we left Abergavenny. Funny, I was thinking about him the other night. Poor sod, do you remember what happened to his son, Graham?'

Edwards nodded. 'George is still kicking about. He's eighty two. His Facebook page is huge, has over twenty thousand followers. They post things every day. You should visit him. He still lives in Lower Monk Street.'

'How the hell did he know it was her?'

'So it was Rebecca. Shit, this is going to mess with your head mate. You coming home and your ex showing up dead.'

'I need to see CCTV footage from that camera at the back of the pub.' Fagan requested.

'Sorry mate, I can't help you with that. It's a dummy camera. We don't get any trouble around here. It's there purely for show. I had some twat smash a window last year. The couple who live in the bungalow opposite recorded it on their camera. Nothing ever happens anymore in Abergavenny. It's full of old people now. Our mam is in Avenue Road old age pensioners home opposite the cricket ground. The last notable murder we had was the old man that Pete Weller murdered. George is going to flip when he sees you. Just last month your name came up in a conversation. He thought the world of you.'

Fagan nodded. 'Tried to keep me out of trouble all those years ago, but I never listened. He was the one who convinced me to join the police. I used to bother with Graham a lot. When he died, George went to pieces.' Fagan stared into his glass. 'I was devastated.'

'You being back is going to stir a lot of memories. Everyone is going to be chuffed to see you again.' Edwards shook his head, smiling. 'Fagan is back home.'

'Did you ever bother with Rebecca?'

'Not really. I'd say hello when I used to pop into Flannel Street chippy where she worked. When you left the old gang split up. I was gutted, thought we'd always be friends.'

'Did she work there long?'

'As far back as I can remember, since the late eighties. She's manager there. Justin Pike now owns the chippy.'

'That boy had some beatings at school.' Fagan recalled.

'Including one or two off you.'

'I thought Rebecca's parents would have pushed her through university after I left.'

'That was the plan.' Edwards said. 'At least that's what she told me about ten years ago, the last time we had a proper conversation. But shortly after you left, she became pregnant.'

'That must have pissed her mum and dad off. Her not going to university and becoming pregnant.'

'It did. They threw her out of that big house they lived

in on Lansdown Road. Said they were ashamed of her.'

'Did she keep the child?'

'Yes, but it was hard bringing up a kid alone. Well, when I say alone, she had an on and off relationship through the decades.'

'Who was the father?'

'Tim Davis.'

'Tim, Jesus, there's a conversation I'm not looking forward to having. Why was it on and off?'

'Apparently, she still held a torch for you. That's what Jackie from the Cantreff claimed.'

'Really.'

'She tried to track you down over the years, but couldn't find anything. You didn't even give her an address to write to. A couple of us have done searches for you on social media, but nothing.'

'I never got into Facebook or Twitter. I had to make a clean break of it. I couldn't take any emotional baggage with me. What about her sister, Susanna?'

'She's living a comfortable life in a nice house on the old Raglan Road. When her parents died, she sold the house on Lansdown Road and moved.'

'Didn't Rebecca inherit any of it?'

Edwards shook his head. 'Her parents wrote her out of the will the moment she became pregnant. When we last spoke, she said she had a massive argument with her sister about it. Told Susanna to shove the money up her arse.'

Fagan finished his drink. 'Listen Simon, I'd appreciate it if you didn't tell anyone I'm back in town. I don't want to muddy the waters regarding this murder enquiry.'

Edwards nodded. 'Sure.'

Watkins walked through the entrance of the pub. 'Boss, the chief constable has arrived. He wants a word.'

'Will I see you again?' Edwards asked. 'It would be

brilliant to catch up on old times. When the time is right, I'll make some calls, tell everyone, Fagan is back in town.'

Fagan stepped away from the bar and nodded. 'It's good to see you again, Simon. We'll catch up soon.'

CHAPTER 4

Incident room – 8:26am

Chief Constable Paul Griffiths shook Fagan's hand. 'I thought I'd pop in and see how you were settling in.'

'Very well, all things considered, sir.' Fagan gestured to his cramped office.

'Temporary for the moment. The old HQ in Cwmbran is going to be houses soon and the new one in Llantarnam is over a year away from being completed. You probably didn't expect a murder case as soon as you started.'

'No, I was not. Where are we at regarding extra bodies to help out?'

'Nowhere I'm afraid, it's just you and DS Watkins. Once the CSIs have scrubbed the scene they'll return to their home constituencies. The uniforms going door to door and guarding the park are on loan from Torfaen.' Griffiths took a breath. 'This town hasn't seen a murder in nearly forty years.'

'To be honest sir, I thought I was done with the murder side of things.'

Griffiths nodded. 'I transferred from the London Met Nearly eight years ago. Had enough of that bullshit.'

'I thought I would end my career tracking down stolen bikes or giving the local kids a ticking off for trampling the flowerbeds in Linda Vista gardens.'

Griffiths mused. 'You know how it is Marc. You scratch deep enough you'll always find dirt. Abergavenny is quiet enough, but like most towns, it has its problems. Mostly drug related. The kids around here have got nothing better to do. These days you have to drive to find a decent job, if you can afford it. The old places like Coopers and the chocolate factory are long gone. There is a turkey factory on the outskirts of town but it employs mainly foreigners. Other than that it's mostly retail and cafés paying out minimum wage.'

'Are you local?'

'I grew up in Monmouth.'

Fagan smiled. 'Gave you boys a good hammering in football a few times.'

'My grandfather was a local. An old school copper, Sergeant Bob Benson.'

Fagan faked a smile, hearing the name. 'Sergeant Bob, I remember him. Collared me enough times back in my youth. A very old school copper. Is he still around? I'd love to say hello.' Fagan had told a barefaced lie. Benson was the reason for him being exiled from Abergavenny.

'He passed away ten years ago. He encouraged me to sign up but I didn't stay local, so I joined the London Met. A tough job back in the day. Like you I moved back to home territory.' Griffiths looked out of the window overlooking the fire station yard. 'In fourteen months I can sit on my patio in Tintern and enjoy the view of the abbey. Anyway, enough of memory lane. How's the investigation going?'

'We're waiting on the pathologist to conduct a full examination of the body. A mobile phone case was found close to the victim. CSIs are running a full analysis. We should have results within a few hours.'

'Any clues how she ended up in the park?'

'Not yet, sir.' Fagan gazed at a photo of Rebecca, which had been grabbed from her Facebook profile. 'This seems to be a random killing.'

'Is it?' Griffiths stared at Fagan.

'What do you mean sir?'

'I keep an eye on social media Marc. You've been mentioned several times on Abergavenny's Facebook page. Rebecca Jenkins was an old girlfriend, wasn't she?'

'An ancient girlfriend sir. And someone I haven't seen in nearly forty years.'

Griffiths nodded. 'Sorry Marc, old habits. You know how it is.

'I'll draw up a list of people who knew the victim, and start conducting interviews. First on my list was her boss at the chippy in Flannel Street.'

Griffiths changed the subject. 'I read your file last week by the way. The incident with Callum Miller.'

Fagan nodded. 'I'll say to you the same thing I have said to everyone else. I have no regrets.'

'Gwent police doesn't need any maverick detectives, Marc.'

'It wasn't about being a maverick sir. It was about giving a man who took part in the torture and murder of his own son what he deserved.'

Griffiths adjusted his cap. 'I'll do a quick tour of the crime scene before returning to Newport HQ.' As he walked through the door he turned to face Fagan. 'Listen Marc, I need to know. You don't have any skeletons in the cupboard do you? You know, growing up here and everything.'

Fagan considered the question before nodding. 'Plenty sir, but nothing that will stop me from doing my job.'

'Good to know.' Griffiths gave a half smile.

C H A P T E R 5

Abergavenny Cinema – 23rd August 1981

'That film was fucking brilliant.' Dean Tyler declared, looking up at a poster outside the cinema. '*American Werewolf in London* has to be the film of the year.'

'*Superman two* was better.' Jamie Evans remarked. 'Plus *Indiana Jones, Raiders of the lost Ark*. Can't wait to see Harrison Ford in the next *Star Wars* film.'

'*Star Wars*.' Fagan mocked. 'What a pile of shit.'

'No, it fucking isn't.' Evans argued. '*Star Wars* is the best film ever. It's a shame they're only making one more. I read in film focus magazine last week they're calling it *Revenge of the Jedi*. It won't be released for another two years. Then that's it. George Lucas says there won't be any more *Star Wars* after the third film. Shame, the storyline has so much potential.'

'A bunch of queers with glowing swords. How original.' Fagan continued to taunt. He looked at Tyler. 'The only reason you liked that film was because Jenny Agutter got her kit off. I saw you fumbling with your balls in the dark.'

'Fuck off.' Tyler barked. 'You wouldn't have been able to get in if it weren't for me.'

Evans shook his head. 'No, if it weren't for your brother being the usher, we would have never have got in.'

'Same fucking difference.' Tyler said.

'I preferred her in *Logan's Run*. She strips naked, you see more than in that werewolf film. *Walkabout* was on BBC2 the other night. Boring as shit, but it's worth watching just to see her naked at the end.'

'Speaking of getting their kit off.' Fagan noticed a group of girls coming out of the cinema.

'Rebecca Jenkins.' Evans said. 'You're dreaming if you think you have a chance with her. Every boy at school has tried his luck. She's way too snobby for you. She'll be a virgin until the day she dies.'

'I wasn't thinking of her, actually. I quite fancy her sister Susanna.'

'She's older than us.'

'Only by a year. That hardly makes her an old lady.'

'I heard Simon Edwards fingered her in the science lab at school.'

'Edwards is full of it.' Fagan stated. 'He told me he shagged Katy Fletcher at the back of the Thursdays youth club. When I asked her about it, she said he didn't touch her.' He looked at the group of girls. 'How were they able to see the film?'

'Because everyone knows the manager is pervy. He likes to spy on the girls in the toilets. That's why he lets them in.' Evans remarked.

A car revved its engine and screeched to a halt.

'Speaking of pervs.' Fagan remarked.

Benny Nelson smiled at the group of girls. 'Any of you girls want a ride home?'

'What's it going to cost us?' Susanna Jenkins asked.

'A blow job off every one of you.'

'Fuck off Benny you spastic. Go and have a wank up the Keepers like you usually do.'

'Diane Marks will give you a blow job for a pack of fags.' Another girl said. 'Or Michelle Pike.'

Nelson spotted Fagan and the other two. 'Well, if it isn't the bummer boys of Abergavenny. Isn't there usually four of you? Oh wait, gormless Graham killed himself last year.'

Fagan stepped forward, glaring at Nelson. 'Why don't you get out of that piece of shit and say that to my face?'

Nelson smiled, revving the engine. 'See you later bummer boys.' The car sped away.

'Fucking prick.' Evans seethed.

'Has anyone seen George lately?' Tyler asked.

'Last week.' Fagan replied. 'He told me he will not be the kid catcher anymore at school.' He pulled out a packet of cigarettes. 'Who wants a fag?'

'Shit, where did you get those?'

'Stole them off the old man. He doesn't take his fags to work. They're not allowed to smoke at the old ammunition factory.'

'That's bollocks.' Tyler countered. 'My uncle works there. He said they have smoking sheds. He told me that some old fella blew himself up ten years ago at the factory. Uncle Chopper said he found his hand once. There were bits of him everywhere.'

The group of girls approached.

'How's it going girls?' Fagan greeted, taking a drag from his cigarette. 'Any of you ladies want a fag?' He held out the box of Woodbine.

'I'll have one.' Susanna Jenkins stepped forward and plucked a cigarette from the box.

Fagan struck a match and lit Susanna's cigarette. 'What did you think of the film?'

'It was ok.' She looked back at the group of girls she was with. 'They hid when they were running from the werewolf on the moors.'

Fagan indicated to Tyler. 'He was wanking off over Jenny Agutter getting her kit off.'

'Fuck off, Fagan.' Tyler barked.

The group of girls laughed.

'So, what are you doing now that we've all done with

school?'

Susanna took a drag from her cigarette. 'I'm going to university.' She glanced at the other girls. 'They're all staying on, in sixth form.'

'Waste of time if you ask me.' Fagan stated. 'Besides, I won't miss that twat, Mr Holder. The number of times he smacked me around the head.'

'That's because you used to piss about a lot.' Susanna added.

'Sue, we should get home. If we are late, mum and dad will go up the wall.' Rebecca Jenkins warned.

'Sod them, its summer holiday. Time to have some fun.'

'I don't want dad to find us with a group of boys. He won't let us out for the rest of the summer. And he'll ban us from watching *Grange Hill*.'

'I was watching that the other night. That new kid in school is a right bastard.' Evans said. 'Gripper Stebson, he's a right dick to that fat kid Roly.'

Susanna glanced at Rebecca smiling. 'She's got a crush on Tucker Jenkins. She wants to marry him so that she doesn't have to change her surname.'

'No, I don't.' Rebecca answered in a defensive tone.

'Where are you boys off to?'

'Thought we might go to the Somerset Arms and have a pint.' Fagan fumbled through his pockets, pulling out some change. 'I've got two quid and thirty pence. That'll get me a few pints and a game of pool or two.' He winked at her. 'You girls fancy tagging along?'

Susanna hesitated before nodding. She glanced behind her. 'You coming girls?'

The group of girls hesitated before nodding, except for Rebecca. 'We can't go into a pub. If dad finds us, he will kill us.' She protested.

'That's the point Becky. Dad wouldn't dream of looking

for us in a pub. It's the perfect hiding place.'

'No, I'm not going.' Rebecca stood her ground. 'I'm going home and telling dad where you are.'

Susanna calmly walked up to her younger sister. 'If you do that, then I'll tell mum you had some of her Cinzano Bianco last night.'

A look of fear spread across Rebecca's face. 'You had some as well.'

'Exactly, so we'll both be in the shit if you say anything.'

Rebecca thought about the dilemma she found herself in before conceding. 'We'll tell mum and dad we went to Lucy's house and played monopoly.'

'I only want to play a game of pool, then we'll go home.'

It took several minutes to walk from the cinema to The Somerset Arms. On the way Tyler scrambled over the back wall of another pub to steal some bottles. He explained the landlord of The Somerset Arms will give them ten pence a bottle, giving them more time on the pool table. When they arrived at the pub they herded the girls past the door that led to the bar. The poolroom was at the top of a spiral staircase. The Landlord didn't like too many people upstairs, especially the younger looking teenagers. A year before, he had been cautioned by the police after a parent complained he was serving alcohol to underage teenagers.

Fagan made sure the girls were upstairs before he entered the bar. A group of old men were in the corner playing dominos. 'Evening Dai, a pint of Harp please.'

Dai, the landlord, eyed the underage drinker for a few seconds before grabbing a glass and pulling a pint. 'On your own, are you?'

'No, Tyler and Evans are with me. They're upstairs in the poolroom.'

'Sounded like a herd of bloody elephants running up the stairs.'

Fagan handed over money for the lager. 'No, just me and the boys.' He said with an innocent tone.

The landlord took the money off Fagan, maintaining eye contact. 'I'll give you half an hour and then I'm coming up to check on you.'

Fagan smiled at the landlord, taking a gulp from his lager. 'Just a couple of games of pool. Then we'll be out of here.'

The group of girls sat in a corner of the pool room chatting away amongst themselves. Occasionally, they would look across at the group of boys and giggle.

The pool room was already occupied by Tim Davis and Simon Edwards.

'Where have you queers been tonight?' Davis mocked. 'Let me guess. You've been bumming each other in the back row of the cinema.'

Fagan looked over at the group of girls. 'More like shagging those in the back row.'

'They're way out of your league, mate.' Edwards said. 'I'm surprised they found the guts to come up here.'

'Fagan wants to get into Susanna's knickers.' Tyler mocked.

Fagan gave him a menacing glare.

'You've more chance shagging Bo Derek than any of those girls.'

'I wouldn't mind giving Bo Derek one.' Evans stated. 'Dudley Moore was bloody lucky shagging her.'

Fagan grinned, holding his glass up in the air. 'Watch and learn boys.' He calmly walked over to where the girls were sitting. 'Mind if I sit ladies?'

'It's a free country.' Susanna giggled.

Fagan drank from his glass.

'What's that you're drinking?'

'A pint of Harp.' Fagan replied.

'Can I have a gulp?'

Fagan handed Susanna the glass.

She eyed the other girls before taking a swig. Moments later she clasped her hand over her mouth. 'That's fucking disgusting.'

Fagan laughed.

Rebecca glared at her sister while the other girls encouraged her to take another gulp.

Susanna held the glass before taking another large mouthful, that she immediately spat out all over Fagan's shirt.

Tyler, Evans and the others burst into laughter.

'Real cool moves there Fagan.' Davis called over.

'Looks like you've got lager all over you.' Susanna pointed out. 'You'll have to take your shirt off now.'

The other girls started chanting. 'Off, off, off.'

Fagan smiled at Susanna before standing and unbuttoning his shirt slowly. He peeled the garment off and threw it onto the pool table.

'Ta da!' He shouted, exposing his upper torso.

The girls cheered.

'What the fucking hell is going on here?' The landlord bellowed as he burst through the door. He pointed towards an open window. 'People can hear you outside. The lot of you can bugger off. You're banned until I say you can come back.' He glared at the girls sat in the corner. 'This is no place for young girls to hang around.'

The girls immediately stood, making for the door.

The landlord blocked the path of the boys. 'I've given you a lot of leeway. Letting you play pool here.' He looked at the pint glass on the table. 'I'm also risking my license serving you alcohol.' He walked over to the pool table, grabbing Fagan's wet shirt and tossing it at him. 'Come back when you're more mature.'

'Well, that's a good night wasted.' Davis complained as they stood outside. 'Thanks to you Fagan, we can't go in there again.'

'Don't be soft, the Farmers will serve you, and they have a pool table.'

'That's if the Wellers will let you play.' Tyler pointed out.

Edwards checked his watch. 'Come on Tim, if we're lucky we'll still be able to get in the Coach before it shuts. The pool table is always free.'

The two of them marched off.

'I suppose I better head home.' Tyler remarked. 'Llanfoist is a long way at this time of night.' He looked at Evans. 'You coming? We'll switch on the ZX 81 and start writing that program for that space invaders game. Our mam says you can stay over when your mam and dad argue.'

Evans hesitated before nodding.

'Looks like you're on your own Fagan.'

In the distance Fagan could hear the girls laughing loudly. He slipped on his shirt and buttoned it up. 'Not entirely boys.'

Susanna turned around and spotted Fagan running up the road towards them. 'Here we go. Romeo is back.'

'At least he's wearing his shirt.' One of her friends remarked.

'Wait up girls.' Fagan panted.

'Are you going to strip for us in the middle of the street?'

Fagan reached for the top button of his damp shirt. 'Only if you want me to.'

Susanna shook her head. 'No thanks, I don't think my stomach will take it.'

Fagan felt a little deflated. 'Can I at least walk you girls home? You know what it's like this time of night.'

'Yeah, boys like you are roaming the streets.' One girl joked.

They all burst into a chorus of laughter.

'What do you want in exchange?' Susanna quizzed. 'For walking us home, that is?'

Fagan shrugged. 'Nothing, I just want to see you girls get home safe.'

Susanna considered his offer. 'Okay then. Tell you what, we'll walk through the park and Debbie will let you grope her tits.'

'No I won't.' Debbie shot back. 'I'm not like that, so don't spread gossip.'

Twenty-five minutes later, it was just Fagan, Susanna and Rebecca left. They meandered slowly up Lansdown Road. Before stopping at the main gates of one of the large houses that lined the street.

Rebecca hurried up the driveway before turning. 'Come on Susanna, we're in enough trouble already.'

'Thanks for walking us home.' Susanna said.

Fagan shoved his hands awkwardly into his pockets. 'I was wondering if you fancy going out next weekend.'

'Why?' Susanna smiled.

Fagan shrugged. 'Do you want to meet me at Luigis?'

'What's in it for me?'

'A milkshake and a plate of chips.'

Susanna nodded slowly. 'Wow, you really know how to wine and dine a girl.'

'We could go to Quo Vadis.' Fagan offered.

'Susanna, come on.' Rebecca called out. 'Look, give him a quick snog then come in.'

'Yes, I will go to Luigis with you.' Susanna accepted, smiling.

'Great.' Fagan said.

Susanna glanced at her sister for a few moments. Then,

without warning, she pulled Fagan towards her, pressing her lips against his.

A surge of adrenalin coursed through Fagan as he felt her warm tongue in his mouth.

She pulled away, gazing into his eyes momentarily before running up the drive towards her sister.

Fagan ducked behind a wall as the main door to the house opened. He could hear their father thundering at the girls for being late home. For a few moments he stayed hidden until the door slammed shut.

Fagan strolled down the street, high on the kiss Susanna had just given him.

CHAPTER 6

Flannel Street chippy – Abergavenny – 11:49am

Justin Pike stared at the man who sat at a table at the back of a small café next to the chip shop. Painful memories plagued his thoughts as he recalled his school days. The constant bullying he had to endure day after day. Being hounded by the other kids who took delight in calling him names and ambushing him in the toilet. One of those kids, now a man in his mid-fifties, was sitting at one of his tables. 'I never thought I would see the day. Marc Fagan, sat in my café.'

Fagan smiled back at Pike. 'Justin, it's been a long time.'

'Not long enough.'

Fagan felt guilt tug at his emotions.

Pike sat down. 'So what brings prince charming of Abergavenny back to the fold? I thought you'd gone for good.'

Fagan placed his identification badge on the table.

Pike glared at it for several seconds. 'Please God, don't say it's true.'

'I take it you've already heard?'

'I thought it was someone fucking around on the Abergavenny Facebook page. George Walker is shit at policing it.'

'Rebecca was found early this morning in Bailey park.'

Pike buried his head in his hands.

'Justin, I need to ask you some questions. Do you need anyone to sit with you?'

'What's that fucking supposed to mean?' Pike growled through his tears. 'You think I murdered her?'

Fagan shook his head wondering why Pike would say that. 'All I was going to do was ask questions about her movements. You were the last one to see her alive.'

Pike wiped his face on his sleeve, doing his best to compose himself. 'We locked up together last night.'

'What time was this?'

'About a quarter past ten. We had to empty the chip fryers because I have a visit scheduled from the food hygiene people this afternoon.'

'Did anyone pick her up from work?'

'I didn't see anyone. She said she was off to the Cantreff to see Jackie Mills. They were good mates. Rebecca spent a lot of her time in the Cantreff. I offered her a lift, but she refused.'

'You drove straight off?'

'Yes.'

'There were no other vehicles anywhere?'

'No, it's usually dead by the time we close. Most of the pubs are shut by ten on a Tuesday night. Since the lockdown and the cost of keeping the lights on most landlords shut up early. I used to have a regular trade come in after ten o'clock. People finishing up after the afternoon shift at the turkey factory. But after ten o'clock, Abergavenny is a ghost town.'

'You said Rebecca spent a lot of time in the Cantreff. Did she drink much?'

'She liked a binge now and then. There were occasions I had to drag her out of bed. But they were far and few between.'

'I spoke to Simon Edwards at the Bailey. He says you had worked with her for over thirty years.'

Pike nodded. 'A few years after you up and left, I

bumped into her in Tesco. She had a young boy in tow and spilled her guts to me. She was in a sorry state. I had just bought this place at rock bottom price from the Morgan family. I was looking for staff, so I offered her a position. We've been close friends for years.'

'Nothing more?'

'No, I never looked at her that way. Yes, she was smart and everything, but I never looked at her beyond friendship. Besides, I had been with Nesta Bradley since school.'

Fagan smiled. 'Your childhood sweetheart.'

'Was my childhood sweetheart. Until I found out she'd been fucking Kevin Carter behind my back for ten years.'

'Ouch.'

'You know what the worst thing was? Everyone knew about it, but thought it was funny not to tell me. I guess certain people never grow out of being twats.' Pike glanced at Fagan. 'What did you call me and Nesta one time? Ah yes, the Ian Brady and Myra Hindley of Abergavenny.'

'Yeah, that was shit of me.' Fagan admitted. 'What about boyfriends?'

'There were a few, but not that many. She hooked up with a bloke from Hereford for a few years. But he ended up fucking her off. Then there was Tim.'

'Tim Davis?'

'Yes, how many Tim Davis' are there in Abergavenny?' Pike barked.

Fagan noticed Pike's left hand shaking. 'You ok.'

Pike clasped his hand. 'It's a sign of getting old. Weren't you and Davis best pals or something?'

'I'd call us more love rivals. But then things got out of hand.'

'Oh yes, the famous showdown in the Farmers. I heard it took six coppers to hold you down.'

'No, it was eight actually. Did you notice anything strange prior to her death?'

'Now that you mention it, she seemed to perk up over the last few weeks. Even cut back on the drinking. There was a new sparkle in her eye. I mentioned it one day last week. She told me she had finally had something in her life to hope for.'

'Did she say what?'

'No. Despite us being close, there were still some things she kept secret.'

'There was no one else in her life?' Fagan continued.

'Besides the revolving door relationship with Tim, no.' Pike stopped in mid-stream. 'Unless you count her regular stalker, Benny Nelson.'

'Still a bit of a wierdo is he?'

'And the biggest perv in Abergavenny. Still walking free despite the number of complaints people have made to the police over the years.'

'Weren't you and him good mates at one time?' Fagan queried.

'Let's get one thing straight. We were never mates.' Pike said in a defensive tone. 'He'd latch on to me every time I went in the Black Lion. Used to make everyone's skin crawl. He'd hang around by the school gates in his Capri waiting for the young girls to come out of school so he could offer them a lift home. He'd fuck off to Thailand twice a year to sample the merchandise. That's what he boasted about twenty years ago.'

'Where is he now?'

'Married to a Thai bride. She's got to be all of twenty-five. He turns sixty-three this year. Put a lot of pictures on Facebook with his child bride.'

Fagan grimaced.

'They live up the Mumbles Close estate.'

'Where?'

'A housing estate they built a few decades back. It runs up by the bypass. Benny was arrested last year. Apparently, he beat the shit out of the poor girl. But she didn't press charges. He still roams the streets eyeing up the younger women. A load of girls told him to fuck off a few months ago when he tried to buy them drinks at the Auberge.'

'The Auberge?'

'Jesus Fagan, you are behind the times. You know, the Old Shire just down from Tesco.'

'Now I remember, the Herefordshire House.' Fagan recalled. 'You say Benny was Rebecca's regular stalker?'

Pike nodded. 'He had been following her for years. At first she felt sorry for him. So she'd go to Wetherspoons and have a drink with him. Then he got creepy, so she had to distance herself. I told her to file a restraining order against him. Always struck me as odd. I joked with her once. She was way too old for him. He'd turn up at the chippy every other day and try to talk to Rebecca. Most days, she would brush him off. You could say Rebecca got used to it. Her son Ricky gave him a hammering a few years ago. During lockdown he would knock on her door almost every day. She phoned the police, but they didn't do anything. Ricky went round his house and kicked the shit out of him. The police arrested him and charged him with assault. While Benny was free to carry on stalking her.'

'Tell me about Rebecca's son.'

'Ricky is a good lad, mostly.'

'But?'

'He hasn't got much of a role model for a father. Tim Davis isn't exactly dad of the year. To be honest, Rebecca never wanted him to be Ricky's dad, despite him being his natural father.'

'Why is that?'

'Rebecca never really loved Tim.' Pike took a moment to choose his words. 'I think she was still in love with you.'

Fagan was suddenly thrust back to 1985. The last time he had seen Rebecca.

'She told me what happened between you two. How you just fucked off up north without as much as an explanation.'

'It wasn't like I had a choice. It was either leave Abergavenny or end up back inside for what I did to Nelson.'

'Time stood still for her. It was still the nineteen eighties for Rebecca. She'd still listen to Wham and Madonna from the early days. Had a wallpaper of Simon Le Bon on her phone.'

'When was the last time Benny had stalked her?'

'Last Saturday night at the Cantreff. But Tim was there to deal with him.'

'Did he beat him up?'

'No, they threw him out of the pub. Rebecca said they had an argument because Benny stole her mobile phone off the bar. He was almost out of the door with it when Tim stopped him.'

'A mobile phone, you say?' Fagan stated, as he remembered the phone case at the murder scene. 'Did the phone have a case?'

'I wasn't there, so I wouldn't know.'

'Do you know if she had a cover for the phone?'

Pike thought for a few seconds before nodding. 'Yeah, she had a wallpaper of Simon Le Bon. And I think on the back of her phone she had a picture of Spandau Ballet. I remember Rebecca saying that Benny and Tim struggled with the phone and the case broke off.'

'Do you know what happened to the case?'

Pike nodded. 'Rebecca told me she threw the case at

Benny and said, if you want a piece of me that much, then you can shove it up your arse'

'Benny kept the case?'

'Yeah, I think so. Why?'

Fagan produced his mobile phone and called up Watkins' number. 'Sean, I need you to track down a Benny Nelson, or Ben Nelson. He lives on an estate called Mumbles Close. We may have our first suspect.'

'Jesus, I thought Benny was many things, but not a murderer.'

Fagan pocketed his phone and looked about the café. 'Looks like you've done well for yourself over the years.'

'It was hard during the pandemic. So, you're a detective Inspector with the police..'

'Just transferred from Merseyside.'

'Why did you come back to Abergavenny? We're not exactly the crime capital of Wales.'

'Let's just say I had seen one too many dead bodies in my time.'

'Now you're back home and the first thing that happens is your ex-girlfriend showing up dead. Have you seen Susanna yet?'

'No. But she's on my list of people to speak to.'

'A lot of painful memories there. You went out with her as well. That's going to be an awkward conversation when it happens.'

'I have to question Benny.' He stood and walked towards the door of the restaurant. 'Listen, if it means anything to you Justin, I'm sorry I was such a dick to you at school. You didn't deserve it.'

Pike stared back, nodding. 'Take care of yourself, Fagan.'

CHAPTER 7

Ty-Affan–Monmouthshire–January 1982

The rain pounded down on the roof of the Ford Transit council van. The two men and five youths sat in the vehicle trying to keep warm, drinking tepid coffee out of flasks. Three of the youths were playing cards. The air was thick with cigarette smoke.

'Fuck me, can't you turn the heating on for five minutes?' Fagan complained, pulling his donkey jacket tight. 'It's fucking freezing in here.'

'No.' Colin, one of two supervisors sat in the front of the van, answered. 'I'm not running the engine. Chambers will have my guts for garters if he finds out we've been using extra fuel. I was nearly sacked last week because we'd been on that jolly to Chepstow.'

'Yeah, but it was worth it.' One youth playing cards boasted. 'I'm seeing that bird again on Friday night.'

'Right, this is what's going to happen.' John, the other supervisor, announced. 'Marc and Tim will scamper up that ladder and finish putting the tiles on that bus shelter roof.'

'Fuck off.' Davis protested. 'Why can't they do it?' He looked at the three youths playing cards.

'Because they're already soaked from cleaning up.' Colin stated. 'You two can get wet for a change. Instead of sitting in the back and gawping at the tits in the Sun.'

'It won't take long.' John added. 'Then we'll pop back to the pub in Dingestow for a quick half and dry off.'

Fagan and Davis jumped down from the van's back

doors. An icy wind enveloped them.

'Fuck, the rain feels like razor blades.' Davis grumbled, pulling his woollen hat over his head.

Colin wound down the window. 'Come on you two. It won't take long. Then we'll be on our way.'

'You go on top and I'll hand you the tiles.' Davis suggested.

Fagan didn't argue. The thought of a pint motivated him. He climbed the ladder and perched himself on the roof of the bus shelter they had been building for the last three weeks. The tilted roof made it difficult to get any kind of gripping. Fagan had to rely on the ability to hold his own body weight, otherwise it was an eight-foot drop onto a concrete footpath.

Davis handed him the first tile.

An explosion crackled across the landscape. Fagan looked towards the horizon. 'Must be two o'clock at the ammunition factory. Our dad will be clocking off now.'

Davis looked in the same direction. 'What is it your dad does there?'

'He doesn't talk about it. Says it's top secret or something like that.'

'They buried Mike's dad last week. Didn't he work there?'

Fagan nodded. 'Dad went to the funeral. He was really cut up about it. They'd been mates for over twenty years.'

'Sarah Armstrong's mother died last year. She worked there as well.'

'Yeah, our mam and dad went to her funeral. They had a blazing row afterwards. Mam hates dad working there. They were taking on at Coopers filters. Mam wanted him to get a job there but dad loves it at the ammunition factory. He has a lot of mates there.'

'It can't be all that healthy working there.' Davis said,

handing Fagan another tile.

'I was thinking about working there myself, but our mam won't allow it.'

'Hey, guess who I shagged last night?' Davis boasted, changing the subject.

Fagan looked at him. 'Who?'

'Michelle Pike.'

'Pissy Pike, Justin the mong's sister.'

'Yeah, and she's up for anything.'

'Benny Nelson reckoned he shagged her when she was thirteen. Said he broke her in.'

'I wouldn't believe anything that twat tells you.'

'I thought you didn't like her. You always said she stank of piss when you had to sit next to her in biology.'

'She still stinks of piss. But she does anything you tell her to do. Swallows and everything.'

'You're a complete twat, treating Rebecca like that.'

'Rebecca.' Davis scoffed. 'I'll be an old man before she opens her legs for me. Tell you what, Michelle and Diane Marks are going down the Cantreff on Friday night. Why don't you come? Diane will hook up with you.'

'No thank you. Diane Marks will open her legs for anyone. I heard the Wetton brothers took turns on her last month.'

Davis smiled. 'There's an idea.'

'I ain't no porridge stirrer, thank you very much. Besides, I promised to take Susanna to the Cartwheel for a meal. Weren't you supposed to be taking Rebecca out this weekend?'

'I was, but since she's yet to do the dirty with me, I cancelled. Besides, she'll make me watch that fucking film again, Casablanca. It's her favourite film of all time.'

'What do you mean, watch it again?'

'Didn't Susanna tell you about the new gadget her dad

bought for Christmas?'

Fagan frowned. 'You know he won't let me in the house.'

Davis grinned. 'Oh yes. Anyway, it's called a video recorder.'

'A video what?'

'It's a machine that tapes TV programs. It's amazing, Rebecca taped Top of the Pops last week with Jimmy Savile.'

'Fucking love him.' Fagan stated. 'Do you remember that charity event he turned up at a few years ago? Evans got his autograph. I was so pissed off at those boys who went to Forest Coalpit dorms with him and Sergeant Bob. So, where did they get this video recorder from?'

'Their dad got it from Rediffusion. Rebecca taped that bloody film. Made me watch it twice over on Sunday. Wouldn't even let me grope her tits.'

'Well, she is all prim and proper.'

'They reckon these video recorders are the thing of the future. Soon you won't have to go to the pictures with Tyler and Evans.'

'The only reason I go with those two is because they can get me in for free. Do the Smith Brothers know about this video thingy?'

'Don't think so. It will piss them off. Their dad is always in competition with Rebecca's dad. Buying all the latest gadgets and everything. Remember when they were the first ones in Abergavenny to get an Atari game machine?'

'Yeah, I remember them losing their door key and making me climb a ladder to get in through a window to open the door. Bernie the bummer Baxter had one of those Atari machines. They reckon he used to invite all the young boys from school to his house to play games. And play with their balls.'

'Wouldn't surprise me.' Davis handed up another tile.

'Listen, don't be such a twat to Becky. She doesn't deserve it.' Fagan advised.

'Growing fond of her, are we?' Davis teased.

'No.' Fagan insisted. 'But she's one of the decent girls in Abergavenny. Every bloke is jealous of you.'

'Including you by the sounds if it.'

'I'm going out with Susanna, remember? And at least we've done the dirty, unlike you and Rebecca.'

'Yeah, and when her dad finds out he'll string you up. So I wouldn't get any ideas about Rebecca.'

After an hour and a good soaking, Fagan and Davis sat in the pub at Dingestow drinking a well-earned pint.

'How long do you see yourself going out with Susanna?' Davis asked.

Fagan gulped down his pint before placing it on the table. 'Not long. She fucks off to university soon. She'll end up with some posh college puke. What about you, any plans for the future?'

'Not really. As soon as I pop Rebecca's cherry, I'll get rid of her and move on.'

'You're a twat if you do that.'

Davis ignored Fagan's insult. 'I don't plan to settle down just yet. There are still plenty of girls left to go through in this town. Have you seen the girls going to the Farmers lately? I wouldn't mind shagging that Jackie Mills.'

'You'll have to Stand behind Edwards. He's got his eye on her. Besides, you know what her brother Tommy is like. Remember last year when he gave Eric Richards a good hiding, just for talking to her.'

'Hey, you two lover boys. You want to get a game of pool in before we leave?' Colin shouted over from the bar.

CHAPTER 8

Newport Central police HQ – 1:56pm

'This is better.' Fagan said. 'I thought we'd have to interview Benny at Morrisons café.'

'A camera has been set up. Nelson's solicitor has been moaning a bit, but everything is legit and by the book. We had to call a duty solicitor. Benny's usual solicitor isn't available.' Watkins explained.

'His usual solicitor?'

'Some bigwig from London.'

'Did Nelson say anything when you arrested him?'

Watkins flipped open his notebook. 'Only that he was being framed and the people of Abergavenny have it in for him. I also bumped into someone called Jamie Evans. He owns a taxi company that operates out of Mumbles Close. He told me to tell you that he was spot on about *Star Wars*.'

Fagan Smiled. 'An old friend who was a bit of a fanboy back in the day. What about tracking down Rebecca's son?'

'No luck yet boss.'

'Anything interesting at Nelson's house?'

'Not yet, but it's a total shithole. He's a hoarder by the looks. There are hundreds of bags of rubbish piled up in his back garden.'

Fagan ran the situation through his mind. 'I'm about to face a man I haven't seen in almost forty years.'

'Do you want me to take the lead on the interview?' Watkins offered.

Fagan considered the proposal. 'No, I should be fine.'

He lied.

Benny Nelson sat relaxed. He sipped from a plastic cup. Waiting to be interviewed by some idiot of a detective. He glanced at his solicitor. 'Don't worry, I've been here loads of times before. They can never make anything stick. This should be quick.'

'Have you ever been accused of murder before?' The solicitor asked in a calm tone.

Nelson hesitated before shaking his head.

'Then don't say anything that might land you in the shit.'

The door opened and two men walked in, sitting down opposite Nelson and his solicitor. One of them placed a tray and a folder on the table.

Watkins pointed a small remote control at the camera.

Nelson scrutinised the other man, finally realising who it was. 'Fuck me, look who the cat dragged back to the valleys. Never thought I'd see you again Fagan.' He leant back in his chair, folding his arms. 'If I remember correctly, Sergeant Bob told you to leave Abergavenny and never come back.'

Fagan looked around. 'And where is Sergeant Bob these days? Oh yeah, he died years ago.' He placed his phone down on the table, pressing the record icon on the screen. 'Interview with Ben Nelson. Present in the room are Mr Nelson and his solicitor, Marcus Andrews. Interviewing officers are Detective Sergeant Sean Watkins and myself, Detective Inspector Marc Fagan.'

Nelson burst into laughter. 'Detective Inspector, now I've seen it all.'

Fagan stared at Nelson. 'Long time no see Benny. How have you been all these years? How's your jaw?'

Nelson glared back. 'Bit of a comedian I see. Is that what you've been doing for the past forty years? Telling jokes about me.'

Fagan noted the thick tangled beard and the bloated stomach. 'You've let yourself go over the years. You used to be scrawny with a skinhead.'

'And you used to be a complete prick.'

Fagan picked up the phone case in the plastic bag from the tray. 'I am showing Mr Nelson a phone case which was recovered at the scene of the crime this morning.'

Nelson gave the item a hard stare.

'Have you ever seen this item before?' Watkins asked.

Nelson continued to glare at the phone case. 'No comment.'

'According to a witness you were caught trying to steal Rebecca Jenkins' phone last weekend when you were at the Cantreff.'

'No, I was giving it her back. She'd dropped it on the floor.' Nelson seemed to be in a panic as he spoke.

'That's not what Rebecca told Justin Pike.' Fagan said.

'That fucking freak! Why are you his mate all of a sudden? I remember you used to pick on him at school.'

'You were seen taking her phone off the bar. Tim Davis caught you going out the door. You struggled for the phone.' Fagan pointed at the bag. 'The phone case was ripped off., Rebecca threw it at you.' Fagan checked his notebook. 'She told you, if you want a piece of me, then you can shove it up your arse.'

'No comment.'

'CSIs have already run it through our fingerprint database. Your prints are all over it.' Watkins revealed.

'So you see Benny, we have you bang to rights.' Fagan explained. 'You can sit there and say no comment all you want. But it won't help you.'

Nelson took a deep breath.

'There's no point lying Benny. You'd been stalking

Rebecca for years. Justin confirmed this.' Fagan explained. 'As I'm sure Jackie Mills will when I speak with her later on today. Where were you late last night?'

'I was in Cardiff Bay at the Odeon, watching a film. Check my credit card records, they'll verify I was there. I even pinged my location on Facebook. And I'm sure I'm on their CCTV system.'

'What film were you watching?'

'*John Wick, Chapter four*.'

'A long way to go to watch a film, isn't it? I see they have a cinema where Fads used to be.'

'I don't like it there. The screens are tiny. And they have uncomfortable seats.'

'What time did the film end?'

'About half-past twelve. I went to a late-night viewing.'

'Did you come straight home?'

'Yes.'

'What time did you arrive back in Abergavenny?'

'Just after one o'clock. I stopped off at MacDonald's for a burger, then went home.'

'You didn't call on Rebecca at her flat in Llwynu Lane?'

'No.'

'Then how did this phone case end up at the murder scene?'

'I don't know.'

'Come on Benny, you've had a thing for Rebecca for decades.' Fagan paused. 'There was me thinking she was too old for you.'

Nelson smirked. 'I know what you're trying to do Fagan.'

Fagan glanced down at a file he had brought with him. 'Your wife is young, isn't she? Twenty-five-years-old. Mon Nelson.'

'Where exactly are you going with this line of questioning DI Fagan?' Andrews enquired.

Fagan ignored him. 'It says here you were arrested last year on domestic battery charges. But you were released after your wife dropped the charges.'

'We had a little tiff, that's all.'

'How long have you been married?'

'Ten years.'

'You've been married since she was sixteen.' Watkins enquired.

'And you are what, sixty three this year?' Fagan pointed out.

'There's no law against it. The legal age of consent in this country is sixteen. I've done nothing wrong. Blokes like you are jealous I can still pull the young ladies.'

'Come on Benny, it's obvious you bought your wife from Thailand. Can't see you pulling an eighteen-year-old local girl. Justin said you've been going to Thailand for years, to sample the merchandise, so to speak.'

'You can't prove anything.'

Fagan leaned forward interlocking his fingers. 'Right now Benny, a team of officers are searching your house. They will strip the place bare.'

'You won't find anything.' Nelson grinned. 'I've been down this road before.'

'So have I Benny. I've been in the force long enough to know what men like you are like.'

Nelson leant forward. 'And I know what you're like, Fagan. What you and Davis did to Rebecca was far worse than what you are accusing me of.'

'What exactly did I do to Rebecca?' Fagan challenged.

'You and Davis played constant mind games with her. Taking it in turns who would shag her.'

'Is that what she told you?'

'When you left, you didn't just break her heart. You shattered it. Then along came Davis to finish the job. Got her pregnant and spent the next thirty-seven years playing mind games with her.'

'And you wanted to give her something else, did you?' Watkins said.

'I could have given her the life you and Davis could have never given her.'

'What, in that squalid place you have at the Mumbles Estate. I was there this morning looking at the hundreds of rubbish bags you've chucked in the garden. Didn't smell very nice. Lots of rats scurrying about. I bet the neighbours love you for that.'

'Why did you murder Rebecca Benny?' Fagan asked.

'I didn't murder her. I wouldn't do anything to hurt anyone.'

'Try telling that to Jenny Lockey.'

Nelson searched his memory. 'Are you for real? That was forty years ago.'

'I bet it still seems like yesterday to Jenny.'

'Detective, I don't' see how this applies to the case at hand.' Andrews protested.

'I can assure you it's relevant. What happened again Benny? You just wanted to give her a lift home.'

'Which I did.'

'Yeah, but along the way you drove her up over the Keepers and tried to rape her. Then you dumped her on the side of the road.'

'It was all consensual. She even admitted that.'

'Only because her parents didn't want the shame.'

'DI Fagan, are these memory lane accusations relevant to my client's current accusation?' Andrews asked.

'You're clutching at straws if you're desperate enough to dredge up the past.' Nelson taunted.

'But it's the past that puts you in the frame Benny. I may have been gone for almost forty years. But from what I have been told, you're still the same as when I left.'

'And never been found guilty of anything.' Nelson boasted glancing at his solicitor. 'See, I told you this won't take long. Detective inspector my arse.' Nelson mocked. 'I remember that time at Ruth Thomson's house when we all played Cluedo. You couldn't have guessed the murderer even if the name was written for you.'

'First off, I wasn't there because of Ruth. I was in the next room with her brother, Paul. We were on the Scalextric. It was you and Ruth playing Cluedo. Only it wasn't ordinary Cluedo was it Benny? It was strip Cluedo. Every time Ruth guessed wrong, she had to remove an item of clothing.'

'She fucking loved it.' Nelson sneered.

'How old was Ruth at the time Benny, twelve or thirteen? How old were you, nineteen? I remember their dad spending six months in prison for beating the shit out of you. Remember that saying you had? If they're old enough to bleed, they're old enough to butcher.'

'I must protest DI Fagan. If you're not here to interview my client about anything else but his past, then I'm ending this interview.'

Fagan composed himself. 'You've been stalking Rebecca for decades. Even her son gave you a hammering a few years back. During lockdown you would knock on her door every day.'

'Little twat, just like his old man. Ricky didn't give a shit about lockdown. He would be out and about. I called on her every day to make sure she was ok.'

'Why did you murder her, Benny?'

'I didn't fucking touch her, ok.' Nelson paused. 'Look, I took the mobile phone case. But I don't know how it ended up with Rebecca, I swear.'

'So it just magically appeared next to her body?'

Watkins said.

'I would never hurt her.' Nelson insisted. 'If you want to arrest someone, then arrest Tim Davis. He used to give her a good hiding every other week. I bet that's something Pike didn't mention. Did he tell you about the time he put her in Nevil Hall for two weeks? I visited her every day. I was the only one who stuck by her. Pike didn't have the balls to stand up to Tim.'

'Did you ever stand up to him?'

'Of course not.'

'Why?'

'Look at me. I'm not exactly Mike Tyson am I.' Nelson inhaled. 'He treated her like shit.'

'She told you this, did she?' Fagan said.

'She used to describe how he would punch her in the stomach. And then there was you, Mr perfect.'

'What did she say about me?'

'She told me the last time you saw her at the train station. Begging you not to leave. But you just upped and pissed off. If you would have kept in touch, it would have been different. She might not have rejected me.'

Fagan glared back at Nelson. 'We both know why I had to leave Benny.'

'She kept on rejecting me, over and over.'

'So that's what this is all about. Her rejecting you. Is that why you murdered Rebecca?'

'For the tenth fucking time, I didn't murder her.' Nelson shouted. 'Don't you have any other suspects you can arrest?'

'The mobile phone case found this morning is covered with your fingerprints Benny. Right now, you are the only suspect. We have plenty of witnesses to testify you had an obsession with her. I'm sure it will only be a matter of time before we find that phone. And when we do, you will be charged with her murder. This town can finally be rid of you. You'll never be able to come back.'

'Despite the mobile phone case, do you have any other evidence to link my client with the murder of Rebecca Jenkins?' Andrews mused. 'Such as DNA evidence on the body.'

'The coroner is due to examine Rebecca's body later on today. I'm sure DNA evidence will conclude that Benny is connected with her murder. I'm going to ask you one more time. Did you murder Rebecca Jenkins?'

'No, I did not. Yes, we had a troubled history. But I didn't lay a finger on her. This is all a setup, you said it yourself. Charge me with her murder and this town will finally be rid of me.'

'If there is nothing else, detective, my client is free to go.'

Nelson stood. 'You've got a nerve coming back to Abergavenny Fagan. Especially after what you did to me, your old pal, and your dead girlfriend. I suggest you let the real police deal with this. You're clearly not cut out for the job.'

'Are you okay, boss?' Watkins questioned.

Fagan looked towards the door. 'Not really. Arrogant prick thinks he can get away with anything.'

'We'll take his place apart and find that phone.'

'What about his wife?'

'She wasn't home when we cautioned Nelson.'

'Find out where we are with the examination of Rebecca's body. We need to find her son asap. We also need to track down Nelson's wife.'

'I'll double down and see if I can reach him.'

'I'll speak with another friend of Rebecca's.' Fagan said.

C H A P T E R 9

Abergavenny Cinema – 12th June 1982

Evans took in a lung full of warm air, spinning around with his arms outstretched. 'Oh my god, that film was brilliant. It was the best. Spielberg has really pushed the boat out.'

'I cannot fucking believe you cried.' Fagan taunted.

'I didn't.'

'Fuck off, I saw you wiping the tears away.'

'It was pretty sad towards the end.' Tyler admitted. 'Especially when ET said come, and Elliot said stay.'

'I thought the BMX bike chase was good.' Fagan admitted.

'So you did like *ET The Extraterrestrial*.'

'It was okay in some parts.'

'It was fucking brilliant all the way through. I'll tell you something else. I have a theory.'

'Here we go, another film theory moment.' Fagan rolled his eyes.

'Hear me out. Think about it. When ET was making all those objects float. When he was showing Elliot and his brother and sister where he lived.'

'On another planet you mean.' Tyler said.

'Yes, but he was moving those objects with his mind.'

'What's your point?' Fagan sighed.

'Don't you get it? The moving of objects with his mind. ET is a bloody Jedi.'

Tyler burst into laughter. 'You're off your fucking head.'

'Stephen Spielberg and George Lucas are best mates.'

'That doesn't mean anything.'

'Yes, it does. They're always playing off each other in their films. In *Close Encounters of the Third Kind*, R2D2 appears on the underside of the mothership towards the end.' Evans waggled his finger at Fagan and Tyler. 'Mark my word, ET will show up in *Star Wars* next year.'

'We'll see.' Tyler said, noticing the sombre look Fagan was expressing. 'You okay Fagan?'

'Yeah, I was just remembering when we went to see *The Empire Strikes Back*. Who were we with?'

Evans nodded. 'Danny, Peter and Graham.'

'Graham is dead, Danny is missing and Peter moved away with his parents.'

A group of girls appeared out of the cinema's entrance. A car pulled up to the side of the curb. Three of the girls got in the car.

Fagan noticed Rebecca walking off alone.

'Come on, let's go to The Somerset Arms before Dai the landlord changes his mind and bans us again.' Evans said.

Fagan watched as Rebecca walked towards the cattle market. 'I'll think I'll pass.'

Evans looked in the same direction. 'I thought you were going out with her sister?'

'We've taken a break. She reckons we were getting too intense.'

'So what? Your solution is to shag her younger sister. Davis will flip his lid.'

Fagan looked at Evans. 'No, but as you can see, she's all alone. Tim won't flip his lid. He's shagging any girl who will open her legs these days.' He looked in Rebecca's direction. 'I thought I'd walk her home.'

'Come on Jamie. We'll visit you in Nevil Hall when Davis gets through with you.'

Fagan sprinted after Rebecca.

Rebecca turned, hearing someone running up from behind.

'Rebecca, wait up.' Fagan stopped, clutching his side.

'You smoke too much. Those things will kill you one day.'

Fagan laughed. 'You could be right.'

'What do you want?'

'I thought I might walk you home.'

Rebecca rolled her eyes. 'Do you say that to all the girls you want to shag?'

'Who says anything about wanting to shag anyone?' Fagan panted. 'I thought your dad would be picking you up.'

Rebecca shook her head. 'No, mum and dad are at the ammunition factory social club. Did your mum and dad go? A comedian called Bernard Manning is there.'

Fagan shook his head. 'Dad hasn't been feeling too well over the last few weeks. He's signed off on the sick.' Fagan reached into his pocket and pulled out a pack of cigarettes. 'Is that a yes to walking you home?' He asked, lighting the cigarette.

Rebecca considered the request, eventually nodding. 'No shortcut through the park. Straight up the Hereford Road.'

'Lead the way, my lady.' Fagan invited.

They walked past the cattle market, emerging out onto the main road.

'So, what did you think of *ET*?' Fagan asked.

'It wasn't bad. Tina cried her eyes out.'

'Yeah, I just took the piss out of Evans. He was blubbering at the end.'

'Still not as good as *Casablanca*.'

'Why are you so obsessed with an old black and white

film?'

'Because it's a simple film with simple values.'

Fagan shrugged. 'Now you've totally lost me.'

'It's about many things. A reluctant hero who doesn't want to be a hero. The heroine who wants to be with the hero. But duty compels her to be with a man she doesn't really love. In the end the reluctant hero saves the woman he loves by shooting a German officer. It's an escape to simpler times. A time when people worried more about what was going on in the wider world. Unlike the world we live in today.'

'Now I'm totally confused.'

'That's easy to do, isn't it, Fagan.' Rebecca chuckled.

'Cheeky little cow.'

Rebecca laughed before inhaling. 'Don't you think the world is moving too fast?'

'Depends what you mean by that.'

'Everyone trying to be like everyone else. Take dad for instance. He's obsessed with buying the latest gadgets, just to show off in front of Robbie and Sam's dad.'

'They;ve been rivals since they were at school.'

'Dad is getting a twenty-inch TV next week to go with the video recorder. He got me and Susanna a black-and-white TV for our bedrooms. I don't really want to watch TV in my bedroom.'

Fagan smiled. 'What do you want to do in your bedroom?'

Rebecca scowled at him.

'I was joking.' Fagan said innocently.

'And then there's that.'

'What?'

'You know, sex.' Rebecca said shyly. 'I'm fed up with being pressured into bed.'

'Has Tim done something?' Fagan asked with concern.

'No, Tim's not like that. Although he's tried on more than one occasion. But he's never forced himself on me. He can be very sweet sometimes, but I know he's only doing it to get into my knickers. It's like I'm some sort of challenge to him or something. So he can go boasting to his mates.' Rebecca paused for thought. 'All the girls I hung around with at school with have popped their cherries. Did you hear about Susan Jones?'

Fagan nodded. 'Saw her brother Robbie last week in the Shire. She's up the poke, isn't she?'

Rebecca nodded. 'Did he say who the father is?'

'No, I tried to get it out of him.'

'They reckon it's Benny Nelson.' Rebecca revealed.

'Fuck's sake, that twat should be locked up. I see Paul Thomson's dad is out of clink. He didn't deserve to go down for beating that shithead up.'

'Susan is fifteen years old and pregnant. She'll end up on the dole for the rest of her life.'

'Just like her dad, who sits in the Labour club every Saturday night getting pissed.'

'Do you know what Katy Prosser told me the other night?'

Fagan shrugged.

'She told me she lost her virginity to a lorry driver in the bus station.'

'No fucking way.' Fagan stated loudly.

Rebecca nodded. 'When she was fifteen. Apparently, she met him at the Chevron one Friday night. He bought her a takeaway and took her back to his lorry. Is it true about you and Jane Thomas?'

Fagan scratched the back of his head, trying to sum up an answer.

'Don't deny it. She told me everything. How you both did it when she was babysitting for a neighbour just down the road from her mum's house.'

'It wasn't anything mind blowing. We started snogging and ended up on the floor.'

Rebecca stared up at the star filled sky. 'I want to keep my innocence for a little longer. I don't want to be rushed. Kind of like Sandra D from *Grease*. I want the moment to be special. I want to find my Rick and fall madly in love.'

'Who the hell is Rick?'

'He's the leading man in *Casablanca*.' Rebecca laughed. 'Played by Humphrey Bogart. You remind me of him.'

'Why is that?' Fagan asked, taking a long drag from his cigarette.

'Because you smoke a lot, just like Rick.'

Fagan tossed his cigarette onto the floor.

'Can I ask you a question?'

'Sure, ask away.'

'What do you think the future is going to be like?'

'How do you mean?'

'Will we still be here in ten years?'

'Probably, I guess. We'll be old.'

'No, we won't. We'll be in our late twenties. That's not old. What do you think you'll be doing?'

'Still getting pissed at the Somerset Arms every weekend.'

'I don't think any of us will be here. Russia and America will blow us all up.'

'My dad says they won't. He says they're winding down production at the ammunition factory. They're laying people off.' Fagan paused for thought.

Rebecca looked at him. 'You okay Fagan?'

'Dad's not very well at the moment. He's having constant headaches. He's seeing some kind of specialist.'

'Your dad will soon be on the mend again.' Rebecca assured him.

They walked up an incline past a grocery shop.

Rebecca looked at the shop. 'No one hangs around Ray's Mini Market anymore?'

'We all go to the back of Dobbins now. They got some cool arcade machines in there. Tim has the highest score on Phoenix. And I have the highest score on Asteroids. There are a couple of fruit machines in there as well. I spent a fortune in there two weeks ago trying to get the highest score on Asteroids. It's way better than going to Tyler's and sitting there writing a computer program all day long just so we can play space invaders.'

'My dad does that. He reckons computers are the thing of the future. So, you'll still be going down The Somerset Arms in ten years.' Rebecca pondered. 'What about in forty years?'

'Forty years, Jesus, probably dead or ancient.'

'No, we'll be in our mid-fifties. My nan and granddad are older than that.'

'I'll have grandkids by then. Probably still drinking in The Somerset Arms.' He looked at Rebecca. 'What about you? Where will you be?'

'Let me see, the year will be 2023. I'll be fifty-four or thereabouts. I think I would have certainly found my Rick by then. He'll be successful. We'll have a bunch of kids and grandkids. And we'll probably be living in Oxford.'

'Oxford, that's posh.'

'My future husband will be a teacher at Oxford University.'

'Is that where you want to go?'

'Not really, but it's what dad wants. He said to me and Sue the other day that he wants us both out of Abergavenny. He doesn't think this town has a future.'

'Your dad is right. I was thinking about going to stay with my nan and grandad in Ormskirk. They're coming down tomorrow to stay with us for a few weeks. As soon as I am done with the YTS, I was going to see if there's anything available up there.'

'So you do have plans for the future. Have you told Susanna?'

'No, and don't you go telling her. Besides, she's about to go off to university. I'm expecting her to dump me any time now.'

Eventually, they reached the front gates of Rebecca's house.

'Well, here we are.' Fagan announced. 'I told you I'd get you home safe and sound.'

'Thanks for walking me home.'

'No problem.'

For a moment, they didn't speak.

Rebecca looked at him, smiling. 'You know, Fagan, you're not the dickhead I thought you were.'

'Thanks, I think.'

Rebecca giggled. 'Not many boys listen to us girls. Tim certainly doesn't. All he wants to do is get down to the nitty gritty of trying to poke me. You have really listened to me tonight.' She stepped forward and kissed Fagan on the cheek.

'So, does this mean you're up for talking another time?'

Rebecca rolled her eyes, smiling at him. 'I knew you were going to try something.'

'What, I haven't tried anything.'

'Then I'll put it in plain English. Are you asking me out?'

Fagan grimaced. 'Maybe.'

'Tell you what, if you come over tomorrow night and watch *Casablanca* with me then I'll agree to go out on a date with you.'

Fagan gave the offer a few moments of thought before nodding. 'It's a deal. Wait, what about your mum and dad?'

'They're going out and won't be back until after midnight?'

'And Susanna?'

'She's going over to Cheryl's house for the night.'

'And what about Tim?'

Rebecca frowned. 'We both know that Tim is shagging around.'

Fagan nodded. 'Yeah, you're right. He's always trying to get laid.'

'So, are you up for it tomorrow night?' Rebecca asked.

A broad grin stretched across Fagan's face.

'I mean watching Casablanca.'

'Ok.' Fagan nodded. 'But if I watch that. You have to watch *the Professionals* with me at nine o'clock.'

'I hate that series, all macho and everything.'

'And what's *Casablanca* about? All soppy shit. I think it's a fair compromise.'

Rebecca considered the proposal. 'Ok, I'll watch *the Professionals* with you.'

'Great, then at ten o'clock we can watch *Hammer House of Horror*.' Fagan suggested.

'No way, Susanna made me watch that last year. It gave me nightmares.'

'You can always cuddle up next to me when the scary bits come on.'

Rebecca shook her head. 'You don't stop trying, do you?'

Fagan smiled back. 'You can't blame a boy for doing that.'

'I'll see you at six thirty tomorrow night. You can bring some Coke and crisps.' She turned and walked up the driveway.

CHAPTER 10

The Cantreff Inn – 3-37pm

Jackie Mills wiped down the bar. The anguish of wondering what happened to Rebecca in her last hours plagued her thoughts. She had seen the post George Walker had put up on Abergavenny's Facebook page. Jackie had also tried to ring Rebecca's phone several times that morning but all she got was an answer phone message. The horror of what happened to Rebecca overshadowed those who knew her.

'Hello Jacks.' A voice called out from the pub entrance.

Jackie looked up, suppressing the urge to break down. She glared at the man standing in the doorway, releasing a snort of derision. 'You're a complete twat. You know that don't you Fagan?'

Fagan grimaced stepping through the doorway. 'Good to see you after all these years.'

'You've cost me a tenner today.'

Fagan responded with a puzzled expression.

'Edwards phoned from the Bailey earlier. Claimed you were back in town. I bet him a tenner he was full of shit. Now here you are waltzing through my door. Nearly forty years after you just fucked off.'

Fagan shoved his hands into his pockets. 'I didn't really have a choice, did I Jacks?'

'Yes you did!' Jackie boomed. 'Rebecca should have been your choice. Instead you just left her. A sobbing wreck at the train station. She would have still been here now instead of.' Jackie fought against her emotions. 'Instead of being murdered by that prick, Nelson.'

Fagan strolled up to the bar, stopping short. His eyes darted around the room. 'Where's that brother of yours, Tommy the tank?'

The grief that had overwhelmed Jackie that morning was temporarily replaced with laughter. 'You don't have to worry about Tommy. Or as he likes to be called these days, Thomas.'

'Really.'

'You'll never guess who he ended up with?'

'Not a clue.' Fagan stated.

'Claire Robinson.'

'Wow, Miss snooty arse herself. How the bloody hell did that happen?'

'They hooked up in the late eighties. She really turned him around. He started his own tarmacking company before selling it to David Podmore.'

'Abergavenny's answer to Alan Sugar.'

'They moved down Cardiff. Tommy started a plastering business and sold it for a mint. Now they have four grown-up children, nine grandchildren and a posh six-bedroom house in Penarth. Overlooking the Bay.'

'Well done, Thomas.'

'Tommy never did you any harm. It was Simon he kicked the shit out of.'

Fagan looked towards the corner of the bar, grinning. 'You had sex in front of everyone in that corner.'

Jackie massaged her forehead, recalling an old memory. 'Jesus, I was beyond pissed that night.'

'What about you Jacks? What have you been up to over the years? Any kids?'

'I have a grown-up boy and girl. They live locally. Bodie is the manager at the turkey factory and Amy works at an estate agent in town. They have three kids between them.'

'Never married?'

'I was with this bloke from Pontypool for about fifteen years, had two brilliant kids. But in the end we went our separate ways. Me and Edwards have a thing every now and then. You know, friends with benefits. How about you, any family, wives?' Jackie paused. 'Husbands?'

Fagan looked back at her frowning. 'What?'

'Everyone is into something these days Fagan. There are no boundaries any more. You are free to switch sides any time you want.'

Fagan shook his head. 'None of the above I'm afraid, including husbands. I've stayed single, mostly. Had a long term relationship.' He sighed. 'But eventually the job came first.'

'You almost sound like you regret it.'

Fagan shrugged. 'You know how it is Jacks. You think you have something special. Then one day, you wake up and discover you're two different people with nothing in common anymore.'

Jackie opened a box of cigarettes, offering it out to Fagan.

'Gave up decades ago.' Fagan declined.

'You used to smoke like a trooper. They called you Fagan the fag.'

'And I gave a few people a good hiding for calling me that. I quit smoking about a year after I moved to Ormskirk.'

Jackie took a long drag before exhaling in Fagan's face.

He wafted the smoke away.

'So, from Fagan the fag to Fagan the filth.'

'Careful Jacks.'

'You hated the police back in the day. You even gave a copper a broken nose that night outside the Farmers.'

'And spent two years in Usk young offenders' prison for it.' He paused. 'Along with what I did to Tim.'

'Why did you join up?'

'About a year after I made the move to Ormskirk, I still couldn't find a job. My criminal record followed me everywhere. Then George Walker visited us. He wanted to see if I'd got into any more trouble. I told him about having problems finding a job. He wrote me a glowing reference. I joined the police, never looked back.'

'Or came back.'

'I wasn't exactly given a choice in the matter. I had to leave it all behind.'

'Including Rebecca.'

Fagan took a deep breath and nodded.

'Besides Simon, who else have you spoken to?'

'Justin Pike at Flannel Street chippy.'

'Did he tell you what happened to his sister, Michelle?'

'No.'

'She committed suicide in the early nineties.'

'Jesus, this town has seen some tragedy.'

'It tore Justin to shreds. Then that trollop Nesta did the dirty on him.'

'Anyone know why she killed herself?'

'There were rumours.'

'Did these rumours involve Benny Nelson?'

Jackie nodded, taking another drag.

'I remember Nelson boasting about her one day. Said he took her virginity when she was thirteen.'

'Then why the fuck did you release him?'

'How do you know that?'

Jackie picked up her phone and scrolled through her Facebook newsfeed. 'He's been bragging about it on his fucking Facebook page.'

Fagan looked at the phone.

'Everyone wants that piece of shit out of Abergavenny. He's been arrested so many times over the years. Released over and over. Now he's married to that poor girl.'

'The Thai bride?'

'He came in here when he first brought her over. The girl was sixteen Fagan. As soon as they stepped in the door, I threw them back out. He was already in his fifties. He'd been grooming her for years. Going to Thailand twice every year. The girl hardly speaks a word of English. And still you lot have done nothing about him.'

'Don't look at me. I've been in Liverpool for the last thirty-odd years.'

'He's Abergavenny's version of Jimmy Savile.'

Fagan glanced at Jackie. 'Jesus, do you remember when he was in town?'

Jackie took another drag, nodding. 'May 1980 if I remember. The same week Danny Llewellyn went missing.'

'I can understand why people want to see Nelson locked away. But it's more complicated than that Jacks. There's a thing called due process and evidence. Do you know how many times the police have been sued over the years? Because we've got it wrong.'

'Then find the evidence to convict that twat.'

'Hopefully the coroner will prove he murdered Rebecca. Then we can put him away.'

'I bloody well hope so, Fagan. For the sake of Michelle and all the other girls he's abused over the years.'

'So, what kind of life did Becky have?'

'She didn't have a life Fagan. You were her life. She thought you were going to be together forever.' Jackie took another drag. 'When you left, she got back together with Tim. Nine months passed, and she gave birth to Ricky. Her dad was furious, wanted to tear Tim apart. He wanted Bec to have a decent education and a decent job. She told me about the day her dad found out she was pregnant. He called her every name under the sun. Slut, slag, trollop, prostitute. He kicked her out of the house. Didn't even let her pack.'

'Where did she go?'

'Here.'

'But you never bothered with her at school.'

'Our nan found her at the bus station all alone, sobbing her eyes out. So she brought her home.'

'Peggy Mills could never turn down a sob story.' Fagan smiled.

'People used to say our nan was the heart and soul of Abergavenny.'

'What did they used to call your nan?'

Jackie smiled. 'The Titanic.'

Fagan nodded. 'That's right, I remember.'

'She died when she was a hundred.'

'Wow, a good old age to reach.'

'The strange thing is, nan was born the day the Titanic sank, and she died exactly one hundred years later. We had a massive party for her. Everyone came around that day.' Jackie looked over at an armchair in the corner of the bar. 'Then in the night when we were all still partying, she just passed peacefully in her favourite armchair.' Jackie paused. 'She had a long and happy life.'

Fagan looked in the same direction. 'Did Rebecca stay here for long?'

'A few years. Nan loved helping her look after Ricky. She tried to get social services to help patch things up with her dad.' Jackie shook her head. 'He didn't want to know. Eventually the council found her a flat up Llwynu Lane and she's been there ever since.'

'What about her sister, Susanna?'

'Susanna Jenkins, don't get me started on that bitch.

Their dad left her the house end everything. He died of cancer in 1993.'

'What about her mother?'

'Drank herself to death within two years of their father's passing. Susanna went to Oxford and got herself a law degree. I didn't think we'd see her again. Then in 2008 she showed up out of the blue with bags of money. She lives in a big fancy house near Raglan Garden centre. With her partner, Victoria and a dozen dalmatians.'

'She's gay?'

'Yup, and proud of it. I was at the Cripple Creek with a bunch of girls from town about three years ago. In strolls Susanna with Victoria. Hanging off her arm like a fucking Gucci bag.'

'Something tells me you couldn't let that go.'

'I laid into her big time. Told her what a cunt she'd been to Bec. And how she should help her out with money. Next thing, I was being manhandled out the door by a couple of coppers.'

'You didn't hit her, did you?'

Jackie nodded. 'I gave her a good slap? Wiped the smug look off her face.' Jackie grinned, recalling the moment. 'Two months later, she had the nerve to show up at my door to tell me she wasn't pressing any charges. She said she didn't want to open up old wounds.'

'When I spoke to Justin earlier, he said Becky was on her way over here when she finished work last night.'

Jackie called up the last text message she received from Rebecca. She handed Fagan her phone. 'That was the last time she messaged me.'

Fagan read the text. 'c u in 5 xx'

'When she never turned up, I thought she changed her mind and went home. Bec always changed her mind at the last moment.'

'Make sure you keep this text message.' Fagan requested. 'Cyber CSIs will want a copy.'

'Ok.' Jackie nodded.

'What about Tim?'

'Tim has been a mess all his life. He still has a limp you gave him outside the Farmers. He only decided to register himself as disabled a few years ago. Said he did it because of the parking charges in town.'

'Jesus, I didn't realise I hurt him that bad.'

'Fagan, you nearly killed him. He spent over a year in a wheelchair.'

'And I did the time for it.'

'You were lucky you didn't give him brain damage, the way you smashed his head against the wall of the Black Lion. Have you seen him yet?'

'What do you think?'

'Well, eventually you'll have to interview him about Bec.'

'Justin Pike said Tim and Rebecca had an on and off relationship.'

'If you could call it that. He tried his best with Ricky, but Bec didn't want him as a father figure. They would argue like cat and dog. I've had to chuck them out of here loads of times over the years.'

'What did they argue about?'

'You mostly.'

'You're kidding.'

'No, every time they argued, it always came down to you.'

'Justin said he put her in hospital.'

Jackie nodded. 'I was in Spain that year. Bec didn't speak to me for six months. Said the only one who seemed to give a shit was Benny fucking Nelson.'

'He's a real piece of work.' Fagan remarked. 'I'm not

supposed to tell you anything about the interview. But there were moments earlier today when I wanted to leap across that table and beat the shit out of him. And when he got up and walked through that door.' Fagan stopped.

'What?'

'It felt like I was in Liverpool again. Interviewing the parents of Aron Miller.'

'The little boy who was murdered during lockdown. I saw it on the news. You were involved with that?'

Fagan nodded. 'I thought I'd seen it all over the years. I've seen prostitutes cut to shreds. Stab victims with their guts hanging out. But when I turned up at the site where they found Aron. I remember his Captain America hoodie. His dead eyes staring skywards. And then interviewing his dad, who didn't show one hint of emotion. Even when we showed him pictures of his dead son. He sat there and blamed everything on his wife and stepdaughter. I saw the same look in Nelson's eyes earlier. The look of someone who didn't give a fuck about the trail of shit he's left over the years.'

'If you want to nail that twat up against the wall, see your old mate, Jamie Evans. He lives up at the Mumbles estate where Benny lives. Owns the main taxi firm in Abergavenny. Jamie has been keeping an eye on Nelson for years. Trying to get dirt on him. Almost came close a few times. But the slippery bastard has always been one step ahead of him. Nelson even got Jamie done for harassment several years back. Not long after, he brought that poor girl over from Thailand.'

'What about Rebecca's phone Benny tried to steal last weekend?'

'Tim caught him at the door. Snatched the phone out of his hand.'

'A broken phone case was found near Rebecca's body

this morning. It had Benny's prints all over it.' Fagan looked over towards the entrance. 'Have you cleaned up much since that night?'

'Of course I bloody have. I keep this place spotless.'

'Where's your rubbish bags?'

'Out back, the rubbish men come tomorrow.'

'Keep everything. I'll get CSIs to pick up the rubbish bags later. If we can find the missing piece of that phone case, then we'll be one step closer to putting that bastard away.' Fagan's phone buzzed. 'Sean, tell me you have something.'

'I'm at Nevil Hall. The coroner wants to see us.'

'I'll be there in five minutes.' Fagan slipped his phone into his jacket pocket. 'The coroner has completed Rebecca's autopsy.' He turned and headed for the door.

'Fagan.' Jackie called out.

He turned to face her.

'If you catch that twat Nelson. Then you'll be the biggest hero this town has ever seen.'

Fagan nodded and walked back towards her. He placed a card with his contact details on the bar. 'Text me your number. I'll do my best to collar that twat.'

CHAPTER 11

Nevil Hall hospital – 4:34pm

Fagan and Watkins put on PPE before entering the examination room. The hospital was once again under strict covid guidelines. Everyone entering the building had to wear a facemask.

'I've received a text on the whereabouts of the victim's son. He spent the night in Newport and is on his way to make the formal identification.'

Rebecca's body was placed on a table at the centre of the room.

'Are you okay, boss?' Watkins asked.

Fagan slipped on a pair of latex gloves. 'Yes, I'm fine.' He lied. Underneath, Fagan tried to control the dread he was about to face. Seeing Rebecca lying dead in the park that morning had shocked him to the core. But he knew he had to hide his emotions if he stood any chance at catching her killer. 'Ready when you are.' He pointed to the door of the examination room.

The coroner was cleaning the instruments he had used to examine Rebecca.

'What have you found?' Fagan asked, maintaining eye contact with the coroner.

'A very nasty killing.'

'Did she even put up a fight?'

'I'm afraid not.' The coroner approached the table and threw the cover back.

Fagan took several deep breaths to contain the shock of

what he was about to face.

'She was hit from behind with a heavy object. Given the indentation in the back of her skull, I'd say it was some kind of metal bar.'

'Jesus.' Fagan gasped

'Why did he go the extra mile and strangle her?' Watkins asked.

'I was wondering that myself. It's possible she could have remained conscious after the murderer hit her. Although given the force of the blow, she couldn't have remained alive for very long. A minute tops, maybe. If she did try to get up after she was struck then the murderer used what I believe to be a cable, perhaps a mobile phone charger. The strangulation marks are quite deep. Our killer was full of rage.'

Fagan spotted a small table containing the driver's licence. 'What about the blood found on her licence?'

'There are no fingerprints. There is however, the shape of a finger.' He picked it up and pointed to an area on the license. 'Our murderer was definitely wearing gloves. Probably disposable ones which are readily available now, thanks to the pandemic.'

'What else have you found?'

'Not a lot, I'm afraid. This is what we in the trade call a clean murder. All the usual signs of a violent death. But little to show who the murderer could have been.'

'Any sign of sexual assault?'

'No, this is a straight up murder.'

'Pike said when they locked up at the chippy last night, he offered her a lift but she refused.'

'Did Pike say where she had gone when they parted company?' Watkins asked.

'He said she was on her way to the Cantreff. She text Jackie Mills to say she was going over there, but never arrived.'

'There are plenty of CCTV cameras around Flannel street. Our victim could have taken any number of routes to the Cantreff. We'll have to trawl through a lot of footage to see if she appears anywhere.'

Fagan ran different scenarios through his head. 'If I wanted to get to the Cantreff from Flannel Street I'd walk straight through the centre of town. Down Frogmore street which comes out onto the Brecon road, where the Cantreff is. I reckon it's a good ten to fifteen minute walk. Most of the town centre has been pedestrianised.'

'Yeah, but there are loads of vehicles who drive through the town centre at night.' Watkins said.

'Something is bound to show up on CCTV.'

'That's a lot of footage to trawl through boss.'

Fagan smiled. 'A job for that useless prick, DI Saddler.' He glanced at the body on the mortuary table. 'So, she is alive when our murderer picks her up. The question is, do they murder in their vehicle or take her somewhere then kill her?'

The coroner pointed to Rebecca's feet. 'The back of the heels of her feet have severe grazes. Meaning she was dragged to the place where she was dumped. I found traces of gravel consistent with the fine gravel near the park gates.'

'Couldn't have the suspect attacked her from behind, then dragged her to the spot.' Fagan asked.

'No.'

'Why?'

The coroner pointed at her face. 'There is bruising around the upper cheek. It's all concrete by the park gates. If she hit her face on that floor, the wounds would have been more severe, but they're not. My guess is that she fell face down on soft ground. I also found traces of horse manure where she hit her face when she fell.' He then pointed at her fingernails. 'There are also traces of horse manure under her fingernails. In the brief time she was alive, she may have tried to get to her feet.'

'Horse manure?' Watkins questioned.

'We scanned the area in the park. No horse manure was present.'

'Could you have been mistaken? A lot of dog walkers use that park. It could have been dog shit.'

The coroner shook his head. 'No, it was definitely horse shit.'

'So she was picked up on route to the Cantreff. The killer takes her off somewhere, murders her, then takes her body to the park before dumping it.' Watkins suggested.

'Right next to the park entrance near the ESSO garage in front of all that CCTV?' Fagan was doubtful. 'Too much exposure on the Hereford Road.'

'Not necessarily. There's a gate up the top end on Park Avenue. Its wide enough to get a vehicle through. The park is well lit. The suspect could have driven through the gate, then dumped her body before driving back through the gate.'

Fagan considered the evidence presented. He produced his phone and checked his text messages. Jackie had texted him a few minutes after he left the Cantreff. He dialled her number. 'Jackie, it's Fagan. Let me ask you this. Does Nelson still own that field out on the Old Ross Road? You know, the one his dad used to keep ponies.'

'Yes, I was coming back from the Copper Kettle the other morning. I spotted him turning into the field on his horse and trap. He had his Thai bride with him.'

'Do you remember the stories about Benny and that stable he had in that field?'

'Oh yeah. I tell you who you should speak to, Katy

Fleming. She told me once Benny lured her up there to look at the horses in the stable. He tried it on with her. She was fifteen at the time.'

'Are you kidding, Katy Flemming. I remember her beating me in arm wrestling.'

'She gave Nelson a kick in the bollocks he didn't forget in a hurry. After that he avoided her like the plague.'

'Good for her.' Fagan smiled.

'Have you found something?' Jackie asked.

'Can't say.' Fagan ended the call.

'What's the plan?' Watkins asked.

'Get hold of uniform and tell them to cordon off the field Nelson owns on the Old Ross Road. But tell them to do it quietly. I'm guessing Benny is back at Mumbles Close. Tell the uniform there to make sure he doesn't disappear.'

Watkins turned on his heels, producing his phone.

Fagan looked at Rebecca's body. 'Let's be clear here. Somehow, Nelson intercepts Rebecca, takes her up to that field. He then murders her. Brings her back down to Bailey Park, dumping her body near the main gates on the Hereford Road. Then discards a mobile phone case plastered with his fingerprints. Plus the bloodied driver's licence.'

'It's a reasonable theory. But we need way more evidence.' The coroner said.

Watkins came back in to the examination room. 'All sorted boss. A couple of uniform are on their way to secure the field.'

'None of this makes any sense.' Fagan said, staring at Rebecca.

'What doesn't?' Watkins asked.

'Why incriminate himself? Why leave all this evidence so that we can catch him straight away?'

'Everyone makes mistakes.' Watkins suggested. 'When

we interviewed him earlier, he admitted to keeping the mobile phone case. After he denied ever touching it.'

'That's my point.' Fagan stated. 'I haven't set foot in Abergavenny in nearly forty years. I've come across loads of people like Benny over the years. Every time I have interviewed a sex offender, Benny has always come to mind. I have spoken to a few people today who have talked about Benny and his perversions over the years. But he's never been caught or convicted of anything. Why?'

'Power.' Watkins suggested. 'Isn't that how paedophiles pray on their victims?'

'What power has he got? He's a fat bald twat with a scruffy beard. Plus, his age doesn't help him. Can't sit outside the school gates in his car anymore like he used to. Probably why he dragged that poor girl over from Thailand. Promised her a luxurious life in Britain.' He looked at Watkins. 'Has there been any sign of her today?'

'No.'

'We'll have to track her down, see how she fits into Benny's sordid lifestyle. We are missing a big piece of the puzzle.'

All three looked in the door's direction that led to the observation room.

Shouting could be heard before the door burst open. A uniform was shoved through the door, losing his balance.

CHAPTER 12

'Where is she?' A man screamed before spotting Rebecca's body on the table. 'Mam!'

The uniform scrambled to his feet and charged at the man, dragging him away from the examination table.

'Get the fuck off me!' The man roared.

Watkins stepped forward. 'Please sir, calm down. Are you Ricky Jenkins?'

'Where is he?'

'Who?'

'Benny the fucking perv that's who!' Jenkins pointed at Rebecca's body. 'He did this didn't he? He murdered our mam. When I find him I'm going to rip his fucking head from his shoulders and shit down his fucking neck.'

A woman in her early thirties entered the room and rushed to the man's side. 'Ricky, don't do this. Please come back outside. Let these officers do their job.'

Jenkins walked back over to the table where Rebecca lay. He dropped to his knees.

Watkins knelt by the side of him. 'Please Mr Jenkins, let's talk outside.'

The woman gently coaxed Jenkins to his feet and led him out of the room.

Fagan waited a few moments before following them out.

Jenkins sat with his head buried in his hands, overwhelmed with grief. The woman beside him was doing her best to calm him down.

Fagan composed himself. 'Mr Jenkins, on behalf of Gwent police, I'm sorry for your loss.'

Jenkins summoned the strength to look at Fagan. 'Who the fuck are you?'

'I'm detective Inspector Marc Fagan.'

Jenkins launched himself at Fagan, pinning him up against the wall. 'So, you're the fucking prick our mam has been talking about for the past several weeks.' He seethed.

Jenkins' girlfriend rushed forward. 'Ricky, let him go, now.' She demanded.

Jenkins ignored her.

'If you assault a fellow officer, then I cannot help you. I will not help you.' She stepped back. 'It's over between us if you touch him.'

'Listen to your girlfriend Mr Jenkins, she's talking a lot of sense.' Fagan gasped.

'Mr Jenkins, you will be tasered if you do not comply.' Watkins warned.

The uniform stood ready to discharge his taser.

Jenkins stood face to face with Fagan for a few more moments before letting him go and stepping back.

'Mr Jenkins, you need to fill in some forms. Please step this way.' Watkins invited.

Fagan brushed himself down.

'Are you okay Sir?' The woman asked.

'Fine thanks, there's no need to call me sir.'

'Sorry, force of habit. I'm a constable with the Newport constabulary. I'd show you my ID, but after Cousins we're not allowed to carry our badge when we're off duty.'

'That was shit for us all.' Fagan looked towards the door. 'Is he going to be ok?'

'Don't worry, I'll make sure he stays out of trouble.' She stood up and left the room.

Watkins walked back into the observation room. 'All

wrapped up now boss, may as well call it a day.'

Fagan replayed the last few minutes through his mind. 'What did he just say to me?'

'I can't remember. Everything happened so fast.'

'He said, you're the prick mam has been on about for the last several weeks.'

'Yeah, I remember now.'

Fagan stood and looked through the window into the examination room at Rebecca's body. 'She knew I was coming back to Abergavenny.'

'Who knew?'

Fagan turned on his heels.

'Boss, where are you going? I thought we might go for a pint at the Bailey.' Watkins called after him.

C H A P T E R 1 3

The Cantreff – 5:09pm

Jackie looked up as Fagan marched into the bar.

'Have you got him? Did Nelson kill Rebecca?'

Fagan ignored the questions. 'What did you say your daughter does for a living?'

Jackie threw back a blank stare.

'Then I'll answer for you shall I. An estate agent in St John Square. Short, pretty with brown hair.'

'Marc, I swear I didn't tell Bec.'

'Then who did?' Fagan shouted.

'Amy.'

'Your daughter.'

Jackie nodded. 'Bec was in here several weeks back when Amy came in. All she did was ask how her day had been. Amy said she had shown this good-looking older man around. You told her you were originally from Abergavenny and that you were looking to moving back. You told her everything, Marc.'

'Including my name.' Fagan added.

'It was just an innocent conversation.'

'She knew I was coming back home.' Fagan slumped down in a chair.

'You should have seen her Fagan. When Amy said your name, it was like a fire lighting in her eyes. It was like she was nineteen all over again. She bought herself some new clothes to look smart when she finally met up with you.' Jackie scrolled through the pictures on her phone before handing it to Fagan. 'When Amy handed over the keys to you she was outside the house.'

Fagan stared at the photo of himself and Jackie's daughter.

'All she wanted to do was get out of her car and say hello. But she was terrified. She thought if she did that, then you'd brush her off.'

'If she would have done that, then she would not have been lying on a slab in Nevil Hall. Jesus, I'm the reason she's dead.'

Jackie shook her head. 'No, don't go down that road. The reason she's dead is because of that twat Nelson. But you can prove he murdered her. You have the evidence.'

'Right now we can't prove shit. There are so many missing pieces. Nelson is running rings around us.'

'Fagan, listen to me. If anyone can crack this, it's you. She's looking down on you. Bec will help you nail that cunt.'

Fagan stood up. 'So you and Becky knew I was coming back?'

'Yeah, but it wasn't like she was stalking you or anything like that. When you moved into your house in Llanfoist a few weeks back she wanted to give you room to settle. She was hoping your old mates would make contact and bring you in here for a few pints. You know, reacquaint you with the old gang.'

'Did you or Becky tell anyone else I was coming back to Abergavenny?'

Jackie shook her head. 'No, not a soul, I swear. It was just me and Bec who knew you were coming back. And Amy, but she didn't know you, so she didn't say anything.'

'Becky must have told Nelson I was coming back to Abergavenny. She wanted him off her back, to stop following her.' Fagan buried his head in his hands. 'Then he murdered her.'

'None of this is your fault Marc. It's all down to that cunt, Nelson. He killed Rebecca.'

Fagan looked at Jackie. 'Not a word of this gets out, understand. If my superiors find out then I'll be booted off the case because I'm personally involved.'

Jackie nodded. 'Ok.'

Fagan marched out of the pub.

C H A P T E R 1 4

Odeon cinema – Hereford – May 1983

'Oh my god, that film was amazing.' Rebecca said spinning around with her arms out stretched. 'What's a feeling.' She sang. 'I'm going to Kestrel records next week to see if they have that song. I hope *Flashdance* comes out on video soon so that I can rent it.'

'It was ok.' Fagan mused.

Rebecca noted the look on his face. 'What?'

'We need to get back to Abergavenny. You told your dad you'll be home by five. Good job the bus station is next to the cinema.'

'Don't worry about dad. Rachel is covering for me, we're safe. I told her what time the bus is back in town and everything.'

'You weren't there at the dugout on the Mardy playing field last week. I thought your dad was going to punch my lights out. I denied ever going near you. I had to, otherwise Tim would have got suspicious.'

Rebecca Laughed. 'Trust me, dad may act like Rambo, but he's a big softy at heart.' She threw her arms around Fagan. 'I love you Marc.' She smiled. 'You're my Kevin Bacon.'

They kissed.

'No more *Casablanca* then.' Fagan said.

'Oh no, *Casablanca* is still my number one favourite film.'

'Come on, we have another half an hour before the bus

leaves. I'll buy you a milkshake and finally teach you how to play pool.'

'Yeah, no Tyler and Evans to put us off.'

They walked the short distance to the bus station café.

'I meant what I just said Marc, I really do love you.'

Fagan smiled. 'I know.'

She turned and blocked his path. 'Then why can't you say it back to me?'

'I am mad about you. We're great together. I don't look at anyone else when we are out and about. Unlike Tim when he went out with you.'

'Tim, don't start me with that boy.'

'Why, what's he done?'

'He knocked on my door last night that's what. Two o'clock in the morning. He'd been up the Chevron. He confessed his undying love for me.'

'Look, why don't we let everyone know we're a couple now? We've been going out for a few months.'

'I'm not ready yet. I love what we have. You have to admit, it's kind of romantic what we are doing. Just like Rick and Elsa from *Casablanca*. Elsa's husband had an inkling there was something between them but he didn't push it. A bit like last night when Tim called.'

'He asked you about us?'

'Not me directly. But I could hear him shouting at the door. He screamed your name half a dozen times. Then dad came up and questioned me.'

'And you denied it?'

'Of course I did.' She took his hand, looking around. 'I love coming to Hereford. Here we can be ourselves. We don't have to worry about being judged.'

'Rachel knows about us.'

'Yeah, but Rachel is good at keeping secrets.' She paused. 'Tell you what, when I turn eighteen, we'll tell everyone we're together.'

'When you turn eighteen.' Fagan groaned stepping back from her. 'That's not until December, another six months away.'

'Dad's planning a big bash for me at the Conservative club, just like he had for Susanna last year. I'll invite you and we'll make the announcement together.'

'Yeah, and it will go down like a lead balloon. When Tim finds out he'll have my guts for garters. And Susanna, plus let's not forget your dad.'

'They'll have to accept we're a couple.'

'Let me ask you this Rebecca. Do you think we have a future together?'

'Of course, what are you trying to get at?'

'You're about to get your exam results. No doubt you'll get top marks. This time next year you'll be going to Oxford.'

'Oxford can take a run and fucking jump.' Rebecca said. 'That's dad's dream, not mine. I want to stay with you. I've got an interview at the Mayflower on Tuesday. I'll be earning money and next year we can get a place together.'

'Where are we going to live, In Avenue Road?'

'I'll put my name down on the council list.' Rebecca offered. 'We can get a place up the Mardy.'

Fagan took a deep breath. 'Rebecca, we need to face the truth. We're not going to go the distance. There are too many differences between us.'

'No, that's not true.' Rebecca said. 'We talk, we have a laugh together. You're not as stupid as dad says you are. You can go back to college, resit your exams.'

'God, I couldn't stomach another two or three years in education. I'm glad to be rid of the YTS. Colin and John barking orders at me all day long.'

'Then what do you want to do?' Rebecca asked.

'I don't know.' Fagan shrugged.

'Couldn't you get a job in the ammunition factory where your dad works?'

'No fucking way. First off your dad is the manager and would make my life a living hell. Secondly, its fast becoming known as the factory of death.' Fagan stopped talking.

'How's your dad?'

'Still on the sick.' Fagan looked at his watch. 'Fuck, I have to go straight back to the house when I get home. Mam and dad said they have something to tell me.'

'Hopefully he'll be back at work soon.'

Fagan shook his head. 'He's lost so much weight lately. He looks totally different than he did before Christmas. It's just like what happened to Toby's dad and the others.'

'Don't think like that Marc. Dad's been working there for years as well. He's healthy. Your dad will get better I promise. Come on, let's not stand here and talk all doom and gloom. You promised me a milkshake and a lesson in pool.'

Fagan gave her a cheeky smile. 'I'd rather give you a lesson in something else.'

Rebecca waved her finger. 'We've plenty of time for that. And when it does happen, I promise you Marc, it will be the best night of our lives.' She turned and walked towards the café entrance.

The bus was ten minutes late leaving the station. When they reached Abergavenny Rebecca's friend, Rachel was standing near the bus depot. Fagan and Rebecca climbed down from the bus.

'Where the fuck have you two been? You're late.' Rachel complained.

'We couldn't help it. The bus was late.' Fagan explained.

'We better get back home. My brother Andrew spotted me in the bus station park on my own. I was supposed to have been with you.'

'What did you say to him?' Rebecca asked.

'I said you'd gone to the toilet so I went off looking for you.'

Rebecca turned to Fagan and kissed him. 'Ring me later on.'

When Fagan arrived back home his mother and father were sat in the kitchen.

'Hi, sorry I'm late.'

'That's okay son, sit down.' His dad invited.

Fagan sat down looking across at his mother. Her eyes were red raw from hours of crying. He looked at his dad. 'What's going on?'

'I went to see a special doctor in Cardiff yesterday. I was getting the results for a test I took a few months ago.'

'How did it go?'

'Not good I'm afraid son.' Alan Fagan took a deep breath before coughing.

Fagan's mother handed her husband a handkerchief.

'Dad, what did the doctor say?'

'It's cancer.'

Fagan stared back at his dad. His heart seemed to stop at the sound of the word, cancer.

His mother started to cry.

'Can't they do anything?' Fagan asked as tears welled up.

His dad shook his head.

Fagan broke down. 'No, no, please no.'

'I'm sorry son.' Fagan's dad sobbed. He reached over clutching his son's arm. 'I am so sorry.'

Fagan choked back the tears. 'How long have you got dad?'

'A few months maybe.'

Fagan threw his arms around his father. 'No, please, I don't want you to die, please dad.'

Fagan's dad held him close. 'I don't want to go either.' He looked across at his wife. 'I love you both so much.'

Fagan pulled away from his dad and sat back down.

'I want you to listen to me son. You have to take good care of your mam. No matter how bad things get you have to take care of her. Please, promise me that.'

Fagan managed to nod.

'You can't get into any more trouble. It will destroy your mam.'

Fagan looked at his dad. 'I promise, I will look after mam.'

'And I want you to promise me something else. I don't want you getting a job at that shit box of a factory where I work.'

Fagan sniffed, nodding. 'I promise dad.'

CHAPTER 15

Mumbles Close estate – 8:23pm

Fagan grinned, studying the logo on the side of the taxi that was parked up.

The sound of a dog barking echoed across the estate.

Fagan heard someone approach from behind.

'Going somewhere, Solo?' The man who had sneaked up, jabbed his finger in Fagan's lower back.

Fagan laughed as he turned around. 'After all these years, you still haven't changed Evans.'

Jamie Evans threw his arms around his old friend. 'I never thought I'd see this day. Marc Fagan is back in Abergavenny.'

Fagan looked at the logo on one of the taxis parked outside Evans's house. 'Does George Lucas know you've named your taxi firm Skywalker taxis?'

'He sold *Star Wars* to Disney years ago. Come on, we'll sit up on the decking and have a natter.'

A woman appeared out of the front door.

'Daisy sweetheart, some beers for me and my old pal Fagan.'

Fagan made eye contact with the woman. 'Daisy Richardson.' He stated.

'Hey Fagan.' Daisy smiled. 'I heard you were back in town.'

Fagan pointed at Evans. 'How on earth did he manage to pull you?'

'I've been wondering that for the last thirty-five years.'

She playfully winked at her husband.

They sat down on some decking that overlooked the street.

Evans waved his hand. 'Welcome to the Mumbles estate. Never will you find such a wretched hive of scum and villainy. We must be cautious.'

'You must know every line of every *Star Wars* film.' Fagan laughed.

'To right I do. Plus, I was right all along. *Star Wars* is massive, despite a lot of it being a load of crap churned out by *Disney*. Do you want to see the memorabilia I have collected? It's my retirement plan. I have some of the rarest action figures, worth a fortune.'

'Another time.'

Daisy reappeared, placing two bottles of beer on the table. 'Here you go boys.'

In the distance two police vans and a lorry with a skip on the back were parked by the curb. Police officers were carrying out bags and throwing them into the skip. Nelson appeared, shouting at one of the officers. Another uniformed officer led him away.

'Slippery twat.' Evans chastised.

'How long has Benny lived in that house?'

'Since they were first built in the 1990s.'

'What happened to the house and the money his dad left him?'

'Blew it all, didn't he. His dad passed just after you left. He was the first one to move in to this estate. Because it's so close to that field he owns.'

'I have a team of officers searching the stable.'

'Good, I hope they find something.'

'We believe it's where he murdered Rebecca.'

Evans looked at Fagan. 'I'm so sorry you had to come home to this mate.'

Fagan gulped down beer. 'There's nothing to be sorry about. I left thirty-eight years ago.'

'You had your reasons. You'd lost your dad. Spent time in Usk prison. Plus, you had to deal with Tim. And then there was Rebecca.' He looked over to Nelson's house. 'Plus that twat had you sent into exile.'

'I should have kept in touch.'

'You owe this town nothing Fagan. Me, Tyler and Edwards never hated you for not keeping in touch.'

'Tyler, where is he these days?'

'Living the dream. Wag for a wife and a four-bedroom apartment with a view of Tower Bridge.'

'How did he manage that?'

'He got a job with the local council. Computer programming or something like that. Started his own software company and made a small fortune. Then is 2009 he hit the jackpot.'

'How?'

'Made a small ten grand investment.' Evans paused. 'In Bitcoin.'

'That jammy fucker.'

'Now he's worth a cool three hundred and fifty million. He hasn't changed a bit. Every one of the last three *Star Wars* films they have made, he's got me tickets to the royal premier. Me and Daisy have been down to London loads of times. His wife is a bit stuck up, but Tyler is the same as he's always been. I messaged him earlier today to tell him you were home. He called me and told me to tell you. The next time he's in Abergavenny, he'll buy the Angel Hotel so we can have a pint.'

Fagan laughed. 'I bet he would.'

Nelson's voice drifted across the street. He was shouting at a uniform.

'How long have we known Benny?' Fagan asked.

'As far back as I can remember. He always used to try to hang around with us as kids. Although he's five years older than us. Nelson was weird growing up. He got worse as he got older. But it was when he became a teenager when he turned to the dark side, so to speak. Rumour after rumour about him touching up the younger girls in school. Plus, rumours filtered out about him touching up young boys.'

Fagan stared at Evans, who nodded. 'Do you remember that police sergeant that used to be at the station?'

'Sergeant Bob Benson.' Evans recalled.

'That's the one. I remember being thrown drunk tank one Saturday night.'

'You were thrown in the drunk tank most Saturday nights.' Evans interrupted. 'The police used to wait outside the Chevron for you to be thrown down the stairs.'

'When I was being processed, there was a woman with her daughter shouting at Sergeant Bob. I can always remember what she said. When are you going to lock up that fucking animal? He stuck his hand up my daughter's skirt. If my old man were still alive, he put him six feet under. Do you know what Sergeant Bob said?'

Evans shook his head.

'Sergeant Bob told her Benny Nelson wouldn't hurt a fly.'

'Different times back then. No one believed any of the girls who made claims about Benny.'

'Jackie told me about Justin Pike's sister, Michelle.'

'Yeah, her and Diane Marks. Both had connections with Nelson.'

'Sergeant Bob's grandson introduced himself to me. He's the Chief Constable for South Wales police. Due to retire in under twelve months.'

'Looks like the apple never fell far from the tree.'

'I've been doing a lot of thinking today.'

'Still picking up bad habits I see.' Evans teased.

'Do you remember the year we left school, 1981?'

'Course I do. We couldn't wait to get out of that shithole.' A memory flashed across Evans's mind. 'Wait, Jesus, why didn't I see that? The charity event on the sports field the year before.'

'The celebrity who attended that event was?'

'Jimmy fucking Savile.'

Fagan nodded, repeating Evans's words. 'Jimmy fucking Savile. That bloke travelled all over the country. TV cameras in tow. There were even TV cameras at the sports field that day. I can remember it all.' Fagan pointed toward Nelson's house. 'Benny had already left school four or five years previous. But I can always remember him running behind Savile. And who was running beside Benny?'

Evans shook his head, shrugging.

'Berny the bummer Baxter.'

'That fucking weirdo PE teacher from school.'

'And running by the side of Savile was none other than Sergeant Bob.'

'Whose grandson now happens to be Chief Constable of South Wales police.'

Fagan nodded. 'And behind them was mayor of Abergavenny, Ernie Brown.'

'I remember him, a scrawny-looking bloke. Dressed like Arthur Daley off Minder. He owned the car dealership opposite the bus station, Mr Brown's cars. Used to speak like he was a member of the aristocracy.'

'Also there that day was the head of the local council, and an MP. Do you remember what the prize was for the best six runners on the field that day?'

Evans leant forward, cupping his hands over his face. 'A night stay over at Forest Coalpit dorms with Uncle Jimmy and Sergeant Bob.'

'And the mayor, and that MP along with Bernie the bummer Baxter.'

'We'd been excluded from running with them that day?'

Fagan mused. 'That's because we'd poured a bucket of paint over the headmaster's car. I was pissed off we couldn't go on that run. I was so jealous of those boys for winning that competition. But we got our picture in the Abergavenny Tribune.'

'They did a big spread the following week. I got Savile to sign my BBC annual. Probably still got it somewhere. Jesus Christ, I just realised. Do you know which boys went to Forest Coalpit that night?'

Fagan rattled off a list of names. 'Andrew Rogers, Ian Williams, Liam Chandler and the Smith brothers.'

'Robbie and Sam, who were both dead before their eighteenth birthday. Andrew Rogers left Abergavenny not long after you. Williams and Chandler died of a drug overdose in the 90s. Which itself struck me as odd because none of them were druggies at school. They were respectable boys from good backgrounds.' Evans swigged back his bottle.

'You forgot someone.' Fagan pointed out. 'Graham.'

'Jesus, of course. George Walker's son.'

'My best mate.'

'Poor bastard committed suicide a year before we left school.'

'I know for a fact that Benny went with them on that overnight stay at Forest Coalpit. I saw him a few months after. He said he had the time of his life. But I don't think Savile stayed the night there. I heard he went back to the Agincourt hotel just outside Monmouth.'

'What do you think Benny meant by having the time of his life?'

'I don't know.' Fagan replied. 'Do you recall the week

leading up to that charity event with Savile?'

Evans thought about the question. 'Christ, I'd almost forgotten.'

'It was the week Danny Llewellyn went missing. Kevin Green was found near the Llanfoist bridge.'

'Half naked and half dead, if I recall.' Evans added. '*The Empire Strikes Back* was at the cinema. I remember, we all went together. Me, you, Tyler, Edwards, Walker, Llewelyn and Greeney, as we used to call him.'

'You had that massive argument with Adrian Lewis outside the cinema.'

Evans laughed. 'I remember. I told him that Vader was Luke's father. He was fuming with me because he was going to watch it on the Saturday night.'

'We all split up when we left the cinema. Danny and Kevin walked home together.'

'Yeah, that's when they disappeared. Or Danny vanished. Kevin was found the next day.'

'Do you remember when we went looking for Danny.' Fagan recalled.

Evans looked at him. 'You got locked in that cellar in that old house on the side of the Deri.'

'That incident still gives me nightmares. Locked in that cellar for two hours in total darkness.'

'Kevin Green moved away from Abergavenny as soon as he recovered from his injuries.'

'I remember our mam and dad talking about it.' Fagan explained. 'He worked with Kevin's dad at the ammunition factory. Dad once said that Kevin had full memory of what happened but was too traumatised to talk to the police. They tried all kinds of specialists that were available at the time. But they couldn't get a word out of the poor bastard.'

'They never found Danny. People still talk about it today. Jesus Fagan, this is a serious can of worms you're opening. You sure you want to go down that path?'

'Right now, it's all about catching Becky's killer. Not summoning ghosts from this town's past.' Fagan glanced up at the cameras fixed to Evans's house. 'Ever caught anything of interest on those cameras?'

'I've got loads of stuff. Residents taking a swing at Benny. Someone chucked a brick through his front window a few years back. He's had paedo spray painted on the side of his van. I caught him on film talking to my granddaughter.'

'That's when he sued you for harassment.'

Evans nodded. 'Slimy little shit. I wanted to beat him to death. Loads of people have complained about him over the years. Trying to get him off the estate. But the local housing authority has refused to budge.'

'How many times has he been arrested over the years?'

'More times than anyone can count. And every time he's got off with it.'

'Can you recall if he had a sister?'

'I think so, but you're talking before our time. My mam said he had a sister. She reckoned Benny's mother died giving birth to him. But again, it's just rumours.'

'What happened to his sister?'

'No one knows. People have said they locked her away in Pen-Y-Fal. Mam said she saw her once. She was way older than Benny, at least fifteen years between them.'

'And no one has ever seen his mother.'

'Not to my knowledge, or my old mam's. If it's local history you're interested in, you need to call on know it all Nigel.'

Fagan smiled. 'Nigel Willard Thomas. Little shit, thought he was the smartest kid in school.'

'That's the one. He's a decent bloke when you get to know him. He's written a couple of books about the history of Abergavenny. I picked him up the other day from the train station. A TV company is making a documentary about local history in South Wales. And Nigel is narrating. He also owns the entire newspaper archives of the Abergavenny Tribune, which went out of circulation decades ago. He lives in Llanover. He'll be able to tell you if Savile spent the night at Forest Coalpit dorms.'

More shouting drifted across from Nelson's house. He appeared on the street and looked in Fagan and Evans's direction.

'Here we go.' Evans said. 'He's spotted us.'

Fagan patted his friend on the knee, mimicking a cockney accent. 'Don't worry sunshine. *The Sweeney* will protect you.'

Evans burst out laughing. 'You used to smoke more than Regan and Carter.'

Nelson marched over. 'Well, well, if it isn't the dynamic duo dimwits. Detective Inspector, I haven't got a clue and Evans the dick.'

'Evening Benny, how's your day been?' Evans asked, trying to sound polite.

Nelson glared at Fagan. 'I didn't kill Rebecca.'

'You know I can't talk about that Benny. I'm off duty.' Fagan held up his bottle of beer.

'You haven't interviewed the one person you should be, Tim Davis. What's the matter? Can't bear to see your old bum chum sent down for her murder.' He then glared at Evans. 'And as for you, cunt. I've got my eye on you and everyone else who's tried to bring me down over the years. I own this town. That's what makes me fucking untouchable.' He turned and walked back towards his house.

Fagan watched as he walked away. 'He's right about one thing.'

'Marc, don't let him do a Hannibal Lecter on you. He's not untouchable.'

'It's not about him being bulletproof. It's about me talking to Tim.'

'You've not seen him at all?'

Fagan shook his head. 'I didn't think I needed to. Our prime suspect is a couple of hundred yards down the road.' Fagan paused. 'Where does Tim live these days?'

'He own's a static caravan on the side of the Skirrid. Next door to the pony trekking centre. He's been an odd job man for the past few decades.'

'Many friends?'

'Yeah, but we're all old and knackered now. He still fancies himself as Jack the lad. Still drinks in the Somerset Arms and the Cantreff.'

'Where Rebecca drank.'

'Yeah, I take it Jackie told you about their hot and cold relationship.'

'She did.'

'I think they kind of love each other.'

'I suppose I'll have to see Tim at some point. Along with Rebecca's sister.'

'Hang on, didn't you mention the police are searching Benny's stable down the road?'

'Yep.' Fagan said, finishing the contents of his bottle.

'What about his allotment?'

Fagan looked at Evans. 'Shit, I forgot about that.'

'You remember where it is? Over at Llanfoist by the graveyard. He's had it for years. Another thing he inherited from his dad. Strange thing about the allotment is, there were never any stories associated with it. Remember Bill, the butcher in the indoor market?'

'Yeah, he used to give our mam a free joint every week after dad died.'

'We buried Bill about four years ago. About six months before he died, he came to me with a story about Benny's shed over at the allotment. Benny has a state-of-the art shed. All the others are falling apart. But Benny's is immaculate. After Bill died, I looked for myself. This was after I confronted him about my granddaughter. He even had video of me walking around the shed. The next thing I know I am being fined for harassment. It looks more like a summer house with no windows. The place is decked out: electricity, telephone and everything. But no windows. Bill said he was walking by the shed one day and Benny had left the door partly open. Bill said he glanced inside.'

'What did he see?'

'Benny's very young wife, sat in front of a laptop with her tits out.'

Fagan was already reaching into his pocket, pulling his phone out. 'Sean, I know it's late but I need a team at an allotment in Llanfoist. Look for the smartest shed on the allotment.'

Evans rubbed his hands together. 'Jesus Fagan, nothing happens in this town for over thirty years. Then the minute you turn up, it's like being in an episode of *Line of Duty*.'

Fagan stood and pointed at the CCTV camera outside Evans's house. 'I want you to go through all the footage you have of Benny. Perhaps we'll find something that may help nail that bastard.'

'I'll call you as soon as I have something.'

Fagan winked at him, mimicking Ted Hastings. 'Heed my words fella. We'll nab that slippery little bastard.'

CHAPTER 16

DAY 2
7:29am

Fagan trudged up the gravel path towards the shed Evans had described the night before. The area was brightly lit with portable flood lights. Police CSIs had been there all night searching the building. Because Nelson's shed had electricity, police set up a mobile operations tent. Fagan sipped from a latte cup and finished the last of a croissant he had bought from a Costa Coffee drive through café near next to a Premier inn.

Watkins walked towards him. 'Everything is there. The murder weapon, the victim's phone, everything. We got him.'

'Where is he now?'

'He's been transferred to Cardiff.'

'Cardiff, why?'

'Orders off the Chief Constable.'

'What about his wife?'

'There's still no sign of her.'

'Come on, let's see what we have.'

Fagan and Watkins entered the evidence tent. Several tables were present containing multiple items wrapped in plastic bags.

'What have we got?' Fagan asked a CSI.

'I reckon this is the weapon Nelson used to kill Rebecca Jenkins with.' The CSI picked up a long tyre iron. 'We've found traces of blood on it. It's only a matter of time matching her DNA to the blood samples we've taken.' The CSI placed the iron back on the table. And moved on to the next item. 'This is the victim's phone. Still has a full charge.'

'Have you had time to check its contents?' Fagan asked.

'We have analysed the information on the phone. It looks like a lot of messages have been deleted.'

'Messages between Benny and the victim.' Watkins asked.

'No.'

'No?' Fagan repeated.

'Nelson has gone to a lot of effort to delete messages from other people except for him.'

'It makes little sense.' Watkins said. 'Why leave messages only from him? He's only digging himself deeper. It's like the mobile phone case found at the scene of the crime. No other prints were found apart from Benny's.'

The CSI moved on to a laptop computer. 'We've analysed the laptop. Full of obscene images of his wife and other young girls. They're mostly Indonesian. There are also images of young boys.'

Fagan stared at the laptop, recalling the story he had told Evans the night before. 'Did you find much in the shed?'

The CSI looked directly at Fagan. 'Go take a look.'

Fagan walked towards the open door of the large shed, slipping on a pair of latex gloves. The shed was as Evans had described. More of a summer house than a garden shed. Taking up much of the space that was supposed to be used for growing. Fagan stepped inside, followed by Watkins.

'It's like the motherload of child porn hauls.' Watkins inhaled.

The walls were plastered with indecent images of both sexes. Fagan stepped through a doorway. Some of the photographs looked decades old. Several old computer tower units were stacked on top of each other.

'All the hard drives have been removed.' A CSI revealed. He was looking at a photograph that he handed to Fagan. 'This is one for the books.'

Fagan stared at a faded colour image. Jimmy Savile was centred in the picture, in a red tracksuit, on one knee. Behind Savile stood several rows of boys. Kneeling next to him was Bob Benson, the Mayor and the MP, along with several other men. Each side of the men were the boys that had won the competition. Benny Nelson stood directly behind Savile, grinning broadly. Fagan scanned the back row of the picture until he spotted his younger self staring back at him.

Watkins was looking over his shoulder. 'Is that you boss?'

Fagan nodded slowly. 'Yes.'

A CSI stepped into the structure. 'The Chief Constable is here.'

Fagan spotted Griffiths marching up the gravel path, leading a team of officers.

'I want this site cleared immediately. Gather everything. It's going to Cardiff.'

'With all due respect, sir. We need to keep this in the hands of the local police.' Fagan challenged.

Griffiths shook his head. 'No.'

'Can I at least ask why?'

'I am taking full charge of this investigation.'

'All the more reason to keep this local until we know what we are dealing with. There is evidence in that building that could suggest a local paedophile ring has been operating locally for decades.'

'Detective Inspector Fagan, your job is to find the man responsible for the murder of Rebecca Jenkins.'

Fagan stood toe to toe with the Chief Constable. 'How am I supposed to do that exactly? When you have the prime suspect locked away in Cardiff, sir.'

'Nelson will be transferred back to Newport central later on today.'

'After what?' Fagan indicated to the shed. 'All the evidence has been removed.'

'What are you suggesting, Detective Inspector Fagan?'

'We can't let another division tamper with vital evidence.'

'Do you have the weapon used in the murder?'

'Yes.' Fagan answered.

'And I understand you also have Rebecca Jenkins' mobile phone.'

'We do.' Fagan sighed.

'Then the rest of this material is irrelevant.'

'Irrelevant.' Fagan pointed at the building. 'Sir, that shed is packed with material that stretches back decades. There's a picture in there of Jimmy Savile and other local officials, including your grandfather, Sergeant Bob.'

'Detective Inspector Fagan, if you do not remove yourself from this crime scene, then you are off the case. The only reason I am allowing you to carry on is because of your local knowledge. Nelson will be transferred later. You will interview him and then he will be charged with Rebecca Jenkins' murder. In the meantime, you are to wait until Nelson arrives. I suggest you cool off until then. Detective Sergeant Watkins, your notebook, please.' Griffiths held out his hand.

Watkins handed over his notebook.

'Dismissed, the both of you.'

Fagan sat in his car, staring out of the window.

'You ok boss?'

'No, I'm fucking not.' Fagan seethed before slamming

his fist against the steering wheel.

Watkins reached into his pocket and pulled out a page he had ripped from his notebook. He handed it to Fagan.

'What's this?'

'I was the arresting officer last night who brought Nelson in. The first thing I did was seize his phone. I looked through his phone records. Since his release yesterday he's only called one number. I tried to dial it, but all I got was an engaged tone. When you told me to secure this allotment last night, I went with a uniform to look at what was in there.'

Fagan smiled at the piece of paper. 'You've not known me long Sean, glad to see I'm rubbing off on you already.'

'When I walked into that shed last night and saw all those images, I knew this was bigger than the both of us. So I ripped the number out of my notebook because I knew it would disappear along with the rest of the evidence in that shed. I have been in the force long enough to know that whenever something massive like this breaks, it's always the ones at the bottom that get charged, never anyone else. So, what's the next move?'

Fagan considered his options. 'I'm going for breakfast at the Bailey. I want you return to the office at the fire station and do as that prick says. Sit tight and wait for word on Nelson. See if you can track down Nelson's missing wife.'

'Understood.' Watkins nodded.

CHAPTER 17

The Labour Club – Abergavenny – July 1983

Hushed conversation drifted across the large dance hall at the rear of the club. Nearly every table was full. With dozens more people in the bar and lounge area.

Fagan watched as Rebecca's father walked onto the stage.

'I'd like to thank everyone today who has turned up for Alan's funeral.' Jenkins pulled out a piece of paper. 'Alan Fagan was one of the hardest working men I knew at the factory. Always ready to help others.'

Fagan's mother smiled as she listened to Jenkins.

'He was a larger-than-life character who can never be replaced. I had worked with Alan for around twenty years. You could say we grew up together. Unlike myself, Alan wasn't interested in job promotions. He was a shop floor worker through and through. An outstanding union representative, always willing to help those in need. On behalf of everyone at the factory I would like to convey my deepest sympathies to Alan's family. I'd also like to assure you that everyone who worked with Alan will stand by you in this time of grief. I would like to ask those of you from the factory who have attended Alan's funeral to put a few quid into a collection box that will be passed around.'

Fagan looked across to where Rebecca was sitting.

She smiled at him, glancing around to make sure no one was looking at her. 'I love you.' She mouthed.

As the afternoon wore on, the room emptied. Coworkers of Fagan's dad said their goodbyes and promised to keep in touch. Fagan was standing by the bar, waiting to be served.

'You're Alan's boy.' A voice asked from behind.

Fagan turned around and faced a man in his early twenties. 'Yeah.' He nodded.

The man offered his hand. 'I'm Colin. I just started working at the factory a few years back. Your dad has really looked after me. I'm so sorry he's gone. I'll never forget what he's done for me.'

'Thank you.' Fagan said.

Colin handed Fagan a piece of paper. 'Here's my phone number. If there is anything I can do for you, please let me know. Perhaps we can go out for a pint some time. I have some hilarious stories to share with you.'

Fagan nodded. 'Thanks, I'll give you a bell some time.'

Evans and Tyler approached the bar.

'Hey mate, how are you coping?' Evans asked.

Fagan swigged from his pint glass. 'How do you think? I'm a fucking mess.' He looked across the room at his mother, who was surrounded by friends. 'But I'm not as bad as our mam.'

'We missed you at the cinema last week.' Tyler remarked. 'Evans had his knob out wanking over princess Leia.'

'Fuck off.' Evans barked. 'It was fucking amazing though, mate. The lightsabre fight between Vader and Luke was brilliant. And the part where they blew up the second death star at the end was mind blowing. Shame they won't be making any more films after this one.'

Fagan forced a smile.

'Listen mate, we have to go. I promised dad I'd clean up the garage.' Tyler said. 'We'll call in on you tomorrow.'

'Cheers lads.'

Davis walked up to the bar and stood next to Fagan. 'Your dad was very popular at the ammunition factory.'

'Yeah, he was.'

'Plenty of fanny here this afternoon.' Davis remarked scanning the room. 'Are you coming out to the Chevron this Saturday? Tony's convinced a load of girls from Llanelli Hill to come down for the night.'

'Tony's a dickhead for inviting them. There'll be twenty boys from the Jolly Colliers following close behind. Besides, if you haven't noticed, my dad has just died.'

Davis didn't show sympathy. He stared over at Rebecca, who was sitting with her sister and mum and dad. 'I reckon I still got a chance.'

'With who?' Fagan asked, knowing what Davis was about to say.

'Rebecca, of course. Look at her, all prim and proper. Virginity still intact. Whoever pops her cherry will be the envy of every bloke in town.'

Fagan glanced over. 'Good luck, her legs are watertight.'

Davis smiled at Fagan. 'Not for long, mate.'

Fagan watched as he walked over. He shook Rebecca's dad's hand and sat next to her.

Rebecca glanced in Fagan's direction and smiled.

Fagan finished his pint.

The rain seemed to come down harder as soon as Fagan left the club. Even though he lived around the corner, he got a good soaking. Changing into a pair of jeans and a t-shirt Fagan came back down the stairs.

The doorbell sounded.

Rebecca was standing on the doorstep in the pouring rain. 'Can I come in?'

Fagan let her through the door. 'Your dad is going to flip if he knows you're here.'

'I snuck out the side entrance. Said I was going to the toilet. Besides, dad has had a few. So he won't notice I've gone.'

'What about Tim?'

'What about him?'

'I saw the two of you together.'

'That's not fair. You know I don't like him anymore. It's you I want to be with.'

'Try telling that to Tim. He's still thinks you and him have a chance.'

'Tim creeps me out sometimes. That's why I finished with him. He can be a bit like Benny Nelson.'

'Listen Becky, I have a lot of things to do. There's stuff in the attic that needs sorting.'

'Where's your mam?'

'She's with a friend for the night. I don't think she could stand being here.' Fagan inhaled. 'I'm not sure I want to be here.'

Rebecca moved closer to Fagan. 'I can't think of any better place to be than with the man I love.' She took his hand.

Fagan looked into her eyes.

'I've been really selfish over the last several months Marc. Today has made me see how much I really love you. All I wanted to do at the club was to hold you close.'

'Same here.' Fagan admitted.

She smiled at him. 'Then let's not waste any more time.' She pulled him towards the stairs.

Fagan put his arms around her, kissing her passionately before leading her up the stairs.

CHAPTER 18

The Bailey 9:16am

Fagan parked his car at the back of the fire station before walking to the pub. He text Jackie before he left the allotment. Telling her to gather everyone and meet in the pub.

'Fagan.' Jackie greeted as he walked through the door.

Dean Tyler stood up and walked over, embracing Fagan.

'I called Dean after you left last night.' Evans revealed.

'As soon as he told me you were investigating Rebecca's murder, I had to come.'

'I appreciate it.' Fagan said with half a smile.

'Besides, I had to see for myself. Detective Inspector Marc Fagan.' Tyler smiled. 'That's the last thing I expected from you.'

'What about you? Elon Musk of Abergavenny.'

Tyler laughed.

'What happened at the allotment last night?' Evans asked. 'Was there anything there?'

Fagan sat down at the table with his friends. 'We hit the jackpot.'

'Yes!' Jackie shouted. 'Finally, after all these years, we got that bastard.'

'I'm afraid it's not that simple.'

Edwards stood. 'I'll put some coffee on.'

'Fagan, why is it not that simple? You said you hit the jackpot.'

'We have.' Fagan said. 'We found the murder weapon,

Rebecca's phone. Plus a shed full of obscene imagery.'

'But?' Evans coaxed.

'Chief Constable Griffiths turned up and said we had to hand the evidence over to him. He was taking charge.'

'Sergeant Bob's grandson.'

Fagan nodded.

'I didn't realise Sergeant Bob had any children.' Tyler remarked.

'Our nan used to talk about them.' Jackie stated. 'They all went to a private school. No one ever bothered with them.'

'How many did he have?' Fagan asked.

'Four.' Jackie replied.

Evans looked at Tyler. 'Dean has something he wants to share with you regarding that conversation we had last night.'

Tyler began. 'In 2019, before all this covid nightmare kicked off, I was at a charity bash in London. It was a celebration of all those who had worked for charities over the past several decades. I had donated 20k to a cancer hospice. I was wandering around doing the handshake thing and meeting people when I came face to face with a ghost from the past, or rather Abergavenny's past.'

'Who?'

'Ernie Brown.'

'Former mayor of Abergavenny?'

Tyler nodded. 'And the fucker is still alive today. Not only that, he's now Lord Ernest Brown. When I said I recognised him being from Abergavenny, he had a look of terror on his face. He left the bash straight after we encountered each other.'

'How long was he mayor of Abergavenny?'

'About ten years, until 1990. He then invested in a property company.' Tyler replied. 'I did a little research on him. He sold his car dealership opposite the bus station, invested in the company and moved to London. He lived with local MP Arthur Thorpe, who rented a flat in Westminster.'

Fagan clicked his fingers. 'I was trying to remember the name of the MP yesterday who was at that charity sports event at the school.'

'In 1994, Thorpe was forced to stand down as MP. Because he was caught on Clapham Common with a young male prostitute.'

'Why am I not surprised?' Fagan said.

Edwards set a tray down on the table with mugs of coffee.

'What about Benny?' Jackie asked. 'If you have the murder weapon and Rebecca's phone, then it's an open and shut case.'

'Not necessarily. Over the years, I have come across several cases that involved what we in the police call an orgy of evidence.'

'What is that?' Evans asked.

'It's when a crime scene has evidence that points solely to a suspect who turns out to be innocent.'

Jackie shook her head. 'No, that maniac murdered Rebecca.'

'Let me ask you this. You all know Benny. I have been away for nearly forty years. In all that time, has he ever been violent towards anyone?'

Jackie and the other exchanged glances.

'No.' Edwards admitted. 'Benny is many things, but not violent.'

Fagan looked at Jackie. 'Rebecca was very fit, wasn't she?'

'Yeah, she went down the gym three times a week. The one at the old chocolate factory that Wetton owns.'

'So, if Benny tried to do something, she'd be able to fight him off.' Fagan looked at Evans. 'We saw how unfit he is when he waddled over to us last night. He was puffing after walking a few hundred yards. During my conversation with Justin Pike yesterday, he said Benny had been stalking Rebecca for years, but she got used to brushing him off. And being the fat bastard he is, he wouldn't have been able to grab an athletic woman like Rebecca.'

'Then who murdered her?' Jackie asked, welling up with tears.

'The person who murdered Rebecca started a domino effect. Benny is at the centre of everything. Whoever murdered Rebecca got hold of the mobile phone case and planted it at the scene of the crime. The case has Benny's fingerprints all over it. The suspect knows everyone hates Benny and wants him gone. They also knew how to gain access to Benny's house.'

'I haven't had time to look through all the footage yet.' Evans said.

'You only need to check footage from the night Rebecca was murdered. Do any of you follow Benny on social media?'

'I do?' Evans admitted.

Everyone looked at him.

'Well, someone has to keep an eye on him. I was expecting him to block me after the incident with my granddaughter, but he didn't.'

'Did he post anything the night Rebecca was murdered?' Fagan asked.

'He pinged himself at the Odeon in Cardiff Bay.'

'Exactly where he said he was when I interviewed him. I'm sure credit card records and CCTV from the cinema will confirm that.' Fagan paused for thought.

'Will Benny get away with having all that stuff in his

shed?' Jackie asked.

'Not if I have anything to do with it.' Fagan thought about the photograph he saw earlier. 'I saw a picture of us at that sports day event that Savile attended. Do you remember how they used to arrange those old photos? The good boys at the front and bad boys at the back. Savile is crouched in the front row with Ernie Brown. Arthur Thorpe, Sergeant Bob, Bernard the bummer Baxter are also in the picture. Plus, Hugh Clarke, head of Monmouthshire county council. All the boys who went on the camping trip were also in the front row. And Benny stood directly behind Savile. Do you know the one person who wasn't there that day?'

Fagan's question was met with a wall of silence.

'George Walker, the school truant officer and local bobby.'

'Your right, he wasn't.' Edwards mentioned.

Fagan continued. 'I know for a fact, George hated Sergeant Bob.' He glanced at Evans. 'On one of the many times I spent Saturday night in the drunk tank, I heard George and Bob screaming at each other.' Fagan paused for breath. 'George mentioned his son Graham several times.'

'No.' Jackie gasped.

'George walked out of the police station that night. I heard him slam the main door hard. The last thing I remember him screaming at Sergeant Bob was, it's all your fucking fault. That's when he walked out. We all know that Graham committed suicide a year before we left school. A few years after I left Abergavenny, George came to see us in Ormskirk. He begged me to join the police force. He said to me, if anyone can spot a rotten apple Fagan, it's you.'

'Do you think George knew what was going on?' Tyler asked.

Fagan nodded slowly. 'I think George knew everything, including his boy being abused by the likes of bummer Baxter. Do you remember what his trademark saying used to be at the end of every PE lesson, particularly football?'

'Come on boys, wrap it up. It's time to hit the showers. I want to see those balls shine.' Evans remembered. 'Then he used to wink at us.'

Everyone nodded.

'Baxter never used to bother with us trouble makers. He preferred the quieter boys.' Fagan said. 'Including Graham and the Smith brothers.'

'How did they keep George quiet?' Tyler asked.

'Probably blackmail.' Fagan answered. 'If you say a word, you're out of the force. If your boy talks, he'll disappear. We'll kick you out of the police if you cause any trouble. All the usual classic blackmail tactics used back in the day.'

'George stepped down from the force literally just after you left Abergavenny.' Edwards revealed.

'Do you know why?' Fagan asked.

'No, and that was the odd thing about it. Some of us have asked him over the years. But he always said he had a guts full of the police.'

'That's not George. He loved that job.'

'After the police George worked security at the old ammunition factory. Just after he retired, his wife died.'

'Poor bastard.' Jackie said.

'Jesus, I just remembered something.' Evans announced.

Everyone looked at him.

'About ten years ago I picked George up from the Crown up at the Mardy. He'd had more than a few to drink. I remember him talking about you, Fagan. He said, Fagan will come back one day, then we'll nab all the rotten apples in this town. My boy will finally know peace.'

Silence enveloped the room.

'What about the twat who murdered Rebecca?' Jackie asked. 'We need to find out who it was.'

Fagan remained silent for a few moments before speaking. 'I know exactly who murdered Rebecca.'

Everyone stared at him.

'We all know Benny isn't the violent sort. So who does that leave?'

'Oh Christ.' Jackie stated. 'Tim.'

Fagan nodded. 'You've all mentioned he's smacked her about over the years. Plus, you were all present that night in the Farmers nearly forty years ago. He broke her nose after finding out we were having a relationship.'

'Go and arrest him then.' Jackie sounded frustrated.

'I can't.'

'Why not?'

'Because all the evidence points to the murderer being Benny. The mobile phone case with Benny's prints. The murder weapon and Rebecca's phone found at Benny's allotment in Llanfoist.' He glanced at Evans. 'That's why I need you to go back to your place and check if there was any movement at Benny's house while he was at the cinema.' Fagan held out his hands. 'There are two major elements at play here. On one hand you have Benny. A known pervert who seems to have committed murder. Then you have Tim, who I believe may have murdered Rebecca. The trouble is both elements affect each other. If we let things carry on and Benny is convicted of murder, then Tim stays free. Not only that, but the murder trial will overshadow everything. Meaning, that evidence at that allotment will quietly vanish. But if we arrest Tim for Rebecca's murder, then the evidence in that shed still disappears.'

'Why?' Tyler asked.

'When I was up there earlier, I saw old computers in the corner stacked high. Some looked decades old. The CSI said all the hard drives had been removed. Meaning Benny has got a stack of evidence somewhere. Don't you see? It's his get out of jail free card. All he has to do is make a phone call and say, if you make the possession of obscene material conviction vanish. I won't expose whoever's left of a historic paedophile ring that operated in the Monmouthshire area. With connections to Jimmy Savile and God knows who else.'

'Who's he going to call, the bloody *Ghostbusters*?' Evans blurted out.

Fagan produced the piece of paper Watkins had ripped from his notebook. He glanced at Evans and winked. 'Maybe.' He pulled a cheap-looking smartphone out of his inside pocket. 'This is called a burner phone. I use it for occasions like this.' He dialled the number on the paper, making sure the loud speaker was active. The phone rang several times before an answer machine message started playing.

'Hello, you have reached Lord Ernest Brown. Sorry I'm not available. Please leave your number and I'll get back to you.' Fagan hung up.

'Ernie fucking Brown.' Tyler said.

Fagan nodded.

'I take it you have a plan?' Edwards asked.

'We have to sit tight. I have been grounded until Benny is given back to us. Sergeant Bob's grandson will go through the motions and expect me to interview Benny and get him to admit to Rebecca's murder. After I'm done, I'll see know it all Nigel to find out if he has any archive pictures of Savile in Abergavenny. I'm pretty sure the picture I saw today was taken by a newspaper. I'll also see George later on today.'

Evans and Tyler got to their feet. 'We'll start trawling through video footage.'

Jackie also stood. 'I better get back to the Cantreff and open up.'

'None of you breathes a word of what we have talked about. If any of this gets out, then it will bring everything down on us, namely my career. I know it may seem agonising, but that's police work for you, slow and methodical.'

CHAPTER 19

Abergavenny cinema–August 1983

'Oh my god that film was absolutely terrifying.' Rebecca said as they appeared out of the cinema entrance. She glanced up at the poster. '*Wargames*.'

'It was ok.'

'My dad is really into technology. He's got an IBM in his office and a Commodore 64 in the study. Writing computer game programs all day long.'

'It was far-fetched. Especially where he hacked the school computer and changed her exam grades. Computers aren't smart enough to do that, yet.'

'Dad says computers will run everything one day. He reckons that computers all over the world will be connected.' Rebecca walked off towards the bottom of Market street.

'We can't go that way.' Fagan said. 'Tim is in the Farmers.'

'But I wanted to go for a drink.'

'Why don't we walk down to the Bridge Inn? It's warm, and your parents have gone away to London for the night. No one goes down the Bridge, it will be nice and quiet.'

'Okay but you can buy me a bag of chips on the way.'

'Deal.' Fagan agreed. 'We'll walk up by Fads, down through the carpark and through the castle meadows.'

'You're not ashamed of me, are you?' Rebecca asked.

'No, of course not. But you know what Tim is like. He's drinking more. He got paraletic last Tuesday with Bonkers.

Evans's mam saw him spewing all over the place outside Woollies.'

'He came to our house last weekend. Dad and him were talking for hours about computers. I can't understand why dad likes him and not you.'

'My dad told me he had a massive argument at the ammunition factory with your dad once. Something to do with the way he was talking to someone. Your dad didn't like it because dad was a shop steward. Dad said he made everyone stop work until your dad apologised.'

'How's your mam?'

'Coping I suppose. She goes and visits dad's grave every week.'

'Have you been with her?'

'No.'

'Why not?'

'I can't face it at the moment. I will one day. Mam is constantly talking about finishing at the sweet factory and moving back up north where her parents are. Dad had no brothers or sisters and his parents died years ago. I guess she feels she hasn't got a connection with this town anymore.'

'What about you? You're not moving, are you?'

Fagan shook his head. 'I've got an interview for Coopers next Wednesday. Plus, I put my name on the housing list last week.'

'You don't sound thrilled about it.' Rebecca pointed out.

'I was thinking the other day. We're all going our separate ways. We're all growing up. It feels like the end of our childhood. School is behind us. Most of us are eighteen. He looked back towards the cinema. I don't really enjoy going to the pictures anymore.'

'Don't tell Jamie that. He'll be really pissed off.'

'What about you? Now that you've finished sixth form.

Got all the top marks in your exams. I expect your dad will pack you off to Oxford.'

'He's already talking about it. We had a bit of an argument the other night. I said that I didn't want to go.'

'So what do you want to do?'

'To be honest with you Marc, watching that film. I'm not sure if we even have a future. The news is always going on about how American and Russia could go to war at any moment. I don't think any of us should make long-term plans.'

'No one knows what the future holds.'

'What about us?' Rebecca asked.

'What do you mean?'

'I thought we were going to be together.'

'Hopefully yes.'

'Hopefully yes, what is that supposed to mean, Marc?'

'It means we have to be realistic. Aren't you even a little curious to see what life has to offer before you settle down? Times are changing. It's not like when your parents were young. Back then, it was about work and family. These days there is more opportunity. I was talking to Derek Bevan the other day. His parents are giving him the money to travel around Australia for a year before he comes home and goes off to university.'

'Derek Bevan is a spoilt twat. Because his dad is the manager down at the TSB.'

'Besides wanting to spend your life with me, is there anything you have always wanted to do?'

Rebecca kicked a crumpled can, that clattered further on down the road. 'I suppose I'd like to travel. See parts of the world no one gets to visit.'

'Such as?'

Rebecca shrugged. 'I don't know, the north pole maybe.'

Fagan laughed.

'Why is that funny?'

'It seems like a bizarre place to want to visit. Unless you're David Attenborough.'

'Isn't there any part of the world that you'd like to see?' Rebecca asked.

'America I suppose. I wouldn't mind going out to Hollywood.'

'Perhaps we can both get jobs, save up and go somewhere together.'

'It would be nice.' Fagan sighed, glancing around the street. 'Sometimes I hate this place. The only excitement that happens is when the fair comes to town. When they're here next, I might ask them for a job.'

'And what about Coopers?'

Fagan shook his head. 'I'm not really holding out any hopes for getting a job there. I've got a criminal record. They'll just look at that and say no.'

'I'd hardly call burglary the crime of the century, Marc.'

'No, but it's enough to put people off giving you a job. Once you've been in trouble once then you're labelled for life.'

'Marc, if you get this job at Coopers, I'll quit the Mayflower and work at the sweet factory. We'll save as much money as we can. Then we'll decide what we want to do.'

They followed the route Fagan had suggested. The summer sun had faded behind the Blorenge mountain that overlooked the town. Rebecca stopped on the bridge, noting that the river was low.

'Charlie Evans jumped off here the other day. I've done it twice. But I wouldn't do it when the river is this low.'

'Andrew Webb jumped off here last year and cut his leg.'

Fagan stared into the river deep in thought.

'You okay Marc?'

'I was just thinking about that time when Graham jumped into the deep pool in the Gavenny. He saved me from drowning.'

Fagan and Rebecca turned towards the pub and carried on walking over the bridge.

The rev of an engine and a horn sounded as a car screeched to a halt.

'Where are you two lovebirds off?' Nelson asked.

'Fuck off, Nelson.' Fagan said sternly.

'Haven't you got any girls in the back of your car you can touch up?' Rebecca mocked.

Why don't you hop in the back. I'll show what a real man is all about.'

'Go fuck yourself mong.'

'What are you doing, looking for twelve year olds to pick up?' Fagan asked.

Nelson glanced at the junction just after the bridge. 'Dad asked me to check on the allotment.'

'I bet you're going to sit in his shed and wank off to porn mags?' Rebecca continued to taunt.

Nelson extended his middle finger. 'Ha ha bitch.' He chided, before speeding off.

CHAPTER 20

Newport central police HQ – 11:46am

'I wasn't expecting to see him so soon.' Fagan commented. 'When you said he'd been transferred to Cardiff, I didn't think we'd see him until this evening.'

'It gets better. He's got a new solicitor. And I don't think this bloke sounds cheap.'

'Name?'

'Wilson Fletcher Crawford. I have had the chance to speak to him. He's switched on. Unlike the duty solicitor yesterday.'

'I wonder how Benny can afford this fancy solicitor? What about his wife?'

Watkins checked his notes. 'She's bolted.'

'Where to?'

'Back to Thailand. She boarded a plane yesterday lunchtime. Manchester airport.'

'The same time we brought Nelson in. He knew he'd be arrested. So he sticks his wife on a plane.'

'Why do you think he sent her back to Thailand?'

'To cover his tracks.' Fagan processed the information he'd learnt. 'I suspect Benny isn't exactly the loving husband type.'

'You think he's violent towards her?'

'He was arrested last year for assaulting her, but was released. I also think he's using her as a sex worker?'

'Pimping her out.'

Fagan nodded. 'Benny has had a reputation in this town

for years. He was different when I knew him. Cruising the streets, looking to pick up any young girls who were naïve enough to get into his car. These days it's a case of log on and get turned on.'

'Why hasn't he been arrested?'

'He's been arrested loads of times. But always released. I think it's related to that allotment. We need those missing hard drives from those old computers we found?'

'It still doesn't make sense Boss. Why have so much material in one place?'

Fagan grabbed a file off a desk. 'I suggest we find out.'

Watkins picked up an evidence box and followed Fagan.

Nelson watched as the two detectives entered the room.

Watkins set the evidence box down on the floor before turning the camera on.

Fagan tapped the record icon on his phone screen. 'Interview with sixty-two-year-old Ben Nelson of Mumbles close, Abergavenny. Present in the room are Mr Nelson's solicitor, Wilson Fletcher Crawford, Detective Sergeant Sean Watkins and myself Detective Inspector Marc Fagan.'

'Let's get on with this, Detectives.' Crawford stated in a firm tone. 'I would like to point out at this moment, my client is here to answer questions about the murder of Miss Jenkins. I would appreciate it if you would not deviate from that line of questioning.'

Fagan stared at him. He had come across many solicitors similar to Crawford. Brash, abrupt and always wanting to focus on singular matters. This was a tactic used to divert attention away from other crimes the suspect may be guilty of.

Watkins lifted the tyre iron out of the evidence box and placed it on the table. 'I am showing Mr Nelson a tyre iron found in a shed in Llanfoist. Mr Nelson, have you ever seen this item before?'

Nelson glanced at his solicitor, who gave a slight nod.

'Yes.'

'Could you tell us what it's used for?' Fagan asked.

'It's a tyre iron. It's for removing tyres.' Nelson said with sarcasm in his tone.

'Traces of blood have been found on this tyre iron.' Fagan pointed out.

Nelson glanced at his solicitor, who remained motionless.

'This item, along with Rebecca's mobile phone, was found in a shed on an allotment in Llanfoist. That allotment is registered to you.'

Nelson inhaled, staring at the iron.

'I'm going to ask you this once, Benny. Did you murder Rebecca Jenkins?'

Nelson inhaled again. 'Yes.'

'So, you're now freely admitting you murdered Miss Jenkins.' Watkins said.

'Yes.'

'When we interviewed you yesterday, you told us you had nothing to do with her murder. Now you say you did murder her. Can you at least tell us why you have changed your mind?'

'I was afraid.' Nelson replied.

'Afraid of what Benny?'

Nelson managed a shrug.

Watkins reached into the evidence box and pulled out the mobile phone. 'I am now showing Mr Nelson a mobile phone that is registered to Miss Jenkins. CSI analysis has revealed that the phone has been tampered with. Messages have been deleted. This phone was also found at the allotment, along with other material.'

'Careful, Detective Watkins.' Crawford warned.

Watkins shot Crawford a glance. 'This phone, along with the iron bar which is suspected to be the murder weapon, was found in a shed at the allotment. The shed registered in your name?'

Nelson nodded. 'Yes.'

'Yes, what Benny?' Fagan questioned.

'Yes, I murdered Rebecca.'

Fagan pointed at the iron. 'You murdered Rebecca with this tyre iron. Is that what you are saying?'

'Yes.' Nelson answered robotically.

'Yesterday, when we interviewed you regarding the murder of Miss Jenkins, you denied everything. Now you are admitting to everything.' Fagan shook his head. 'Help me understand all this Benny.'

'I murdered Rebecca after she rejected me.'

'Where did you murder her?'

'At her flat.'

'In Llwynu lane?' Watkins pressed.

'Yes.' Nelson said. 'I murdered her because she told me to fuck off last Saturday night.'

'This was when you tried to steal her mobile phone?' Fagan pursued. 'At the Cantreff pub on Brecon Road.'

'That is correct, yes.'

Fagan sensed frustration welling up from within. 'Benny, talk me through what happened last Saturday night. You were in the Cantreff and you saw Rebecca. Was she with anyone?'

Nelson considered the question. 'She was with Jackie Mills. Tim Davis came into the pub around nine thirty.'

'What happened?'

'Rebecca talked to Tim about things.'

'Things, what things?' Watkins questioned.

'Something he borrowed from her. I couldn't really make out the conversation they were having.'

'Then what happened?' Fagan asked.

'Rebecca left her phone on the bar. Tim was talking to her over by the fruit machine. I grabbed the phone.'

'Go on.'

Nelson recalled that evening. 'Tim saw me as I was going out of the door. He grabbed the phone from my hand. The back broke off.'

'The back that was found with Rebecca's body yesterday morning.'

Nelson gave his solicitor a sideway glance before answering. 'Yes.'

'What happened after you had a struggle with Tim?'

'Like I just said, he snatched the phone from my hand.'

'Did he say anything to you?'

'He called me a thieving cunt and a paedo.'

'Did Rebecca say anything to you?'

'She Had a go at me about how her son had bought her that case.'

'Did you give her an explanation why you took her phone?'

'Not really, I may have said I wanted something to remember her.'

Fagan sat back in his chair, feeling perplexed by the interview he was giving. 'Something to remember her by? Does that mean you were already planning to murder her?'

Nelson shrugged, glancing at Crawford, who remained silent while scribbling notes. 'Yeah, I guess so.' Frustration was clear in his tone.

'You guess so.' Watkins stated. 'You don't sound very sure of yourself Benny. Either you did or did not plan to murder her.'

'Yes, I planned to murder her, ok? Is that what you want to hear?'

'Perhaps.' Fagan responded casually. 'But is that what

you want to tell us, Benny?'

'Exactly where are you going with that question DI Fagan?' Crawford enquired.

Fagan looked at him. 'Yesterday your client denied murdering Rebecca Jenkins. But today he wants to shout it from the rooftops.' He looked back at Nelson. 'Why is that Benny?'

'Because I want to ease my conscience.'

'I didn't realise you had one.'

'DI Fagan, you are out of term with that statement.' Crawford said. 'You are putting my client under unnecessary pressure.'

'Exactly what pressure are we applying?' Watkins spoke up. 'We're hardly using thumbscrews on your client. He's singing like a little canary.'

'Ok, let's back up for a moment.' Fagan said. 'You had the argument last Saturday night. Tim gave you an ear bashing and Rebecca let you have her mobile phone case. So you went home and thought, fuck it, I'm going to murder her.'

Nelson hesitated before nodding. 'Yeah, that's about the size of it.'

'So, you had a week to organise. You needed to come up with a plan. A plan to get her to speak to you. A plan detailing how you were going to dispose of her body?'

Nelson nodded. 'If you say so.'

Fagan looked at Crawford. 'If you were a decent solicitor, you'd be stopping this interview. I mean, what I just said could be classed as leading the suspect.'

'My job, Detective, is to make sure you stick to the matter in hand. Which is the murder of Miss Jenkins.'

Nelson sat staring at the space in front of him. Drumming his fingers on the table.

'Okay then.' Fagan said. 'We'll get on with it. So, Benny,

you had a full week to plan for Rebecca's murder. How did you make preparations?'

'What do you mean?'

'I mean, you must have done something to plan for that event. It's not like you were planning your weekly shop. You planned to murder Rebecca. Did you buy anything to help dispose of the body? She was struck on the back of the head. There was massive blood loss. You must have bought cleaning products to scrub the crime scene.'

'I bought a couple of items.' Nelson confessed.

'Such as?'

'The tyre iron.'

'That tyre iron was brand new when you bought it.' Watkins said.

'Yes.'

'Do you own a DeLorean Benny?' Watkins asked. 'You know, the car from *Back to the Future*.'

'No, I drive a Mercedes van. What is that supposed to mean?'

'The tyre iron is at least forty years old. So either you travelled back in time, buried it somewhere, then dug it up forty years later before murdering Rebecca. Or you're not being truthful.'

'Look, I'm confessing aren't I. It's a fair cop and all that.'

'If I didn't know any better Benny, I'd say you were acting under duress.' Fagan made eye contact with Crawford.

Crawford pointed a bony finger. 'I'd watch your tone DI Fagan. If you accuse me of anything, I'll come down on you like a tonne of bricks.'

Fagan considered Crawford's words. 'Alright then, I'll dance to whatever tune is being played out here. Let's skip forward a week to the day you claimed you murdered Rebecca. After getting out of bed, you thought, today is the day. I'm going to strangle that bitch until I squeeze every last breath out of her.'

Nelson sat up straight. 'I didn't strangle her. I hit her with the tyre iron.'

'The pathologist said that she had also been strangled.' Watkins pointed out.

Nelson glanced at Watkins. 'Oh yeah, I remember now. Yeah, I strangled her.'

'With what?'

'A rope, of course.'

'A rope.' Fagan nodded. 'Funny, because the medical examiner said that Rebecca had been strangled with a phone cord from a charger. Probably the one that she used with her phone.'

'Yeah, that's what I strangled her with, a phone charger cable thingy.'

'You strangled her with the phone charger cord? Then you left the tyre iron along with her phone in your shed. What did you do with the phone cord?'

Nelson shrugged. 'I don't know, must have chucked it somewhere.'

'Ok, moving on to the night you murdered Rebecca. You obviously knew she was working at Flannel Street chippy. So you waited until she came out.'

'No, I told you yesterday, I was in the cinema in Cardiff watching *John Wick*.'

'Oh yes.' Fagan nodded before looking down at his notes. 'You sat in the cinema, munching away on your popcorn planning Rebecca's murder.'

Nelson's mood seemed to change. He smiled at Fagan. 'Lee Harvey Oswald sat in the cinema after he had assassinated Kennedy.'

'We're not interested in a history lesson Benny.' Watkins sighed.

Fagan checked his notes again. 'You claimed yesterday that you got a burger from MacDonalds in Abergavenny.'

'Yeah, I did.'

'Then you went up to Rebecca's flat and murdered her.'

Nelson sat back, folding his arms. 'Yeah.'

'How?'

'How what?' Nelson snapped.

Fagan could sense his frustration rapidly increasing. 'How did you murder her?'

Nelson shrugged. 'I smashed her over the head with the iron bar.'

'Just like that, with no warning. You belted her with the tyre iron.'

'Yep.'

'Ok, tell you what. Why don't we take a break?'

'What purpose is that going to serve DI Fagan? My client has confessed to the murder of Rebecca Jenkins. He needs to be processed.'

'I'm afraid I'm going to have to disagree with you on that matter, Mr Crawford.' Fagan looked at Benny. 'We'll break for an hour, then reconvene. Interview suspended.' Fagan pressed the stop icon on his phone.

Crawford stood and led Nelson out of the interview room.

'Talk about taking the piss. We're being played by that fat twat and his fancy solicitor.' Watkins complained.

'You think.' Fagan replied with sarcasm.

'He didn't murder Rebecca, did he?'

'No.'

'Why is he suddenly confessing? DNA evidence will eventually clear him of her murder.'

'Yes, it will.'

'Ok, so why are we playing along? This is a complete waste of time.'

‘I don’t think it is.’

‘Why is that?’

‘We’re being stalled. My guess is it has something to do with what was found in that shed last night.’

‘But why is he saying he murdered Rebecca when he clearly didn’t do it?’

‘That’s what I’m trying to find out.’

‘But the actual murderer is still out there.’

Fagan thought back to the conversation he had earlier with his friends. ‘Yes, they are. But they won’t stay hidden for long.’

CHAPTER 21

The Chevron–Abergavenny–July 1983

'Fuck me, it's warm in here!' Fagan shouted over the din. He picked up his pint glass and took a swig, grimacing. 'Even the fucking lager is warm.'

'I know, it's fucking brilliant!' Davis yelled back.

A group of girls danced around their handbags to Wham's latest hit, Club Tropicana.

'There's fanny everywhere.' Davis said scanning the room. 'Look at the tits on her.'

Fagan stood. 'I can't be bothered with this. It's a fucking shithole in here. I'm off to the Abergavenny. At least they have cooling fans.'

'I'm not going there. I paid fifty pence to get in here. Besides the girls are stuck up in the Abergavenny. At least you're guaranteed to get laid here.'

'I'm not staying here when all hell is about to kick off. The Abergavenny only allows local people in.'

'What's your fucking problem Fagan?' Davis barked. 'You've been a miserable twat all fucking night!'

'I'm sorry. I don't mean to be a miserable twat. But I guess that's what happens when your dad dies.'

'You know I didn't mean it like that.'

'I'll tell you why I don't want to hang around here.' Fagan looked towards a corner of the club where several young men stood. 'There are Brynmawr boys in that corner, eyeing up the Ebbw Vale boys in the other corner. Then you have the Llanelli Hill boys gawping at the

Abergavenny boys. It's like Little Big Horn. I'm not waiting around for a black eye and a night in the drunk tank.'

'Suit yourself. It's more tits for me to grope.'

Fagan turned and headed for the nightclub entrance.

'Look who it is, Fagan the fag.' Nelson blocked Fagan's path.

'Fuck off Benny, I'm not in the mood.' He looked at the young girl Nelson had his arm around. 'I see you've pulled another twelve-year-old.'

The girl looked awkward standing in Nelson's shadow.

'Do yourself a favour love, go home and don't bother with this twat.' Fagan carried on walking towards the entrance.

'Poor little Fagan.' Nelson called out. 'Missing his daddy.'

Fagan stopped.

'What's the matter, missing that sad twat of a father?' Nelson continued to taunt. 'Or are you missing your little friend, Graham the wanker Walker? You know, the one who killed himself. I reckon his old man was slipping Graham one.' Nelson laughed at his own twisted humour.

Fagan stood still with his arms by his side, clenching his fists. Urging himself to walk away. He took another step towards the entrance.

'That's it, keep walking little Fagan.' Nelson continued to taunt.

Rage coursed through Fagan. He spun around launching himself at Nelson who was still laughing until the moment Fagan's fist collided with his nose.

The young girl tore herself away.

Fagan was still in forward momentum. Like a locomotion he pummelled Nelson again. Punching him on the side of the left cheek.

Nelson stumbled backwards into a group of girls. A girl

who had held on to her drink threw it in his face.

Fagan wasn't finished. He threw himself onto Nelson, pinning him to the floor. Repeatedly punching him in the face.

On the other side of the nightclub chaos erupted as two groups of young men charged at each other. Like two sides of a medieval battle screaming as they clashed. The club's DJ, who was protected by a mesh barrier, switched records as soon as the chaos engulfed the nightclub. He pumped up the volume to drown out the screaming mob. *Survivor's Eye of the Tiger* played over the din as groups of youths fought a ferocious battle with each other.

Fagan continued to rain blows down on Nelson's bloodied face. He suddenly felt two brawny arms pulling him away.

'Must be Saturday night.' One of the Wetton brothers shouted as they dragged Fagan towards the top of the stairs.

Fagan looked over the precipice before experiencing a momentary sense of weightlessness. His body slammed hard against the edge of each individual step. After what seemed to be an eternity, Fagan landed in a heap at the bottom of the stairs.

'Evening Fagan.' Sergeant Bob Benson greeted as he hauled a bruised and battered Fagan to his feet. 'Room for one at the Abergavenny Savoy is it my boy.'

Fagan was bundled into a police car. He looked out of the window and saw a police van pulling up by the door of the nightclub.

At least a dozen officers poured out of the van and raced into the club.

Fagan opened his eyes. His upper arm was severely bruised from being thrown down the stairs the night before. For a few moments he was sure he had broken something.

The cell door swung open with a loud creak. A familiar face holding a cup of coffee strolled in.

Fagan yawned. 'Morning George.'

George Walker sat down next to Fagan, handing him the hot coffee.

'Thanks, just what I needed.'

'The usual Saturday night for you was it?'

'Not exactly. I was trying to leave the Chevron.'

'What happened?'

'Benny fucking Nelson, that's what happened.'

Walker hung his head.

Fagan looked at him, noting his expression. 'You alright George.'

'I'm fine.' Walker sighed.

'If it's any consolation, I smashed his face in.'

'I know. He spent the night at Nevil Hall getting his face stitched up. His old man has been in here threatening to press charges.'

Fagan gulped down the coffee.

'You can't keep doing this Marc. You can't keep getting into trouble.'

'Nelson is the one that started the trouble last night, not me. He insulted dad.' Fagan paused. 'Then he slagged Graham off.'

'I see.' George said in a calm tone.

'I couldn't walk away from that prick. He had it coming.'

George nodded. 'He did.'

'How's Mary?'

'Coping, if you can call it that. She hasn't worked since Graham died.'

'I'll tell our mam to look in on her.'

Walker nodded before standing. 'Do me a favour Marc.'

Fagan looked at him. 'Sure.'

'Leave Abergavenny. Leave before you do something you regret. This town will consume you. Then it will drag you down and grip you until you've no fight left in you.'

Fagan nodded. 'Ok.'

'I'll leave the door open. You know the way out.'

CHAPTER 22

12:59pm

'Resuming interview with Ben Nelson in connection with the murder of Rebecca Jenkins. Present in the room is Mr Nelson and his solicitor, Wilson Fletcher Crawford. Also Detective Sergeant Sean Watkins and myself, Detective Inspector Marc Fagan.'

Crawford glanced at his Rolex watch.

Fagan quickly scanned his notes. 'So, Benny, where were we? Ah yes, you turned up at Rebecca's flat. Remind me, what time was this exactly?'

Nelson inhaled. 'It was after I got a burger from MacDonalds.'

'What did you get from MacDonalds exactly?'

'Just a burger and fries and a drink, and an apple turnover.' Nelson replied casually.

'What did you do after you had eaten your burger?'

'I went to Rebecca's flat.'

'But you don't remember what time it was.'

Nelson thought for a brief moment. 'About two o'clock, maybe a little after.'

Fagan noted Nelson's attitude had changed. He seemed more confident in the way he answered questions.

'So, it was in the early hours of the morning when you went up to Rebecca's flat. How did you get through the main door? Those doors have magnetic security locks. Residents have to have a key fob to gain access.'

'I have a gadget for getting into those flats. It

deactivates the magnetic lock.'

'Handy, you had one of those on you.' Watkins commented.

'Handy for me, tragic for Rebecca.' He said, staring at Fagan.

'Ok, you are in the building and climbing the stairs towards Rebecca's flat. What's going through your mind at this moment Benny?' Fagan asked.

'Mainly how I was going to kill the bitch.'

'And how did you plan to kill her?'

'Well, as soon as I gained entry to her flat, I knew I had to be quick. The tyre iron would have done the job nice and neat. One smash over the head and she would have been gone.' He looked at Fagan. 'I'm sure during your career, you've encountered a lot of murders that have happened like that.' Nelson almost sounded excited in the way he described his actions.

Fagan stared back it him, remaining silent. In his training over the years he had learnt to switch himself off while listening to suspects relay their stories. Especially if their statements involved a suspect giving detailed accounts of how they murdered their victims.

'When you reached Rebecca's door, what did you do?' Watkins asked.

'I rang the doorbell.'

'Did Rebecca answer straight away, or did she take her time?'

Nelson considered the question. 'I rang it three times.'

'And then she answered.' Fagan said.

'Yes.'

'Then what happened?'

'She opened the door, and I barged in.'

'Did Rebecca have a chain on the door?' Watkins enquired. 'I mean, it was the middle of the night. The woman would have been alone. She probably had a peephole on her door to see who it was.'

Nelson gave an enthusiastic nod. 'Oh yeah, she did.'

'And she let you in?' Fagan said. 'She didn't put the chain on her door?'

'Yeah, the door had a chain.'

'Those chains are pretty hard to break Benny. You must have made a lot of noise. Enough noise to wake the neighbours in the block of flats where she lived.' Fagan remarked. 'You would have had to ram the door.

'I had a pair of heavy-duty cutters on me. As soon as Rebecca opened the door with the chain on, I snipped it. Next thing I knew, I was in her flat.'

'So with the tyre iron in one hand and the cutters in another, you snipped the chain.' Fagan stated.

Benny paused momentarily. 'I had a rucksack.'

'Still, it must have taken a few seconds for you to burst through the door after you cut the chain. I suspect Rebecca must have had time to call out for help.'

Nelson shook his head. 'No.'

'Did she tell you to leave?'

'No.'

'Why not?'

'She was terrified.'

'Of you?' Watkins said.

'Yes, so I took advantage of the situation. Most victims when they are in a terrified state never call out for help.' Nelson leant back, folding his arms. 'I've watched a few episodes of Dahmer.'

'What did you do next, after you gained entry?'

'What do you think? I murdered her.'

'OK, you had forced your way into her flat. You had to get the tyre iron out of your rucksack. You dropped the cutters straight away to free up your other hand so you could grab her, then what?'

'I smashed her over the head with it.' Nelson answered abruptly. 'I don't think she even saw it coming.'

'Where did you hit her?'

'Over the head, as I just said.'

'No Benny, what I meant was, did you hit her on the front of her head or on the side?'

Nelson seemed to stall on an answer.

'Benny, where did you hit Rebecca?'

'On the front of the head. She was facing me, but she was backing away from me at the same time.'

'Thing is Benny, the CSI report has already revealed that Rebecca received a massive blow to the back of her skull. Not the front.'

'Yeah.' Nelson said. 'I remember now. Rebecca turned and ran towards the living room. I gave chase and smashed her on the back of her head.'

'Where did she fall?' Watkins asked.

'In the hallway.' Nelson thought for a moment. 'No, wait. The upper part of her body was in the living room.'

'Did she move after that?'

'Yeah, she was still conscious just about. I remember her crawling into the living room.'

'Is that when you went looking for the mobile phone charger to finish the job?'

Nelson nodded.

'Where was the phone charger, Benny?'

'In the living room.'

'So, you stepped over Rebecca's semi-conscious body and unplugged the charger?' Fagan stated.

'Yes.' Nelson replied. A wry smile appeared on his face.

'What's so amusing Benny?' Watkins questioned.

'It's nothing, well it's something I remember, that's all.' Nelson seemed to be in a trance as he spoke.

'What?'

'The look he gave me, as he lay in a crumpled heap on the floor.'

Fagan and Watkins exchanged glances.

'The look he gave me, as he lay in a crumpled heap on the floor.' Fagan repeated, feeling perplexed. 'Who is he, Benny?'

'I mean, the look Rebecca gave me.'

'And what kind of look was it?'

Nelson inhaled, recalling the scene. 'The look of total hopelessness, vulnerability. It's when a person knows they're going to die.' Nelson said hypnotically. 'She looked at me and that's when I saw it.'

'Saw what?'

'Her invite, for me to kill her. That moment when the light fades in their eyes. It's the moment when they say I am yours, do what you want with me.' Nelson closed his eyes. 'It was pure ecstasy.'

Fagan and Watkins exchanged another glance.

Nelson's solicitor sat silently scribbling down notes.

Fagan gathered his thoughts. 'You took the charger cable and wrapped it around Rebecca's neck and strangled her.'

'Yeah.' Nelson replied, nodding. 'It only took a minute for her to die.' He tapped the back of his head. 'I thought that smash on the head I gave her was the death blow. I used the cord to aid her on her way quicker. I didn't want her to suffer, you see.'

'After you had murdered her, what was your next move?'

'I knew I had to get rid of the body, so I had to act fast.'

'That's when you picked up her body and rushed out of the door.' Watkins suggested.

'Yeah.'

'Was there much blood around Benny?' Fagan asked.

'Tonnes of it. I thought about scrubbing the scene, but I thought it wasn't worth it. I knew your CSIs would find something no matter how hard I cleaned.'

'After you murdered Rebecca you carried her down to your van. Which was parked outside the block of flats, and threw her in the back. You then drove down to Bailey park where you dumped her body.'

'Yes, that's about the size of it.'

'But why wait all these years to kill her Benny? Why wait until that moment? You told us yesterday that you would never hurt Rebecca.'

'That's exactly what happened.' Nelson said. 'Everything I have said is true.'

'Only it isn't, is it Benny? 'None of it happened.'

'No, I murdered her. I confess. You've got your man DI Fagan. You can process me now.'

'What happened Benny?'

'I murdered Rebecca. That's what happened.'

'Why are you lying to us?' Watkins questioned.

'Why would I lie? I murdered Rebecca ok.' Nelson insisted. 'Now you can charge me. Isn't that what you want to do? The people of this town will finally be free of me.'

Fagan shook his head. 'You've sat there today just to spin some fantasy bullshit story about murdering Rebecca. You've done this to distract us.'

Nelson shook his head rigorously. 'I murdered Rebecca. I want to go to prison, so charge me.' Nelson started to get agitated. 'All these years in this town, people have accused me of doing all kinds of things. Benny the perv is what the kids shout at me in the street. For years, people have labelled me as being a paedophile, although I'm not. You want to know why I murdered Rebecca? Because I wanted to be released. Released from the prison, which is this town.'

Fagan remained unphased by Benny's words. 'What's in the shed at that allotment, Benny?'

'DI Fagan, I told you earlier to stay focused on the case involving Miss Jenkins.' Crawford stated.

Fagan stared at him. 'Now you decide to say something. As soon as I go off topic, you suddenly pipe up.'

'Be careful with your tone of voice DI Fagan.' Crawford looked at the camera.

Fagan couldn't stop himself from laughing at Crawford's gesture. 'This interview has been bullshit from the word go. So don't threaten me. I know I'm on camera. This interview is being recorded. I also know that none of what has transpired here today is admissible as evidence. I've been a serving detective for over thirty years. I have sat in on enough interviews in my time. Interviews with murderers. Nine times out of ten, they'll sit there and repeat over and over, No comment, no comment. It's usually what their solicitor advises.' Fagan stared at Nelson. 'But Benny here is singing like a bloody canary. Cleansing his soul for the world to hear. This isn't an interview. It's a diversion.'

Nelson smiled.

'I'd wipe that smug look off you face if I were you Benny. Especially when it involves a murder enquiry. I'll make sure you get at least ten years for perverting the course of justice.'

'I doubt whether you'll be able to do that, DI Fagan.' Crawford remarked.

Fagan glared at him. 'Why is that exactly?'

'I'm recommending Mr Nelson be given a full psychological evaluation before any charges can be brought before him.'

Benny stared straight ahead. 'You've no idea how much I have suffered in this town, DI Fagan. Decades of ridicule, trapped in an endless nightmare. There goes Nelson the perv. There goes Nelson the paedo. There goes Nelson the fat cunt. You will never know the mental abuse I have had to endure from the people of this town.'

'Why haven't you moved?' Fagan suggested. 'I did.'

Nelson stared at him. 'And now you've returned. And your teenage sweetheart is dead. I find that more than a coincidence that Rebecca was murdered soon after you roll back into town.'

'What about your wife Benny?' Watkins asked on purpose.

'My wife.' Nelson responded.

'Do you love her?'

'Of course I bloody well love her.' Nelson snapped.

'How old is she? Twenty-four, twenty-five maybe.'

'Twenty-six actually.' Nelson boasted.

'How long have you been married?' Fagan asked.

'Ten years this year.' Nelson replied smugly. 'Lovely wedding. You should have been there.'

'Where did you get married?'

'Thailand.'

'If you truly love your wife, then why have a shed full of obscene images at the allotment?'

'I won't tell you again, DI Fagan. Stay on topic.' Crawford interrupted.

'Where is your wife Benny?' Watkins asked.

Nelson summoned up an answer. 'She had to go back home. Her mother died suddenly. I bought her a ticket so that she could fly back to Thailand.'

'This was yesterday?'

Nelson nodded.

'Do you know what I saw when I was in that shed, Benny?' Fagan said. 'I saw an old photograph of us. Do you remember the summer of 1980 Benny? When Jimmy Savile attended a charity event at the sports field. We all had our photo taken with him. Do you remember that?'

'DI Fagan, is this trip down memory lane absolutely necessary?' Crawford enquired.

A smile stretched across Nelson's face. 'Of course I remember. Best summer ever.'

'How old would you have been back then, twenty?'

'DI Fagan, this pointless questioning will get you nowhere.' Crawford interrupted. 'I have constantly reminded you this interview is about the murder of Rebecca Jenkins.'

'Didn't you go to Forest Coalpit dorms with Savile and those six boys who won the competition?'

Nelson maintained his smile. 'Like I just said, best summer ever.'

'I think we're done here.' Crawford stood. 'For the record, I would like to say that I will make a full complaint to the Chief Constable of South Wales police. I will contact an appropriate psychiatrist to make a full assessment of Mr Nelson, who I'm sure has found this whole affair very stressful.'

Nelson also stood, maintaining his stare on Fagan. 'I'm going to make sure the people in this town pay for what they have done to me over the years.' He stepped up to Fagan. 'That includes you Fagan. Don't think you've got away with beating me up all those years ago.'

'Arrogant prick.' Watkins seethed after Nelson had left. 'He wasted our time on purpose. While the actual murderer could be in another country by now.'

'No.' Fagan said.

Watkins looked at him, noting the look on his face. 'You know who it is, don't you?'

'I have a good idea, yes.'

'Well, wouldn't it be a good idea to arrest whoever that

is? Instead of wasting our time on that twat.'

'There is far more going on here than the murder of Rebecca. Benny Nelson has been a thorn in this town's side for over fifty years. For some reason he seems to be totally immune to prosecution. That pimp of a lawyer who was with him will contact some high up psychiatrist to rule that Nelson has an unstable mental health issue. By the end of today we won't be able to touch him.'

'And the suspect who murdered Rebecca Jenkins? What about them?'

'Don't worry, they won't be going anywhere.'

'So what, they're going to sit on their arse and wait for us to turn up.'

Fagan glanced at Watkins. 'No, it's just me they're waiting for. I want you to analyse the interview. I'm sure the Chief Constable will return later on today after Crawford has a moan.'

Fagan threw his jacket on.

'Where are you going?'

'For a long walk down memory lane.'

'Ok, I guess I will hold the fort until you come back.'

'I know you have just met me Sean. I can tell you are a by the book officer. Unfortunately, that's not the true meaning of a good officer. I have trusted my instincts for the last four decades. It hasn't let me down yet.'

Watkins nodded, looking back at his superior. 'Okay, boss, it's your show.'

Less than five minutes later, Fagan was driving towards Llanover. He hit the speed dial on his phone. 'Tanner, you old devil.' Fagan smiled.

'Fagan, how's life in the land of the sheep?' Wayne Tanner asked in a broad scouse accent.

'Fine and dandy. Listen, I need a favour.'

'Bloody hell Fagan, you've only been gone a few weeks.

You must miss me.'

Fagan laughed. 'Terribly, and you're the only one I know at the moment I can trust. I need you to look for a brief called Wilson Fletcher Crawford. Nothing too heavy, just a light background. Any notable people he may have represented over the years.'

Tanner scribbled down the name.

'I also want a detailed search on a Ben Nelson, known locally as Benny Nelson. Arrests dates everything that he's been pulled up for. I'll text you his address.'

Tanner jotted down the second name. 'Everything okay at your end?'

'Mostly yeah.'

Tanner noted his tone. 'Fagan, you're not pissing in someone's pool, are you?'

Fagan smiled. 'Yeah, and I'm fresh out of chlorine tablets. Give me a bell when you have something.' Fagan hung up and put his foot on the accelerator.

CHAPTER 23

9th August 1983

Fagan entered the kitchen, hearing his mother talking to someone.

His mother looked in his direction. 'Hi sweetheart.'

Fagan looked at the man sat the other side of the kitchen table.

'This is Victor Adams.' Fagan's mother introduced. 'He's a local estate agent.'

'Estate agent?'

'I'm putting the house up for sale.'

Adams looked at Fagan, noting his expression. 'I'll give you a phone tomorrow and we can arrange another meeting.' He got up and left the kitchen, shutting the front door behind him.

'What do you mean selling up?' Fagan questioned.

'Your nan and grandad are coming down the week after next. We need to make plans for the future.'

'We can't leave mam. What about dad?'

'We'll make arrangements to come down on his birthday, and at Christmas. To lay flowers on his grave.'

Tears welled up in Fagan's eyes. 'We can't leave him alone.'

'We won't be leaving him alone. I have already spoken to George. He promised to look after your dad's grave.'

'What about everything else? What about all our friends?'

'I can't stay here Marc. Yes, I've got friends, but now we

have a new opportunity to start fresh. Your dad's work is giving us a massive pay out.' She handed him a letter she had received that morning. 'Twenty thousand pounds. It's called a death in service pay out. I'll be able to pay off the mortgage and sell the house. We'll have enough money to move to Ormskirk and buy a house. It's a fresh start. There's nothing for us here, Marc.'

'Maybe not for you mam. But what about me? What about the mates I have here? I have a life. I can't bugger off.' Fagan thought about Rebecca. He was starting to realise how much he loved her. Although he could not bring himself to tell her.

'Your so-called friends, Marc, have brought you nothing but trouble. Do you know who I had around here shouting on my doorstep yesterday? Bill Nelson, Benny Nelson's dad. Greasy little toad. He's threatening to press charges for the beating you gave his son.'

'That fucking twat deserved it mam. First, he called dad useless. Then he slagged off Graham. I couldn't ignore him. He would have kept on.'

'But you should have ignored him.' His mother shot back. 'How many more fights are you going to get into Marc? No one will employ you in this town with a criminal record.'

'No one will employ me where nan and grandad live.'

Fagan's mother shook her head. 'I have already had a word with grandad. He says there's a job for you at the car plant. He also knows people at Liverpool docks.'

'More fucking dead-end jobs, mam.'

'Since where have you been fussy about where you work?'

'I don't want to end up like dad. Working my bollocks off until I die. Besides, I am thinking of going back to college. Redo my exams.'

'Why the change all of a sudden?' Fagan's mother frowned. 'Oh I know, it's that girl from Lansdown Road, Rebecca, the stuck up one.'

'She's not stuck up. When you get to know her.'

'How well do you know her exactly?'

Fagan looked at his mother. 'Don't worry, I haven't got her pregnant or anything like that.'

'Marc, girls like Rebecca are not cut out for life on a council estate. You only have to look at their house on Lansdown Road. They live in a palace for Christ's sake.'

'Are you saying your own son is not good enough for her?'

'I'm saying that she's not good enough for my son.' Fagan's mother said defensively. 'Do you honestly think her father will accept you? He never meant any of those things he said about your dad at his funeral. He hated your father because he stuck up for the shop-floor workers.' She paused. 'Now that your dad has gone, he'll treat those factory workers like shit. What chance do you think you've got with that girl Marc? If you don't even stand a chance with her father. I've seen plenty of girls like her during my life. The first moment something better comes along, she'll dump you in a heartbeat.'

'Well, I guess you don't know her as well as you think. She doesn't want to go to university and been all prim and proper like what her father wants. She wants a life here in Abergavenny.'

'What life Marc?'

'There are jobs around. As soon as I get the money, I'll learn to drive. There's a chicken factory in Hereford that pays good wages. Sam Stephens' dad works there.'

'You just said you don't want a dead-end job. I've been fed up with the sweet factory for years. The only reason I got the job was because me and your dad had to be working to buy the house. Both of us need a fresh start. I don't want you to throw your life away Marc. Moving to Liverpool will give us a new outlook on life. When we are settled, then you can go back to college. You can make a real go of your life.' Fagan's mother paused. 'It's only a matter of time before you get into another fight. I don't think I can take much more of Sergeant Bob or George showing up at my door. Look, if it means anything to you, then it will be a while until we can move. At least next May. You've got plenty of time to say goodbye to everyone.'

Fagan turned and headed for the door.

'Where are you going?'

'Down the bloody pub.' Fagan barked.

'Marc, we really need to have this conversation.' His mother gave chase. 'Marc, you can't bugger off down the pub. This is something we really need to talk about.'

Fagan turned to face his mother. 'Didn't take you long, did it mam?'

'What didn't?'

'Deciding to move. Did you make the decision while they were burying him, or did you decide at the wake?'

'That's not fair.' Fagan's mother retorted.

Fagan slammed the door behind him.

CHAPTER 24

Llanover – Monmouthshire – 1:31pm

Nigel Thomas watched from a recliner as Fagan navigated the winding garden path. He stood up and walked towards him. 'Marc Fagan, as I live and breathe.' Thomas offered his hand.

Fagan smiled. 'Know it all Nigel.'

Thomas laughed. 'Haven't heard that one in a while.'

Fagan glanced around the sprawling garden. A mixture of lawn, vibrant coloured flower beds and a large vegetable garden. Surrounding an impressive 17th century stone cottage.

'Nice place.'

'It suits my purposes.' Thomas said.

'Evans said you're some kind of historian.'

Thomas nodded. 'Studied at Cambridge, worked in several museums around London over the years. I've written over a dozen books. Narrate for the BBC, the history channel, Discovery and the National Geographic channel. And narrate a lot of audio books.'

'Impressive.'

He looked at the cottage. 'Life has been good to me. But there is always a catch. I lost my wife to cancer two years ago.'

'I'm sorry.'

'The pandemic has claimed more lives through other illnesses. The NHS ground to a halt. When she was diagnosed, it was devastating. The cancer clinics had all shut down. We had some wonderful years together. Had three beautiful children. Even though she is gone, I am still blessed.' Thomas looked at Fagan. 'How about you, Detective Inspector Marc Fagan? You've seemed to have carved out a career for yourself. Serving with the Merseyside police for over thirty years. I bet you've got more than a few stories to tell. As a matter of fact you sprang to mind about ten years ago. I was writing a piece on the history of Usk prison for the Telegraph. I was going to write a book on the subject and you came to mind. Didn't you spend time as a guest of her majesty?'

'I did.' Fagan answered, recalling his experiences at the young offenders' institute. 'Back when I was banged up there, it was a brutal place. The guards and the prisoners were as bad as each other.'

'Well, at least you redeemed yourself by joining the police. Which is more than I can say for many people we went to school with.'

'People have done all right for themselves, for the most part.'

'What do you think of Abergavenny compared to when you left it?'

'I have to admit, the town has grown up over the years. The last thing I expected to see was a MacDonalds. I remember many people being opposed to the idea when it was first suggested before I left.'

'The town has had to change with the times. Unlike a lot of the towns in the valleys. Can I offer you a tea or coffee?' Thomas asked.

'No, not at this moment, thanks. How did you know I was a copper?'

Thomas smiled. 'I spoke to Jackie last night. I'm sorry to hear about what happened to Rebecca. Not the cushy last few years on the job you were expecting.'

'No, it certainly was not.'

'Do you think it was Benny who did it?'

Fagan shook his head. 'He's a total fantasist. His story this morning was a complete work of fiction.'

'So the murderer is still out there?'

Fagan nodded. 'He's still out there.'

Thomas glanced at Fagan. 'He?'

'I haven't had the chance to interview him. Anyway, I'm here on another matter. Evans told me you bought the entire archives of the Abergavenny Tribune.'

'Yeah, about sixteen years ago. A man called Arthur Forbes was the last editor. He had a massive shed in his back garden. It was stuffed with every copy and other stuff stretching back over a hundred years. He told me the Chronicle had offered him a considerable amount of money about twenty years ago. But he declined.'

'Why?'

'The Chronicle is owned by a newspaper group. Arthur said he didn't want the archives being swallowed up and disappearing forever.'

'How much did you pay for the archive?'

'Not one penny.'

'Really.' Fagan stated with surprise.

'When I told Forbes I was a historian, he was more than happy to let me have it for free. I had to assign an entire team to digitise the archive. It took three years to scan everything and file it. Photos, negatives and documents. A hell of a project. What is it you want to know?'

Fagan took a few moments. 'Do you remember when Jimmy Savile attended that charity event in 1980?'

Thomas inhaled. 'Yeah, I remember, although I didn't go to it. The Summer of Savile was the headline in the Tribune. If they knew back then what we all know now. A week before Savile visited Danny Llewellyn went missing.'

Fagan nodded. 'Me and Evans were talking about that last night.'

'And they still haven't found him. Next to Sally Anne Price, who disappeared in 1963. It's one of the biggest mysteries of this town.'

'I'm looking for pictures that were taken when he attended the event.'

'You're not the first person to ask for pictures of Savile at that charity event.'

'Who else has asked?'

'That's the thing, I don't know. He wouldn't give his name. I got a phone call about eighteen months back from a chap who offered me ten grand for all the pictures and negatives that may exist from that time. The weird thing about the bloke who asked, was that he was very specific about the details of the photos. That's when I became suspicious.'

'Suspicious, why?'

'He was interested in pictures taken of a camping trip that Savile attended.'

'The camping trip at Forest Coalpit dorms.'

'Yeah.' Thomas nodded. 'Anyway, I told him that archives prior to 1983 had been destroyed in a fire. He then hung up on me quickly. He almost sounded relieved they'd been destroyed.'

'Smart move.' Fagan remarked.

'The minute he asked me about surviving negatives of photos taken at the charity event, I knew he would have made them all disappear. No one asks for something specific like that unless it's for the sole purpose of erasing history.'

'I seem to remember you not going to that charity sports day.'

'It wasn't my thing. I hated PE, remember.' Thomas put

his hand on his chest and pretended to wheeze. 'Asthma.'

Fagan smiled. 'You faked asthma.'

Thomas smiled back, nodding. 'I could never stomach all that PE macho crap. I was too much into my history. Mr Julian Pask, the history teacher used to stick up for me. Said I would benefit more from having extra history lessons.'

'I remember us taking the piss out of you. Accused Pask of bumming you.'

Thomas nodded. 'Yeah, the kids were really cruel back then.'

'We also used to take the piss out of Pask. He used to have that limp. We used to call him limpy.'

'No one bothered to ask him how he got that limp.'

Fagan inhaled. 'We didn't give a shit. Just used to laugh at him as he limped towards his car after school.'

'His wife and two children were killed outright in a car crash in Oxfordshire in 1977. He was driving the car, when a drunk driver ran them off the road.'

'Jesus.' Fagan stated, imagining the scene.

'Jullian moved to Goytre in 1979 before starting work at the school.'

'You were obviously close to him.'

'Yeah, well, he was the father I always wanted. Instead, I got a violent drunk for a father. As for those rumours of Pask bumming me.' Thomas shook his head. 'You couldn't have met a more stand-up bloke. He was decent and brilliant. When he died ten years ago, I was devastated.'

Fagan stared out over the garden. 'When you look back at your school days. And you think about the other kids you took the piss out of. You never realise the damage you were doing back then. We used to call kids spastics, mongs, morons, thickos, retards and queer. It never entered our heads what we were doing.'

'That's why I have only lectured at university. Had no

trouble with older people.' Thomas stood. 'Come on, let's see what I have in the archives.'

A few minutes later, Fagan was sitting in Thomas' study. Pictures of Thomas and his wife were everywhere.

'Why are you looking for these pictures?'

'We raided a shed at an allotment yesterday evening belonging to Benny Nelson. I came across a picture of a line-up of boys who had their picture taken with Savile in 1980. I was in the picture. Unfortunately, the Chief Constable of South Wales police assigned his own team to clear out the shed this morning. The Chief Constable who is Bob Benson's grandson.'

Thomas smiled. 'Who himself was Chief Constable of South Wales police. At least that clears up that mystery.'

Fagan looked at him.

'My mystery caller. He had an official sounding voice. Question is, why would he want those pictures?' Thomas tapped away on the Keyboard.

'My guess is not to tarnish his grandfather's legacy.'

'Or to protect his own. Over the years, the police have been rocked by scandal. Most recently, the murder of a young woman by a serving police officer. Protecting his grandfather's legacy is a bit of a stretch. Unless, of course, his grandfather had something to hide.' Thomas clicked on the mouse, opening a file. 'Here we go. There are eighteen photographs that were taken in all. Not many when you considered how big Savile was back then. They were all taken by a photographer called Victor Clegg. I remember old victor, long dead now. He was the chief photographer for the Tribune.'

'Any negatives with the pictures?'

Thomas studied the information in front of him. 'Five in all.'

'Can you bring up the pictures?'

Thomas clicked a file, and a picture appeared on the screen.

'That's it.' Fagan pointed at the screen. 'That's the picture I looked at this morning.'

'I knew every one of these boys in the front row.' Thomas revealed. 'All but one are dead.'

'Andy Rogers is the one still alive.'

Thomas pointed at a young teenage boy on the screen. 'The other five are long dead. Three suicides and two overdoses.'

'Or five suicides.' Fagan added. 'Victims of abuse can often self-harm in later life. Suffering from flashbacks. Can you scroll through the rest of these pictures?'

Thomas started clicking.

'Stop.' Fagan said as Thomas clicked on the last picture. 'Do you have a date for this picture?'

'It was taken on Sunday, 1st June 1980, at Forest Coalpit. You can see the bus in the background that picked them up.'

'Savile didn't spend the night at the dorms did he?'

'No.' Thomas clicked on another image. 'This image was taken at the Regent Hotel in Monmouth. MP, Arthur Thorpe hosted a charity dinner that Savile attended. He spent the night at the Hotel. Then on the Sunday morning he travelled back to Forest Coalpit dorms to meet the boys and bring them back to Abergavenny. He boarded a train at the station at eleven o'clock.'

Fagan looked at Thomas. 'How do you know that by just looking at a picture?'

Thomas smiled. 'When the mystery caller asked for all information regarding Savile. I took the liberty of trawling through all the articles in the Tribune. Because I have had a few jobs narrating for the BBC I have avoided the news stories about Savile. The BBC can be very funny, when you start asking the wrong questions. I didn't want to lose the job.'

'Go back to the first group photo of all of us with Saville.' Fagan instructed.

Thomas scrolled back through the images.

'Now go to the picture taken on 1st June 1980.'

Thomas scrolled back to the last picture.

Fagan stared at it for several moments. 'Go back to the first.'

'Have you spotted something, DI Fagan?'

Fagan pointed at the picture. 'This image here where I am stood at the back. We're all smiles. Everyone is happy.'

'Of course, Mr Fix it himself was in town. The whole of Abergavenny was on a high that day.'

'Now go back to the other image.'

Thomas flicked through to the last image.

'Look at this image, with Savile the other adults and all the boys. Benny is there on the left, standing next to Bernard Baxter. What do you see?'

Thomas stared at the image before realising what he was looking for. 'None of the boys are smiling. In fact, they look downright miserable. All the adults are happy as Larry, including Savile.'

Fagan glanced at Thomas. 'Makes you wonder what went on at that camping trip.'

'Jesus, that's going to give me nightmares.' Thomas stared at the image of Baxter. 'He's still alive, Bernard the bummer Baxter. Living in Llanellen, just down the road. He also owns a house on Trinity Street somewhere. I was talking to someone the other day. He's been diagnosed with Alzheimer.'

'Must be into his nineties by now. I remember him being quite old when we were in school.' Fagan remarked. 'You heard the rumours then, mentioning his nickname.'

'Why do you think I avoided PE? I mean, they were just rumours back then. But it was enough for me to steer clear of the man. Julian told me he and Baxter had an argument about me. Baxter tried to force the headmaster to make me do PE. But Tomkinson wasn't having any of it.'

Fagan smiled at the name, rubbing his hand. 'I remember having a ruler across the back of my knuckles more than once because of that bloke.' He stared at the computer screen. 'All this started with the arrest of Benny Nelson yesterday.'

'Looks like you're the stone that's been thrown across the pond.'

'How do you mean?'

'Like ripples on a pond. You turning up out of the blue has set a series of events in motion. Starting with the death of your ex-girlfriend. Whether you like it or not Fagan, you are part of a bigger picture here.' Thomson looked at Savile. 'He was top of his game, wasn't he. Have you seen that two-part documentary series on Netflix about him? Worth a watch. I have watched it several times and have thought about that summer when he visited Abergavenny. He groomed an entire nation into thinking he was some kind of hero.' Thomas inhaled. 'When in fact he was a depraved monster who preyed on kids.' Thomas pointed at the photograph Fagan appeared in. 'I'd be very careful about the road you travel.'

'Why is that?'

'You've got two tasks on your hands. The first one, solving the murder of Rebecca Jenkins.' Thomas pointed at the photograph. 'The second one, uncovering a conspiracy about a highly organised group of paedophiles that may have operated within the community during the 1980s and before that. If Savile wouldn't have visited the town back in 1980, then we would not be having this conversation.

Abergavenny is a small community. It's not as closely knit anymore, but people still have long memories. There are many communities in the valleys that are still split because of the miners' strikes that took place back in the 70s and 80s. Families that haven't spoken to each other in decades. It's the same with Brexit. Exposing what could have happened back then could tear the local community apart. People don't like to be reminded of a past that connects them. They can sit there all day long watching the history channel. But when it comes to personal history, people would rather bury the past.'

Fagan absorbed Thomas' lecture. 'I have worked many cases involving child abuse over the years. Each one has left its mark on me. Especially the last one involving a six-year-old boy. A boy that should have been loved. But instead, his parents murdered him and dumped him like he was nothing.' He looked at the picture on the screen. 'The men who commit acts of depravity against innocent children have no souls.' His train of thought was interrupted by his ringing telephone.

'Boss, the Chief Constable is here. He wants to talk with you.'

'I'm on my way.'

'Trouble?'

'You could say that.' Fagan sighed, looking at the photograph. 'Can you print a copy of these photos? I need them if I'm going to bring Nelson to his knees.'

'And Rebecca's killer. What about him?'

Fagan inhaled. 'I'll bring him in. He's not going anywhere soon.'

CHAPTER 25

September 1983

'When were you going to tell me?' Rebecca screamed, pointing at the for-sale sign outside Fagan's front gate. 'Or were you going to fuck off without as much as a goodbye?' Tears streamed down her face.

'I was going to tell you as soon as the time was right.'

'When the time was right. And when will that be? On a phone line two hundred miles away in Liverpool.'

'Of course not.'

'So that's it. You're moving out of town and just going to leave me.'

'You know it's not like that, Rebecca.' Fagan paused. 'Next week I am due in court. All because I gave that twat Nelson a good hammering several weeks back. What happens if I get into trouble again? It means a custodial sentence. Do you really want to be with someone who beats people up?'

'Nelson deserved it. He should have been locked up years ago.'

'But he's not. Instead, I'll be the one who they'll be locking up. I don't want to throw my life away like that. And I don't want you wrecking your life by having to wait for me to get out of prison. Right now, the best thing you can do is listen to your dad. He may be a twat most of the time. But he doesn't want you throwing your life away. Go to Oxford, become a doctor or whatever he wants you to be.'

'And what about what I want?' Rebecca shot back.

'You're both the same. Always telling me what's best for me, but not having the first fucking clue what I want. I thought we had something special Marc.'

'Jesus Christ Rebecca, we're still bloody teenagers. You really want to decide what you want to do with your life before you have had a chance to live it. You're talking about settling down when we're barely out of school. There's more to life than kids and a mortgage.'

'So let's go travelling together. We can get jobs and save up. Go out to Australia, or America even. We could see the places we've always wanted to see.'

'And then what? Come back to this miserable shit hole of a town and set up house.'

'Then tell me what you want and I'll follow.'

'I don't want you to follow me anywhere, Rebecca. I want you to do what you want to do.'

'Then why did you just tell me to do what dad wants me to do?'

'Because I don't want you making mistakes you're going to regret later on in life. Look at all the people we know from school. The couples who are together and are planning to spend the rest of their lives together. How long before most of them are divorced?'

'But I love you.' Rebecca sobbed. 'Why can't you say it once, Marc? That's all I want to hear from you.'

'You know I'm crazy about you. I have jumped through your hoops, haven't I. Sneaking around pretending we're just good friends. How long can we carry on that charade for? The minute Tim finds out we're a couple he's going to flip.'

'So fucking what? There's not a lot he can do about it, is there.'

'Come on Rebecca, he's had his eye on you for the past few years. Once he finds out about us, he'll come looking for me. Have you seen him lately? He's slowly going off the rails.'

'Are you finishing with me?' Rebecca demanded to know.

'No.' Fagan struggled to say.

'I'm not stupid Marc. I can see the look on your face.'

'I have been trying to talk mam out of selling the house for weeks. I don't want to leave this town.' Fagan paused. 'But we have to face reality. It's either clink for me or a new start somewhere else.'

'When we announce we're together, I'll stand by you no matter what. I wouldn't worry about Tim. We can deal with him when the time comes.'

'You mean I'll have to deal with him. And then there's your dad, who's going to blow his stack when he finds out what we've been up to when him and your mother have been away.'

'I don't care about any of that. When we tell everyone, whoever is pissed off, can take a run and jump. All I want Marc, is for us to be a couple.'

'And I want you to have a life, Rebecca.'

'I can have a life. We can have a life.'

'I'm sorry, but I need to go. I have a meeting with my probation officer about the hammering I gave Nelson a few weeks back. I'm lucky I'm not doing time already.'

'Marc, we need to talk more.'

'About what?' Fagan shouted. 'There's nothing to talk about anymore.'

'So that's it. We're over. I obviously meant nothing to you. Perhaps I should be with Tim.'

'What is that supposed to mean?'

'It means you've treated me no better than he would.'

'Fuck off, that's not fair. I didn't pressure you into anything. You turned up at my house the day of dad's funeral. It's not like I dragged you up those stairs. Unlike Tim, who would have eventually forced you into shagging him.'

Rebecca stared back at Fagan.

'Yeah, he's fast becoming that type. I heard the way he talks about all his conquests. Like their meat down the market.'

'Are you finishing with me?' Rebecca demanded to know.

Fagan felt the mounting urge to slam the door in Rebecca's face.

'Are you finishing with me?' Rebecca repeated the question with a darker tone.'

'I think we should take a rest, yeah.'

'And how long should this rest be for?'

'Look Rebecca, I am doing my best here. Trying not to make it look like I'm shitting on you.'

'That's exactly what you're doing, isn't it? What's the next step? Go boasting to Tim and your other mates about popping my cherry.'

'That's unfair. You know I would never do that to you.'

Rebecca looked Fagan up and down. 'I should have known.'

'You should have known what.'

'That you were going to do this, that's what.'

'Rebecca, all I'm suggesting is that we take a break for a few months. With what happened to dad, plus that prick Benny Nelson, my head isn't in a good place right now.' Fagan paused. 'I just want some space.'

'Ok.' Rebecca nodded. 'I'll give you all the fucking space you want.' She turned and walked away.

CHAPTER 26

Newport Central police HQ – 3:12pm

'Do you want to tell me what the hell you're playing at, DI Fagan?'

'Sir?'

'Don't play fucking games with me!' Griffiths shouted. 'The interview with Ben Nelson. His lawyer is filing a complaint against Gwent Police. He claimed we've totally mishandled this investigation. And that you should be reprimanded regarding your conduct during the interview.'

'That's total bollocks. Nelson has been wasting our time.'

'Why didn't you charge him with the murder of Rebecca Jenkins?'

'Because I don't think he did it.' Fagan held back. He didn't want to indicate to Griffiths that he might have another suspect.

'But he confessed to murdering her.'

'Did you even listen to the interview? The man is a total fantasist. He's playing us, to amuse himself.'

'The murder weapon and the victim's phone were found at the shed Nelson owns. The phone case found in the park had his fingerprints all over it. What more evidence do you need?'

'Sir, during my career, I've come across an orgy of evidence on a number of occasions.'

'Don't lecture me Fagan.' Griffiths rumbled. 'I am aware of what an orgy of evidence is.' He collected his thoughts.

'Any ideas who has a grudge against Nelson?'

'Probably the entire town sir. The man is a serial sex predator who should have been locked up years ago. It's no secret he likes young girls. His wife is twenty-six years old. Nelson is approaching sixty three. I've been away from this town for thirty-eight years. Nelson has always had a reputation for being a pervert. It's almost like I never left. Here's my question. Why hasn't he ever been charged with anything? My local sources informed me he's been arrested many times over the years. But the man is still able to prowl the streets.'

'Your local sources, you mean mates from school who have had it in for Nelson? He mentioned you were hanging around near where he lived last night.'

'I don't believe I'm hearing this from a senior officer.'

'Watch your mouth Fagan.' Griffiths warned.

'I am free to visit whoever I want when I am off duty. It's a coincidence Nelson happens to live on the same street as an old friend.'

Griffiths looked down at some notes on his desk. 'A man who was prosecuted for harassment against Mr Nelson.'

'Oh, so we're calling him Mr Nelson now are we?'

'DI Fagan, it is the job of the police to show everyone respect. Both suspects and the innocent. We may not like it, but that's what we have to do. Innocent until proven guilty. Or have you forgotten that part?'

'What about the shed with all the explicit material? It was being used as some kind of sick twisted porn hub. There were possibly thousands of images in there. I haven't seen a haul that large in almost twenty years. The man had it decked out, electricity, phone lines. Despite all the times police arrested Nelson, no one has thought to look at that location.'

'Your job is to apprehend the person behind the murder

of Rebecca Jenkins. Given your past relationship with this woman, this should be your number one priority.'

'What exactly do you want me to do? Charge a man who did not murder her. Nelson will have our guts for garters in a court. It will cost Gwent police dearly. I will charge him for possessing illicit material and indecent images of children. And wasting police time. Provided I have access to the material.' Fagan paused. 'If I have to, I will contact the Commissioner of South Wales police to get results on this.'

Griffiths stared back at Fagan. 'Are you threatening me DI Fagan?'

'Is that how you see it, a threat? Forgive me sir, but I thought we were both police officers who've signed an oath to uphold the law. To serve the people of this country and to protect the public from men like Nelson.'

'Again with the lecture.' Griffiths rolled his eyes.

'I want access to the material in that shed.'

'It's out of your hands. A special division connected to cybercrimes has been assigned to examine all the material. If any illegal material is found, Mr Nelson will be charged accordingly. His lawyer has put a case forward the Mr Nelson is suffering from AMI.'

'Apparent mental illness.' Fagan mocked.

'Yes, an approved mental health professional is coming later to assess Mr Nelson to see if he is a danger to himself.'

'And what about the wider community? This all started with the murder of Rebecca Jenkins.'

'A matter you should focus on DI Fagan.'

'And that's exactly what I'm doing, sir. But I've also discovered another crime. One that Nelson has been getting away with for years. And you're sitting there acting as if it doesn't matter. The man is a danger to the community.'

Griffiths glanced at some notes. 'It says here you've a bit of a history with Mr Nelson. In 1983, you were charged with GBH after assaulting him. Then again, in 1985.'

'Jesus bloody Christ, you're talking about forty years ago.'

'Exactly what did Mr Nelson do to you?'

'Nelson was a complete prick. He'd constantly put himself in the line of fire with everyone. You think I was the only one to give him a hammering? Every time I saw him, he had a fresh black eye. Because he mouthed off to the wrong person. I'm not proud of what I did back then. But when it came to giving Nelson a kicking, I've no regrets. Neither does anyone else I doubt. Nelson was the reason I had to move from this town.'

'So, now the truth comes out. You've got a grudge against him.'

'No I haven't. Yes, I hated the man's guts forty years ago. But he wasn't the only reason I left. Truth is, I didn't want to end up back inside. Because that's exactly what would have happened. If it wasn't for George Walker, then my life would have turned out differently. Speaking of old school coppers. The one that had a soft spot for Benny was your grandfather. No matter how many people complained about Nelson back in the day, your grandfather protected him time and time again.'

Griffiths stared back.

'When I was up at that shed this morning, there was a picture of Jimmy Savile when he attended a charity run in the summer of 1980. Your grandfather was pictured next to him, along with several other men, including the MP for Monmouthshire. He was forced to resign because he was found with a rent boy.'

'I'd be very careful where you are going with your accusations DI Fagan.'

'Five out of six of the boys in the front row are now dead.' Fagan continued. 'The remaining boy is God knows where.'

'I suggest you rein in wherever you are going with this. My grandfather was an outstanding officer with a distinguished career.'

'I'm sure he was.' Fagan added, not wanting to push it too much. He had a habit of pushing senior officers until he was one step away from being kicked out of the force. 'But what about the others? We all know about Savile and what he was like. Over five hundred lines of enquiry being investigated by police forces across the UK. When I was working with the child protection unit in Liverpool, the scandal about Savile unfolded. We had three hundred people step forward with allegations regarding other people he was involved with. Pop stars, footballers, celebrities. Do you know what the senior ranking officers did? They shelved all lines of enquiry pending investigation. In other words, they didn't want to make themselves look bad. I mean, the police back in the day were an entity to be seen with the likes of Savile. Working alongside him at his charity events.'

'They were different times.'

'So everyone keeps telling me.' Fagan stated. 'Innocent times. A time when nothing like that was supposed to happen. Savile painting a perfect picture of himself. No one ever questioned him. And those who did were silenced. After all, how can uncle Jimmy do such terrible things? He raised millions for charities. No one was ever going to challenge Jim'll fix it. He was a money tree. Every time an organisation, hospital or institute needed money; it was a simple case of shaking the Savile tree. The thing about the Savile case is that it exposed an ugly underbelly of what goes on in the world of celebrity. When we were dealing with all these cases that flooded in, it became perfectly clear that abuse is like a disease. It spreads to every corner of society and has always been there. The woke generation of today are too busy wanting to cancel the past. Pretend none of it happened.' Fagan pointed towards the door. 'Out there, living and walking within our community is another version of Savile. Those who have come forward over the years have been silenced. I want to know why. I want to know how someone like that can walk amongst us for so long and stay free.'

'I'm not saying Nelson is without controversy. The man himself is a criminal enigma. You're right. He's been arrested time and time again and not charged.'

'Why not?'

Griffiths ignored the question. 'Can I trust you, DI Fagan?'

Fagan sensed a change of tone in Griffiths. 'Of course.'

'The National Crime agency sent out a new directive several months ago. Any large haul of illicit material found has to be handed over to them. This includes both adult porn and indecent pictures of children. It's part of a new drive following cases like the Jimmy Savile allegation and the Rotherham abuse scandal. My grandfather helped to bring down a paedophile ring that operated in Swansea in the mid-nineties.'

'What's the purpose of this new directive?'

'To establish a link between paedophile gangs currently operating in the UK. The pandemic has put all the UK police forces back five years. When everything stopped three years ago, crime kept going. It became far easier for criminal networks to share pictures and videos. The NCA is coordinating its efforts with constabularies across the country in the hope they can build a map of paedophile hubs in the UK. So you see, I had to take charge this morning. This was a massive find. You will be recognised for discovering the contents of that shed. I am not cutting you out of the picture altogether.'

'But that still leaves the question of what's being done about Nelson. Surely you can contact the NCA and give them his profile. They'll be able to take action.'

Griffiths frowned. 'Unfortunately, because of the fancy lawyer Nelson had representing him this morning, it's going to take a lot of wrangling to get him locked up for anything.'

'I'm trying to figure out how Nelson could afford that kind of brief. From what I know of the man he wasn't well off.'

'I've read your file DI Fagan.' Griffiths revealed. 'You've got a bad habit of pissing people off, especially senior ranking officers.'

'Who are more interested in not upsetting the apple cart than catching criminals.' Fagan added.

'You have to go by the book on this Fagan. Let's focus on one thing at a time. And right now, that's catching the person who murdered Rebecca Jenkins. Now, you say there was an orgy of evidence stacked against Nelson.'

'Yes.'

'Then you need to find who had the biggest grudge against him.'

'That's going to be a long list sir. I'm even near the bottom somewhere.'

'Nevertheless, we have to find the killer before the people of this town get too jittery. I have already had Wales Today phoning me. Asking when I plan to make a statement about her murder. I want you to give a brief statement to the press later this evening.'

'Me.' Fagan pointed at himself.

'You are the SIO. You need to show your face. I'm sure

plenty of people in this town still remember you from the old days. This will make it easier for people to come forward. You're a familiar face, one the people of Abergavenny can trust. Over the years, the trust of the police has diminished, especially in the wake of recent scandals involving serving police officers.'

Fagan nodded. 'I'll contact the press office at the BBC and arrange a conference later today.'

There was a knock on the door before Watkins walked in. 'Sorry to bother you sir. They have found a second set of fingerprints on the phone case belonging to the murder victim.'

Fagan and Griffiths exchanged glances.

'CSIs are running them through the national fingerprints database. But it will be a few hours before we get a positive match. It's only a partial thumbprint.'

'Good work.' Griffiths complimented. 'Well gentlemen, it seems you have a second suspect in the murder of Rebecca Jenkins. I suggest you hop to it.'

'Come on, pick up.' Fagan whispered, looking around.

'Fagan, you old devil.' Evans greeted.

'I hope you and Tyler haven't been sitting around watching bloody Star Wars all day long.'

'No, of course not. We've been steadily going through the Transformers movies.'

'Please tell me you're joking and you've found something.'

Evans laughed. 'As a matter of fact we have.'

'Superb.' Fagan almost punched the air. 'Come around my place tonight. Call Jackie and Edwards and tell them to be there for seven. Bring a takeaway and a box of bud. I'll have a chicken tikka masala and garlic naan.'

CHAPTER 27

Abergavenny cinema – September 1983

Fagan, Tyler, Evans and Edwards exited the cinema's main entrance.

'Best Bond film ever.' Tyler declared.

'Roger Moore is getting too old to play Bond. He's got to be in his mid-fifties by now. I prefer Live and Let Die, then Man with the golden Gun. Followed closely by Moonraker.' Evans said.

'The only reason you liked Moonraker is because it had space shit in it.' Fagan mentioned.

'Moonraker was brilliant.' Evans looked up at the poster, smiling. 'I love the names the producers come up with, Octopussy. Get it Octopussy as in pussy, like Pussy Galore in Goldfinger.'

'Sean Connery is doing another Bond film later on in the year. I read it in film UK last week.' Tyler mentioned.

'Fuck me, how old is Connery?' Edwards questioned. 'He must be in his fifties, like Roger more.'

'Guess what's on next week?' Evans smiled at a smaller poster. 'Porky's Two, the next day.'

'It's a fucking sequel Evans.' Tyler pointed out. 'It's bound to be shit. And I still haven't forgiven you for dragging me to see Jaws three. Biggest pile of shit ever.'

'Yeah, but the effects were cool.'

'Where are we going then?' Fagan asked.

'I thought we might go to the Black Lion until closing time.' Edwards suggested.

'Why can't we go to your dad's pub?'

'I'm not going there, when I have to fucking live there.'

'I say we go to the Black Lion. There's always decent totty there.' Tyler suggested.

All four agreed and walked towards the choice of pub they had made.

Nelson drove by in his car, briefly making eye contact with Fagan, grinning as he sped off.

'Prick.' Fagan seethed.

'He's just trying to wind you up. Still pissed off at the hammering you gave him up the Chevron several weeks back.' Edwards said, giving his friend a pat on the back.

'Someone is going to put him six feet under one day.' Tyler said.

'Yeah, probably be me.' Fagan stated. 'I felt like killing him when I beat the shit out of him. Sergeant Bob gave me a lecture when they threw me in the drunk tank. He accused me of being a nasty little bully who will one day get his comeuppance.'

'That's because Benny is his favourite.' Evans said.

The music from the Black Lion drifted down the street. But the shouting coming from the Farmers was louder. The sound of smashing glass cut through the air. A young woman appeared out of the entrance covered in blood, sobbing.

'Looks like Daisy's had another good hiding from her boyfriend.' Edwards despaired, looking over at the girl.

'I'll see if she needs help.' Evans offered, quickening his pace.

Fagan grabbed him by his shirt collar. 'Easy tiger, that's Daisy Richardson, Craig Parry's girlfriend. If you as much as blink at her, he'll rip off your head and shit down your neck. It may as well be a death sentence having a fight with him.'

'I've seen him at one of the garages in Charles Close

training the local kids.' Tyler said. 'He's got a punch bag hanging up. Pretty cool, actually.'

In the distance wailing sirens approached. A police van and an ambulance sped down Market street, screeching to a halt outside the pub. Several police officers, including Sergeant Bob poured out of the back of the van. He spotted Fagan and the others on the other side of the street, watching as police officers wrestled people out of the pub's entrance.

'Get the fuck off me! I'll kill the fucking lot of you!' Parry yelled as four officers dragged him to the van before tossing him in.

Benson marched towards Fagan's group. 'You planning to join those arseholes in the drunk tank tonight Fagan?'

'No.' Fagan replied, glaring back at Benson.

Benson took a step forward, standing nose to nose with Fagan. 'No, what?'

Fagan took a moment to answer. 'No, sir.'

Benson stared at him for several seconds before spinning on his heels and strolling back towards the police van. 'Right, come on. Let's get this miserable lot to the cells!'

A few curious onlookers stood around the entrance to the Black Lion.

An ambulance driver helped the girl covered in blood into the back of the vehicle. Her friend climbed in after her.

'I should go to Nevil Hall.' Evans said.

'Jesus Evans, you're madly in love with her, aren't you?' Tyler stated.

'I've been mad about Daisy since school.'

'And Parry will munch on your head if you as much as look at her.'

'Well, well, if it isn't the four musketeers of Abergavenny.' Davis greeted as he emerged from the pub entrance.

A surge of rage coursed through Fagan as he made eye contact with Rebecca, who looked away quickly.

Davis had his arm wrapped tight around her. He looked over at the Farmers before peeling himself away. 'Rob.' He shouted before jogging across the street.

The others had lost interest in the commotion and had disappeared into the pub.

Fagan glared at Rebecca before looking across the street at Davis. 'What the fuck is this?'

'Don't know what you're on about.' She shrugged.

'Fuck off Becky, don't play games with me. You're with him now, are you?'

'So what if I am? You couldn't give a shit.'

'All I said is that I wanted a break. I didn't say we were finishing for good.'

'Yeah, well, I decided to finish us.'

Fagan glanced at Davis across the street. 'I thought you weren't interested in him. Said all he wanted to do was get into your knickers.'

'I'm entitled to change my mind, aren't I.' Rebecca sounded as if she didn't have a care in the world.

'What's wrong with you Becky? All I wanted to do was take a break. You know, while I got my head together. It's been a shit year with losing dad and that prick Nelson. I didn't want you having to put up with that. I was even going to ring you next week. Thought we might go to Hereford and watch a film. Shit, I was even going to rent Casablanca on video and invite you over. Show you I still care.'

'Well, I guess things change.' Rebecca sniffed the air.

Fagan took a step back. 'So, it's like that, is it?'

'Yeah, it's like that. If you have a problem with it, then you'll have to deal with it.'

Davis marched back across the street, wrapping his arms around Rebecca. 'Everything okay Becks?' He asked, making eye contact with Fagan before kissing her on the neck.

She stared at Fagan. 'Yeah, everything is fine. Come on, let's go up the Chevron.'

Fagan watched as the couple walked away.

'Fagan.' Evans called out from the pub entrance. 'You coming or what?'

C H A P T E R 2 8

7:56pm

'Fine art, are you bloody joking Fagan?' Evans said, gawping around the dining room at the pictures that lined the walls. Leonardo Da Vinci, Michelangelo along with several other renaissance artists were on display.

Fagan smiled, tearing a naan bread in half. 'What can I say? You love Star Wars. I love fine art.'

'Never figured you as an art lover, Fagan.' Tyler said. 'Unless you count looking at the tits on page three back in the day.'

Fagan laughed.

'You should come down to London some time. There are some big art exhibitions this year. It's part of the coronation to celebrate the King's love of art. I can get you in all of them.'

'I might take you up on your offer.' Fagan stuffed naan bread into his mouth.

Evans stepped up to a picture of the Mona Lisa. 'Hang on, these aren't paintings. They're bloody jigsaw puzzles mounted on the wall.' He looked back at Fagan. 'I remember you joining the chess club at school. You didn't have a lot of patience for that.'

'Yeah, and I remember giving Norman Finch a bloody nose. What did he say? I had no scope for the game because I lacked intelligence.'

'But why Jigsaw puzzles?'

'Why not?' Fagan Shrugged. 'I got into them about four years after I joined the police. My first murder investigation as a detective constable was an old man in Southport. At first, it looked like he had taken a nasty fall down the stairs in the middle of the night and smashed his head open. But it turned out his own son had murdered him to claim the inheritance. Anyway, this old fella owned a lot of jigsaws, thousands of them. Some of them were rare and worth a fortune. A couple of weeks after solving the case, I bought a jigsaw. Didn't really think anything of it at first. But as I started to put it together, I noticed it had a calming effect. It also helped me deal with the job. Every time I got a tough case, I bought a jigsaw and put it together. It has helped me through some difficult cases.'

'Including the murder of Rebecca.' Tyler said, indicating to a table with a new puzzle. A box displaying the movie poster Casablanca was placed next to the puzzle.

Fagan stared over at the table, nodding. 'The more complicated the case, the more complicated puzzle I buy.'

Jackie and Edwards walked into the dining room.

'I got some red wine from Waitrose. Cost me a bloody fortune.'

'Nice one Jacks.' Fagan looked at the wine label.

'What happened today when you interviewed Benny?' Jackie asked.

'A total nutter. Yesterday, he denied everything. Today he was admitting to everything. None of it makes sense.'

'So he did murder Rebecca.' Evans said.

'No.' Fagan shook his head, dumping rice onto a plate. 'He didn't murder Becky. CSIs found a second set of prints on the phone cover.'

'Who's?' Edwards asked.

'That's the thing. They're only a partial match. It will take time to come up with a full match. Hopefully, we should know before the day is out.'

'Why haven't you questioned Tim yet?' Evans asked.

Fagan thought about the question. 'I'll be honest, Tim should have been my first port of call.'

'But?' Jackie said.

'I almost killed him forty years ago. He was in a wheelchair for over a year and he still has a limp because of what I did to him. I can't bring myself to face him.'

'Fagan, we were all there that night in the Farmers. He belted Rebecca in front of all of us. Her nose exploded. You were trying to protect her.'

'By almost killing him.' Fagan said. 'That makes me no better. Has anyone even seen him since Rebecca was found yesterday morning?'

'I have.' Edwards admitted. 'I spotted him coming out of Flannel Street chippy at lunchtime. Which is odd. Tim only goes to Market Street chippy.'

Evans produced his mobile phone and slid it across the table. 'This footage may interest you.'

Fagan tapped on the screen and a video played of a car pulling up outside Nelson's house. The video showed Justin Pike getting out of the car and talking to Nelson's wife.

'I did an edit earlier and zoomed in.' Evans explained.

'The video showed Nelson's wife handing over what appeared to be a set of keys.'

Fagan checked the timeframe on the video. 'This video was taken around midnight. Nelson would have still been in Cardiff. I bet those keys are for Benny's shed at the allotment.'

Jackie stared at the footage. 'So what? Justin murdered Rebecca. I find that hard to believe. They've worked together for over thirty years. They had a real close friendship.'

'Not close enough for Pikey.' Evans said.

Jackie shook her head. 'Rebecca never mentioned Justin fancying her, or anything like that. If he had a thing for her, he kept it well hidden. He always kept their relationship professional.'

Evans retrieved the phone and played another video. 'This was taken less than fifteen minutes after Pikey shows up at Nelson's house.'

Fagan watched as Pike returned to his car. Again Nelson's wife was waiting for him. The window slid down and Pike held up the keys. Nelson's wife snatched them away and quickly disappeared.

'Nelson's wife boarded a plane yesterday morning for Indonesia.'

'What?' Edwards queried.

'Benny somehow knew he would be questioned over the murder of Becky. So he bundled his wife on the first flight out of the UK. I'm guessing he may have been using her as a sex worker.'

'Funny you should say that Fagan.' Evans said. 'I have footage dating back several months. Every other Friday night, around eleven o'clock. Pikey turns up outside Nelson's house to pick his wife up. They're usually gone for three hours before he brings her back.'

Fagan stared at the video as it played.

'And that's not all. Every day, twice a day, a different car pulls up to Nelson's house and his wife gets in. She's usually gone for an hour, then gets dropped off back at Nelson's house. Once around ten in the morning and again around three o'clock in the afternoon.'

'And no one has noticed this in all the time she's been there.' Jackie stated.

'Not really no. There are people coming and going all the time on that estate. There are a lot of dealers that come into the estate and drop off supplies. A regular dealer drives a black BMW with blacked out windows. He's like an Amazon delivery driver. All kinds of shit goes on. Nelson's wife blended into the background. Everyone has got used to Benny over the years. Unless he goes out of his way to fuck someone off, no one questions him anymore. We let him get on with his life.'

Fagan took a good swig of red wine, watching the video play. 'Benny, you piece of shit. You've been pimping out your wife.'

'Fucking hell, just when you think that man couldn't get any worse.' Jackie said in disgust.

'My guessing is he married her to get her a British passport. Bring her over and set her to work earning money.'

'Don't forget what I told you yesterday. She's been in that shed getting her tits out as well.' Evans mentioned.

'I'm sure the laptop will confirm that.' Fagan glanced at Evans. 'I want you to e-mail all this footage to me.'

'Hang on a minute here.' Tyler said, crunching on a poppadum. 'We don't know anything at the moment. Those keys could be for anywhere. For all we know Justin could have dropped his house keys, and she found them.' He looked at Fagan. 'You could get into a lot of shit for not considering Tim as a suspect in Rebecca's murder.'

'True.' Fagan responded. 'But Benny has been such a distraction. Up until another set of prints were found he was our only murder subject. It's like I mentioned last night. An orgy of evidence has been deliberately planted to implicate Benny in Rebecca's murder. Plus, his arrest has opened another can of worms. Suggesting that at some point in his sordid life Benny could have been involved in a paedophile ring that stretches all the way back to 1980, and before that.' Fagan stood and walked over to a chest of drawers, and pulled out some photographs that he tossed onto the table. 'Nigel printed these out for me today. Apparently, someone phoned him last year and asked if he had any pictures of Jimmy Savile attending that charity gala in the summer of 1980. They offered him a lot of money to buy up any pictures he had, including negatives.'

Everyone stared at the pictures.

Fagan looked at Tyler. 'You're absolutely right. I should have spoken to Tim as soon as Rebecca's body was found. I was about to visit him when the prints produced a result. Then Benny came squarely into frame as the prime suspect. He's got plenty of form over the years for being the town's pervert, but never been charged with anything. CSIs found a load of old computers at his shed at the allotment. But the hard drives were missing.' Fagan thought back to the interview he gave Nelson. 'Something Benny said earlier today rattled my cage and sent me into a cold sweat.'

'What did he say?' Evans asked.

'It was when he was describing the way he killed Rebecca. Nelson claimed he smashed her over the head, before looking for a phone charger cord to finish the job. Until that point in the interview he was rattling off pure fantasy. I've heard the things he was saying a thousand times before. But then he smiled and looked at me.'

'What did he bloody say?' Evans repeated his question with more enthusiasm.

'Nelson said; The look he gave me, as he lay in a crumpled heap on the floor.'

'What's that supposed to mean?' Jackie asked.

'That's what intrigued me. I repeated back to him what he told me. Nelson seemed to snap out of a trance and carried on rambling, but not before he said something else.'

The room plunged into silence as everyone hung on to what Fagan was telling them.

'He said. She looked at me, and that's when I saw it. I asked Nelson what he saw. He answered, her invite, for me to kill her. The moment when the light starts to fade in their eyes. It's a moment when they say, I am yours, do what you want with me. It was pure ecstasy.' Fagan gathered his thoughts. 'I reckon Benny was reliving a moment.'

'Reliving a moment?' Edwards repeated.

'Benny has killed before.' Fagan stated.

The others exchanged looks of shock.

'Who's he killed?' Evans asked.

'That's the sixty-four-thousand-dollar question, isn't it? Who indeed?'

'The last person to be murdered in this town was old Fred up Underhill. About thirty-five years ago. Until yesterday this town hasn't seen anything like that.' Edwards said.

'Unless you count the suicides over the years.' Evans added.

'If what you say is true, and Benny has murdered someone. Who do you think it is?' Jackie asked.

'It has to be someone from the distant past.' Fagan said. 'When did Benny learn to drive?'

'He's been driving since he was seventeen.' Evans revealed. 'I remember when he got his first car, a Mini.'

'That would be around 1977.'

Evans nodded.

'He used to cruise around Abergavenny looking to pick up young girls.'

'And he used to wait outside the school gates.' Jackie said, shuddering.

'But he used to go out of Abergavenny. All over the valleys, even as far as Hereford.' Fagan pointed out. 'Which means he could have committed murder anywhere.'

'What about Danny Lewellyn.' Evans suggested.

'Shitting hell.' Jackie cursed. 'You think he murdered Danny?'

'We all remember that week.' Evans looked at Fagan. 'It was the week you got locked in that cellar for a couple of hours.'

Fagan nodded recalling the incident. 'The night before Danny went missing we were all at the cinema together.'

'Watching *The Empire Strikes Back*.' Tyler added glancing at Evans.

'You nearly had a fight with Adrian Lewis who was going to see it on the Saturday night.'

Evans smiled. 'Lewis was fuming when I told him Vader was Luke's father.'

'Danny and his mate Kevin Green came with us.' Fagan mentioned. 'The next day Kevin was found under the bridge at Llanfoist and Danny went missing.'

'Are you saying that Benny could have something to do with that?' Jackie quizzed.

Fagan inhaled before nodding. 'It's possible.'

'This is all well and good, but where's your evidence?' Edwards questioned.

'I haven't any. But the way Benny spoke to me today. I can tell when someone is reliving a memory.' He looked down at the photograph of the line-up in which Savile appeared. The six boys stared at the camera, smiling, full of hope and excitement. They were meeting one of the biggest celebrities in the country. Then he looked at the other photograph taken the next day. The boys staring blankly at the camera. Their faces deprived of the happy smiles the day before. 'We need to find out what happened at Forest Coalpit dorms in the summer of 1980.'

'All the boys are dead except one.' Evans said. 'Andrew Rogers.'

'It'll take time to track him down. What about the

parents of these boys?'

'All have passed away, except for George.' Edwards said. 'The man lost his son, then lost his wife to cancer. Anyone else would have given up. But somehow George has clung on.'

'Perhaps he hasn't given hope of finding some kind of resolution to Graham's suicide.' Fagan said. 'And perhaps he could be ready to talk about his son's death.'

'Are you fucking mad, Fagan?' Evans questioned. 'The poor bloke is eighty years old, for fuck's sake. What are you going to do? Knock on his door and ask, George, do you think your son could have been raped by Savile and those other paedos at Forest Coalpit in 1980?'

'But Savile didn't stay the night at Forest Coalpit dorms. He stayed at a place called the Agincourt Hotel just outside Monmouth. It was Sergeant Bob and a few others that spent the night at Forest Coalpit.' Fagan pursed his lips. 'I think George will talk to me. I suspect Graham might have told him what transpired that night.'

'And if you mention it, the poor fucker could have a heart attack and drop dead.'

'No.' Fagan said quietly. 'You're right, George has hung on for so long. It's because he wants to expose this.' Fagan's phone rang.

'Boss, we have a match for the second set of prints.' Watkins revealed. 'They belong to a Justin Pike.'

Fagan massaged his forehead. 'Right, send a couple of uniform to arrest him. We'll interview him first thing tomorrow morning.'

Everyone in the room glared at Fagan as he hung up.

'Well?' Jackie was the first to speak.

'Justin Pike's prints have been confirmed as the second set of prints on the phone case.'

'Fuck.' Evans cursed.

'Let's get on with our takeaway.' Fagan suggested. 'I'll go and see George in an hour.' He got to his feet and walked over to the table where the new jigsaw was. Fagan stared at it for a few moments before placing some of the pieces into place. 'Listen, regarding Tim.' He turned to face the group. 'I promise he will be questioned about Becky's murder.'

'And what if he does a runner?' Tyler said.

Fagan shook his head. 'Tim won't run. In fact, it's a sure bet he's waiting for me to arrest him.'

'Why do you think he hasn't handed himself in?' Jackie asked.

'This is personal to him. He wants to face me. After forty years, he still has something to say.'

CHAPTER 29

The Farmers Arms—16th October 1983

'Watch this for a shot.' Evans said with confidence as he thrust the cue forward. The white ball rebounded off two cushions before gently nudging the black ball into a corner pocket. 'Come on!' Evans shouted triumphantly, punching the air. Several other people joined in, cheering him on.

Fagan frowned at the pool table. 'You jammy fucker, that was a total fluke.'

The sound of Michael Jackson pumped out of the juke box.

Evans marched over to Fagan, who reluctantly reached into his back pocket.

'Come on Fagan, cough up, two quid please.'

Fagan thrust two crumpled pound notes into Evans's hand. 'Here, shove it up your arse.'

'Don't be like that. Just because I have beaten you three times in a row.' Evans boasted. 'Tell you what, double or nothing. Best out of three again. A chance to win your money back.'

'Don't be a silly twat Fagan.' Edwards warned. 'You know he'll hustle you out of another two quid.'

Fagan considered the proposal before nodding. He glanced at the clock, which read 9:30pm. 'We'll have to be quick. The pub shuts in half an hour.'

'I want to get home, anyway.' Evans said, chalking his pool cue.

'Why, you going to swing by Daisy's place and finally ask

her out?' Tyler mocked.

'What did I tell you a few weeks back?' Fagan recalled.

'No, I want to get home to watch a program I taped off the telly this afternoon.' Evans looked about, lowering his voice. 'Something called Terrahawks.'

'Terra what?' Fagan said.

'It's a new TV show from Gerry Anderson.'

'Who, the bloke who made Thunderbirds?' Edwards guessed.

'Yes, the bloke who made Thunderbirds.'

'Don't say it's got puppets in it again.'

'So what if it has?' Evans responded defensively.

Fagan, Tyler and Edwards burst into laughter.

'You're a fucking spastic sometimes Evans.' Tyler laughed. 'What was that you were talking about last week? Something you read in a film magazine. Remember, you were going on about that bloke who directed Piranha two. He's working on a new film.'

'James Cameron.' Evans said. 'And he's working on a script for a film about a robot that comes from the future to kill this girl.'

'If the sequel to Piranha is anything to go by, James Cameron will be lucky if he's a future in Hollywood.'

'You're not still wasting your money on toys, are you, at your age?' Edwards asked.

'It's not a waste of money.' Evans replied. 'And they're not toys, they're collectables. One day my Star Wars figures are going to be worth a fortune and then you lot can suck my dick.'

'I watched that new TV show last night on HTV Wales, The A Team.' Edwards remarked.

'I saw that.' Fagan piped up. 'Fantastic, loved all the stunts in it. Had the bloke from Rocky three.'

'Mr T.' Tyler stated. 'I still like the Dukes of Hazzard.

Daisy Duke's tits are spectacular.'

A group of young women piled through the entrance to the pub laughing. Jackie Mills led the group. Her jet black hair was tied up. She wore a short skirt with fishnet stockings with a small black leather jacket. She casually strolled over to the juke box and made a selection. A few moments later Dead Ringer for love came on.

'Speaking of spectacular tits.' Edwards said, eying up the group of women at the bar. 'Hey Jackie, get your tits out for the boys.'

Jackie turned to face him, stooping over, clutching her ample cleavage. 'You wouldn't know what to do if I rubbed them in your face.'

The group of women she was with laughed.

'Come on then Fagan. Set them up before they call time.' Evans challenged.

Fagan reached into his pocket and pulled out two ten pence pieces he slotted into the pool machine to release the balls.

'Get off me, you fucking twat!' Rebecca shouted as she was shoved through the pub entrance.

Everyone looked in her direction.

'Where is he?' Davis shouted, staggering into the bar. He spotted Fagan. 'There he is. There's your fucking lover boy.'

Fagan placed the cue he was holding on the pool table.

Everyone looked on.

'What's going on?' Fagan asked in an even tone.

Davis glared back at him. A look of hate and anger etched into his expression. 'I'll tell you what's going on, shall I twat. Me and Becky have been having a little chat. Turns out you and her have been fucking each other for the last few months.'

Fear mounted as Fagan stared back at Davis. He knew

he wouldn't beat him in a fight.

'Cat got your tongue, has it Fagan?' Tim slowly approached. 'Not like you to be stuck for words. You've usually got more than a few things to say.'

Fagan glanced at Rebecca. Black streaks ran down her cheeks.

'Don't look at her twat, look at me.' Tim demanded.

'What's the problem Tim.' Fagan asked, trying to stay as calm as possible.

'I'll tell you what the fucking problem is.' He pointed at Rebecca. 'You fucking her behind my back. That's what the problem is. Kept that a secret, didn't you Fagan.' He looked at Fagan's friends. 'Did you tell your little band of queers here?'

'Fuck off, Davis.' Edwards snarled.

'Oi, you lot.' The landlord shouted from behind the bar. 'If you're going to fight, you can fuck off outside.'

'No one is going to fight, are they Fagan?' Davis said. 'I mean, we're all good mates here. And good mates tell each other everything.'

Fagan nodded slowly.

'Then why didn't you tell me you've been fucking Rebecca?'

'Because it's none of your fucking business.'

'None of my business.' Davis said with a mocking tone.

'Back off, Tim.' Jackie ordered.

Davis grinned at her. 'Fuck off slut.'

Jackie glared back. 'Try calling me that if Tommy was here. He'd rip your fucking head off.'

Davis ignored her and took another step towards Fagan.

Fagan stood his ground. 'Fuck off home Tim. Everyone can see you're pissed.'

'Come on, Tim let's go.' Rebecca spoke up.

'Fuck off cunt. I'll deal with you later.' Davis snarled at

her.

'Tim, don't fucking start.' Fagan advised. 'Do as Rebecca says. Go home and sleep it off.'

'I'm not going anywhere until you admit you're a lying little cunt.'

'I don't have to answer to you. Who the fuck to you think you are?'

'I thought we were mates.'

'We were never mates Tim.' Fagan glanced at Evans, Tyler and Edwards. 'They're mates. They've stuck with me this year after dad died. The only reason you turned up at his funeral was to see if there were any women that needed a good shag.' He glanced at Rebecca.

'I told you not to look at her.' Davis took another step forward.

'Is this what you want, Rebecca?' Fagan looked Tim up and down. 'Someone who'll just shit on you all your life. You may not want to go to university, but you can't stay here in this shit box of a town.' Fagan pointed at Davis. 'Full of pricks like him who will drag you down to his level and use you. Then throw you aside the first moment another conquest comes along. Because that's all you are to him.'

Davis took another step forward, clenching his fists. 'You want to call me a prick again, Fagan. I'll lamp you into the middle of next week.'

'Fuck off, Tim. I don't want to fight. I know you can handle yourself. Maybe you will punch my lights out. But it won't make me respect you. You have to earn respect, not beat people up to get it.'

Everyone in the bar nodded silently.

Tim took another step forward, bringing him within striking distance. 'I bet you both had a good laugh, didn't you, behind my back?' He turned his head, glancing at Rebecca.

'No, we didn't, actually. You think when we were doing it, your name came up. You really are full of yourself.' Adrenalin coursed through Fagan as he remembered the day of his father's funeral. The afternoon when Rebecca showed up at his house. 'I'll tell you something shall I. When we did fuck each other it was beautiful. We didn't rush. I didn't just get on top and pump away like you usually do with the girls. It was a perfect moment.'

Davis glared back, blood rushing to his rage filled expression.

'Then after we had fucked each other, we fucked each other again, and...'

Tim grabbed Fagan, launching his head forward.

Fagan felt agonising pain as the bridge of his nose collapsed. Blood exploded in all directions, splattering across the pool table.

'That's it!' The landlord screamed. 'I'm calling the fucking police.'

Davis wasn't finished. He launched his fist, striking Fagan just below his right eye.

Fagan stumbled backward. As his body headed for the floor, he smashed his head on the side of the pool table. The room spun violently as Fagan fought to stay conscious.

Davis lunged forward, booting Fagan squarely in the stomach.

Fagan felt the air rush from his chest. For a fleeting moment he considered the possibility that this was the end.

Rebecca lunged at Davis, screaming. 'Get off him!'

Davis spun around and punched Rebecca. She stumbled backwards falling into a table of empty glasses. Davis stooped over, grabbing a handful of her long blonde hair.

'Fuck off me!' She screamed.

'I just said to you, cunt, I'll deal with you later.' Davis

struck Rebecca hard across the cheek before flinging her aside.

The air rushed back into Fagan's lungs. Rage coursed through his body as he watched Rebecca sobbing, clutching her bloodied nose.

Davis stood over her, positioning himself for another blow.

'Get off her, you twat!' Jackie shouted, rushing forward.

'Take another step forward cunt, and I'll smash your fucking face through the back of your skull.' Davis growled.

'That's it, I'm calling the Cantreff. When Tommy gets here, he's going to rip your fucking head from your shoulders.' Jackie rushed to the payphone by the bar.

Davis looked down at Rebecca. 'Give me one reason why I shouldn't fucking kill you right here.'

Fagan's strength had returned. He jumped to his feet and flew across the bar, grabbing the pool cue.

Davis turned to face his opponent, but it was too late.

Fagan swung the heavy end of the cue, striking Davis across the face.

Davis stumbled, crashing into a table where a group of people sat. The sound of smashing glass echoed around the bar.

Fagan launched himself at Davis, who was scrambling to his feet.

People scattered, trying to distance themselves from the ensuing battle.

Davis barrelled towards Fagan, grabbing his waist. The two of them fell to the floor, with Davis having the advantage.

Evans, Tyler and Edwards rushed forward, dragging Davis off Fagan.

Davis staggered backwards toward the bar entrance.

Jackie had finished on the phone and was comforting

Rebecca.

Davis pointed at Fagan. 'This isn't over you twat.' He turned and fled the bar.

Fagan looked over at a sobbing Rebecca before glaring at the pub entrance.

Tyler grabbed Fagan's arm. 'Leave it mate, the twat ain't worth it.'

Fagan wrenched himself away, heading for the pub entrance.

Davis stood on the pavement on the other side of the street, catching his breath.

Drinkers from the Black Lion had poured onto the street after they'd heard what was going on at the Farmers.

Fagan spotted Davis panting against the wall. Rage thrust him forward, hurtling towards his opponent.

Evans and the others flooded out of the Farmers.

'Fagan, let it go!' Tyler shouted.

Jackie rushed out of the entrance. Rebecca was close behind.

Fagan sprinted across the street, aiming at Davis, who had barely time to look up. Fagan shouldered Davis against the wall of the Black Lion.

Davis let out an agonising gasp.

Fagan smashed Davis' head up against the wall.

Blood sprayed in all directions across the wall.

Fagan smashed his head again, then again.

Davis' eyes lolled upwards as he lost consciousness.

Fagan threw him to the floor before launching a series of devastating kicks into his back.

Tyler, Evans and Edwards rushed forward, dragging Fagan away.

Jackie knelt by the side of Davis. 'Jesus, he's not breathing.'

'What?' Evans rasped.

Jackie glared at Fagan. 'He's not breathing, you twat. You've fucking killed him.'

Sirens from approaching police vehicles could be heard fast approaching.

Tyler rushed back into the Farmers to call an ambulance.

'What have you done?' Jackie screamed at Fagan.

Two police vans and a squad car hurtled down Market street, screeching to a halt in front of a bloodied and battered Fagan.

CHAPTER 30

Lower Monk Street – Abergavenny 9:23pm

George Walker stared back at the man he knew as a boy. He opened his arms, beaming. 'I never thought I'd see this day.'

Fagan embraced the old man who had mentored him as a teenager. 'I'm sorry I didn't come to see you sooner George.'

'From what I've been hearing, you've been up to your neck in it.'

Fagan nodded as he stepped through the door. 'You could say that.'

'It's so good to see you my boy.' Walker smiled. 'A detective inspector, no less. You've really done me proud.' He paused. 'The others told me about your mam, so sorry.'

'Thank you George.'

'Me and your dad used to be best mates back in the day. A lot like you and Graham.'

They sat opposite each other in two Chesterfield armchairs.

Fagan glanced around the room, which was filled with pictures of Walker, his wife, and son. A young Fagan also appeared in a few of the pictures. Walker stood and walked over to the mantlepiece, picking up a picture in which Fagan appeared with his young friend.

'The good old days.' Walker handed the picture to Fagan.

'I remember. We were inseparable.'

'You were all close back then. You, Graham, Evans, Tyler and Edwards.'

'We used to go everywhere together. I owe Graham my life, literally. When I jumped into the deep pool in the Gavenny. He had to jump in after me. I couldn't even swim.'

'Graham loved his sports, especially swimming. He also liked his footie. Remember when you two played for the Mardy?'

'Yeah.' Fagan nodded. 'What did old Mack Jacobs used to call us, the cream of the Mardy crop. He contacted that Leeds United scout to come and watch us play.' Fagan rubbed his knee. 'That was the day I bloody knackered my knee up.'

'Did Graham ever tell you, that scout offered him a place?'

Fagan looked at the old man sat in the chair opposite. 'No.'

'He turned up at the front door a few days after he saw him play. Graham turned him down.'

'Why an earth did he do that?'

'Graham said he didn't want to go anywhere without you.'

'He never said anything.'

'He didn't want to undermine your friendship. Graham always said you were his best mate.'

Walker stood and walked over to a drink cabinet, pouring two glasses of brandy.

'Thanks.' Fagan took the glass and tasted.

Walker sipped from his glass. 'You're not here for a trip down the pleasant part of memory lane I take it.'

'I'm afraid not George.' Fagan placed his glass down on a small coffee table. 'I meant to see you yesterday about the post you put on social media. How did you know

Rebecca had been found?'

Walker produced his mobile phone. 'The dog walker who found her text me this image.'

Fagan stared at Rebecca's dead body in the undergrowth.

'I didn't post this picture on social media or share it. I only mentioned that she had been found.'

'Did you know Rebecca?'

'Yes, we used to have lunch at Wetherspoons at least once a month. We struck up a friendship a couple of years after you left. I saw her one day in Kwik Save. We got talking about that night in the Hospital. You know, the night you gave that lad a good hammering.'

'I remember.' Fagan recalled the fight as if it was yesterday. 'So lucky I didn't kill Tim.'

'Have you spoken to him? You know, since you come back to town.'

'No.'

'What did that fat bastard Nelson have to say?' Walker asked.

'Not much, and too much. Yesterday, he denied murdering Rebecca. Then earlier today he was shouting it from the highest rooftops. The man has serious mental health issues.'

'Twat should have been put away years ago. Instead, the system has allowed him to roam free and do whatever he wants.'

'Why do you think that is, George?'

'Because of the people he had connections with. The nonces who got away with everything back in the day. Shitty little errand boy. That's all he is.'

'Arresting Benny has opened up a can of worms.'

Walker nodded. 'A lot of old ghosts are about to be exorcised. Ghosts people of this town thought were long gone.'

Fagan flicked through the pictures on his phone. 'While police were searching a property of Nelson's last night, we came across a stash of images.'

'I told them years ago to search that little porn paradise of his at the allotment. All I got was ignored.' Walker had an air of resentment in his voice.

Fagan passed Walker his phone. 'This was taken in the summer of 1980.'

Walker stared at the image. 'The summer when Uncle Jim came to town.'

'I know this will be difficult. We don't have to do this if you don't want to.'

Walker shook his head rigorously. 'We have to do this.' He paused, gathering his thoughts, glancing at a school photo of his son that hung on the wall over the fireplace. 'I have waited forty-three years to tell my story. You have to understand Fagan, no one was interested back then.'

'Take your time, George.' Fagan coaxed gently.

Walker composed himself. 'Graham was so excited when the Tribune published an article about Savile coming to town. And when he found out about the competition to meet Savile, he was determined to win and be part of the gang that went to Forest Coalpit dorms. Graham had written to Savile many times before. Asking if he could get to meet and swim with David Wilkie.'

'Christ, there's a name I haven't heard in a while.'

Walker continued. 'On the day that Savile was due to arrive in Abergavenny, Graham was like a kid on Christmas morning. He got up early and went for a run.' Walker smiled. 'I think his mother was just as excited as he was.'

'If I recall George, you weren't that that day.'

'No, I was on patrol around Gilwern. There'd been a spate of burglaries, so I had to go out and look for any suspicious activities. I was in Gilwern until at least two o'clock. When I got back, Savile and the group had already left for Forest Coalpit. One of the teachers at the school told me that Graham was the fastest runner in the competition.' Walker sniffed. 'I was so proud of him that day.'

'Where was Mary?'

'She pulled an all-day shift at the Mayflower café. They were struggling for staff, so she pitched in. We were both home by half-past five when Graham rang from Forest Coalpit.'

'How did he seem?'

'Over excited. He said they'd been playing football all afternoon. And that Uncle Jimmy had brought a load of chocolate for the others who had won the competition.' Watkins paused for a moment. 'It was only later when Graham told me they'd also brought a lot of alcohol.'

'Go on, George, you're really doing well.'

'The next morning they arrived back at the school. There were crowds cheering Savile as he stepped down from the bus. He didn't spend the night with the boys. Bob Benson and several other men stayed with them. I remember the boys stepping down from the bus. Not one of them was smiling. Then I saw Benny Nelson put his arm around Graham and whisper something in his ear. When we got Graham home, we were both so excited to hear about the time he spent with Savile. I mean, at the time, the man was a national treasure. The things we know about him now were decades away from being revealed. We asked what he got up to.'

'What did he say?'

'Graham said they'd been playing football all day long, and that was about it. He didn't seem as excited as he was the day before. Me and Mary thought he was tired, and all that running around had knackered him out.'

Fagan recalled a memory. 'We all wanted to know what it was like at Forest Coalpit. He seemed withdrawn, wouldn't talk to us about it.'

Walker sniffed, wiping a tear away.

'George, if you want to stop, we can.'

'No.' Walker said defiantly. 'I need to say my bit. I need to make peace with myself.'

Fagan nodded.

'The nightmares started almost straight away. Graham would wake up screaming for his mum, or me. We would try to calm him down as best we could. He wouldn't go to sleep unless the light was on. Eventually we took him to see a doctor.'

'What did they say?'

'The boy was going through puberty. It was natural for boys his age to experience nightmares. Bloody some doctor he was.' Walker mocked. 'As time went on it got so bad me and Mary took turns sleeping in his room. I had an old army camp bed my old man used during the first world war. Used to sleep on that.' George swallowed hard. 'Graham seemed to become more withdrawn, retreating into himself. We took him back to the doctor, and he said that Graham was having a nervous breakdown and that he should be admitted to Maindiff Court.'

'Was he?'

'No, there was no way I was putting him in there. You hear the stories about that place. Electroshock treatment and other forms of barbaric therapy. Mary had to give up her job to take care of him. We took him out of school, which landed us in a lot of trouble with social services. Social workers came around and threatened to take Graham away if we didn't send him back to school. Then in mid September, I went up to his room. Mary had called him to dinner, but he didn't respond. 'I knocked on the door, but still couldn't get an answer. But I could hear the lad sobbing, so I opened the door.'

'George, look at me.' Fagan said. 'We can stop if you want.'

'No.' Walker rumbled.

'Ok, take your time George.'

'When I opened the door, Graham was sitting on the bed. In one hand he was holding a razor blade. I rushed forward and slapped it out of his hand. I remember shouting at him as he sat there sobbing his eyes out. Calling him stupid.' Tears welled up in Walker's eyes. 'Mary came running up the stairs. She had to calm me down. I was fuming with the boy.' Walker broke down and began to cry. 'I shouldn't have called him stupid. What kind of father was I?'

Fagan got up and knelt down by Walker and put a comforting hand on his arm. 'You were the best father ever George. That's what kind of father you were. Graham worshipped you. He used to tell us boys he was going to be a police officer, like his dad when he grew up.'

Walker managed a smile. 'After we all calmed down, we all sat on Graham's bed. I asked him what happened that night at Forest Coalpit. That's when he told us everything.'

'What did he say?'

'Up until the time he rang us that afternoon it was all fun and games, you know. Football, a bit of rugby and general running around. But then Graham said that it all changed throughout the evening. Savile said his goodbyes and went back to the Agincourt Hotel with the journalist from the Tribune and the photographer. He promised he would return the next morning to take them back to Abergavenny. That's when the evening took on a very dark turn. Bob Benson started to hand around the alcohol.

Graham said that he refused time and time again. But Benson promised him that if he had alcohol, then he would make sure Savile would introduce him to his sporting hero David Wilkie, and that they could go swimming together.' Walker took a deep breath. 'Naturally, Graham accepted the alcohol.'

Fagan felt emotion building up from within.

'As the night wore on, things took on a darker tone. Graham said the abuse began when the men started to pull down the boys' trousers and underpants. They were too drunk to put up any kind of fight. But Graham put up a fight. He told me he gave one of the men, Bernard Baxter a good punch in the jaw. That's when Sergeant Bob and another man held Graham down. Graham looked at me sobbing his eyes out. He said, dad, they raped me.' Walker broke down. 'They raped my boy, and I wasn't there to save him.'

Fagan clutched Walker's arm, wiping away tears that streamed down his face. 'I am so sorry George.'

'I couldn't save him, for Christ's sake.' Walker continued to sob uncontrollably. 'I couldn't save my boy from those bastards.'

Fagan spotted a box of tissues on a coffee table. 'Here you go George.'

Walker wiped his eyes. 'I'm sure, as you know, as a copper, you have to deal with all kinds of situations. Until that moment I had never heard the word rape come out of a bloke's mouth. It was something that was never spoken out aloud back then. Yeah, sure, I heard it time and time again from a woman.'

'George, I know this is hard for you. But did Graham say if Benny Nelson was there that night?'

Walker nodded, blowing hard into the tissue. 'Oh yeah, Nelson was there. Graham said he was the worst of the lot of them. Like some kind of depraved, sadistic monster as Benson and the other men cheered him on. When Graham had finished telling us what happened that weekend, I blew a fuse.'

'What did you do?'

'I went straight to the station and confronted Benson. Of course he denied everything. Said that Graham had been a disruptive influence that weekend. I told him exactly what Graham had told me and Mary. Arrogant prick, laughed it off.'

'I take it you didn't just stand there.'

'I gave him a good punch in the face.' Walker replied.

Fagan couldn't help smiling, picturing the scene in his mind. 'Benson couldn't stand me.'

Walker looked at him. 'It's because of me he hated you. Because I was fond of you, because you were best mates with Graham. I was put on a six-week suspension for striking a senior officer, no pay. But it was only the start of our nightmares.' 'Walker composed himself. 'The 30th November 1980 was the worst day of our lives. The day Graham turned sixteen. One of the ladies from the Mayflower café baked him a big birthday cake. We were trying to get his mind off his troubles. We climbed the stairs singing happy birthday as loudly as we could, candles blazing, the works. We scrimped together for the latest Leeds United shirt. When we opened the door to his room, we saw he was still in bed. Wake up, my little prince, Mary called out.' Walker shook his head. 'He wasn't moving. So I sat on the bed looking at him. He looked so peaceful. I gently shook his arm. Mary just stood there, staring at our son. Her hands trembled so much she dropped the cake. Had to stamp out the candles before they set fire to the house. It was only when we peeled back his bed covers did we see the bottle of sleeping pills, empty.' Walker buried his head in the tissue and sobbed again.

Fagan looked on, feeling utterly helpless as George cried.

'In the months following Graham's death, it was terrible. Mary was in and out of the hospital with stress. Fucking doctors said she belonged in Pen-Y-Fal. I tried my best to look after her. Her sisters rallied around as well. I carried on with the job.'

'What about Benson?'

'The twat hardly spoke to me after Graham died. He was also going places, on his way up.' Walker paused. 'Funny thing, I always knew Benson was a rotten apple as we called them back then.'

'What do you mean?'

'He was a bent copper through and through and in more ways than one.' Walker recalled. 'Back in the 60s there was a place called the London Hotel. All kinds of unsavoury characters used to hang out there. Criminals from the valleys, Newport and Cardiff would meet to fence stolen goods. Benson was a regular, along with his pal, Ernie Brown. Loads of other people used to go in there from other places. It used to attract a lot of toffs.'

'You just mentioned Ernie Brown. The former Mayor of Abergavenny.' Fagan said.

Walker nodded. 'Crooked bastard if ever there was ever one. Now Lord Ernest Brown. Bloody makes me sick to my stomach. He used to fence stolen cars through that dealership he owned, Mr Browns Cars. Lags would steal cars from all over and bring them to him to sell on. I tried on more than a few times to bring him in, but Benson was his protector.'

'You said that Benson was bent in more ways than one. What did you mean by that?'

'I received a complaint from a young cleaning lady in

1968. She worked at the London Hotel, which was at the top of Lower Monk Street. She said that while cleaning the rooms at the London, she'd entered a room thinking it was empty. There was Bob Benson with two other men stark naked. She described one of the men as being very young.'

'Did she say who the other men were?'

'She identified Benson and Ernie Brown. She didn't recognise the other man, but it didn't stop me from guessing. Back in the day the London had a reputation for being a hangout for poofters and queers, that's what we'd call them.'

Fagan nodded.

'My guess it was a male prostitute.'

'Rent boys in Abergavenny?' Fagan said with scepticism.

'You'll be surprised what this town was like in the sixties. Abergavenny was a real boom town back then. I remember when the Beatles played at the town hall in 1963.' Walker looked at the picture on the phone. 'Jimmy Savile eh, who knew? Back in the day, he was massive. Friends with royalty and prime ministers, and totally untouchable. I couldn't believe the day when I saw Bob Benson on TV bumped up to Chief Constable of South Wales police. I remember when he went on the news to say that he had helped crack a gang of paedophiles operating in Swansea grooming young girls. It was the end of Mary when she saw him. Seven months later, she was gone. I've lingered on ever since.' Walker broke down again. 'I've fucking lingered on for almost thirty years carrying the burden.'

'George, look at me.' Fagan coaxed.

Walker lifted his head.

'I swear I will get Nelson for what he did to Graham. I swear on mam and dad's grave I will bring him to justice.'

'I know you will.' Walker patted Fagan on the shoulder.

'The moment I knew you were back in town, I knew. This would be the beginning of the end for that fat bastard.'

Fagan thought back to an earlier conversation. 'I was talking to some of the boys about you. Tyler said you resigned from the force just after I left.'

Walker nodded slowly.

'Why?'

'To save you.'

'I don't understand.'

'The second time you gave that Nelson boy a good hammering, Benson wanted to send you back to prison. I couldn't cope with that. You were living with me and Mary.'

'What made you resign from the force?'

Walker composed himself. 'Have you ever heard of Operation Countrymen?'

Fagan thought about the question. 'Yeah, it was a police operation regarding bent coppers in the seventies and eighties. A lot of London Met officers were put under the spotlight. But nothing really came of it. A few were charged, but it mostly fizzled out.'

Walker nodded. 'It wasn't just the London Met who was under investigation. There was a secret team recruiting officers across the country to collect information on bent coppers. It wasn't very popular. No one likes a grass. That's what Benson said to me once.'

'You were one of those recruited?'

Walker Nodded. 'I had already been collecting information on Benson for years. He hung around with some shady people back in the day. Especially at the London Hotel. I was part of a raid one night. We found these two blokes in bed together. You know they were together.'

Fagan nodded.

'Anyway, there was another officer working with me, collecting information on all the bent coppers on our patch. But turned out, he was bent too. He was feeding information back to Benson. When you beat up that Nelson boy just after you got out of Usk, Benson came to me and gave me a choice. Either I destroy all the information I had on him and drop any further enquiries into his activities. Or, you go down for another stretch in Usk. So I dropped everything. After you left, I couldn't stay in the force. I couldn't work with that bent bastard. But I didn't destroy the information. I kept it hidden. It's all in a shed out back if you want to have a look sometime.'

Fagan stared at the old man, wiping away more tears. 'George, you gave up everything to save me.'

'I had to. It would have killed your mother if you'd been sent down again. There was no alternative. Benson gave me no choice.'

Fagan thought back to the day Benson told him to leave. 'I remember him saying that I could either spend the next ten years in clink, or I could fuck off and never come back.' He took a breath. 'I guess I had no choice either. But why didn't you say anything when you visited us?'

'Because knowing you, Fagan, you would have come back to Abergavenny and gone after Benson.'

Fagan nodded. 'You're right, I would have. I'm surprised I managed to get into the police. After doing a two year stint in Usk prison.'

'When I visited you and encouraged you to join up. I'd already had a word with a senior ranking officer in Merseyside. He was part of Operation Countryman. Detective Chief Inspector Leslie Chapman. He had a lot of connections. We had a long chat and he said he would give you the chance you needed. Chapman silently helped with your application.'

Fagan smiled remembering the old school copper. 'DCI Chappy we used to call him. He took me under his wing when I joined Merseyside CID.' He stopped for a moment. 'I remember the application form dropping through my door. I didn't even send off for one. Next thing I knew I was being signed up, and never looked back.'

'And now you're a detective inspector. I'd love to see the look on Benson's face if he could see you now.'

Fagan smiled. 'You should have seen the look on Nelson's face when I walked into that interview room.'

Fagan and Walker sat in silence.

'There's something I need to tell you Marc. When you hear what I have to say I don't want you doing anything rash.'

Fagan nodded. 'Ok.'

'The day after the events at Forest Coalpit. When they were getting off the bus, Nelson threatened Graham.'

'What did he say?'

'He told Graham, that if he breathed a word of what went on that night he would come after you. And that he would kill you.'

Rage coursed through Fagan.

'Promise me, you won't go after Nelson off your own back. The law will punish him.'

Fagan calmed himself down. 'Listen George, now I know everything. I will make things right. Thank you for helping me all those years ago.'

Walker smiled. 'It was nothing. Now go get that fat bastard and put him away for good.'

Fagan and Walker agreed to meet a week later before they parted company.

C H A P T E R 3 1

DAY 3

Newport Central Police HQ – 8 32am

Fagan placed a latte cup down in front of Watkins.

'Cheers boss, I was about to go out for one.'

'Any fresh developments?'

'CSIs found a discarded pair of blue latex gloves in a rubbish bin near where the victim's body was dumped. One finger on the gloves has a hole. I reckon Pike was wearing the gloves at the time and didn't notice they were torn.'

'Stupid to leave a pair of disposable gloves that would have his DNA all over them.'

'You know how it is boss, heat of the moment thing. Most people who kill don't have a proper plan. That's why they're caught so quickly.'

'I don't get it. When I interviewed Pike, he said he left Rebecca outside Flannel Street chippy. That's the last time he saw her alive. He said he went home. But the CCTV footage Jamie Evans has submitted suggests otherwise. Call up the video he sent us. I want to watch the CCTV.'

Watkins clicked the mouse on his laptop and the video played.

Pike pulled up outside Nelson's house. Less than a minute later, Nelson's wife appeared.

'Pause it and zoom into Nelson's wife.' Fagan instructed.

Watkins slid the mouse across the pad.

Fagan pointed at the screen. 'There, she's holding up more than just a set of keys.'

Watkins squinted at the screen. 'Fuck, the phone case.'

'I bet that's the third set of fingerprints.'

'It's not like we can arrest her when she's on the other side of the world.'

'I take it Pike is in the interview room?'

Watkins glanced at his phone. 'He's been in there for half an hour.'

'I'm sure the duty solicitor will have a whinge at us, but I don't really give a shit.'

Fagan and Watkins sat down and set up the equipment.

Pike looked withdrawn and tired after sleeping on a hard cell bed all night.

'Interview with Justin Pike.' Fagan dictated. 'Present in the room is Mr Pike's duty solicitor Sarah Fraizer, Detective Sergeant Watkins and myself, Detective Inspector Fagan.' Fagan fixed his glare on Pike. 'It would appear Justin, you have a lot of explaining to do.'

Pike sat there in a sulking position, arms crossed and slouching.

'When I spoke to you about Rebecca, you told me you went home immediately after leaving her outside Flannel Street chippy?'

Pike shrugged. 'No comment.'

'CCTV shows you outside Ben Nelson's house the night Rebecca Jenkins was murdered.' Watkins explained. 'What were you doing there at that time of night, when you already said you went home?'

Pike stared into the space in front of him. 'No comment.'

'A set of partial prints were found on Rebecca Jenkins' phone case. These prints have been identified as belonging to you. The CCTV reveals Nelson's wife handing over a set of keys and the case. Could you tell us what these keys unlocked?'

'No comment.' Pike sighed.

Fagan studied him for a moment. 'Why are you protecting him Justin? I thought you hated Benny Nelson.'

Pike shot Fagan a brief glance. 'No comment.'

'What was your relationship with Nelson's wife?' Watkins asked. 'We have CCTV footage of you and others, regularly picking his wife up, disappearing for a few hours then bringing her back.'

'No comment.'

'Is this how this interview is going to go Justin? Are you going to sit there and defend Nelson?'

Pike shifted in his chair. 'No comment.'

'Why did Nelson's wife hand over the mobile phone case found at the murder scene? It's as plain as day on the CCTV footage.'

'No comment.'

'Did you have anything to do with Rebecca Jenkins' death the other night?' Fagan questioned.

'No comment.'

'Justin, I can understand you not wanting to implicate yourself any further. But you have to help us out here mate.'

'I ain't your fucking mate Fagan.' Pike seethed. 'I remember in school, the beating you gave me that day.'

Fagan remained calm. He hunched forward interlocking his fingers. 'Help us piece together what happened to Rebecca the other night. You were friends with her for over thirty years. How can you sit there and make out any of it doesn't matter?'

'No comment.'

'Do you want to go down for Rebecca's murder?'

Watkins asked. 'You've lost everything. Your business, your reputation. It's all gone.'

Pike placed his palms flat on the table. 'No comment.'

'Justin, listen to me.' Fagan said. 'Right now, it looks as if you had a hand in Rebecca's murder, along with Nelson. You are looking at a maximum of thirty years in prison. Jesus, they'll be bringing you out in a box. Is that what you want?'

Pike tapped his foot on the floor nervously. 'No comment.'

'A set of blue latex gloves was found at the scene. Our labs are doing a DNA test as we speak. We know your DNA is on record.' Fagan glanced down at his file. 'In 2013, you were charged with assaulting Benny Nelson outside his house. And now here you are aiding the man in Rebecca's murder.'

'I didn't fucking murder Rebecca!' Pike yelled. 'I didn't touch her.'

'Then who did?' Fagan persisted.

'No comment.'

'Justin, help us understand the situation. You maintain you didn't murder Rebecca. If you didn't do it, then who did?'

'Fucking Nelson did. Can't you see that? The evidence is there. The mobile phone case. You found the iron bar and her mobile phone at Nelson's shed, didn't you?'

Fagan and Watkins exchanged glances.

'How do you know what we found at the allotment?' Fagan asked.

'No comment.' Pike answered quickly.

'So you had nothing to do with her murder? Even though the CCTV footage shows you handling the phone case on the night Rebecca was murdered. The same phone case that was found with her body.'

'No fucking comment.' Pike barked.

Fagan leant back in his chair. 'What was your relationship with Nelson's wife?'

Pike shook his head. 'No comment.'

'You have been seen regularly picking her up.'

'I'm not saying anything more.'

'Was Nelson pimping her out to you? Is that what this is all about Justin? You were paying Nelson to have sex with his wife. Along with other men in the area.'

'She's not part of this.'

'Part of what, Justin?' Watkins asked.

'Fucking prick.'

'Who?' Fagan asked.

'Who do you fucking think? Nelson of course.'

'Why is he a prick?'

'Because of the way he treats her.'

Pike's solicitor sat quietly scribbling notes.

'And how does he treat her?'

'He doesn't love her. He uses her. Fucking pervert has been grooming her since she was twelve years old. Visiting Thailand twice a year. Fucking prick needs to be shot.'

'Do you love her, Justin?' Watkins asked.

Pike looked at him for several seconds before nodding. 'She started to trust me.'

'Even though you were paying her husband to have sex with her.'

'It was never like that. I didn't pay her for sex because I saw her as a prostitute.'

'How did your relationship start with Nelson's wife?' Fagan asked.

Pike sat with a defiant expression. 'No comment.'

'Justin, don't punish yourself like this. Tell us about your relationship with Nelson's wife.'

Pike took a few moments to say something. 'It started

about a year ago. She came into the chippy with Nelson. Gave me this smile. After she had left, Rebecca warned me not to go anywhere near her. But Nelson messaged me on WhatsApp. He sent me naked pictures of her.'

'You were in contact with Nelson through social media?' Watkins stated.

'No, but I kept an eye on him. We all did, given his reputation in this town for being a pervert.'

'How did the relationship start with his wife?'

'When she was in the chippy that day Nelson was with her. He saw the way I looked at her. At first he sent me naked pictures. Then a few weeks later, he turned up at my house. Offered me a taster.'

'Taster?'

'A freebie, you know, free sex.'

'What did you do?'

'I fucking refused.' Pike answered. 'Then a few weeks later, she turned up at my door dressed to the nines. Short skirt, makeup, heels, the lot.'

'And?' Watkins said.

Pike looked at him. 'What do you think? I invited her in and we had sex.'

'How often did you have sex with her?' Fagan asked.

'Usually every other week. After a while she opened up to me. Mon said she was unhappy. She didn't want to marry that twat. She knew she was being trafficked to the UK for prostitution. Mon told me everything. How Nelson had spotted her on the dark web. How he went to Thailand to meet her for the first time.' Pike struggled with the next sentence. 'How he raped her for the first time. Or as he likes to put it, broke her in. She was twelve years old for fuck's sake.'

'So, she opened up to you. Which means you must have opened up to her.'

'I told her everything. I told her about Nelson's reputation in this town over the years.'

'How did Rebecca factor in to all this?' Watkins questioned.

'No comment.'

'Justin, why are we back to this shit now? You've openly admitted to having a sexual relationship with Nelson's wife.' Fagan said. 'How did Rebecca play a role in all this?'

'She didn't ok.' Pike paused. 'It was an accident, a stupid accident.'

'An accident you murdered Rebecca?' Watkins remarked.

'I didn't murder her.' Pike stalled.

'Go on Justin. You said you didn't murder Rebecca. If you didn't murder her, who did?'

'Nelson, he murdered her. All the evidence points to him.'

'All the evidence you planted Justin.' Fagan suggested.

'Careful DI Fagan, you are leading my client.' Pike's brief cautioned.

'Okay then Justin. How did all the evidence end up at the murder scene and in the shed at the allotment? At the moment everything points to Nelson as being the prime suspect. But the fingerprints on the phone case suggest you aided in her murder.'

'I didn't murder Rebecca!' Pike shouted. 'I didn't lay a finger on her. It was Nelson., you have all the evidence, why aren't you charging him?'

'Benny Nelson admitted killing Rebecca yesterday.'

A look of shock appeared on Pike's face. 'He did?'

'Yes, he gave a full confession.'

'Then charge him. Why are you interviewing me? I had nothing to do with her murder.'

'Your fingerprints are on the phone case. If you say you

didn't murder Rebecca and Nelson did, then you must have aided in the disposal of her body.'

'I didn't touch her, ok.'

'You've already stated that, Justin. What we want to know is if you helped Nelson dispose of the body.'

'No, it was all him. Benny murdered her. You just said he confessed. All the evidence points to him.'

'Who else are you protecting, Justin?'

'What?'

'Who else are you protecting?' Fagan repeated the question.

'I'm not protecting anyone. If Benny has admitted murdering Rebecca, then why haven't you charged him?'

'Because I don't think he murdered Rebecca.' Fagan answered. 'I think someone is out to frame him and make it look like he murdered her.'

'Why are you sticking up for that fucking twat?' Pike screamed. 'Do you have any idea what he's done?'

'I'm not sticking up for him, Justin. All I want is to find out who murdered Rebecca.'

'You told me that Nelson confessed.'

'And he did, but as I have just stated, I don't think he murdered Rebecca. But I suspect that you know who murdered her.'

Pike glared back at Fagan. 'No comment.'

'Why did you assault Benny Nelson several years ago?' Watkins quizzed.

The question seemed to throw Pike off. 'What?'

'Why did you assault Nelson ten years ago?' Watkins glanced down at the notes. 'Your record showed you were charged with GBH and had to pay Nelson two grand in damages. This was in May 2013.'

'Fucking cunt.' Pike seethed.

'Why did you assault him?' Fagan pursued.

'Because he said shitty things about Michelle. He took the piss out of her committing suicide.'

'Michelle, your sister.'

'Yes!' Pike screamed again before breaking down. 'Benny Nelson raped Michelle when she was only thirteen.'

'I think we should leave it there. As you can see, my client is very upset.' Pike's solicitor advised.

Fagan ignored her. 'Is that why she took her own life, Justin, because of what Benny did to her?'

Pike choked back tears, nodding. 'For years, the blokes of this town pegged Michelle as an easy ride. The local bike, just like Diane Marks.' He glared at Fagan. 'What was it you lot used to call her? Pissy Pikey, Michelle the minger, Pike the pisser.'

Fagan was thrust over forty years into the past. Remembering the cruel names he called Pike's sister when they were at school. 'If it's any consolation to you Justin, I'm sorry. I never realised what I was doing back then was hurting her. What happened between her and Nelson?'

Pike fought to regain composure. 'Nelson was always one for buying the underage girls alcohol. Go to Benny if you want a flagon of cider. It will only cost you a blow job. Michelle was on her own, walking home from a friend's house, when Nelson pulled up in his car. Asked her if she wanted a lift. That was Michelle's problem. She was always too trusting. One of the other girls had got her into smoking the year before.'

'What happened Justin?'

'Her friend lived in Llanfoist. Underhill was a long walk. Nelson stopped when she was crossing the Usk bridge. He said he would give her a lift home. Michelle told me years later that Nelson drove her up the Deri lanes to the sub-station carpark and offered her alcohol.'

'So she took it.' Watkins guessed.

Pike nodded. 'Michelle is what they would call vulnerable in today's world. Back then, it was the local bike, an easy ride. Give her a flagon of Old English, she would do anything. That's what Nelson used to say about her. He was the one who started the rumours about Michelle being easy.'

Fagan stared at him for what seemed to be a long time before terminating the interview. He also told Pike that he would be remanded in custody until further notice.

'How come you ended the interview?' Watkins questioned.

'Because he's being used.'

'You know his lawyer will kick up a fuss about him being remanded in custody and Nelson being set free.'

'True, I'll bet she doesn't cost a thousand pound an hour, unlike Nelson's brief. Speaking of which, I want to bring him in for questioning.'

'Why?'

'Because of the number of allegations made against him over the years. I want to see if I can rattle that lawyer of his.'

CHAPTER 32

Nevill Hall Hospital—October 1983

'Jesus.' Fagan winced as the nurse gently tried to clean up his bloodied face.

'Well, there's no doubt about it. You'll need to have your nose reset. Looks like you'll be here for a good few hours.' She continued to clean the wounds on his face carefully. 'Was she worth it?'

Fagan pondered the question. In his mind's eye he could see himself spending a large chunk of his life in a prison. The final scene of the fight with Davis played in his mind. Like a TV playing a slow motion rerun of an event. A police officer rushed to Davis to administer mouth to mouth resuscitation.

Jackie jumped to her feet and charged at Fagan, screaming at him. Another officer stopped her before she could get to him.

A police officer grabbed Fagan's arm, and dragged him towards the police van.

Fagan lashed out, punching the constable squarely on the nose. The officer fell backwards.

Four more uniforms rushed at Fagan, pinning him to the ground. He was cuffed before being hauled to his feet and thrown into the back of the van.

'No.' Fagan said. 'She wasn't worth killing another boy for.'

'Being melodramatic, aren't you?' The nurse stated.

Fagan glanced at her.

'The young lad you had a fight with isn't dead. Not yet anyway. But they have had to revive him twice.'

'Christ, I thought I had killed him.' Fagan winced again as the nurse applied more pressure.

'He is unconscious and stable. You want to tell me what happened?'

'A stupid fight, that's what happened.'

'Well, love will make you do all kinds of silly things.'

George Walker pulled back the curtain of the cubical.

'I guess I better let this constable take a statement from you.' The nurse smiled before gathering up the bloodied swabs.

Walker sat on the bed next to Fagan. 'Dare I ask what happened at the Farmers?'

'I wish I knew myself, George.'

'Benson wants you sent down for this. He said a spell in Usk might sort you out.'

Fagan felt his stomach tighten at the prospect of serving time in a young offenders' institute. While he was working at the council, he had passed the place many times. Occasionally there would be guards and prisoners tending the ground that surrounded the prison.

'I'm not sure if I can help you, Marc. Benson wants your guts for garters. My only advice to you is to keep your head down. Serve your time and then get out of this town.' Walker looked at Fagan's bloodied face. 'This place will be the end of you Marc. There is no future for you in Abergavenny. This is not what your dad would have wanted for you.'

Fagan tried to sniff, but the pain took over.

'What happened?'

'Just a stupid fight, that's all.'

'I heard it was over a girl.'

Fagan recalled the moment Davis punched Rebecca. He

relived the rage that had given him the strength to take on Davis. In the past Fagan hadn't even considered the possibility of being able to beat Davis in a fight. They'd wrestled as kids, but Davis had the superior strength to pin Fagan to the ground. 'Tim came into the Farmers with Rebecca and we started arguing. Tim head butted me and started kicking the shit out of me. Rebecca tried to pull him off me but he punched her.'

'Which was when you flew at him.' Walker added.

'Before I knew it, we were outside the Farmers and Tim was on the floor. Jackie screamed I had killed him.'

'Well, you came damn close, I'll say that. You gave his head a good bashing.'

'I know.' Fagan swallowed blood. 'I'm sorry George, I didn't mean for it to kick off the way it did.'

Walker patted Fagan on the knee.

'How's Mary?'

'She's fine.'

'Marc.' A voice called out.

Fagan looked at Rebecca. Her eyes were swollen and her nose had been taped up.

Walker glanced at her before standing. 'I'll leave you two alone to talk.'

Rebecca stared at Fagan's injuries. 'Jesus, are you ok?'

'Not really. I had my face smashed in.'

'I'm sorry Marc. I never meant for any of this to happen.'

'I take it you told him about us. Is that why he came looking for me?'

Rebecca nodded.

'What did you tell him exactly for him to act like that?'

'He was drunk and all over me. I was pissed off with him because he was seeing another girl behind my back, Alison Gordon. I mentioned that you wouldn't treat me the way he does. That's when he started shouting at me.' Rebecca began to tear up. 'He asked me if I have ever gone out with you. He was hurting me, so I had to say yes, and that we had slept together.'

'That's why he came looking for me.'

'Yes. He went looking all over for you. He dragged me into the Vine Tree. One of the boys said he had seen you playing pool in the Farmers.' Rebecca began to cry. 'I tried to stop him Marc, honestly. But I couldn't. I am so sorry.'

'I know.' Fagan said quietly.

'You must hate me now after what has happened. I don't blame you if you don't want to go anywhere near me again.'

Fagan looked at her. 'No, I don't hate you Rebecca. But I suggest we steer clear of each other for now.'

Rebecca massaged her forehead, continuing to cry. 'Ok.'

Fagan looked towards the treatment area entrance. The shouting grew louder until Rebecca's dad burst through the door.

A police officer was trying to coax him back into the waiting room.

Rebecca's dad saw his daughter's bandaged nose before fixing a glare on Fagan. 'I thought you would be at the centre of all this, you shitty little twat.'

'Mr Jenkins, please, let's go back into the waiting room. I don't want to arrest you for disturbing the peace.' The constable asked sternly.

'You're a useless piece of shit. You know that don't you boy. You're no better than that lazy twat of a father of yours.'

Adrenalin coursed through Fagan. He glared back at Rebecca's dad, lifting himself off the examination bed. 'What did you fucking say about my dad?'

'You heard, you little twat.'

The constable stepped between the both of them, glancing at Fagan. 'You're due for a spell inside, so I wouldn't get clever.' He then glared at Rebecca's dad. 'I suggest you fuck off back to the waiting room. Unless I'll throw you in the cells for the night.'

'Rebecca, let's go.'

Rebecca looked back at Fagan. 'I'm so sorry Marc.'

'Come on young lady.' The constable coaxed. 'Let's get you home.'

Shortly after they had left, Benson stormed into the treatment room. Fixing a steely glare on Fagan. 'I knew it was only a matter of time before you did something like this, you shitty little runt. You will not get away with what you did tonight Fagan. You broke a police officer's nose when he was trying to get you into the back of the van. Assaulting a police officer is a term inside. Right now, that boy you beat up is lying in a critical condition. I'll make sure you do at least two years in Usk for this. But if he dies, you'll go to proper clink for the next twenty-five years. Think about that, you little shit. Making a right mess of your life aren't we.'

Fagan was in too much pain to say anything.

'I'll let the doctors clean you up, then you're mine, you little bastard.'

CHAPTER 33

9:43am

'Detective Inspector Tanner.' Fagan greeted. 'I take it you've got something interesting to tell me?'

'Bloody hell Fagan, what shitstorm have you stirred up in the land of Taff?'

'I take it you've found something juicy.'

'I did a search on the two names you gave me and stumbled into a right hornet's nest.'

'Give me the dirt then.'

'First of all, your old pal Ben Nelson. Born 6th July 1960. This man has an arrest record as long as your arm. But here's the thing. He's never been convicted of anything serious. He's been charged with lots of minor stuff.'

'Tell me about the serious stuff.'

'Amongst other things, twelve counts of indecent exposure.'

'But not one conviction?'

'No, and I've been reading some of the cases. Many of the women who accused Nelson of something have always been shown as leading him on.'

'How is that possible?'

'It's not supposed to be. Nelson has also been accused seven times of rape over a period of thirty-five years. But again, all the cases were thrown out because of lack of evidence. He's also got twenty-three cases involving sexual assault, the youngest being a three year old girl. It happened about twenty-five years ago in Cardiff swimming pool. Despite CCTV footage, there was evidence the jury tried to force a guilty verdict. The case was thrown out. The mother of the victim tried to get a retrial, but it never happened. This Nelson sounds like a piece of shit. He's been arrested over one hundred times during his lifetime. He's got fines for shoplifting, speeding and being drunk and disorderly along with other bits and bobs. But anything to do with dangerous sexual behaviour he's got away with.'

'What's your theory?'

'Who says I have one?'

'Because you always do. Which is why I called you.'

'Ok, so Nelson has a string of minor offences which he has always been tried for. And a string of serious offences that he's always got away with. For all his minor offences which have been fines or court appearances for various trivial things he's always used a duty solicitor. For all the serious allegations regarding sexual misconduct, he's been represented by Wilson Fletcher Crawford.'

'The brief who was with him yesterday.'

'This guy is super old, and is still representing people today. He's known as the Fixer and he specialises in two types of cases. Murder and serious sexual offences. He's represented a lot of people over the years. Footballers, politicians, music stars, TV personalities, MPs, you name it.'

A notion entered Fagan's mind. 'Has he ever represented an MP called Arthur Thorpe?'

There was a moment of silence before the answer came back. 'Yeah, in 1993. Thorpe was caught on Clapham Common with a rent boy. Crawford defended him in court and he was cleared. The court convicted the rent boy of sexual assault against Thorpe. Crawford stated that Thorpe happened to be walking through the common at eleven o'clock at night.'

'Yeah, because that's what all MPs do at that time of

night.' Fagan joked. 'Has Crawford ever defended anyone in the House of Lords?'

Another few more moments of silence followed. 'Yeah, a few.'

'Lord Ernest Brown wouldn't be amongst those few, would he?'

'Yeah, but nothing juicy like the MP. In 1990, someone called David Podmore tried to sue Brown for damages regarding a car dealership they had joint ownership in. When they sold the business, Podmore never saw a penny.' Tanner paused again. 'Mr Browns cars in Abergavenny. I found one little thing about Crawford that you might find interesting. He was arrested in 1968 at a place called the London Hotel, in Abergavenny.'

Fagan's ears pricked. 'Go on, I'm listening.'

'He was arrested with twenty-three other men regarding alleged rent boys being hired out.'

'Alleged rent boys?'

'Yeah, the case never made it to trial. An official investigation was launched in 1967 into illicit activities at The London Hotel by the Chief Constable of South Wales police. The only reason Crawford is mentioned is because one of the arresting officers took all their names. But they were withheld from the press and public. Probably to prevent embarrassment to the government of the day. At least four of the men arrested were MPs.'

'Who was the arresting officer?'

'Someone called George Walker.'

'Does it say anything about who launched the investigation into the London Hotel?'

The line went silent for a moment. 'Chief Constable Arthur Portman, hmm, that's odd.'

'What?'

'The investigation was shelved.'

'Does it give a reason?'

'No, but whoever made these notes wrote the Chief Constable's name, then in brackets wrote deceased with a question mark.'

'As in deceased with a mystery.'

'Looks that way. I'm guessing the investigation was one of those brush under the carpet deals which happened loads of times back then.'

Fagan scribbled the name on a piece of paper.

'Exactly what have you been up to down there Fagan? It's only been a few weeks since you left Merseyside.'

'We've arrested Nelson on suspicion of murder. He confessed to everything. But I know for a fact he didn't do it.'

'Who's the victim?'

'An ex-girlfriend from nearly years ago.'

'Jesus Fagan, it's a wonder they haven't taken you off the case.'

'I haven't had any contact with this woman in all that time.'

'Do you know who committed the murder?'

'I've a good idea, yeah.'

'But you're more interested in Nelson. Which means you've got a personal connection to this whole affair.'

'You could say that.' Fagan responded, recalling his meeting with George the night before.

'Still think moving back home was a good idea?'

'Not really. What's the earliest file you have on Nelson?'

'Let me see. It's before the computer age. They're more or less scribbles. His first alleged sex offense was in 1974. The mother of a seven-year-old girl put a complaint into local police. Nelson apparently groped her in an open air swimming pool. The complaint was made to a Bob Benson. Oh Wow, who later became Chief Constable of south

Wales police. Benson convinced the judge that the mother had a grudge against Nelson.'

'What was after 1974?'

'He's got a string of minor shoplifting offences. He was caught several times in a store called Richards and Woolworths. Hmm, here's something worth noting. Nelson was apparently a person of interest regarding a missing schoolboy, fourteen-year-old Danny Llewellyn.'

'I remember him going missing.'

'Danny Llewellyn was reported missing on 23rd May 1980. His friend Kevin Green was found the next morning half naked on the banks of the river Usk. He had severe neck injuries.'

'Because some twat tried to strangle the poor lad.'

'Green survived the incident, but Llewellyn was never found. Police questioned quite a few people back then, including Nelson.'

Fagan Googled Danny Llewellyn. A website called Abergavenny.history.org was top of the search result. Fagan clicked on the link. 'According to this, the search for Danny Llewellyn was the largest that South Wales police had ever carried out. It involved over five hundred officers, but no trace of the boy was ever found.'

'Sounds like you're opening a hell of a can of worms at your end Fagan.'

'It certainly looks like that. But you know me when I've got a feeling. I'm like a dog with a bone. What do you make of Nelson's solicitor?'

'From what I can see here, Crawford sounds like a get out of jail free lawyer for nonces. He's defended hundreds of cases throughout his career. Mostly sexual harassment, rape or assault.'

'If you ask me, he sounds like one of those black bag lawyers. Operating in shady circles.'

'There were plenty of those types about in the day. Still quite a few kicking around..'

'Could be a nonce himself if he's defending them.'

'He could be, but try proving it. You can guarantee the guy will know ten more nonce lawyers to represent him in court. There are still a lot of cockroaches left in the woodwork from Crawford's generation. Who will only crawl out when one of their own is in trouble.'

'Nelson definitely fits that profile.'

'The fact he seems to have a history with your home town definitely suggests something dodgy about him.'

'It does indeed.'

'I'd watch your back with this one Fagan. Looks like he could cause you a lot of grief. If you already know who the murderer is, then he might be clever enough to figure that out. And he will fuck you harder than a rent boy. Do you want me to come down to Taff and offer support regarding your murder victim?'

'No mate, it's all in hand.'

'I'll e-mail you everything I have so you can sort through it.'

'Cheers Tanner, I owe you one.' Fagan hung up and scrolled through a list of numbers until he came to Nigel Thomas.

'Detective Inspector Fagan. I never expected to hear from you so soon.'

Fagan skipped the greetings. 'Nigel, what do you know about a place called the London Hotel?'

Thomas chuckled. 'I could write an entire book about that place.'

'Just the basics please?'

'What do you want to know exactly?'

'Anything regarding male prostitutes.'

Thomas smiled, tapping away on his keyboard. 'The

London Hotel was located at the top of Lower Monk Street. It's flats now. The old police headquarters used to be opposite. Its history is rich with scandal and skulduggery. Back in the day, it was the Soho of Abergavenny.'

'You're kidding.'

'No, the London Hotel was a veritable den of iniquity back in the 50s and 60s.'

'I'm looking for something regarding the mass arrest of a number of high-profile people.'

'I can certainly help you with that one.' Thomas said, furiously tapping away. 'In 1967, twenty-four men were arrested after a tipoff. According to the article the hotel was a hub for male and female prostitutes.'

'Who were the men arrested?'

'No one knows which makes the story more interesting. According to an anonymous source who contacted the Tribune the men arrested were a mixture of local officials, MPs, serving police officers and other prominent men from London. Abergavenny was quite the meeting place back in the day. people used to flock to this town from all over, including London.'

'I don't suppose you have any pictures of the London Hotel, do you?'

A moment of silence followed. 'Yeah, there's quite a few dozen.' Thomas paused. 'I'll have a sort through them and e-mail any that might apply to your case.'

'If you can, cheers Nigel. Also, see if there is anything in the Tribune that mentions a Chief Constable Arthur Portman.'

'Quite a shopping list you have for me Fagan. I'll get back to you later.'

CHAPTER 34

Usk young offenders institute – November 1983

'Name?' The head guard barked.

'Marc Fagan.'

The guard glared at Fagan. 'I'm not interested in your first name you cunt. So don't think we're going to be best mates or anything like that. I am here to make sure you serve your time. And serve time you will. You have my fucking word on that. Let's try again, shall we, name?'

'Fagan.'

A guard standing behind punched Fagan hard in the ribs.

Fagan dropped to the floor, groaning, clutching his side.

The head guard smiled at his colleague.

Fagan fought for air as he staggered back to his feet.

'Did you go to school, you stupid twat?' The head guard demanded to know.

Fagan gulped down a lungful of air before nodding.

'What did you call the male teachers?'

'Sir.'

'Then what do you call me?'

Fagan coughed. 'Sir.'

'Right, from the top shall we, name?'

'Fagan, sir.' He answered as quickly as he could.

The other guard circled him. Like a bird of prey looking for its next meal, sizing him up. 'I heard you put some lad in a wheelchair. And that you broke a copper's nose.'

'Is this true Fagan?' The head guard asked.

'Yes sir.'

'Fancy yourself, do you Fagan?' The circling guard questioned. 'Think you're hard as nails, do you?'

'No sir.'

The guard punched him again on the other side of his ribcage.

Fagan dropped again, clutching his opposite side. He glared at the guard.

The guard looked down, grabbing a fist full of hair yanking Fagan to his feet. 'What was that look for Fagan?'

Fagan was too winded to answer.

'Did you hear me cunt? I asked, what was that look for you twat?' The guard punched Fagan in the jaw.

Fagan stumbled backwards, toppling over a chair.

The guard kicked the chair aside and pulled Fagan to his feet.

The head guard glared at him. 'Name?'

'Fagan sir.' He struggled to say.

'Now listen here, you little cunt. Playschool is over. You have no friends here. Do you understand Fagan?'

Fagan nodded. 'Yes sir.'

'You belong to the system. You answer to the system. And you will play by system rules. If you piss me off, you'll wish your father never fucked your mother so she could push out a useless shit like you. Do you understand, cunt?'

Fagan nodded stiffly. His frame was now hurting in several places. He suddenly longed for home. The urge to burst into tears nearly got the better of him, but Fagan stared at the space ahead. 'Yes, sir.'

'Your number is three two, eight seven. When the guards address you, it's number first and name second. So, name?'

'Three two eight seven, Fagan Sir.'

The head guard nodded. 'Good, you grasped that

quickly. Now you listen to me Fagan. You'll have to grasp things quickly here. The boys at this institute can be a little, aggressive. They don't like new boys, especially those who think they're hard as nails. Do you understand what I am saying to you?'

Fagan nodded. 'Yes sir.'

'You see Fagan, you have a choice. Either you behave. Or you bend over and get fucked like a twelve-year-old choirboy after chapel on a Sunday morning.' The head guard scribbled some notes. 'Since I am feeling in a good mood today, I'm putting you in a single cell.'

A wave of relief washed over Fagan. The last thing he wanted was to be shoved into a dormitory with a bunch of hard cases. He needed time to think and prepare for the two year stretch he'd been given.

'I wouldn't get too comfortable Fagan. It's just for a week, then you're in a dorm with the big boys.' The head guard smiled at him. 'I want you to acclimatise yourself before the big boys have fun with you.'

Fagan's heart fell into the pit of his stomach.

'My name is Mr Howell.' He indicated to the guard who had punched him. 'This is Mr Duncan. You will address us as Sir.' Howell looked Fagan up and down. 'Fagan is it? Have you ever read Oliver Twist Fagan?'

'No sir.' Fagan answered abruptly.

'Well, you'll be pleased to know that we have the full works of Dickens in our library. But I will tell you this. If you as so much as piss me off, I'll make Oliver Twist look like Peter fucking Pan when I'm through with you. Now, name?'

'Three two eight seven Fagan, sir.'

'Mr Duncan here will take you to get your shit. Then you can report to the canteen. You can spend the rest of the day scrubbing your cell. I'll inspect it later. If I see as much of a speck of dust, you're on report, understood?'

'Yes, sir.'

Howell looked at Duncan. 'Get this twat out of my sight.'

Half an hour later, Fagan was taken to the main canteen. As he walked through the door, the room plunged into silence. Fagan felt vulnerable.

'Get your food and sit.' Duncan ordered.

Fagan sat down and stared at the metal tray.

'I wouldn't stare at it too long. It's likely to get up and walk away.' The youth sat opposite quipped.

Fagan picked up a half cook potato and shoved it into his mouth.

'Chew, don't spit it out. Otherwise everyone in here will think you're a poofter.' The youth advised.

Fagan chewed on the disgusting tasting potato. He maintained his stare on the tray in front of him, summoning the strength to swallow without gagging.

'There's a good boy.' The youth smiled. 'You'll get used to the food in here.'

Fagan scooped up a fork of what he guessed was mushy peas.

Next to the youth was a much younger looking boy, fourteen or fifteen. The boy stared at the space in front of him. His face telling the story of pain and misery.

Two youths strolled into the canteen. They scanned the room, spotting the young boy sat at the same table as Fagan.

Fagan watched the two youths navigate the maze of tables in the canteen. One was lanky, with black hair. The other youth was much shorter with blonde hair.

They reached the table where the young boy was sitting.

'On your feet little Gobbler. Sandy wants to see you.' The tall youth ordered, staring across at Fagan. 'Oi, cunt.'

He called over.

Fagan maintained his nerve and carried on eating.

The tall youth walked over to him, clearly agitated at being ignored. 'I said, oi, cunt.'

Fagan glared at him.

'What are you fucking staring at?'

'You.' Fagan answered, standing.

The youth sized him up. Besides the height difference, Fagan was definitely the wider built. The youth turned his attention back to the prisoner.

His companion yanked the young boy to his feet. 'Did you hear us Gobbler, you little poofter? Sandy wants his daily special.'

Tears streamed down Gobbler's cheeks as he was frogmarched out of the canteen.

Duncan smiled as he watched them leave.

'Poor bastard.' The youth opposite said, chewing on an under cooked piece of ham. 'Only been here six weeks. Didn't take Sandy long to size him up.'

'What's a daily special?'

The youth looked at Fagan. 'Gobbler will be led to the coal shed and raped by Sandy. And those two who you've met.'

'Jesus.' Fagan shovelled more food into his mouth.

'In here, you're a survivor, a hunter, or prey.' The youth indicated to Duncan, who was patrolling the canteen. 'The inmates are not the only sodomites in here. So, how did you become a guest of her Majesty?'

Fagan gulped down some bitter tasting water. 'Had a stupid fight.' He glanced over at Duncan before looking back at the youth. 'What are you in for?'

'Helping my dear old dad fiddle the books for his haulage company just outside Gloucester. When the taxman found out, my dad decided I was to blame. The judge told me, locking me up with these animals would teach me a valuable lesson in life. The only thing it's taught me is how to avoid shower time.'

'How have you managed that?'

'I'm a number cruncher, a useful pet for the warden. Don't know how he's going to manage without me when I get out.'

'What's your name?'

'Outside I am James Harper. In here I'm Dodger. What do they call you?'

'Three two...' Fagan stopped in midstream.

Dodger smiled. 'It doesn't take long to sink in, does it.'

'Fagan.'

Dodger laughed. 'We're a right pair, aren't we, Dodger and Fagan. Is that Fagan spelt like Dickens' Fagin?'

'No, with an a.'

'Most of the inmates in here haven't even seen a book, let alone know who Charles Dickens is.' He looked at Fagan. 'I'll give you one piece of advice Fagan. Don't be a grass. No matter how bad things get, don't grass anyone up. You have no friends here, not even me. The only reason I'm talking to you is because you're sat there. The fact you've stood up to one of Sandy's henchman states you could be of use to me one day.'

A siren blared through a loudspeaker.

'Right, you bunch of twats. Lunch at the Savoy is over.' Duncan shouted. 'Line up, put your trays on the stacker and fuck off back to your cells.'

Everyone lumbered to their feet.

'Move, you lazy cunts!' Duncan bellowed. 'Or I'll put every one of you twats on report.' He checked his watch before heading in the same direction as the two boys and Gobbler.

Fagan lay on his bunk, contemplating his circumstances. He replayed the night outside the Farmers in his mind. Davis lying motionless on the pavement. The scene played over in his head several times. Fagan raged at himself for being so stupid.

A door unlocking broke Fagan's concentration.

'Move Gobbler, you fucking little poofter.' Duncan shouted.

Fagan listened as the metal door slammed shut. Its echoes rebounded off the prison walls for what seemed an eternity. Mattress springs squeaked as the young boy fell onto his bunk. For a minute or two, nothing but deathly silence. Then, the sound of a sobbing boy, as he cradled himself to sleep, crying out for his mum.

For a moment in his mind's eye, Fagan found himself doing the same.

CHAPTER 35

Newport central police HQ – 12:18pm

Nelson sank his overweight body in to the interview chair.

Crawford marched into the room within seconds of Nelson sitting down.

Fagan observed Crawford's behaviour as he entered. A man in a rush. Overstayed his welcome to represent an imbecile like Nelson. He plonked his briefcase down on the table and opened it quickly, pulling out a large writing pad before stashing the case under the table. Crawford reached into his inside pocket, plucking out an expensive-looking pen. He clicked the pen with a sense of purpose and scribbled a brief note at the top of the page.

'What are we talking about today? My favourite colour, what I ate for breakfast.'

Fagan looked down at the notes he had printed a few minutes earlier. 'This is quite the arrest record you have Benny. Shoplifting In Woolworths fifteen times.'

'I had a thing for their pick and mix.' Nelson remarked with a smug attitude.

'Plus, you've been arrested for stealing from Richards.' Fagan smiled. 'I remember Richards. They used to sell the most amazing toys upstairs. And Christmas was brilliant. My mam used to take me to see Father Christmas.' He glanced at Nelson. 'Did yours ever do that, Benny?'

Nelson scowled at him. 'You absolute cunt Fagan.'

Crawford glanced at his client before looking back at his

pad.

Fagan glanced down at his file. 'Let me see, several speeding fines, parking tickets. Oh, and urinating in a public space at least six times.'

'Yeah, well, I have a childlike bladder. I'm unable to hold it sometimes. I paid all the fines, so don't think you can pin something trivial on me.' He glanced at Crawford, who scribbled in an agitated manner.

Fagan observed closely, smiling briefly at Nelson. 'Yes, I can see that. But what I'm interested in, is your successful career as a sexual predator.'

Crawford looked up.

Nelson rolled his eyes, smiling. 'Here we go. Dragging up the past again. If you think you're going to get me to answer for crimes I never committed, then you can forget it. The people of this town have always had it in for me. Ever since I was born. They had it in for my dad who died of a heart attack because people labelled him as a weirdo.'

'What about your mother?' Fagan asked, purely to see what kind of reaction Nelson would give.

A look of loss flashed across Nelson's face. 'Why are you talking about my mam? What has she got to do with anything?'

Fagan mused. 'I'm curious. I mean, we all knew your dad when we were kids. But never saw your mum, or sister.'

'They're not here, they're gone.' Nelson sounded like a child who had lost something but never understood why he felt that way.

'Must have been hard for your dad to raise you alone.' Watkins remarked.

'I'll tell you what was hard. Having to endure the people of this town being total twats to me and my dad. He couldn't even get a job locally because no one would employ him.'

'DI Fagan, is this history lesson necessary?' Crawford asked.

Fagan made eye contact with him. 'Then there's your lawyer here. Travels all the way from London to defend you.'

'Exactly where are you going with that line of questioning, Detective Inspector Fagan?'

Fagan glanced down at the file he had in front of him. 'July 1968, you were arrested, along with two dozen other men at a place called the London Hotel.'

Watkins glanced at Fagan, wondering where the conversation was going.

Crawford pursed his lips. 'Let me get this straight, You have dragged me and my client down here to put us both under the spotlight. Give me one good reason why I shouldn't have you reprimanded and suspended without pay.'

'It's just a question. I haven't formally accused you of anything. The London Hotel was classed as being a seedy den of inequity back in its day.'

Crawford searched his memory. 'Yes, I am vaguely familiar with this establishment.'

'Have you always lived in London?'

'Yes.'

'A long way to go for a quick pint.'

'I had relatives in Gilwern. I used to visit them regularly until they passed away in the 70s. Get to the point, DI Fagan?'

'I'm merely stating that someone like yourself doesn't come all that cheap. And let me go on record as saying that for most of your career, you've represented some very high-profile clients. Footballers, celebrities, politicians, along with other high-class individuals. But here you are, defending a lowlife like Benny.'

'I'd watch your mouth if I were you Fagan.' Nelson warned.

'Or what?' Fagan gave Nelson a rigid stare before refocusing on Crawford. 'How is it that such a high-profile lawyer is representing a nobody like you?' He looked back at Nelson, folding his arms.

'I have money?' Nelson boasted.

'What money?' Watkins asked. 'I doubt you've worked a day in your life. And we've been told you squandered all the money your dad left you.'

'The shed your lot raided. It's my primary income.'

'What, selling child pornography?' Fagan remarked.

Nelson smiled back. 'Every picture in that shed is of someone who is of legal age. You won't find anything that suggests what you are accusing me of.'

'And what about your wife?'

'What about her?'

'I saw the layout Benny. You've got a pole in there, camera, internet and everything. Broadcasting all over the world.'

'It's a legitimate business. Everything is legal.'

'Even the consent of your wife?' Watkins added.

'Yes, she loves doing what she does.'

'Including paid for sex, which is illegal.'

'Can you prove it?' Nelson smirked.

'We've interviewed Justin Pike, who has already confessed to paying for sex with your wife.'

'Paid sex, using what a credit card?'

'Cash, I know you're not that stupid Benny.'

'Do you have any idea how long Pikey has held a grudge against me? Ever since I allegedly raped his sister when she was thirteen.'

'A bit specific on age aren't you Benny.' Watkins remarked. 'You must have known she was underage to come up with a specific number like that?'

Nelson ignored the comment. He side glanced at Crawford. 'Another crime I have been accused of, but didn't commit. Part of a long list of crimes I have never committed.' Nelson paused for thought. 'I can hardly walk down the street, because of certain people in this town,. The kids used to chase me around, calling me pervy. Do you have any idea what it's like? To endure ridicule for over fifty years. Constantly having to rely on antidepressants to get me up in the morning. To keep me going. You've no bloody idea what I have had to go through.'

Fagan almost rolled his eyes.

'You don't give a shit about me. All you want to do is dredge up some imaginary past. Hoping that I will crack, eventually. Well guess what. I'm not going to crack, not ever. I'm sick of this kind of bullshit from people like you. People who used to claim to be my friends.'

'I can assure you Benny. I never classed you as a friend. You were always the one who used to hang on to people who didn't want you there.'

'Fuck you Fagan.' Nelson seethed. 'You and your perfect life, with all your mates. Do you have any idea how many times I dreamt of having friends to hang around with? Instead, I had to content myself with hanging around all the outcasts in Abergavenny. Those who were seen as odd or weird. I would have given anything to have the life you and your mates used to enjoy. All in your own little group. Popular with the girls at school. I never stood a chance from the very start!' Nelson was now screaming at Fagan and Watkins. Tears streamed down his face. 'An old man who didn't give a fuck about me.'

'You used to go everywhere with your dad when you were younger.'

'Oh, yeah, that's because he barely let me out of his

sight. I was jumping for joy when the fucker died, couldn't stand the twat.'

'Not very nice, considering he left you that big house on the Mardy.'

'So glad they demolished that place.' Nelson exhibited a bitter tone, as if he was recalling a terrible memory.

Fagan looked back at his file. 'Let's see, fifteen accounts of indecent exposure and not one conviction.' He looked at Crawford. 'You've represented Mr Nelson on all of these accusations and every time you've got him off. You're very skilful at getting people cleared of sexual misconduct.'

Crawford smiled. 'I have been practicing for over sixty years, detective. You get to learn a few things on the way.'

'How do you know Benny?'

Crawford seemed to show frustration. 'None of this applies to the case at hand Detective. Which, in case you've forgotten, is about catching a murderer. All you've done is harass my client and made him relive some very painful memories. Which is why I am ending this interview. Please note that I will submit a full complaint to the police federation regarding your actions towards my client. This interview is now over.' Crawford stood and grabbed his briefcase from under the table.

Nelson heaved himself out of his chair, glaring at Fagan. 'You should have never have come back to Abergavenny Fagan. I'd tuck your tail between your legs and fuck off back under that stone you crawled out of.'

Crawford threw him a disapproving glance. 'Let's go.' He barked.

Fagan watched them leave.

'What do you reckon?'

'They've both got something to hide.'

'His brief is right, boss. We should concentrate on finding Rebecca's murderer.'

Fagan cleared his thoughts, nodding. ‘I’ll speak to her son. I want you to find out if there is any truth to what Nelson is saying about running a reputable adult entertainment business. Hopefully Rebecca’s son will have something useful to tell me.’

Watkins gathered his notes and walked out of the interview room.

Fagan thumbed through his speed dial list. ‘Jacks, do me a favour. Gather everyone together at the Cantreff. Nine o’clock tonight.’

‘Everything okay Fagan?’

‘I need a stiff drink and some old friends to talk to.’ Fagan hung up.

C H A P T E R 3 6

Usk young offenders institute — 18th December 1983

Fagan had been at Usk for nearly a month, adjusting to life in prison. He had experienced a few minor skirmishes with other inmates, but nothing too bad. The head boy, Sandy, as others called him, stayed out of Fagan's way. Dodger explained to him, this was Sandy's usual routine, to size up a new inmate. When an inmate least expected it, Sandy would strike. Fagan had received a visit from his mother the previous day. She'd brought with her some Christmas presents that were confiscated as soon as she had left. Duncan, the prison guard, told him, shitty little gutter snipes didn't deserve a Christmas.

The recreation room was sparsely populated. Dodger sat in the corner reading a copy of Dickens' A Christmas Carol. The room was large and mostly empty except for a table with a net and a couple of worn table tennis bats. A pool table stood in the centre. Chairs and other old furniture lined the walls.

Fagan had beaten one of the prisoners five times in a game of pool. 'Come on, hand them over.' Fagan held out his hand.

The other prisoner scowled at him. 'You're a fucking wanker Fagan.' He said, handing over a packet of Embassy number ones.

Fagan smiled. 'No, I'm better at pool than you are.'

'That's the third pack you've had off me in two weeks.' He grumbled.

'Then learn to play pool better, you twat.'

The double doors to the recreation hall flew open. Gobbler was shoved through. Blake and Ellis, Sandy's henchmen, were close behind.

Dodger looked up from his book briefly before returning to the ghost of Christmas past.

Blake pulled Gobbler to his feet. 'Over there, poofter.' He ordered, shoving the young boy towards a wooden bench. Gobbler stumbled forward onto his face.

Blake and Ellis laughed out loud as they watched him scramble to his feet.

Other prisoners in the room did their best to ignore the commotion.

Fagan watched as the young inmate sat down. Blood streamed from his nose. He stood up to fasten his prison trousers.

Blake and Ellis strolled around the room, looking for their next target.

'Another game.' Fagan offered, holding up the pack of cigarettes.

The inmate glanced over at Blake and Ellis, shaking his head. 'Na, I'm going back to my dorm.'

Ellis zeroed in on the pack of cigarettes Fagan was holding. He marched over with Blake close behind. 'Oi Fagan, you cunt, hand them over.'

Fagan glanced at the pool table. 'Set them up and we'll play the best of three. Winner takes the fags.'

Ellis looked behind at Blake. 'You hear that? This twat thinks he's going to play pool with us.' Ellis stepped up to Fagan, who stepped back out of head butting range. 'You don't understand, do you, cunt? I wasn't asking for a game of pool. I'm fucking telling you to hand over the fags.'

Fagan stared down at Ellis, who was considerably shorter. He slipped the cigarettes into his back pocket.

'They're not for sale.'

Ellis grinned. 'I wasn't going to buy them from you.' He held out his hand. 'Hand over the fags, now twat, or else.'

Fagan knew Ellis and Blake were no match unless Sandy was in tow. He was the one that made them dangerous.

'Or else what, shorty?' Fagan mocked.

Dodger burst out laughing.

Ellis shot him a glare. 'Shut it cunt, warden's lapdog.'

Dodger smiled back and carried on reading.

Ellis glared at Fagan for several seconds. Before turning and marching quickly towards the hall entrance. He glanced over his shoulder. 'It's time you started paying tribute Fagan.'

Fagan imagined Ellis running off to tell Sandy about the awkward cunt who wouldn't hand over the cigs. Fagan looked towards Gobbler, who sat on his own. His head bowed, staring down at the bench. Fagan sat next to him, staring at the anguish and torture clear on the young boy's face. 'What's your real name?'

The young boy looked at Fagan. 'Alan.' He sniffed. 'Alan Clark.'

Fagan put a comforting hand on Clark's shoulder.

Dodger walked over. 'Well, you've thrown down the gauntlet now Fagan. Sandy will come for you. I'd watch your back.' He walked back to where he was sitting and buried his nose in his book.

CHAPTER 37

Llwynu Lane – 4:05pm

Fagan climbed the two flights of stairs to the top of the three-story block of flats. He waited about a minute before going over a brief conversation he had with Rebecca's son earlier that day. Ricky seemed uninterested in talking to Fagan, brushing him off. Telling the DI he was too busy organising his mother's funeral arrangements to talk to some copper. Fagan could hear his girlfriend in the background. Advising him it would be a good idea to talk to the police now, rather than later. Ricky conceded and told Fagan where he lived.

Ricky's girlfriend answered the door, smiling at him. 'Come in, please. Ricky is in the living room. I'm sorry I didn't introduce myself properly yesterday. I'm Stacy Flynn, Ricky's other half.'

Rebecca's son was sitting in a recliner, staring out of a large window that faced the street below.

'I'll make some coffee.' Stacy offered.

'Two sugars please.' Fagan requested.

Ricky looked as if he'd been crying since he had to endure the task of identifying his mother's body.

Fagan sat down on a comfortable recliner sofa. 'Ricky, there's no other way of putting this. I need to ask you a few questions regarding your mother.'

Ricky sniffed, wiping his nose on his sleeve. 'How long had she been in the park like that?'

'We believe her body was dumped sometime after

midnight. It was found several hours later at first light.'

'How was she killed?'

'She was hit over the back of the head with a tyre iron.'

Ricky buried his head in his hands and sobbed.

'We are close to catching the murderer, I promise. We are interviewing everyone.'

'Then why did you let that fucking paedo go?'

'I'm afraid Nelson has an alibi at the time your mother was killed.'

'But people on Abergavenny's Facebook page have been saying police found the murder weapons used.' Ricky composed himself. 'To kill her.'

'Yes, we located the murder weapons. But it's more complicated than that. We believe someone deliberately planted the items in the shed to make it look like Nelson killed your mother.'

'He's been stalking her for years. Constantly sending her shit like flowers and chocolates. Turning up at the front door.'

'Do you know why?'

Ricky shrugged. 'Fucked if I know. I thought he always preferred little girls to adults.'

Stacy entered the living room handing the mug to Fagan.

'Thanks.' Fagan took a sip.

'How close are you to catching Rebecca's killer?'

'We are interviewing two suspects at the moment. One is still in custody.'

'Yeah, Justin Pike. Why is he still in custody and not that fucking perv?' Ricky snorted. 'Justin wouldn't hurt our mam. Jesus, they worked together for years. Why would he do something like that?'

Fagan inhaled. 'Justin was seen outside Nelson's house the night your mam was murdered.'

'What does that prove exactly?'

'Justin was allegedly having some sort of relationship with Nelson's wife.'

'Every fucker knew that. It wasn't exactly a secret. That twat would tout his wife all over town.'

'You knew Justin was paying to have sex with Nelson's wife?'

Ricky nodded. 'There are always rumours coming out of Mumbles Close about Nelson's wife being a prossie. It wasn't exactly the world's greatest secret.'

'Did anyone complain?'

'Not really. It wasn't like Nelson was knocking on everyone's door and offering her up. A mate of mine told me out of towners would turn up at Benny's house. Take her off for a few hours, then bring her back.'

Fagan nodded. 'We have CCTV evidence that would support this.'

'Why haven't you charged Nelson with soliciting his wife for sex?' Stacy asked. 'If you have CCTV of men picking up his wife outside their house, then it's a simple case of doing a PNC check, isn't it? Track down the owners of the vehicles and question them. Then you should have sufficient evidence to charge them. Plus, convict Nelson on several accounts of soliciting his wife for prostitution.'

'Nelson has a very expensive lawyer to represent him. This bloke knows all the tricks of the trade. It's very hard to charge him at the moment. We found a load of illicit material in the shed he keeps up at the allotment. A team is going through it. So far, it looks as if nothing has been found that might get him charged with possessing indecent imagery. Also, Nelson's wife has fled the UK.'

'In the meantime, he's free to roam the streets looking for the next ten-year-old girl to eye up.' Ricky stated.

'I'm sorry, but that's how the way things work. Justin

Pike is still in custody because we're waiting to see if he will give any more information. He hasn't got a fancy lawyer like Nelson to bail him.'

'Fucking twat should have been put away a long time ago. Everyone knows what he fucking well is. He's lucky I didn't kill him during lockdown.'

'Exactly what happened between the two of you?'

'He wouldn't leave mam alone. During lockdown he kept knocking on her door. Claimed he was just making sure she was ok.'

'Why do you think he was so fixated on your mam?'

'Fucked if I know. I always assumed he was into young girls.' Nelson paused. 'And young boys.'

'Where have you heard those rumours?'

'He's older than mam. She used to tell me all about him. How he would wait outside the school for her and her friends to come out. They reckoned he raped so many girls in the back of his car. Aunty Jackie down at the Cantreff talks about him all the time. She said she didn't understand how he stayed out of prison for so long.'

Fagan noticed a photograph and Ricky and Rebecca on a sideboard. 'She looked after herself.'

Ricky looked in the same direction 'Yeah, mam was always trying to find ways of staying young. Many of the women she hung around with at school let themselves go. I saw a picture of aunty Jackie once. She was a looker back in the day.'

Fagan smiled. 'Yeah, but no one would dare go near her because of her brother.'

'You're the one who gave dad his limp, aren't you?'

Fagan recalled the fight at the Farmers all those years ago. It was the one thing that had stayed with him all his life. The image of Davis lying motionless on the floor would haunt his dreams. 'A stupid thing that got out of hand. We were young and very foolish.'

'Weren't you and dad going out with our mam at the same time?'

'Not at first. I was actually going out with your mam's sister.'

'Rich bitch.' Ricky scoffed. 'Mam hated her guts.' He paused. 'What happened between you and my dad?'

'I was in the Farmers one night.' Fagan recalled the scene as if it were yesterday. 'I was with a group of mates. Your aunty Jackie had just walked in with a group of her friends. And then Tim marched in with your mother. He was ranting about me and Rebecca seeing each other behind his back. The next thing I knew, he head-butted me and I was on the floor. Your mam tried to drag him off me, but he hit her.' Fagan could sense his emotions getting the better of him. 'I snapped when I saw your mother on the ground. The next thing I knew, your dad was lying on the pavement outside the Black Lion. I thought I had killed him at the time.'

'Typical dad, he was always knocking mam about.' Ricky mentioned.

'Did they argue a lot?' Fagan asked.

'All the time when I was young. Dad never lived here. He would just hover, you know. He'd usually get violent after he had a drink.'

'Did he ever hit you?'

Ricky nodded. 'A few times when I was young. As soon as I turned into a teenager, I fought back. Gave him a broken nose once.'

'Your relationship was estranged?'

Ricky nodded. 'He wasn't much of a dad. Never being there when I really needed him. Mam always used to struggle with money. Aunty Jackie would help. She always got me the best presents for Christmas. But all dad used to give me was excuses.' Ricky shook his head. 'I remember him getting me a Sega Mega drive one Christmas. A couple of days later, the police knocked on our door and took it away. Apparently, dad had been arrested for handling stolen goods. Broke my heart.'

Fagan changed the subject. 'How long have you two been together?'

Stacy looked at Ricky, smiling. 'About two years now, isn't it babes?'

Ricky nodded.

'How did you meet?'

Stacy smiled. 'I was on patrol in Abergavenny when I saw our Ricky pissing against the town hall.'

Ricky laughed.

'I jumped out of the car and shouted, come on, put your Johnny wobbler away. I bumped into him the next week in Weatherspoon and we got talking.'

Fagan smiled.

'What about you?' She asked. 'You used to live in this town, didn't you? Why did you leave?'

Fagan hesitated before answering. 'First up, I wasn't good for your mam. I didn't want to make her life a mess.' He glanced at Ricky. 'Second, it was because of Nelson. After a spell in Usk prison I came back to Abergavenny. Me and your mam started seeing each other for a brief time. And then one night Nelson rubbed me up the wrong way. I beat the shit out of him and put him in the hospital. I was given a choice: either go down again, or get out of town.'

'You have a history with Nelson?' Stacy asked.

'Yes, we have a history. Many people in this town have a history with him. During the investigation into your mother's murder, I believe I have uncovered evidence that Nelson was part of a paedophile ring that operated during the 1980s. And some time before.'

'Jesus.' Stacy gasped.

'While up at the shed, I came across a photo that was taken in 1980. It was of a charity event that Jimmy Savile attended.'

Stacy looked at Ricky. 'We watched that documentary on Netflix with your mam a while back. She mentioned he had come into town once.'

'At least you got out of this town.' Ricky said. 'I would love to get out.'

Fagan looked at Stacy. 'Why don't you join the police like your girlfriend?'

Ricky laughed. 'I'm not cut out for the police.'

'That's what I thought. But when I moved I decided I didn't want to spend my life in and out of trouble. I sat my exams, joined the police and the rest is history.'

'Mam wanted me to travel. She said I should see the world. Travel to all the exotic places like Casablanca.'

Fagan laughed out loud. 'Your mother loved that film. I lost count the number of times she made me watch it. Whenever she would sneak over to my place, she would bring the video with her.' Fagan looked at Ricky. 'I get it now.'

'What?'

'She named you Rick, after the main character in that film.'

Stacy smiled. 'Don't get him started on his middle name. It's Humphrey.'

'After Bogart.' Fagan guessed.

Ricky nodded, smiling before looking across at Fagan. 'Did you love her?'

Fagan hesitated before nodding. 'Yes, which is why I put your dad in a wheelchair.'

'Why did you leave town?'

'I didn't want her to have a boyfriend that was in and

out of clink. She deserved better than that.'

'She deserved better than dad as well. He's shit on her all her life.'

'It would seem that way. If it means anything, I'm sorry.'

'How long until you sort this out? You know, mam's murder?'

'Nelson confessed to her murder, but I'm convinced he didn't do it.'

'Which means the suspect is still at large.' Stacy remarked.

'Yeah.'

'Have you any other suspects to interview?'

Fagan didn't have the heart to say that eventually he would have to bring Ricky's dad in for questioning. 'At this moment, we're hoping that Justin Pike can provide more information. I think eventually he will reveal something that will lead to the arrest of whoever killed your mother.' Fagan stood. 'I have to go, but I will keep you up to date with any developments.'

'Thank you.' Ricky said.

CHAPTER 38

Usk young offenders institute – 25th December 1983 – 1:03am

Fagan barely had time to open his eyes before Blake and Ellis were on him. His mouth was strapped with tape and his hands were tied before he realised what was going on. The dorms were locked at night by the guards. Fagan assessed Duncan must have left the door open for them to gain access to the dorm. Blake and Ellis hauled him to his feet. As he was being dragged out of the dorm, Fagan noticed the other boys cowering under their prison issue covers.

The coal shed was on the back end of the prison, nestled against the imposing stone wall that surrounded the compound. Fagan knew it was the place Sandy would bring vulnerable prisoners he and others would abuse. The shed was lit by a dim light bulb, a hastily constructed electrical job by an amateur electrician. Fagan hated turning the light on when it had been raining. The coal shed was large and freezing cold.

Fagan fought wildly against his captors as he was hauled across the prison yard like a sacrificial lamb. He knew what was waiting for him in that coal shed. He'd prepared himself for the moment when Sandy would have him alone.

Sandy was leaning against the wall near the entrance, smoking a cigarette.

Blake kicked Fagan's legs from under him.

Fagan hit the ground hard, landing on a sharp piece of coal that dug into his back.

Sandy circled Fagan, looking down at him with a hungry expression on his face. He glanced at the other two, rubbing his hands. 'I reckon we're going to enjoy this lads. I always love a fresh young virgin. Especially on Christmas Day.'

The tape was torn away from Fagan's mouth.

Sandy continued to circle his prey. 'I heard you gave my boys grief last week in the rec hall. Wouldn't give them any tribute.'

Fagan spat on the blackened floor. 'Fuck you. They were trying to steal cigs off me. I gave them a fair chance to win them in a game of pool.'

'No one plays games in here Fagan, unless I allow it. Rules must be followed.' Sandy glared down at his captive. 'And I make those fucking rules. Understand, you worthless cunt. You see Fagan, what many fail to understand. Is the moment they walk through them gates. When that cold hard steel door slams shut, they belong to me. That includes you Fagan.'

Fagan glared back at him.

'Do you know what day it is Fagan? It's Christmas fucking day. And I want a present.' Sandy walked over to a box and pulled out the parcel Fagan's mam had brought him a week earlier. Sandy pulled off a card that was stuck to the side. He slid the card out of the envelope, struggling to read the message his mother had written. 'To Marc, love, mam.' He stared at the word. 'And, George.' He looked down at Fagan. 'Where's your daddy Fagan? Who's George? Is he fucking your mother? Or does she like to suck him off?'

Fagan tried to break free of his bonds, but they were too tight.

Sandy tore the wrapping away from Fagan's present, revealing a thick jumper. 'Look at this Fagan, a nice jumper to keep you warm.' He tossed the jumper on the filthy floor spitting on it. Using his boot to rub the jumper on the blackened wet floor.

Fagan felt the rage he had unleashed on Davis outside the Farmers.

Sandy turned to face him. He walked towards a kneeling Fagan, unzipping his fly and pulling out an erect penis. 'Now then Fagan, here's what you're going to do. You're going to open your mouth and I'm going to stick my cock in it. Then you will suck. And when I cum in your mouth, you will swallow every last drop. Then you will lick my cock clean of any cum that's left. After, you are going to do the same to my two boys here. You are going to suck them off and swallow all their cum. And lick their cocks clean.'

Fagan stared up at him with a defiant look. 'You stick that in my mouth and I shit you not. You'll fucking lose it.'

Sandy laughed out loud. 'You hear that boys? The big man here thinks he's going to bite my dick off.'

Ellis produced a razor blade, waving it in front of Fagan. 'You do that Fagan, and I will slit your throat as you suck him off.' Ellis held the blade against his jugular.

Fagan could feel the edge of the blade against his skin. 'Go ahead, but I should warn you that any sudden pain causes the victim to bite down hard.' He looked up at Sandy with a sinister grin. 'The bite is so intense they have to pry the victim's jaws open with a crowbar.'

Sandy stared down at Fagan with a look of apprehension. 'You're full of shit. Where did you hear that?'

'I spend a lot of time in the prison library reading books. They have a lot of medical books in there.' He glanced at the Christmas card Sandy had thrown onto the floor. 'From the way you read my mam's card, I'd say you can't read.' Fagan looked up at Blake and Ellis. 'Can any of you read?' He locked eyes with Sandy. 'You dull cunts.'

Sandy stepped back and put his penis away, zipping up his fly. He turned his back on Fagan for a few moments before spinning around kicking Fagan viciously in the chest.

Fagan felt his chest implode.

Blake and Ellis let go of Fagan, who dropped to the floor.

For a few minutes all three inmates kicked and punched Fagan until he was semi-conscious. They dragged him back to his dorm, removing the binding tape. The guards found him the next morning, still drifting in and out of consciousness. Fagan spent the rest of Christmas in the prison infirmary recovering from his injuries. Dodger would be allowed to visit. No one owned up to the attack. Despite an interrogation by the prison governor Fagan insisted he had fallen down a staircase. The governor said that Fagan couldn't have sustained such injuries from a simple fall, putting him on report for a month.

CHAPTER 39

The Cantreff - 8:14pm

'He looks a happy chappy.' Evans remarked as Fagan strolled through the door.

Fagan parked himself on a barstool they had set aside for him. Apart from a few locals who were glued to the football on the TV in the lounge, the bar was deserted.

'What's new then Fagan?' Jackie asked, placing a glass of brandy on the bar.

Fagan picked it up, knocking it back in one go.

'Easy tiger.' Tyler advised. 'Another few like that and we'll have to carry you home.'

'I take it you haven't had a good day.' Edwards guessed.

'Bingo.' Fagan replied.

'Come on, what happened? Don't say you released Nelson again.' Jackie said.

'Yep.'

'Shit, what is wrong with the police? Haven't you got anything to hold him on?'

'Not at the moment.'

'What about Justin?'

'Still in custody.'

'Why the fuck is he still in custody?' Evans asked.

'Because he hasn't got a shit hot lawyer like Nelson. Who can bail him in a heartbeat.'

'So we're stuck at square one then.' Tyler said.

'Not necessarily. I reckon a spell in the clink will sober Pike up. Since his fingerprints were also found on that phone case, we'll have to keep him in. We'll interview him again tomorrow. With any luck he'll come to his senses and reveal who the murderer is.'

'You mean he'll tell you that Tim did it.'

Fagan nodded.

'You know you're risking your job by not arresting Tim. I mean, I'm no police expert, but when you have a murder enquiry, you have to round up everyone who knows the victim. That includes husbands and boyfriends. Tim should have been on the top of your list.' Edwards pointed out.

'I guess I have been preoccupied with Benny.' Fagan sighed.

'I know why?' Jackie said. 'That twat is the reason you left Abergavenny.'

Fagan looked at her and nodded.

The others looked at him.

'You never told us that.' Evans pointed out.

'Because I didn't want you going round to Benny's and giving him a good kicking.' He looked at Jackie. 'I never told you that either.'

'Who do you think told me?'

'Rebecca.'

Jackie nodded. 'She told me everything that happened at the train station that day.'

'What happened?' Tyler asked. 'How was that slimy twat able to run you out of town?'

'It wasn't just him. It was Sergeant Bob. After I gave Benny another good hiding I was given a choice. It was either get out of Abergavenny. Or end up in Usk prison for another five years. I didn't want that.'

'So you left.' Evans said.

'I beat the shit out of Benny because he took the piss out of me for being inside.' Fagan recalled that day. 'Then he said something shitty about Graham committing suicide.' Fagan stared at his empty brandy glass. 'I snapped there and then.'

Everyone stared at Fagan

'When I came back home I hoped things would be different in this town. I thought people would have moved on and got on with their lives. I'm not saying none of you have. You've all done really well for yourselves.' He paused. 'But there are things that are still the same. When I saw Rebecca's body in the park the other day, it resurrected a lot of old ghosts. Graham's suicide, me having that massive fight with Tim. Spending time in Usk prison. I suddenly remembered how much I hated this town because of what Nelson did. And when I faced him in that interview room for the first time in nearly forty years it all came flooding back. I wanted to beat the shit out of him there and then. Do you remember what it was like growing up in this town? It was one big adventure for us.'

'We were like the *Goonies*.' Evans remarked. 'Albeit an earlier version. Or like the kids from *Stranger Things*. But without the Demogorgon or the secret lab run by a nazi scientist.'

'I always thought we were like the kids from *Stand By Me*.' Tyler said.

Fagan nodded. 'We *were* like the *Goonies*. Always off on some crazy adventure on our bikes.' Fagan reflected on the past. 'Then Graham committed suicide and everything changed. We had never experienced tragedy until then.'

'There was a time above, a time before. There were perfect things, diamond absolutes.' Evans recited.

Everyone looked at him.

Evans grinned. 'Sorry, I was quoting the opening line to Batman versus Superman.'

'Really.' Tyler clipped him across the back of the head.

'No, think about it. They were glorious times for us.

There was nothing we couldn't do.'

'But they weren't happy times for everybody, were they? There were kids that didn't have the families that we had. I hate to say it, but this included Benny.' Fagan pointed out. 'Do you remember Katy and Andrew Finch?'

Jackie nodded slowly. 'I remember. They were taken out of school. A mate of mine who lived next door to them said they'd been taken away from their mam and dad, because the dad had been interfering with them.'

Fagan continued. 'The things we know now were taboo back then. Whispers in darkened rooms and the corner of the classroom. Now everything is out in the open. We know more about the past. The likes of Savile being paedophiles. Over the past couple of days, we've peeled back the dark history of this town. Back then, rumours about Benny were just rumours. We all knew what he was like. But most of us took it with a pinch of salt.' Fagan recalled the conversation he had with Walker. 'I went to see George last night. He told me everything. Why Graham took his own life.'

'Oh fuck.' Evans cursed.

'The boys who went on that trip were all raped by Sergeant Bob, Nelson and the others.'

Jackie poured another brandy into Fagan's glass. 'It's on the house.'

'Then we got the bastard.' Tyler said.

'We haven't, because all the boys that went to Forest Coalpit Dorms are now dead.' Fagan knocked back the second glass of brandy.

'Not everyone.' Evans recalled. 'Remember when we were talking the day before yesterday? Andrew Rogers left town not long after you. It's only a case of tracking him down.'

'If he can testify to what happened that night, then Benny will go away.' Edwards said.

'But it will still take time to track Rogers down.' Fagan delved into his pocket to retrieve his ringing phone. 'Evening Nigel.'

'Not disturbing you, am I?'

'No mate, listen, I am putting you on loudspeaker. All the old gang are here.'

'Hi Nigel.' Everyone called out.

'What have you got?'

'I researched information regarding the London Hotel.'

'My nan used to talk about that place.' Jackie interrupted.

Fagan put his finger to his lips. 'What have you found out?'

'It was a real hotspot back in the day. The main police station for Abergavenny used to be opposite. The pub history goes back quite a while. But in the sixties, it was always making the local headlines. The Tribune reported several accounts about the pub being a den of iniquity and vice. The police raided it quite a few times. They reported the pub was a go to place for homosexuality. The biggest raid on the place was the one I mentioned earlier, in 1968. At least two dozen men were arrested, along with several young boys. MPs, local council officials, a journalist that worked for the Mirror and several serving police officers.'

'But there are no names.'

'No, sorry.'

'Another thing, I came across an interesting article regarding the London. It just so happens that the newly appointed Chief Constable was the bloke you mentioned earlier, James Portman.'

'What was the article about?'

'The headline for the article read, local police chief vows to rid town of filth. Portman said he would do everything in his power to make sure The London was shut down. But it didn't shut until the early seventies.'

'Any theories on why?' Fagan asked.

'You're going to love this. An article a few months later reported a serious house fire on Western Road. Two people were killed.'

'Let me guess, one of them was James Portman.'

'And his wife.' Thomas added.

'That explains why the investigation was shelved.'

'The fire brigade at the time said the cause of the fire was a chip pan being left on. I've also had a sieve through pictures of the London Hotel. Lots of group photos stretching all the way back to 1920. However, there is one I emailed you which will interest you and the gang there. It was taken in 1968.'

Fagan called up the picture on the small screen. A black and white group photo, a wide-angle shot of a few dozen men and women, stood outside the hotel.

'Right at the centre.' Thomas instructed.

Fagan and the others focused on the image of a young boy stood next to a teenage girl.

'Oh my god, that's.' Jackie stated.

'A very young Benny Nelson.' Evans finished her sentence.

'Listen, Nigel. I want you to look for everything regarding the missing paperboy Danny Llewellyn.' Fagan instructed.

'Will do.'

'Thanks Nigel.' Fagan hung up. 'Jackie, have you got a tablet? I need a larger screen. I'm emailing you this picture.'

'Yeah, sure, it's upstairs.' Jackie hurried out of the bar.

'Hang on.' Edwards said. 'One minute you're talking about this pub full of queers. The next you've mentioned Danny Llewellyn, care to share.'

'I got hold of Nelson's arrest sheet earlier. Besides a stupid number of allegations regarding sexual conduct made against him. Nelson was also questioned regarding the disappearance of Danny Llewellyn in 1980.'

Jackie returned with a large iPad, looking at the photo Fagan had e-mailed her.

'Look, let's concentrate on one thing.' Fagan advised. 'Let's not go off track. We'll talk about Danny Llewellyn at another time.'

Jackie placed the tablet on the bar.

Fagan pointed at the picture. 'That's Benny in the centre. And there's his dad stood to the left.'

'Who's the young woman he's got his arm around? stood next to Benny.' Edwards asked.

'It has to be Benny's sister we talked about the other night.' Evans offered, looking at Fagan.

'So where's his mother?' Jackie asked.

Fagan shook his head. 'There was never a mother. At least not that I can remember. I went to Benny's house once, the big one up on the Mardy. Really creepy place. Me and Graham used to do the Mardy paper round. We had to collect money from his dad who owed on the papers. I remember the place stinking of fags. Really old place full of old furniture. Like something from the Adams Family.'

'Shit.' Evans cursed for the second time.

'What?'

'I just had a really dark thought.' He pointed at the young woman in the photo. 'How old does she look?'

Fagan studied the picture. 'I'd say, early to mid-twenties.'

'So, no one has ever seen Benny's mother. But here we have his sister in her early to mid-twenties. And we have Benny who's around eight years old if this picture was taken in 1968.'

'What are you suggesting?' Jackie asked, pointing at the picture. 'The girl in the photo could also be Benny's sister and mother.'

Evans nodded. 'Yup.'

'Jesus Christ, it's like having the family from the Texas Chainsaw Massacre living in the same bloody town as you.' Tyler said.

Evans slapped his palm on the bar. 'And Benny is fucking leather head.'

'The only way to be sure is to go to the local registry office.' Jackie suggested.

'I don't believe it, look who we have here.' Fagan said loudly, pointing at a man in the picture.

'What now?' Tyler responded.

'That man there, on the end. It's Nelson's lawyer.'

Everyone stared at the young man in a smart suit.

'Think about it. Fresh out of law school. Wanting to take on the world.' Fagan studied the picture. 'He's in his twenties there, but it's definitely Crawford.' Fagan felt sick to his stomach. 'Jesus, I just realised. I was talking to a colleague in Liverpool earlier on today. We were talking about Nelson's lawyer being a nonce. What if this London Hotel wasn't just a meeting place for gay men?'

'It was also a grooming shop for young children.' Evans speculated.

Fagan nodded.

'Ok, fair enough.' Jackie said, pointing at Nelson as a young boy. 'Benny obviously didn't deserve to be abused as a child. But as an adult, I don't feel sorry for him.'

'In my years as a police officer I have come across adults who were abused from an early age. Many of them became abusers themselves. This is the case with Benny. When you're used to something from childhood, it becomes second nature.'

'All this dark history has come from Rebecca's murder.' Edwards said.

'Perhaps it's fate.' Fagan suggested.

'Didn't think you were the philosophical type.' Evans remarked.

Fagan looked at Edwards. 'You're right, I could have gone and questioned Tim straight away. He would have confessed and been behind bars by now. But within hours of Rebecca being discovered, Nelson had been arrested because of an orgy of evidence planted at the scene of the crime. Justin Pike hated Nelson because of what he did to Michelle, his sister, who committed suicide. So he makes it look as if Nelson murdered Rebecca to get back at him. And on top of all that, because we've been looking into Nelson's background, its churned up all this mystery surrounding why he's always got away with stuff. The expensive lawyer, his involvement with the incident at Forest Coalpit Dorms. The possibility he could have been involved with the disappearance of Danny Llewellyn in 1980.' Fagan pointed at the photo. 'Plus, you have this London Hotel, which was basically the porn hub of Abergavenny back in the day. You have a police chief who wanted to shut this place down. He obviously knew enough for someone to murder him.'

'But where does Tim fit into all this?' Tyler asked.

'That's what I need to find out. I need to interview Justin again early in the morning. Has anyone seen Tim since Rebecca was murdered?'

'He drove by me today.' Edwards revealed. 'He saw me but didn't wave like he usually does.'

'If he murdered Rebecca, then why hasn't he skipped town?' Jackie questioned.

'Where's he going to go?' Fagan asked. 'He's an only child and both his parents are dead. The only connection to this town is his son. When I spoke to Ricky today, it doesn't sound as if they have a loving father son relationship.' Fagan paused. 'He's waiting for me to confront him, I'm sure of it.'

Fagan's phone buzzed.

'Boss, we have a situation at Mumbles close with Nelson.' Watkins revealed. 'He's been rushed to the Grange. Looks like a suicide attempt.'

'I'll be right there.'

'Jesus Christ, if he dies, then everything we've discovered over the past few days will quietly vanish.' Evans stated.

Fagan stepped away from the bar. 'He better not die, not until I have the chance to fucking kill him myself, for what he did to Graham.'

CHAPTER 40

Mumbles Close – 8:32pm

Evans dropped Fagan outside Nelson's house. He was given instructions not to be nosy by hanging around, and to pull any CCTV from his security cameras that might be relevant.

'What happened?' Fagan sipped strong black coffee from a disposable cup. Better to have coffee breath than smelling of alcohol.

'The call was made about five past nine. The paramedics were here within twenty minutes. Someone phoned an ambulance after Nelson had posted a video online. When paramedics arrived, they found Nelson semi-conscious on a sofa in the living room. I've already been in the house. CSIs found paracetamol. And it looks like he consumed a bottle of Jack Daniels. The video he posted appears to be some sort of video suicide note.'

'Video suicide note?'

'That's what his followers are calling it.' Watkins handed Fagan his mobile phone. 'It's already had over a thousand views. Lots of comments calling the police bastards. He also mentions you in that video.'

Fagan tapped the play icon on the screen.

'This is a message to all my followers and those of you who don't know me. My name is Ben Nelson. I have lived in the town of Abergavenny in Monmouthshire all my life. And all my life I have been the target of systematic bullying by the town's residents. The people of this town see me as the oddball.'

Tears seeped from Nelson's eyes.

'I have been called weirdo, mong, spastic, Quasimodo, thicko, moron, perv, paedo and other hurtful things by certain people in this town. I have been beaten up more times than I can remember. My house has been targeted by thugs who have smashed windows and vandalised my cars. The things that I have been accused of over the years have been totally made up by those who have held a grudge against me. I'm talking about Justin Pike, who claims I raped his sister, but has no evidence to back up these claims. Neither have I have ever been questioned in connection with her death. Then there is Jamie Evans, who has had a grudge against me for years. He is constantly filming me, going about my everyday business. And finally, there is Marc Fagan, who has attacked me twice. Putting me in the hospital.'

Fagan glared at the screen. 'You piece of shit, Nelson.'

'Marc Fagan is nothing but a thug who served time in Usk Prison for nearly killing someone. To add insult to the mental and physical injury I have suffered over the past five decades. Marc Fagan holds the rank of Detective Inspector of the Monmouthshire constabulary. I believe he is still capable of acts of violence and ask that his superior officers should look into his past actions.'

'Fuck!' Fagan screamed.

A few police officers, together with curious residents, all looked in his direction.

'And now I have been accused of murdering Rebecca Jenkins. I didn't touch this woman. I am completely innocent of this crime and every other crime I have been accused of. However, the people of this town will always hold me accountable, whether I am guilty or not. So the people of Abergavenny leave me no choice. My priority is my wife and her safety. We both decided she should leave this town and return to her native home for protection. From the vile people who have persecuted me. I am absolutely heartbroken, as a few weeks ago we found out that we were expecting our first child. For her safety and the safety of our unborn child. I have sent her back home to her family in Thailand. I want her and our child to be safe.'

Nelson wiped tears away from his eyes.

'I have tried to be tolerant all my life with those who have brought me pain and misery. But clearly the people of this town have not shown me the same courtesy. Therefore, I have made the only choice open to me, which is to take my own life. To those from the online community who have been supportive I thank you. I hope lessons can be learnt from my death. As a final act I have donated five thousand pounds to a charity that supports people who have been abused. Thank you and see you on the other side.

'You complete bastard Nelson.' Fagan sneered at the screen.

Evans was already marching towards Fagan and Watkins, holding up his smartphone. 'Have you seen this?' He thundered.

'Calm down Jamie, you know he's playing us.'

'Well, it appears to be working. Have you seen some of the replies people have been posting?' Evans scrolled through the comments section of the video. 'Evans should be hung over this. That sad twat Evans is going to get his comeuppance. Oh, and here's my favourite. Anyone know where that twat Evans lives, so I can go round there and rape his wife and kids in front of him.'

'Jesus.' Fagan gasped.

'You're in the firing line yourself.' Evans scrolled further on down. 'Fagan will go straight to hell for this. The police should sack him immediately. Probably a nonce copper. All coppers are bent as a butcher's hook.'

Fagan scrolled through the screen on Watkins' phone. 'This isn't Facebook is it, or any other mainstream site?'

'No, it's one of many social media platforms that have sprung up since the major sites started clamping down on hate speech.' Watkins explained.

'According to this, Nelson has five thousand followers.'

'What are we going to do about this?' Evans said in a worried tone. 'The last thing I need is someone targeting me and my family.'

'Oi Evans you fucking cunt, feeling guilty, are we? Now that Benny has committed suicide.' A man on the other side of the street shouted.

'Fuck off Merrik, you sad crackhead.' He pointed at the man. 'See, now I have to deal with the likes of him.'

Fagan stared at the screen, noting the time frame. 'Hang on a minute. This video was recorded at eight o'clock last night. But it was posted at nine o'clock tonight.'

'It's a timed, preloaded video by the looks.' Watkins pointed out. 'Nelson must have recorded it last night for it to be released this evening at nine o'clock.' Fagan glanced at Watkins. 'Didn't you just say the paramedics found him semi-conscious?'

'Yes.'

'And this video was released at nine o'clock this evening?'

'According to the time frame, yes.'

'Nelson couldn't have taken those pills long before he posted that video.'

'Meaning?' Evans said.

Watkins looked at Fagan. 'Meaning he took the pills and

made a gamble. Betting that someone would phone an ambulance not long after the video was posted.'

'No.' Fagan responded. 'It's too much of a risk to take, hoping that someone was going to call an ambulance just because he posted that video. The only way to execute that kind of plan is if you have an accomplice.'

'Who the fuck would help that prick out?' Evans asked.

'I have no bloody clue.' Fagan inhaled.

'Boss.' Watkins said sternly, indicating further on down the road.

Chief Constable Griffiths was climbing out of a Police Land Rover. Crawford stepped out of the back passenger seat.

Fagan glared at the eighty-three-year-old lawyer, who seemed very agile for his age. 'But I have a pretty good idea.' He spun on his heels, grabbing Evans by the arm. 'Do they still have shut-inns at the Cantreff?'

'Yeah.' Evans replied, confused as to why Fagan was dragging him away.

'Good, tell the others to meet me there at midnight. Now, follow my lead. Mr Evans, you cannot be here. This is a matter for the police.' Fagan said loudly, before pushing him away.

Evans immediately got the gist, faking a stumble. 'Hey, you can't silence the people copper. I know my rights.'

Fagan returned to the group.

Griffiths held up his smartphone that was playing the video. 'Care to explain this, DI Fagan?'

'I have seen the video sir, and I have reason to suspect Nelson may have faked a suicide attempt to throw this murder enquiry into chaos.'

'Really Detective Inspector Fagan. Is that the best you can come up with?' Crawford stated with an arrogant tone. 'For two whole days, you have done nothing but harass my client. Causing him great anxiety and depression. You have dredged up the past, weaponizing it. An excuse to antagonise Mr Nelson.'

'Bullshit.'

'That's enough Fagan.' Griffiths shouted.

'Chief Constable Griffiths, it's clear to me DI Fagan is unfit to handle this murder enquiry. May I suggest you assign this case to a more competent officer.'

Griffiths considered the proposal for a few moments before nodding. 'Very well, as from now Detective Inspector Fagan, you are to cease all operations concerning the Rebecca Jenkins murder enquiry. You will hand over all relevant data to your team coordinator, who will assign a new detective.'

Crawford exhibited a wry smile at the corner of his mouth before turning and walking back to the Land Rover.

Watkins looked on, dismayed at what he was witnessing.

Fagan stared at the two men before producing his phone. He hurried towards the vehicle Crawford was about to climb into. 'Is this what you wanted Crawford? For me to be pushed aside. So that you can sweep everything under the carpet.'

'Is that the best you have DI Fagan?' Crawford smirked.

'You just said to me I was purposely dredging up Nelson's past to antagonise him.'

'Which is clearly the case.'

'What about your past?'

'My past has nothing to do with you DI Fagan.'

Fagan called up the black-and-white picture of Crawford outside of the London Hotel. 'This is you, isn't it?' Fagan observed Crawford's reaction. 'It's a photograph taken of you back in 1968.'

'I haven't got my glasses on.' Crawford seemed to

stumble over his words.

'Another word from you Fagan, and you'll not only find yourself thrown off the case. You will be booted off the force.' Griffiths threatened.

'With all due respect sir, you don't have the balls.'

Rage stretched across Griffiths' face.

'How many others?' Fagan looked at Crawford.

Crawford shrugged. 'How many other what?'

'Let me put it in plain English shall I. How many kids were groomed and abused at the London Hotel? Did you groom Benny Nelson? Is that the reason he became an abuser himself?'

Griffiths' look of rage was replaced by shock.

Fagan glared at the Chief Constable. 'I have growing evidence that a prolific group of paedophiles operated in the Abergavenny area as far back as the 1960s. Jimmy Savile visited Abergavenny in May 1980. He and six other adults plus Nelson took six young boys to Forest Coalpit dorms where they were subjected to sexual abuse and rape.'

'And you know this because?' Griffiths stated.

'I have a statement from a former serving police officer.'

'Would that be the former disgraced police officer, George Watkins?'

'George Watkins served the force with distinction. It was your grandfather, the former Chief Constable of South Wales police, who got him kicked out of the force. The same Chief Constable who cracked a gang of paedophiles in Swansea in 1995, shortly before his retirement. Your grandfather, who accompanied Savile to Forest Coalpit and took part in the systematic rape of six young males.'

It was Crawford's turn to look shocked.

Fagan stepped closer to Griffiths. 'One of those boys

was George Walker's son, Graham.' He fought to control his emotions. 'A year later, Graham committed suicide. Weeks before he took his own life, Graham told his mam and dad everything that had happened that night. But by then there was nothing George could do but stand by and watch his son slip into a deep depression. The result being his suicide. Graham was my best mate at school.' Fagan fought to restrain his tears. 'All but one of the young boys who went with Benson and his paedo cronies are now dead. But I promise you this. I will find the surviving member of the group and get him to testify about what happened that night.'

'I'm not going to listen to any more of your fantasies DI Fagan.' Crawford climbed into the vehicle.

'And then the was the mysterious house fire that killed a former Chief Constable and his wife. An officer that was planning to shut down that paedophile paradise you used to visit.'

Crawford paused before heaving himself onto the back seat.

'This time tomorrow I will have Rebecca Jenkins' murderer in custody.' Fagan offered. 'Unless you still intend to boot me off the case.'

Griffiths stood his ground and nodded. 'You have twenty-four hours. Then I'm shutting you down.' He turned and climbed into the vehicle, which drove away at speed.

Watkins walked up to Fagan. 'You ever play poker, boss?'

'No.'

'You should. You'd make a bloody good card shark.'

CHAPTER 41

Usk young offenders institute – May 1984

Blake and Ellis frogmarched a dishevelled-looking Gobbler through the double doors of the recreation hall. Their smug look on their faces told a story Fagan had witnessed dozens of times over the past few months. The nightly sobs of the young inmate became intolerable. Fagan had even fashioned earplugs to drown out the cries of the anguished boy.

'Over there you fucking poofter and be quiet?' Blake ordered, shoving Gobbler forward.

The two inmates did their usual patrol of the rec room, selecting their next target. A young boy was playing pool, desperate not to be the next victim. He decided to make a break for the main doors.

Ever since the incident at the coal shed, Sandy and his two henchmen had mainly ignored Fagan. However, over the past week Blake and Ellis had exchanged verbal insults with him. Indicating they were going to make Fagan succumb to their depraved behaviour.

Ellis spotted the young boy heading for the main entrance to the rec hall. 'Oi cunt, where do you think you're going?'

The young boy froze and slowly turned. 'I'm going to take a piss.' He trembled as they approached.

Ellis grinned at Blake. 'He was going to take a piss.' He mimicked the young prisoner.

Fagan looked on with growing anger.

‘I know what you’re thinking Fagan.’ Dodger said quietly, reading a battered copy of Orwell’s classic, Nineteen Eighty-Four. ‘But ask yourself this. Do you really want to travel down that road?’

Fagan hunched forward, rubbing his hands together. ‘I can’t let them carry on. It’s fucking killing me.’

‘But they have left you alone after your brief encounter on Christmas Day.’

Fagan smiled as he remembered the threat he had made to Sandy. He glanced at Dodger. ‘Yeah, but for how much longer? I need to make a stand. Show that nonce prick Sandy he can’t pick on these boys anymore.’

‘Okay then consider this.’ Dodger mused. ‘Say you go over there and give those two the pasting they deserve. Then you find Sandy and give him a good walloping. What then?’

‘They leave these younger ones alone, that’s what.’ He looked across at Gobbler, who was staring at the floor. ‘That poor bastard is only fourteen, for fuck’s sake. Sandy is twenty.’

‘So you become head boy after you have dealt with Sandy. And everyone is happy. Then what?’

‘I just said didn’t I. They won’t touch any of these boys, that’s what.’ Fagan began to get frustrated with Dodger’s pointless banter.

‘And after you get out.’ Dodger stated. ‘How are you going to protect these boys?’

Fagan hadn’t considered that scenario. Dodger knew it and took the initiative.

‘You’re only doing a two year stretch. I’m doing two and a half years. I got here about six months before you, which means we’ll be released together.’ Dodger looked at Gobbler. ‘Poor Gobbler over there is doing a three-year stretch for setting fire to his second school. He arrived a month before you.' He then looked at Blake and Ellis. 'Those two are doing a five year stretch along with Sandy. We'll both be out of here before all those lot. If you do something now Fagan, they will rain down holy terror on Gobbler and the rest of the boys when you get out.'

'I take it your solution is let them get away with it?'

'Fagan, look around you for fuck's sake. We're in prison. What do you think it's like in other prisons? You think it's all jam and cream sandwiches elsewhere?'

Fagan looked over at Ellis, who was shoving the young boy taunting him. Blake laughed out loud.

'You serve your time. You get out, and if you have any sense, you won't be back.' Dodger advised.

Fagan continued to watch as Ellis and Blake bullied the young boy.

'Go on then, take a piss.' Ellis ordered.

The young inmate turned towards the door.

Ellis grabbed him. 'That's not what I meant, you little cunt. What I meant was, you take a piss here.'

The young boy looked confused at the request.

Ellis slapped him hard across the cheek. 'Didn't you hear me cunt? I told you to take a piss here, in your pants.' He glanced at Blake, who was grinning. 'Come on, piss in your pants you little cunt.'

The boy's face turned purple as he nursed his stinging cheek.

Blake stepped towards the boy, delivering a hard jab to his abdomen.

The young inmate stayed on his feet. His face was bright red as his bursting bladder unleashed into his trousers.

Ellis and Blake looked down at his light coloured trousers that turned dark as the urine cascaded down his leg.

'Look at this Blake. The little baby has pissed his pants.'

Ellis mocked.

The boy sobbed.

'Aw, don't cry. We'll have the warden get you a nappy, you sad little twat.' Blake offered.

The inmates laughed together as the young boy continued to sob.

'Hey Dolly, you fucking twat!' A voice shouted from behind.

Ellis was still laughing as he turned to face the thick end of a pool cue that pummelled his face.

The pool cue splintered in two.

Before Ellis had a chance to launch any kind of offensive, Fagan kicked his legs from under him. He then launched a devastating kick so powerful Ellis slid across the floor into a stack of plastic chairs.

For a few moments Blake looked like a rabbit caught in headlights as he observed the scene unfold. He snapped out of his temporary trance and headed for the door.

Fagan grabbed a plastic chair and threw it across the room.

Blake was caught by surprise. His lanky frame toppled over the chair.

Fagan glanced behind at Ellis, who was curled up in a ball screaming like a wounded animal. He then focused his attention on Blake, who was scrambling to his feet, reaching for the door handle. Fagan flew towards him, scooping up the heavy end of the pool cue.

Blake clenched the door handle.

Fagan brought the cue down on Blake's knuckles.

Blake screamed in agony.

The other inmates in the canteen looked on.

Fagan wasn't finished yet. Gripping the cue, he swiped Blake across the face.

Blake's nose exploded in a crimson mist.

Fagan shoved the lanky inmate who fell backwards onto the floor. He lashed out, kicking him in the stomach.

Blake let out an agonising gasp.

'Where is he?' Fagan screamed at the bully, who had assumed the foetal position.

Blake gasped for air.

Fagan booted him again. 'I said, where is he you bastard?'

'In the coal shed.' Blake groaned in agony.

Fagan turned towards the door, noticing Ellis scrambling to his feet. He picked up the chair he had used on Blake, hurling it at the inmate.

Ellis didn't even have time to shield himself as the chair came crashing down on him. One of its metal legs smashed him in the jaw.

A guard marched through the entrance at the other end of the rec hall. 'What the fuck is going on here?'

'Nothing sir.' The inmates replied in a chorus.

The guard walked over to Blake, who was propped against the wall, nursing his shattered knuckles. 'What happened to you?'

'Nothing sir.' Blake wept.

'What happened to your hand?'

'It's nothing sir. I fell sir.'

'Bullshit, you slimy little twat.' The guard spotted Ellis nursing his broken nose. He marched over to him. 'What happened to you lad?'

Ellis spat out a front tooth. 'Nothing sir, I fell sir.'

'Don't give me that nonsense, you sad cunt.' He turned and faced the rest of the inmates. 'Right, that's it. Every one of you fuckers is on report.'

Sandy stared down at the terrified young boy who had arrived the day before. He clenched a fistful of the boy's hair. 'Now I want you to listen carefully. You're going to swallow what I fucking give you to swallow. Do you understand, you little bitch?'

The terrified boy could barely manage a nod.

Sandy unzipped his fly, pulling out his erect penis.

Fagan had crept across the yard and stood at the entrance to the coal shed. He spotted a coal shovel propped up against the wall next to the entrance.

Sandy strained to glance over his shoulder as he heard a boot scuffle. A coal shovel smashed into the side of his face. The inmate was sent flying into a bay filled with coal.

Fagan looked at the terrified boy, who was still kneeling. He grabbed his arm, pulling him to his feet. 'Go.' He urged.

The young boy gave him a grateful stare before sprinting away.

Fagan loomed over Sandy.

His face was splattered with blood from the coal shovel that had shattered his nose.

Fagan noticed Sandy's penis was still protruding through his trousers. He lifted the shovel above his head. 'You won't be using that any time soon.' Fagan brought the coal shovel down on Sandy's groin with ferocious speed.

The inmate's scream echoed across the yard, causing two crows perched on a wall to take flight, cawing as they rose into the air.

Fagan threw the coal shovel to one side and grabbed Sandy's donkey jacket collar. 'I swear, if you touch any of these boys again, I'll fucking bury you under that mound of coal. Do you hear me, you fucking cunt? I'll fucking kill you. You're not the head boy anymore. I am.' Fagan pointed to himself. 'I'm the head boy now, cunt, understand?'

Sandy spat out a mouth full of blood. 'Yeah.' He gasped.

Fagan let him go, watching him drop to the floor. He turned his back and walked away before stopping. He then turned and ran at Sandy, kicking him in the back. Fagan stopped, panting heavily, looking down at a terrified Sandy. He suddenly found himself outside the Farmers Arms. Davis lying unconscious on the ground. Fagan then turned and left the coal shed.

Blake and Ellis were nowhere to be seen when Fagan returned to the rec room. All the inmates in the room stared at Fagan as he walked back to his seat.

Gobbler watched him for a moment before walking over.

Fagan looked at him.

'Thanks Fagan.' Gobbler said before walking away.

Dodger casually flicked through the pages of his book. 'Now you've done it Fagan.' He glanced across the rec hall at the other prisoners, who were looking in their direction. 'You're both their saviour and their damnation.'

Fagan nodded slowly. 'Maybe.' He looked at Dodger. 'But it felt good giving those twats what they deserved.'

CHAPTER 42

DAY 4

The Cantreff – 12:43am

Jackie let Fagan through the door, locking it behind him.

'How did it go?' Evans asked. 'You looked like you were having an intense discussion with those two blokes.'

Fagan parked himself on a bar stool. 'It was intense. I had to play my trump card to stop Griffiths pulling me off the case.'

'Your trump card.' Edwards stated.

'I showed Nelson's lawyer that photo with him in it.'

'I bet that went down like a lead balloon.' Tyler remarked.

Fagan yawned and nodded at the same time.

'Have you been to see Benny at the Grange?' Jackie asked.

'I didn't get to see Benny, but I spoke with the doctor who treated him. Nelson didn't take enough paracetamol to put his life at risk.'

'It's like you said. He faked a suicide attempt.' Evans suggested.

'It looks that way. He's a complete twat. He did it on purpose to stall us.'

'Stall you.' Tyler said.

'Any further investigation into Nelson is being forbidden.'

'That's what the lawyer wanted.' Evans said.

Fagan nodded. 'I think we've uncovered more here than

we were supposed to. From now on I have to focus on finding out who murdered Rebecca. My superior has given me twenty-four hours.'

'Well, he's sitting in his caravan on the side of the Skirrid.'

'I know, but I have been so obsessed with Nelson. If I go up there and arrest Tim, there will be fingers of suspicion pointed at me. I should have gone up there the moment they discovered her body.' Fagan drew breath. 'Because of what happened with us all those years ago, I couldn't bring myself to go up there and arrest him. I guess after all these years and having destroyed his life once before, I didn't have the heart to destroy it again. Truth be known, I was glad when they identified the prints on that phone case as Nelson's.'

'But it kicked off something else.' Evans said.

'So when are you going to arrest Tim?' Jackie asked.

'It's not a simple case of going up there and arresting him. I have to have probable cause. There is only one option now. Turn the thumbscrews on Justin and hope he gives Tim up. I will interview him tomorrow morning. Maybe I'll be able to get the truth out of him if I use the right language.'

'Perhaps you may not be able to carry on investigating Nelson, but that doesn't mean the rest of us can't.' Evans pointed out.

'True, but none of you are police officers and could get into serious trouble if he finds out. You've already got done for harassment once before. And it could land me in deep shit.'

'But no one knows we have helped you with Nelson yet. And the police always have to rely on members of the public half the time to help solve crimes.'

'He's got a point, Fagan.' Tyler said. 'The police in

London are always asking for help from the public, because they haven't got a clue.'

'Thanks for the vote of confidence.' Fagan frowned at Tyler.

'Come on, I have heard police officers moaning about not having the resources to carry out operations. It's always on the news. Lack of funding and all that. Not enough officers. Tell you what, you concentrate on proving that Tim murdered Rebecca. And we will focus on Benny Nelson. We've already found out shit loads about Nelson. We haven't had access to police resources like you. After what George said he did to Graham, you of all people want to see him hang for what he did.'

Fagan nodded slowly. 'Ok, you lot can go after Nelson. But under no circumstances are any of you to approach him, or interrogate him about anything. He's not stupid. He knows I am friends with all of you. So if any of you go at him, he'll push the panic button straight away. Just like he did with his wife, sending her back to Thailand. He'll lie low for the moment. I'm sure that lawyer of his has already instructed him to do so.' Fagan suddenly had an idea. He looked at Evans. 'Remember earlier when we suggested the idea Benny had an accomplice?'

'Yeah.'

'It has to be his lawyer. That's the only person who knows Nelson's dirty little secrets. And faking a suicide attempt is a good way to get people onside. Especially what he did earlier with social media.'

'Speaking of media, look at this on the Mail's website.' Tyler handed Fagan his phone.

'Fucking bastard!' Fagan swore as he read the headline on the web page.

Police drive vulnerable man to attempt suicide

‘How did they get hold of the story so quick?’ Jackie questioned.

‘Isn’t it obvious.’ Fagan replied. ‘It has to be Benny’s lawyer. Prick knows all kinds of people that can hold the front pages. This will slow us down again. There’ll be gutter press hanging around the office tomorrow. Especially since he mentioned my name.’

‘What exactly are we trying to achieve here?’ Edwards enquired.

‘To prove Nelson is the pervert we all knew he was.’ Jackie responded.

‘But by doing that we’ve uncovered something much bigger. A paedophile ring that operated when?’

‘From what we have discovered so far, it could have been operating back in the sixties, seventies and eighties.’

‘But what about now?’ Jackie asked.

Fagan looked doubtful. ‘Highly unlikely with all the cyber security monitoring agencies the police work with. I mean, think about it. Back when Savile was prowling the hospitals and schools, there was virtually no one to challenge him. We now know there were many people who questioned his behaviour but were ignored. It’s the same with most paedophiles back in the day. The police simply weren’t interested. Or the witnesses wouldn’t testify in court because of the shame. Back in the day, it was illegal to be gay. If you were caught, then it would mean a prison sentence.’

‘And then some kind of medical treatment to cure homosexuality.’ Tyler added. ‘They reckon that’s why computer genius Alan Turin killed himself.’

Fagan spotted Jackie’s tablet on the bar. He called up the picture Thomas had sent him. ‘Who have we got here exactly?’ He pointed at the picture. ‘Benny, his alleged sister and his dad in the centre.'

'Nelson's lawyer is on the end.' Evans pointed. 'Sergeant Bob, Bernie the Bummer and Ernie Brown are also in the picture. What about the others who went on that weekend with those boys?'

Fagan scanned the photograph. 'It doesn't appear they're in the picture. But it doesn't mean they didn't go in that place.'

'So Benny was groomed at the London Hotel.' Jackie speculated. 'Which means there could be other pictures with kids in them. Kids who were also groomed. If they're Benny's age and they're still alive then it's simply a case of identifying them.'

'Hold on Jackie.' Edwards said. 'Do you think they'll will want to be contacted?'

'He's right.' Fagan countered. 'Many children who are abused want to forget it and get on with their lives. Unfortunately, the media has turned this sordid kind of thing into a cottage industry. Offering money to anyone who will come forward and speak. Especially if the person who abused them is famous.'

Tyler considered something. 'Has anyone seen that documentary on Netflix about Savile?'

Everyone nodded.

'It highlights the power that Savile had back in the day. I mean, they put him in charge of a top committee at Broadmoor. They gave him full access to the hospital. He mixed with everyone there. The Yorkshire Ripper, Ian Brady and loads of other psychos. He was given access to hospitals and institutions all over the country. He had royalty asking him for advice and Prime Ministers inviting him around for tea. How anyone didn't see what he really was, I'll never know.'

'Everyone was blinded by the money he was making for

charity.' Fagan mentioned. 'Savile raised tens of millions for good causes. When he was raising all that money, he was a national hero.'

'But what about others like him?' Evans asked. 'Whenever a story breaks, they always focus on the weakest link in the chain. Look at Epstein. He's arrested, allegedly committing suicide in prison. Then they catch the Maxwell woman leading to the downfall of Prince Andrew. But what about the other rich and powerful people out there who like this kind of shit?'

'I take it you've seen Taken?' Fagan asked Evans.

'Of course, brilliant film.'

'You'll be surprised how much of that film is true. When I was on the force in Liverpool, we cracked a gang who would target girls specifically because they were virgins. We raided this warehouse one night. There was an actual bidding war going on to buy this girl's virginity. She'd been bred especially for that purpose.'

'What do you mean, she'd been bred?' Evans questioned.

'One of the girls we rescued from that warehouse said that she'd literally been brought up in captivity in Russia. Apparently Russian women desperate for money are paid to get pregnant. When they give birth, the baby is taken away from them and raised in trafficking farms across Russia and other countries. When they reach a certain age, they are sold for their virginity. Most are raped, then killed and discarded.'

Jackie put her hand to her mouth. 'You're not pissing about, are you Fagan.'

Fagan shook his head. 'You think that seeing a story about Savile abusing kids on the news is bad. Trust me, the things I have seen will give you nightmares.'

'Why isn't any of this reported on the news?' Evans

questioned.

'Would you want that kind of thing reported all the time? Just the murder of a child is bad enough. The press are aware of a lot of things but avoid certain subjects like the plague.'

'I always knew the media was manipulated. You only have to look what's happened over the last three years.'

'Can we focus here please and get back on track with Benny. How are we going to prove that he's got away with so much shite over the years?'

'Right now, there's not a lot we can do.' Fagan stated. 'His lawyer is about to slap the police with a gagging order regarding Nelson.'

'What does that mean?'

'It prevents the police from mentioning Nelson being part of our enquiries. It's also like a restraining order. Which is why the police had to stop searching Benny's house.'

'All this started when you came to town, Fagan.' Evans stated.

Fagan shook his head. 'All this started with the murder of Rebecca. The last thing Nelson expected was him being thrust into the spotlight over her murder.'

'Because he didn't murder her.' Jackie said.

Fagan looked at her, nodding. 'Because Justin planted that mobile phone case at the scene of the crime, it brought him into focus. Which is the last thing he expected. That's why he hits the panic button and calls that expensive solicitor. Then the next thing that happens is all this history suddenly comes to light.' Fagan looked at Evans. 'It's when we started talking about the weekend Savile came to town. And the boys who were on that trip to Forest Coalpit dorms. When I interviewed Justin, he refused to tell us what he was doing at Nelson's house the night Rebecca was murdered. He didn't say anything about Nelson's wife handing over the keys to the shed up at the allotment.'

'Then you need to be a little more persuasive with him.'

Fagan nodded. 'I want to know how Justin got caught up in all this. He was close to Rebecca.'

'What about Ricky?'

'Poor sod.' Edwards said. 'When he finds out who killed his mam, he will flip.'

'Has he got a temper?' Fagan asked.

Jackie nodded. 'I'd say it was fiercer than Tim's.'

'I know you all want to get Benny for the shit he's caused over the years. But let's all be patient. We'll focus on getting justice for Rebecca and then we'll deal with Benny. I'll text Nigel tomorrow. See if there are many pictures from the sixties and seventies from the London hotel. I'll also check on Benny's family background.'

'Sounds messed up, if you ask me.' Evans remarked.

Fagan stared at the photo of a young Nelson.

CHAPTER 43

Usk Young offenders institute – September 1984

Fagan stared across the visitors' room, perplexed at his visitor.

Rebecca spotted Fagan approaching. She smiled at him as if she hadn't seen him in a few years.

Fagan sat down opposite Rebecca. 'What are you doing here?'

'I wanted to see you.'

'After what happened, after what I did to your boyfriend.'

Rebecca seemed hurt by the statement. 'He's not my boyfriend Marc. We split up after your fight.'

'How is he?'

'Still in a wheelchair.'

'Fuck.' Fagan seethed.

'I thought you'd be happy to see me.'

'I'm stuck in prison Rebecca. Why would I be happy to see you?'

'I see your mother has sold the house.'

Fagan nodded. 'She wrote a letter to me last week from Ormskirk. She's got a job in a local shop and has already put a deposit on a house.'

Rebecca looked dismayed. 'I suppose you'll be leaving as soon as you get out.'

'Actually, George Walker came to visit last week. He said that I am more than welcome to stay with him and Mary.'

Rebecca smiled. 'That's great.'

Fagan had an idea where the conversation was heading. 'Rebecca, when I leave here I'm not looking to get back together with you. It's too much.'

'But I thought we could at least try to work something out.'

'Why haven't you got on with your life? Why haven't you gone to university?'

'I told you. That's dad's dream, not mine. I have a job at the sweet factory now. It pays good money. I have passed my driving test. I've got a car. When you get out, we can go places. We don't have to hang around Abergavenny all day.'

'And what about your dad? I expect he'll be monitoring me when I get out.'

Rebecca shook her head. 'I wouldn't worry about dad. So, what will you do when you get out of here?'

Fagan shrugged. 'It all depends. I'll be an ex-convict. Perhaps I can get a job working at Mr Browns cars opposite the bus station. Earnie reminds me of Arthur Daley.'

Rebecca smiled at Fagan's attempt at humour. 'I have put my name on the council list. Hopefully, they'll get me a flat soon and I'll have a place of my own.'

'I doubt if your dad will allow that. How's your sister?'

'Doing well at Cambridge. She's got her eyes set on a law degree.'

Fagan looked at Rebecca. 'Why do you want to hang around Abergavenny Becky? There are better places out there. You can do whatever you want. I'll be stuck in here for over a year.'

'I don't want to rush my life. Before you know it, Susanna will have got her degree. And the first thing dad will expect her to do is settle down. It seems such a waste of time going to university if you're not going to do anything with the degree. I had an argument with dad the other night. I told him to stop trying to tell me what to do with my life.'

Fagan smiled. 'I bet he didn't like that.'

Rebecca shook her head. 'Nope.'

'Have you heard from the others?'

'I saw Edwards, Evans and Tyler at the cinema last week. They watched a film called Ghostbusters. As usual Evans was all excited about it. They invited me to the cinema next week. Apparently Harrison Ford has made another Indiana Jones film. The Temple of Doom.'

Fagan recalled the nights he and Rebecca would curl up on the sofa at his mam's house and watch a film.

'Still in love with Rick from Casablanca, then.'

She smiled back at him, nodding.

'Time ladies and gentlemen!' The guard shouted.

'I guess I better go.' Rebecca stood.

Fagan also stood. For a moment, he gazed at Rebecca. 'I'll see you around.'

Dodger had been watching Rebecca and Fagan talking. 'Nice-looking girl.' He remarked.

Fagan watched as Rebecca waved goodbye.

'I guess.'

Dodger smiled. 'Forbidden love, eh?'

Fagan watched as she disappeared from sight. Dodger was right, he was madly in love with her. 'No, not a chance.' Fagan lied.

CHAPTER 44

Newport central police HQ – 8:56am

Fagan went through all the start-up procedure for the benefit of the recording.

Justin Pike looked tired and withdrawn.

Fagan Began. 'So Justin, is there anything new you would like to tell us today?'

Pike shrugged.

'For the benefit of the tape, Mr Pike is shrugging. Look, Justin, you know what I want to hear from you. I want to know who murdered Rebecca Jenkins. You say you didn't do it. But you're adamant that Benny Nelson murdered her.'

'He did.' Pike insisted. 'How many times do I have to tell you?'

'And how many times have I got to tell you Justin? Nelson didn't murder Rebecca.'

'You're trying to mess with my head.'

'Why would we do that? The only one messing about here Justin is you. Let me ask you this. Are you ready to spend the next twenty years in prison for something you didn't do? Do you think Rebecca would want that?'

Pike glanced at Fagan, shaking his head. 'I wanted to make that bastard look like he murdered Rebecca. We knew if we could plant all the evidence, you lot would arrest him and charge him with her murder.'

Fagan glanced at Watkins. 'We?'

Pike stared at the table. 'No comment.'

'Justin, who is we?' Watkins asked.

'No comment.'

Fagan inhaled. 'Look, Justin, I really want to help you. But the longer you hold out, the worse it will look for you. If you tell us who murdered Rebecca, then it will go a long way towards reducing whatever sentence they will give you.'

Pike glared back at him.

'Tell us who murdered Rebecca and I promise, you will receive a lesser sentence. I can tell you've been pressured into this.'

'Tim Davis!' Pike blurted out before Fagan could say anything else.

'Tim Davis?' Fagan repeated.

Pike broke down, sobbing.

'Tim, is that who murdered Rebecca?'

Watkins slid a box of tissues towards Pike.

'It was an accident.' Pike blew his nose. 'He didn't mean to do it. At least that's what he told me.'

'Okay Justin, let's back up. You said the other night that you left Rebecca outside the chippy in Flannel Street. Then you went home.'

'I did. That part is true.'

'And then?' Watkins pressed.

'About an hour after I got home, Tim phoned me. He sounded like he was in a panic. He said Rebecca had a serious accident and that I need to meet him.'

'Where did she have an accident?'

'He didn't say. He just said to go to his place.'

'And Rebecca was already there when you arrived?'

Pike nodded.

'For the benefit of the tape, Justin Pike is nodding. What happened when you got to Tim's?'

'Rebecca was already there.'

'Was she conscious?'

'No.'

'Do you know if she was still alive?'

Pike shook his head rigorously. 'No, I think Tim had already killed her.'

'So you didn't know how she died?'

'Tim said they'd had some kind of argument. And that it got out of hand.'

'Do you know what they were arguing about?'

'No.' Pike sniffed.

'Where was Rebecca when you arrived at Tim's?'

'He'd put her into the back of his pickup. God, there was blood everywhere.'

'And then what happened?'

'He said there was a way we could get out of it. He knew I was having a relationship with Benny's wife. Benny pinged himself at the Odeon cinema in Cardiff.'

'What happened next?'

'He asked me to go to Nelson's house and get the phone case he knew he kept. He asked me to find the keys to the allotment shed in his house. When I went in, Mon helped me find them.'

'And that's when you showed up on CCTV.'

'Yes.'

'What did you do next?'

'We had to come up with a plan to put Rebecca where someone would easily find her.'

'In Bailey park?'

'Yes.'

'Taking a bit of a risk, weren't you? There are usually kids hanging around until the early hours. It's open twenty-four hours.'

'That's what I said to Tim. So we checked. There wasn't anyone around.'

‘So what, you simply drove to the park and dumped her body?’

Pike nodded.

‘For the benefit of the tape, Mr Pike is nodding. Surely you knew that eventually you’d be caught.’

‘Everything was so fucked up. Tim was in such a hurry to dump Rebecca.’

‘But you don’t know how he murdered her?’

‘No, I swear. All he said was they had an argument. Things got out of control.’

Fagan leant back in his chair. ‘Why did you go along with it?’

‘What choice did I have?’

‘You did have a choice, Justin. You could have walked away and come straight to us. But you chose to help a murderer. Perverting the course of Justice can carry up to life imprisonment. You’ve signed your own life away helping Tim.’

Pike buried his head in his hands, sobbing profusely. ‘I wanted that bastard Nelson to pay for what he did to Michelle.’ He looked at Fagan. ‘You know what he was like all those years ago. How many girls did he get drunk and rape? He’s been getting away with shit all his life. Everyone wants to see the back of him. That’s why I did it.’

‘Plant the evidence in the park?’ Watkins said.

Pike nodded. ‘When I was at Nelson’s house I grabbed the phone case.’

‘Not knowing you had a hole in the latex gloved you were wearing.’ Watkins continued. ‘It was careless of you to leave them in a bin close by.’ He picked up an evidence bag containing the gloves. ‘You thought the council would empty the bins, didn’t you? You assumed the police wouldn’t search the bins.’

‘No.’ Pike sniffled. ‘I thought you’d find Rebecca and

just take her for an autopsy or something like that.'

'How did Tim get Rebecca in the back of his truck, considering he's got that limp?' Fagan asked.

'He's still pretty fit, despite having that disability you gave him.'

'Which park entrance did you use?'

'We knew the top gate in park avenue is wide enough for a vehicle to get through. Although Tim scraped the side of his truck on the gate. He drove down to the place where we left her.' Pike broke down again.

'Perhaps we should take a recess while I discuss this matter with my client. He has provided you with the name of the suspect responsible for the murder of Rebecca Jenkins.' Pike's solicitor requested.

Fagan stared at Pike for several moments before nodding. He ended the interview and allowed them to leave.

'Organise a couple of bodies.' He threw his jacket on. 'We'll arrest Tim Davis.'

Watkins stared at Fagan. 'You knew Pike would give up a name.'

Fagan looked back at him. 'How do you mean?'

'The argument you had with Griffiths last night. He gave you twenty-four hours to clear this up. Less than twelve hours later you have a name.'

Fagan took a deep breath. 'Nelson has taken up a majority of the past few days. Playing games with us. He enjoys that kind of thing. The only reason he owned up to her murder was to taunt me.'

'What did he have to gain out of it?'

Fagan thought about what Nelson had said to him in a previous interview. 'Let's just say, for the time being, we haven't heard the last of Nelson.'

CHAPTER 45

Usk young offenders institute – 2nd December 1985 – 2:09pm

Dodger stretched out his arms, taking in the fresh air. 'You know what that smell is Fagan? That is the sweet smell of freedom.'

Fagan was staring back at the main prison gates.

Dodger read the look on his face. 'I warned you Fagan. You would be their saviour and their damnation. And dammed they will be now that you're no longer there to protect them.'

'I had a word with the governor this morning.' Fagan revealed.

'Let me guess. He said that he would make sure the boys are treated in a civilised manner.'

'Something like that.'

'All that twat will do is laugh behind your back.' Dodger put his arm around Fagan. 'I guess this is where we part company.'

A car pulled up to the side of the road. George sounded the horn.

'Do you need a lift anywhere?' Fagan asked.

Dodger shook his head. 'I thought I might go into Usk. Spend the four pounds I have to my name in the pub. Then phone my dear dad to pick me up.'

Fagan and Dodger shared a quick hug before saying their goodbyes.

‘I’m sure you’ll want to meet up with friends when you get back.’ George made conversation as they headed back towards Abergavenny.

‘I’ve got no money to go down the pub George.’

Walker smiled. ‘I’ll give you a fiver so you can go out and meet up with someone.’

Fagan shook his head. ‘You’re giving me a place to stay George. You don’t have to give me money as well.’

‘Nonsense. Besides, who else are you going to stay with? You would have been on the streets. I couldn’t have that. We’ve made up your room and Mary is cooking you a big meal later on. I’ll expect you’ll be fed up with that prison muck.’

‘You can say that again.’ Fagan looked forward to home cooking.

‘That young lady friend of yours, Rebecca, has knocked on the door a few times. She is eager to meet up with you. She’s a lovely girl. Might be good for you to have a girl like that on your arm. You know, to keep you occupied.’ Walker winked at him.

Fagan smiled. ‘I suppose I better go and see her.’

‘I spoke with Kenneth Barker last week. He says he’d be more than happy to take you on as a labourer and learn you the ropes of bricklaying. It’s cash in hand, so you’ll have some money in your pocket.’

‘You don’t have to do all this for me George.’ Fagan paused for thought. ‘Not after what I did to Tim.’

Walker spotted a layby and pulled in.

‘Your mates told me what happened that night. It sounds to me you were sticking up for that girl of yours. Tim hit her, didn’t he?’

Fagan nodded.

‘So you let loose a little. Perhaps you should have backed away. You cannot change the past. All you can do is create the best future for yourself.' Walker pulled out of the layby. 'I spoke to your mam last week. She wants you to move up with her as soon as its possible.'

Fagan shook his head. 'I'm not ready to move yet.' His thoughts turned to Rebecca.

Twenty minutes later, Fagan stepped through the door of George's home. Mary fussed around him, taking his bag and dumping it in front of the washing machine. She immediately set about making a bacon sandwich for Fagan and George. Later on in the early evening, they all sat down to a full roast beef dinner. George gave Fagan a five pound note so he could go out and meet up with everyone in the Somerset Arms.

Tyler was the first to throw his arms around Fagan as he walked into the pool room. 'You are a sight for sore eyes.'

Every one gathered around.

'What was it like?' Evans asked.

'Don't be such a twat.' Edwards jibed.

'I just want to know if you were the daddy.' Evans attempted a cockney accent.

Fagan couldn't help laughing. 'I wasn't the daddy.' He reflected on his time in prison. 'But I had to deal with a few twats.'

'It doesn't matter.' Tyler said. 'Fagan is no longer in that shit hole. Let's get pissed and play pool.'

'I have a brilliant idea.' Evans announced. 'Saturday at Abergavenny cinema. There's a film called Back to the Future playing. We'll watch the film. Come back here for a few bevvies then have a late night at the Dragon.'

Fagan mused over the idea. 'Sounds like a plan to me.'

Evans pushed the release switch on the side of the pool table and the balls cascaded out.

'Has anyone seen Tim?' Fagan asked, supping on his first pint.

‘I saw him last week. He’s been free of his wheelchair for a few months now. He’s hobbling around on a walking stick.’ Edwards said.

Guilt stabbed at Fagan as he recalled the night outside the Farmers.

‘Don’t let it get to you mate.’ Tyler said. ‘He started that fight. Don’t forget he broke your nose. After which he set about giving Rebecca a good hiding. No one hates you for what you did.’

‘Except for Tim.’ Fagan responded.

‘Come on Fagan, he had it coming. He was turning into a right dickhead. Even the girls got fucked off with him. Pestering them all the time so he could get laid. So don’t over think anything.’

Everyone stopped talking and looked towards the door.

Fagan stood in awe as Rebecca glided into the room. She was wearing full makeup and a blue mini dress that her father would have considered as way too short. Her long blonde hair cascaded over her shoulders and down her back like a golden waterfall. Even in the dimly lit pool room, she seemed to glow.

‘Hey Marc.’ She smiled at him.

‘Wow, Rebecca. You look amazing.’ Fagan gasped.

She smiled as her cheeks blushed. ‘I called at George’s house. I hope you don’t mind. I knew you were coming out today. I would have been here sooner, but I had to work on at the sweet factory.’

‘No, it’s fine. I’m just a little surprised to see you, that’s all. Can I buy you a drink?’

‘I was hoping we could go somewhere to talk.’ Rebecca requested.

Fagan looked at his friends, who were already giving him eye signals to go.

Rebecca and Fagan walked back through town and

headed up the Hereford Road. Rebecca explained her parents were in Paris for two nights and they would be back the following afternoon. A day later, the family will be flying out to the family villa in Spain for several days.

'It's a shame. There's a big night out at the cinema on Saturday. Evans is really excited.'

Rebecca laughed. 'Evans is a huge nerd when it comes to films.'

'Perhaps you should make him watch *Casablanca*.'

Rebecca looked at the darkened silhouette of her house on Lansdown Road. She then gazed at Fagan with an inviting smile. 'I'd rather watch it with you.'

They walked up the driveway and disappeared into the house.

CHAPTER 46

Penlan Farm – Abergavenny – 11:45am

Fagan, Watkins and four officers in stab vests, armed with tasers, trudged up the gravel track towards the farm entrance. The farm was at the base of the Skirrid mountain. Fagan had instructed all police vehicles to park at a distance. A black Toyota pickup was parked near the entrance to the farm.

'Boss.' Watkins pointed at a gash on the side of the truck.

Fagan glanced at one of the officers. 'Call this in. Get a team of CSIs here.'

As they carried on walking, four large static caravans came into view. They were evenly spaced out, giving each caravan room for a garden. The structures overlooked the valley, which on a clear day, gave a majestic view of Abergavenny and the surrounding mountains that stretched in all directions.

Fagan stopped, spotting a man sat on decking outside one of the caravans.

'Is that him?' Watkins asked.

Fagan stared at the man sat on a deckchair watching the party approach. A man he hadn't seen in forty years. A walking stick was propped up against the chair.

Fagan nodded. 'Yeah, that's him.'

Watkins and the police officers continued their march towards where Davis was sitting.

'Wait.' Fagan ordered.

The group turned to face him.

'I'll go alone.'

'Are you sure boss?' Watkins glanced towards the caravan. 'He could be armed.'

Fagan shook his head slowly. 'No, he wants to speak to me, and me alone.'

'Ok, but if he tries anything we'll move in.'

'He won't try anything. He's been waiting for me. He's been waiting forty years.' Fagan carried on alone to where Davis was sitting.

Davis stooped over and pulled two bottles of beer out of an icebox sat by the side of him.

Fagan stopped short of the decking that surrounded Davis's static.

Davis flipped the tops off the bottles and placed them on the table.

Fagan walked up the decking steps.

Davis picked his bottle up and took a swig. He savoured the taste before placing it down on the table. 'Took your time, didn't you?'

Fagan nodded. 'Benny has been giving us the runaround for the past few days.' He picked up the bottle of beer.

'I knew he would. You know what that slippery twat is like. He'll taunt you and play with you as long as he finds it fun. I have to admit, I wasn't expecting Pikey to hold out for so long. I was expecting you to be here yesterday. It was a shitty plan to say the least.'

'Why didn't you run?'

Davis frowned at Fagan, glancing at his walking stick. 'Where am I going to run to? I've been a fucking cripple for most of my life.' He took another swig of beer. 'No thanks to you.'

'Jesus Christ Tim, are you still blaming me for that?'

'Yeah well, I've had nothing else to do for the past few

decades but reminisce about the good old days.'

'Tim, you did that to yourself. You decided to walk into the Farmers and start that fight, not me. Perhaps if you wouldn't have broken Rebecca's nose I might have been contented to have left you alone.'

'And perhaps you should have told me you and her were seeing each other behind my back.'

'Seriously, after all these years, you're still clinging on to a pointless grudge. I served two years for what I did to you. And let me tell you, it was no bloody picnic.'

Davis kicked his walking stick. 'And I have served a forty-year sentence for what you did.'

'Fuck off Tim. Is this what you've been doing all these years? Wallowing in your own self-pity. Blaming everyone else for your mistakes. Everything you have done is down to you. If it's any consolation, I'm sorry.'

'Shove your fucking pity up your arse Fagan. As soon as you got the chance, you just fucked off. Now you decide to waltz back into Abergavenny to take everything from me again.'

'Is that why you murdered Rebecca? Because you were afraid she'd side line you if we got back together.'

'That's exactly what she was planning to do.' Davis revealed.

Fagan stared at him.

'I bet Jackie has been nattering, hasn't she?'

'We've had a chat, yeah.'

'But she didn't tell you I was in the pub several weeks ago when her daughter mentioned you'd been looking at a house in Llanfoist. Rebecca literally jumped off her stool when Amy mentioned your name.' Davis had a look of revulsion on his face. 'All she would go on about after that was you. I can't wait to see Fagan again. I hope he's not married. She was so full of herself, knowing that you were coming back to town. Bought new clothes and tarted herself up.' He glared at Fagan. 'You said you wouldn't be back and that you'd be gone for good. So, why have you come back?'

'If you well remember Tim, I was run out of town by Bob Benson and Benny. I had no choice after I gave Benny another beating. Unlike you, I didn't want to throw my life away by going back to prison for another five years. I didn't want to subject Rebecca to that kind of life.'

'So, you were planning to play happy families. At least I know the truth now.'

'Tim, you had your choice of any woman back then. Until you became a dick. I remember the women tripping over themselves to be with you.'

'And now they're tripping over my walking stick in Morrisons.'

'What happened?' Fagan asked. 'Why did Rebecca deserve to die?'

Davis took another swig from his bottle. 'I didn't mean for things to get out of hand.' His voice trembled as he talked. 'Because she knew you were coming back home, the arguments got worse. It started off as bickering and then turned into full-blown screaming matches.'

'So that's it. You snapped and decided to kill her.'

'No, I didn't decide to kill her. I'm many things Fagan, but I ain't no murderer.'

Fagan looked at him. 'What happened?'

Davis took a deep breath. 'I wanted to talk to her, that's all.'

'So you drove to Flannel street chippy?'

Davis nodded. 'You'd been home a few days. She was planning to bump into you the minute you contacted old friends down here. She was so excited and nervous. She thought you wouldn't want to know her. Perhaps you'd moved on with your life and all that. Not interested in old flames. I thought I could try to patch things up between us. We'd been arguing so much lately because of you.' Tears seeped out of his eyes. 'I spotted her walking down Market street. I asked if we could go somewhere and talk, that's all.'

'Where did you take her?'

'Here.'

Fagan looked back down the road and noticed horse manure dotted all over the place.

Davis's hands trembled as he spoke. 'I begged her to give us one more chance. But she didn't want to know. All she could think of was you being a couple again.' He rubbed his hands together, looking down at them. 'She said she had enough of me, wanted me gone from her life. I begged her not to do this. But her mind was made up.'

'And then?' Fagan coaxed.

'She said that she didn't want a lift. She'd phone a taxi. I, uh, was furious as she walked away from me.'

'And that's when you went after her?'

Davis nodded. 'I totally lost it. You know, that moment when you are totally blinded by rage.'

Fagan nodded, recalling the night in the Farmers.

'I don't even remember grabbing the tyre iron from the back of the truck. She turned to me and saw me holding it. Becky started running down the gravel track. One of her heels broke loose from her shoe. She stumbled to the ground. The next thing I knew, I was upon her.' He shook his head. 'I only meant to give a tap on the back of her leg.'

'The pathologist said the blow was extreme.'

Davis buried his head in his cupped hands. 'I didn't mean to do it. I just wanted to talk to her.'

'Why did you call Justin?'

'Panic set in. There was blood all over the place. Saw

she'd already dialled Justin's number, so I hung up.'

'That's when you called him?'

'Yeah, it all happened so fast. I wanted to call the police.' He swallowed hard. 'Rebecca was still conscious, just about.'

'What did you do?'

'I rifled through her handbag and found her mobile phone charger.'

'And then you finished the job by strangling her with the cable?'

Davis nodded. 'I lifted her body onto the back of my truck. Rebecca was very fit. She didn't weigh much. I grabbed a hosepipe quickly and started to jet wash the area she had fallen. God, there was so much blood.'

'When did Justin arrive?'

'He got here within ten minutes of me calling him. When he saw Rebecca's body, he was fuming at me. He was already phoning the police.'

'How did you stop him?'

'I told him I knew he was seeing Nelson's wife. I knew he was giving him money to screw her. It wasn't exactly a secret. You know what Benny is like. I told him we could fix this. I said if we could somehow plant evidence that Benny had killed her, then we'd be in the clear. Everyone knew Benny had been stalking Rebecca for years. I knew Benny was at the cinema. He'd pinged himself in Cardiff about half an hour before. I told Justin to go to his house and get the phone case he had stolen a week before. I thought he'd only be five minutes, but he took at least twenty minutes to come back. That's when I panicked. I'd already decided to dump her body in the carpark on the other side of the Skirrid, opposite the café. But when he didn't show up, I left her in Bailey Park.'

'Justin wasn't with you when you dumped Rebecca's

body?'

Davis drank greedily from his bottle. 'No. I went back up to Nelson's before driving back to the park with Pike. We chucked the phone case by her body before driving to the allotment in Llanfoist to dump the rest of the stuff. We drove back to Nelson's, handed the keys back and went home.'

'Did Nelson's wife have any idea what you had done?'

'No, we told her we wanted the keys to the allotment. She handed them over without saying anything.'

Fagan took a moment to imagine the scene.

'It all happened so fast. By the time Justin came back I couldn't think straight. I said we should leave her in Bailey Park. I didn't want to leave her where no one would find her. I wanted her to be found.'

Fagan looked back at Watkins and the officers nodding. 'Timothy Davis, I'm arresting you for the murder of Rebecca Jenkins. You do not have to say anything. But it may harm your defence if you do not mention when questioned something which you later rely on in court. Anything you do say may be given in evidence.'

Two officers stepped forward and pulled Davis to his feet. His hands were cuffed behind his back.

'Hold on.' Fagan called out as they led him away. 'Everything you have done has led to this moment Tim. No one else is to blame, least of all me. I didn't come back to upstage you. I came home to serve out the rest of my time in relative peace and quiet. I have seen enough death over the last three decades.' Fagan paused. 'All you've done here is end the life of someone who was loved. Rebecca never deserved you. And you certainly didn't deserve her. That's why she had the good sense to walk away. But you couldn't let go, could you. You had to have her all to yourself, even if it meant killing her. You've let everyone down, most of all your son.'

'You dull twat.' Davis growled. 'You have no fucking idea what has happened. When Rebecca found out you were coming home, she wanted you to be ready.'

'Ready for what?'

'For the truth, you stupid cunt.'

'What truth would that be Tim?'

'You don't get it do you Fagan. You left Rebecca a sobbing wreck at the train station. She hated you for what you did. Fucking off, without as much as leaving any kind of contact address.'

'I had no fucking choice!' Fagan shouted. 'After I put Nelson in the hospital, Bob Benson said I could either go back to clink or leave for good. He also told me I couldn't have contact with anyone, including Rebecca.'

Tim struggled against his handcuffs. 'To spite you, Rebecca came crawling back to me. And then nine months later Ricky was born. I tried to be the best father I could. I tried to be the father that you should have been. But instead you were busy playing cops and fucking robbers.'

Fagan stared back, too stunned to say anything.

'Don't you fucking get it? Ricky is your boy. Not mine, yours. When Rebecca found out you were coming back, she confronted me with the truth. She was pregnant before we got back together. She only got back with me to save herself the humiliation, being labelled as the town bike.' Davis stopped talking, fighting to keep his composure. 'She's had thirty-eight years to tell me, but she waited until now. And when she revealed the truth, the look on her face. The look that finally told me it was over between us.' He glared at Fagan. 'There was no fucking way I was going to let you just turn up and take them both away from me.'

Fagan nodded to the officer. 'Take him.'

C H A P T E R 4 7

The Somerset Arms – December 1985 – 9 58pm

'I don't get it.' Fagan said, taking a shot on the pool table. 'That kid, Marty, what's-his-face?'

'McFly.' Evans remarked dryly, chalking his pool cue.

'Yeah.' Fagan nodded. 'Goes back in time to shag his own mother.'

Evans rolled his eyes. 'No, Marty accidentally goes back to 1955 in the DeLorean after the Doc is shot by those Libyans. He saves his dad from being hit by the car his grandad is driving.'

'Because his dad is a perv who spying on his mother undressing.' Fagan summarised.

'Yes, now you're getting it. And because he was brought into the house instead of his father, his mother Lorraine, fell in love with her own son.'

'But she should have known he was her son?'

'How the fuck could she have known that? Marty hadn't even been born yet. She hadn't even got together with George.'

Fagan was even more confused. 'I didn't get that film at all.'

'I loved the part near the end when Marty played Johnny Be Good and then broke into that heavy metal track. Did you see the looks on their faces?' Edwards said.

'I liked the part where George punched Biff's light's out.' Tyler added. 'Everyone went wild in the cinema.'

'The only thing that made little sense was the ending.

When Doc Brown comes back and tells Marty he's got to go back to the future with him.' Evans explained. 'Something has to be done about their kids.'

'How do you mean?' Tyler asked.

'Well, think about it. If Marty gets in the DeLorean and goes forward in time, he will not be able to see his kids, or himself. All that's going to happen is that he's going to disappear in 1985 and turn up in the future. It's like a car journey. The moment you jump in the car at point A, and arrive at point B, you exist only in the car and nowhere else.'

'I wonder how far they're going to travel?' Tyler questioned. 'Could be another thirty years, but forward in time and not back. What year will that be?'

'2015.' Evans answered.

'Wonder if they'll have flying cars?'

'We'll have to wait until they make a sequel. I loved the last thing the doc said. *Roads, where we're going, we don't need roads*.' Edwards finished his pint. 'besides, we'll still be waiting for Fagan to take his shot.'

Fagan sneered at him before smashing the white ball that hit the black ball into the corner pocket. 'I'll let you geeks talk about time travel. Anyone want a fresh pint?'

Edwards held up his glass. 'Yes please mate, another Carlin.'

Fagan looked at Evans, who was shaking his head.

'Got no more money.' He moaned.

Fagan entered the bar.

'Well, well, well. If it isn't tweetie pie, the jailbird. Abergavenny's favourite convict. How's it going?' Nelson was slouched at the bar, clearly drunk.

'Two pints of Carlin please Dai.' Fagan ignored Nelson.

'Aren't you talking to me then Fagan?'

Fagan gave Nelson a sidewards glance. 'Fuck off. There,

I said something.'

'How was your time inside? Is your arsehole any bigger? Did they bend you over in the showers and have their way with you?'

Fagan shut Nelson out.

Nelson pulled up his stool by the side of Fagan. 'Not good enough to talk to, am I?'

'I told you to fuck off. That's enough talk.'

Nelson grinned at Fagan. 'Come on Marc, you can tell me. Were you a good fuck in prison?'

Dai had finished pouring the first pint. The phone behind the bar rang. 'Got to answer this. Be back in a moment.'

Fagan supped from his full pint glass.

'What's the matter Fagan? Too scared to tell me if you were fucked up the arse.' Nelson taunted.

Fagan could feel agitation building.

The landlord was talking to someone on the phone and showed no sign of hanging up.

'I bet you were a good fuck, weren't you Fagan?'

Fagan could smell the stench of whiskey on Nelson's breath.

'I bet they bent you over and had the time of their lives with you.'

'Benny, if you don't fuck off, I'll fucking lamp you.'

Nelson laughed. 'You'll be inside by Monday if you do that Fagan. I heard sergeant Bob wants to see you go away again.'

'I said fuck off Benny.' Fagan seethed.

Nelson flopped a drunken arm around an enraged Fagan. 'Come on mate, you can tell me. Were you a good fuck in prison?' He shovelled peanuts into his mouth from a bowl on the bar. 'Did you squeal like a pig, boy? I'll tell you who was a real good fuck. Your mate Graham, when we all took it in turns fucking him at Forest Coalpit. Fair play to Graham. He really put up a fight. And the more he struggled, the harder I fucked him. It was pure heaven.'

Fagan exploded, kicking the bar stool from underneath Nelson.

Nelson dropped like a stone, smashing his chin on the edge of the bar.

The landlord slammed the phone down on the receiver. 'That's enough!'

Fagan grabbed Nelson before he crumpled to the floor, kneeing him in the chest.

Nelson spat out a mouthful of peanuts.

Fagan punched him in the jaw. Before throwing him across the bar, scattering tables and chairs. Glasses smashed onto the floor. Pub residents scattered, trying to avoid the one-sided fight. Fagan dragged Nelson to his feet. 'You talk like that about Graham again and I'll fucking kill you.' He spat into Nelson's face before head-butting him.

Nelson's nose exploded.

Fagan let go and watched as he crumpled to the floor. He then let loose a barrage of violent kicks.

Evans, Tyler and Edwards flew into the bar. Looking on in horror at a semi-conscious Nelson sprawled out on the floor.

The landlord was already dialling 999.

Tudor street police station – 11:15pm

Fagan strained to listen through the cell wall. Walker and Benson were screaming at each other. But Fagan could not make out what was being said. He lay on the cell bed and considered his not so bright future. He had no regrets about attacking Benny. But he felt guilty about letting George down. Who had taken it upon himself to give Fagan a home. After about half an hour of intense shouting, the door to the cell opened.

Bob Benson stood there glaring at Fagan. 'Out, you little shithead.'

Fagan was escorted to Benson's office. George wasn't on the front desk.

A few minutes later, Benson marched in and sat down opposite Fagan. He stared at him before opening a folder. 'I've just got off the phone to Nevil Hall. Let's see, broken nose, fractured jaw, two broken ribs and internal bleeding. Looks like Benny will be spending Christmas in the hospital.' He slapped the folder shut. 'You're a complete piece of shit. Do you know that Fagan? You do nothing but fuck people's lives up. It would seem that stint you did in Usk wasn't enough. You like doing porridge, do you?'

Fagan didn't answer.

'You're looking at another five to ten years inside. Your dad must be looking down on you now and shaking his head in shame. And as for your poor mam when she finds out. It's enough to give her a heart attack.' Benson pushed the file to one side. He leant back in his chair that creaked under his weight. 'There is an alternative, you know Fagan. Unless, of course, you want to go back to prison.'

Fagan remained silent.

'Is that what you want? To spend the better half of the next decade behind bars?'

'No.' Fagan replied.

'No.' Benson repeated. 'Therefore, I am giving you another option.'

Fagan looked at Benson.

'You can fuck off from Abergavenny and never come back. Go and live with your mother in that shit box English town she's from.'

Fagan considered the proposal.

'So, what's it going to be? More time spent in prison?

Or move on and start fresh. Although I'm sure you'll be in Liverpool nick at some point.'

Fagan nodded.

'Did you say something Fagan?' Benson held his hand to his ear.

Fagan cleared his voice. 'I'll go.'

Benson nodded. 'That's what I wanted to hear. You're very lucky I know people who can make this all go away. Otherwise you'd be sitting in a cell in Cardiff nick by midnight.' Benson paused. 'I'll give three days to say goodbye to your mates and George. Then you are on the first train up to Liverpool.'

Fagan stared wide eyed at Benson. But he had no choice but to agree.

'One more thing. When I mean I want you gone, I mean I want you gone forever. No letters or swapping phone numbers. This time next year no one is going to remember you in this town. Is that clear?'

Fagan nodded slowly.

'Good.' Benson said, getting to his feet. 'I'll make arrangements for your exile.'

CHAPTER 48

Llanfoist cemetery

Three weeks after Tim Davis' arrest.

Fagan stared down at his father's grave. He was expecting it to be unkept. To his surprise, there were flowers that looked as if they'd been replaced regularly. He stared across the cemetery towards Rebecca's grave. A large group of people, including her weeping son and girlfriend were at her graveside. Jackie had started a crowdfunding appeal to pay for the funeral and had raised over eleven thousand pounds in two weeks. Dozens had turned out to pay their respects. Fagan looked back at his father's grave.

'She came up here twice a month.' Jackie said, appearing at his side. 'Your dad was her only connection she had to you. George used to tend it regularly. But over the past few years he's become too old to walk up here.'

Fagan nodded silently.

Jackie looked across the graveyard. 'I love it out here. It's so peaceful.'

'I'm having our mam's ashes transported down here so she can be with dad.' Fagan looked on as Rebecca's son walked back towards a waiting limousine.

'What are you thinking Marc?'

Fagan inhaled. 'All that's happened over the past few weeks. I never expected to come back to any of this.' He watched as Ricky and his girlfriend drove away. 'Now I've discovered I've had a son for the last thirty-seven years. I didn't know I had. That's the one thing about being in the police force. You have to give up your visibility to stop criminals tracking you down. That's why Rebecca couldn't find me. I'd become a ghost. I never really took an interest in social media. A few weeks before I came back, I had a friend look her up.' Fagan smiled. 'She looked amazing. It was as if she hadn't aged a day. I considered the possibility of getting in contact with her as soon as I got back. But when I saw she had a son, I thought she had moved on with her life. Forgotten all about me and found a new life with someone else.'

'She never forgot about you Fagan. She never stopped loving you.'

Fagan turned to Jackie. 'Did you know? You know, that Ricky was mine?'

Jackie took a deep breath. 'I had an inkling. But nan always said you were Ricky's dad. She didn't make it public.'

Fagan shoved his hands in his pockets. 'I shouldn't have come back.'

'What?'

'I shouldn't have come back to Abergavenny. If it wasn't for me, she would have still been alive.' Fagan felt a cascade of emotion engulf him. He dropped to his knees in front of his father's grave and cried.

Jackie knelt, putting her arm around him. 'Now you listen to me, Marc Fagan. None of this is your fault. That bastard Tim took her away from us, not you. So don't go blaming yourself for anything. Rebecca certainly wouldn't want that.'

Fagan wiped the tears away and stood. 'What happens now?'

'We are going to remember her together, and we are going to celebrate her life.'

'And what about Ricky?'

'Ricky is a strong lad, just like his dad.' She smiled at him. 'Tim was never any kind of father. Ricky even told me once that he didn't want Tim to be his father. And he wished for a better dad.' Jackie cuddled Fagan. 'You are that better dad. Just give it a little time. I think he knows.'

Fagan nodded. 'If your nan were here, I thank her for taking Rebecca in when she needed someone the most.'

Jackie glanced skywards. 'She knows. She's always looking down, watching over us. Come on, let's get back to the Cantreff. Nothing like a good wake after a good funeral.'

CHAPTER 49

The Cantreff

Guests at the wake said their goodbyes. The pub was empty except for Fagan, Tyler, Evans, Edwards and Jackie.

'Thanks for coming up from London for the funeral, Tyler. Really appreciate it.' Fagan said.

Tyler dismissed his comment. 'Rebecca was a good friend. There was no way I was going to miss her funeral.' He raised his glass. 'To Rebecca, never to be forgotten.'

Everyone else raised their glasses.

'I saw Benny today outside his house looking smug. He's gained a lot more followers on social media since that stunt he pulled a few weeks ago.' Evans revealed.

'Our cybercrimes division couldn't find anything that could get him charged with what they found in that shed. All the images are traceable and the men and women in those photographs are of legal age. No one has been able to track his wife after she left the country. Although we have Justin's statement he'd been paying for sex, we still don't have enough to charge Nelson. All the number plates we collected have been traced. But so far, no one has admitted to anything. I'm guessing they all paid by cash, which is untraceable.'

'Fuck.' Jackie swore. 'That slippery bastard still gets away with everything.'

'No.' Fagan shook his head. 'My coming back to town has set a chain of events in motion.' He reached inti his inside pocket, pulling out a few pieces of paper. 'Nigel called around this morning and found some more information on Benny. His father Bill Nelson married a woman called Annie Pugh in 1943. In 1945, she gave birth to Joan Nelson.' Fagan paused. 'Annie died, giving birth to Joan.'

'I knew it.' Evans said. 'I said there was a possibility Benny could be this Joan's son.'

'The girl in the picture, outside the London Hotel.' Jackie speculated. 'Which means Benny's father got his own daughter pregnant with Benny.'

'That's my thinking.' Fagan said. 'Because there was no other record of Bill marrying again.' He produced another piece of paper. 'It gets even more interesting. In 1969, the Abergavenny Tribune ran an article about a 24-year-old woman being arrested for attempting to strangle a nine-year-old boy. Who do you reckon that was?'

'Benny Nelson.' Edwards guessed.

Fagan nodded. 'The article mentions Benny but doesn't say who the woman is. It says she was arrested and admitted to Pen-Y-Fal hospital to undergo psychiatric treatment. However, resourceful Nigel has access to old hospital records from Pen-Y-Fal. In 1969, a woman called Joan Pugh was admitted for evaluation. I'll bet any money that's Benny's mother forward slash sister. She was admitted under Pugh, her mother's maiden name.'

'Why do you think she tried to murder him?' Tyler asked.

'Probably because she saw Benny as an abomination.'

'When was Pen-Y-Fal shut?'

'1997.' Fagan answered. 'At the time of its closure, Joan Pugh was still alive. She was transferred to Broadmoor.'

'No fucking way!' Evans exclaimed.

'And she's still there, in her late seventies.' Fagan revealed.

'That's worth the trip just to see her.' Edwards said.

'Providing she's in any fit state to talk.' Jackie pointed out. 'She's been locked up in mental asylums all her life. That's got to do a lot of damage.'

'There's a lot of fucked up shit that has gone on in this town.' Evans remarked. 'I mean, I know everyone hates the bloke, but you can't help feeling sorry for Benny at the same time. He was probably abused at the London, his mother tried to strangle him. It's enough to make anyone go mental.'

'But he's an adult now.' Jackie pointed out. 'He should still be brought to heel and locked up.'

Fagan nodded. 'Benny will fuck up in the future. He still has secrets to give up. Believe me when I say this, it's far from over when it comes to Benny. In fact what we've learnt so far, is just the tip of the iceberg.'

Evans slapped Fagan on the back. 'Well, I for one am glad you're back with us. So, let's raise our glasses to the new sheriff in town. To Detective Inspector Marc Fagan, to new beginnings, and to, a new hope.' Evans held his smart phone up and played the *Star Wars* theme tune.

Fagan chuckled. 'Trust you to get a line from *Star Wars* in there.'

Everyone laughed.

E P I L O G U E

Abergavenny train station—December 1985

'Take care of yourself Marc. Don't get into any more trouble.' George hugged Fagan.

'I'll try not to.' Fagan said. 'Tell Mary that I am sorry for everything. I wish things were different.'

George nodded. 'Say hello to your mam. I promise me and Mary will visit in time. We have to let things die down. Nelson is still pissed off because he can't press charges. He wanted you to do more time.'

'Do you know why Sergeant Bob gave me the choice? Either go back to clink or leave Abergavenny altogether.'

George shrugged. 'I don't know.'

Fagan stared back, knowing there was something George wasn't telling him.

In the distance a train sounded its horn, coming into view further on down the track.

George turned and walked down the platform, out of sight.

The rumble of the train grew louder as it approached the station.

A wave of sadness cascaded over Fagan. He didn't want to leave. He still had a life here. But it would have been a life in and out of prison.

'Marc.' A tearful Rebecca came into view, sprinting up to him.

Fagan sensed his heart sink. He knew Rebecca was coming back the same day he was leaving. But he was hoping to be gone before she found out he had left Abergavenny for good.

'Where are you going?'

'Where do you think? I have to leave Becky. It's that or spend another five years in prison for what I did to that prick, Nelson.'

'There must be something we can do. Someone we can talk to.'

'I've already tried. It's leave now or clink for me.'

'But I don't want you to go.' She sobbed. 'I thought we were back together.'

'I thought so as well. But I fucked up again Rebecca. I couldn't stand another five years inside. It would be unfair to mam, and I couldn't do that to you.'

'But I love you Marc. I want to be with you.'

Fagan stared back at her. 'I love you too, which is why I have to leave. Do you have any idea what it would be like if I stayed here? I'm not good for you Rebecca. I want you to have the life you deserve. Look, I'm no genius. But even I can see the problems of two young people doesn't amount to shit in this stupid world. You're intelligent enough to understand that.'

'Please Marc, don't go.' Rebecca sobbed.

The train signalled its arrival at the platform, grinding to a halt. Passengers disembarked.

A station guard approached Fagan. 'You getting on or what?'

'Yeah, just a sec.'

'Please Marc.' Rebecca sobbed. 'I don't want you to go?'

'And I don't want to leave.' Fagan sniffled.

'I can go with you. We can have a life away from this stupid town.'

'Becky, listen to me. Where I'm going, you can't follow.

What I have to do now, you can't be a part of. If you get on this train with me, I guarantee you'll regret it. Maybe not today, maybe not tomorrow. But you will end up regretting it later in life.'

Rebecca continued to cry. 'But what about us?'

Through the heartbreak Fagan smiled at her. 'We'll always have *Casablanca*.' He tucked his hand under her chin and kissed her gently on the cheek. 'Here's looking at you kid.' He turned and stepped aboard the train.

The train horn sounded before pulling out of the station.

Rebecca dropped to her knees, sobbing.

The guard stepped onto the train and slammed the door. 'Young love, eh.'

Rebecca watched the train pull away. An uncomfortable sensation rose from the pit of her stomach. It was the fourth day in a row she had been sick. She stood and rushed to the toilet.

Detective Inspector Marc Fagan will return in the Dead and the Buried

May 31st 2023

Help an independent author.

Many thanks for buying a copy of The Dead Will Beckon.

Before you take to Amazon and hammer me about grammar please stop to pause.

Please e-mail and tell me if there are any problems with the book. I do spend time going over my books making sure you, the reader enjoy the stories that I write.

If you have enjoyed what you have read then please by all means spread the word to other avid readers.

You can also click the follow button on my Amazon page.

Many thanks

Jason Chapman

Jasonchapman-author@hotmail.com

Other books by Jason Chapman

The UFO Chronicles

The fallen

Codename Angel

The Angel Conspiracy

The Angel Prophecy

Detective Sergeant Samantha Drake series

Dystopia

Avalon Rising

Signals

Project Genesis

Quality declaration

Please note, this book has been written in UK English. US English and UK English differ slightly.

I have taken every care to produce a quality item. As an independent author, it is hard to find people who will edit for a fair price. With the cost of living crisis biting down, it gets harder with every passing day. Most editors and proof-readers cost thousands of pounds. Way beyond the budget of most struggling indie authors. As a result, independent authors are often criticised for producing sloppy work. Packed with mistakes and a poor use of grammar. It can be an uphill struggle against reviewers who ignore the storylines and concentrate on missing full stops or speech marks. I am constantly updating my books, reading through them. Making sure you the reader enjoy the stories I write. I use AI software to help me with my writing and editing. It's not perfect, but it's better than just giving up.

Mainstream publishers label independent authors as desperate, inexperienced, self-published cry-babies. There are many indie authors who work hard to perfect their craft. Producing exciting stories for an ever-hungry reading public. Often writing better stories than many of the top bestselling authors. It comes down to two choices. Chase the dream, or give up because you simply can't afford it.

O F F W O R L D
P U B L I C A T I O N S

Printed in Great Britain
by Amazon